Melissa M Marlow

It's Not Over/Losing You combined novel. Copyright© 2014 by Melissa M Marlow. All rights reserved. Printed in the United States of America. For information address Poehler Publishing, Ramsey Minnesota. Book design provided by Melissa Poehler with Poehler Publishing.

Photos from 123RF

www.mmmarlow.com
ISBN   -10:   0983524564
        -13:   978-0-9835245-6-4

First Edition: November 2014

Losing You

By

Melissa M Marlow

Preface

Paul

As a man, sex is important to us as a group. We want it, desire it, and will beg for it, if we have to, but love completes you by filling your heart with happiness. I wanted Jessica Jenson to be mine and only mine. It's a nightmare thinking of someone else kissing my Jessica. I cannot put my finger on just one thing that makes her the one, because I love everything about that girl. Her scent a mixture of jasmine and lavender, not only did it fill my nose I could taste it on her ear, neck, and lips. The only thing that she wanted happen to be me and I didn't understand that when I should have. I wanted to show her what she means to me, and how it will be for the rest of our lives if we stay together.

I traced the back of my hand from her neck down the middle of her chest, but never taking my eyes off of hers. Those deep green colored eyes sucked me in as she looked innocently at me. I could tell she wondered what we were about to do. I wanted to make her want me so bad that she would beg me to make love to her forever. When you love someone it's not just sex, it happens to be so much more than that. Making love is a way to express the trust, loyalty, respect, and dedication to this person that fills every part of you that is missing a piece. Someone once told me that sex happens in mind, not in body. I have found that to not be true for me. It happens in body and mind, not really sure which gives you pleasure for it's a fusion of all senses; love, lust, touch, and a whole lot more.

I slowly lowered the sheet wrapped around her and pulled her to me. Our time to complete the connection happened to be now. I lowered her to the bed moving between her legs wear the warmth of her could rest against me. She smiled as I enticed her with my desire rubbing against her throbbing with need to dive deep within her.

"Jessica, will you marry me?"

She shook her head no, but with the cutest grin on her face. I enticed her more with little kisses against her neck and under her ear asking again, "Jessica, you must tell me you will marry me."

She shook her head *no* yet again.

My ego hurt but determined to make her say she would be mine I brushed kisses against her cheeks while my membrane rubbed against her wet folds. I pleaded again, "Please tell me you will marry me?"

I could see the tears well up in her eyes. She gave me a slight grin as I took the ring from the box and pulled it out. Taking her hand in mine I slid it on her finger, "Jessica, will you honor me by telling me you will marry me?"

She nodded as the tears trickled from her eyes and down the sides of her face. At the moment she said yes I pushed into the depths of her core where the warmth surrounded me. She gasped for a breath of air, but I captured her squeal tasting those sweet lips. Not moving an inch of my body allowing her body to adjust to the intrusion I kissed, sucked, and licked her mouth. The throbbing reminded me of where my penis happens to be at this very moment. As slow as humanly possible I withdrew until just the tip touched her. Her hands trailed down my back until she gripped to pull me into her. Gliding back into her with a little more ease; her body engulfing me pulling me deeper. The tightness of her enticed chills up my spine. Not taking my eyes from hers for one reason only, I wanted to see her face as we made love for the first time.

I wasn't doing as well as I had expected. I had jacked off to build my tolerance for this moment, but nothing compared to the way this filled every dream I had about the first time with her. The warmth of her interior added to the sensation making the release come to fast. I knew she didn't have the same feeling as me because her face hadn't changed at all. I blew it because I wasn't able to give her the pleasure that she had given me.

I rolled over pulling her with me just to hold her to me. As I closed my eyes to cherish this moment with her I promised that I would make it up to her as soon as I regained some energy.

When I opened my eyes she wasn't there. I sat up looking around my room and she wasn't here at all. I looked where we had left our clothes and not only were her clothes missing, but I was still in mine. I still tasted her on my mouth, her scent filled the room, and the sensation still throbbed in my membrane; finding that I had ejaculated in my dreams. It's crazy, God she's mine. Grabbing my phone I made the call yet again.

"Paul?"

"Jess!" My voice betrayed me with a hint of torment.

"Are you okay?"

Subduing the agony I replied with the truth, "No, you?"

"Not really."

We sat in silence listening to each other breath. I know she broke up with me, but for a good reason. I left her lonely and sad most of the time, but I did it for her. She wasn't ready to take that next step and my needs were getting harder and harder to suppress. I wanted to give her time to grow into herself without pressure from me. We're both sad and lonely now, and neither of us wanted to let go. To deal with it we call each other listening to each other breath….

1

Jessica

Paul, my ex-boyfriend of three years, happened to be one of the most amazing guys in the world. He had sandy brown hair that always seemed a mess, hazel green eyes that melted me when he looked into my eyes. A great muscular body, an amazing smile; featuring the best dimples that I had ever seen. I am one hundred and ten percent still in love with him, but the last two years of our relationship didn't go so well. In fact it was hard for me. We spent a lot of time apart, because of his business and going to college. Neither of us wanted it to end, but to go through another year of missing him would be too painful. I didn't want to stand in his way, so I let him go. I have regretted it ever since, but I had plans, boy did I have plans!

I tried a date with a guy from school, Greg, another great guy. The problem of me comparing everything he did to Paul happens to be the problem. I still loved Paul when I kissed Greg. My only intention was to see if there could be anything between us. After the kiss, we both looked at each other and laughed. He didn't have it for me and I definitely didn't have it for him. We had the best hug and agreed that we're much better off being friends than anything else. Besides, his kiss didn't make my toes curl like Paul's did. Oh yeah, comparing them again. This needed to stop because it didn't matter anymore. I had to face my fears head on and fight for what I wanted, Paul.

Mom and dad drove me to school. I hadn't told Paul this yet, but I got accepted to the same school he attended. I wanted to surprise him. I needed to figure out his schedule and then I'd find a way to spring it on him.

He turned over all his work to a few guys that he called foremen, and then he also had workers to handle all his accounts. If we have a chance at all it would have to be now when he had the time. All he had to concentrate on is school, and me, of course.

Mom and dad stayed to get me moved into my room. Before they left they wanted to make sure I had everything.

Dad seemed more worried about Paul than me, "Jess, we should stick around and say hi to Paul ourselves."

"Dad, you are not ruining my surprise for him and no, you are not saying hi to him."

Mom had to get her input, "Are you sure he is still interested, Jess. I mean you broke his heart. It is possible that he is dating."

"No, he's not dating. Besides, we still talk a little. If he did date he would have told me. I told him about Greg."

Watching my mom and dad exchange glances worried me a bit. Did they know something that I didn't? My dad and Paul had this weird relationship where they talked like friends. Hopefully they were concerned for our wellbeing. Paul had been through so much in his life already with his last girlfriend dying next to him in a car. Or it might have been the three weeks I wept in my room.

"If you are sure, but I don't want you to be disappointed."

"I won't."

I walked them down to their car; I have my own now. Thank god I wouldn't be stranded at school and if I needed to go home for a weekend I had the means to go. I pushed them in their car and I kept looking over my shoulder worried that Paul may show up to ruin my surprise. The campus happened to be smaller than I believed, and I didn't have a clue what floor he lived on, even though housing consisted of one building.

When I walked back in I went to the director's area in the resident hall and asked what his room number is. They didn't have anyone staying in this hall by that name. Sure that he still went to school here, I wondered why he didn't have a room number.

I went back to my room, where my roommates worked to organize their rooms. We had three bedrooms and two bathrooms, so I walked into the room that I had decided on being my bedroom. When I walked in a girl had already moved in arranging her side of the room the way she wanted. I sat down on my bed and introduced myself. She told me her name, "Karlie Brown. She explained that she's a junior. Getting acquainted I filled her in on my plan. We seemed to get along fairly well.

After about two weeks of getting comfortable I set my mind on finding Paul. Going to admissions proved that he definitely went to school here. Sweet talking the student aid guy gave me what I needed, Paul scheduled, which had to be against school policy. Side tracked with school work; it's harder than I assumed it would be I didn't have much time to work on my surprise. My roommate asked me if I really wanted to find him. Telling her our story she agreed that we belonged together. She even had tears in her eyes at the end of it.

Cross referencing our schedules together, I found that the possibility of running into him would have to be planned out. I tried to fit it in and watched for him, but day after day I kept missing him. I did a glance one day as he drove off and my heart sank. Wanting to hear his voice deeply I called him that night.

"Jess?"

"Hey."

"So, how is school?"

"Frustrating."

"It gets better. Tell me where you are. I'll come visit you."

"No, not yet Paul, but soon."

He chuckled, "You are giving into me."

"A little."

He laughed. We talked about his school too, but he didn't stay on campus, that explained a few things. He lived in an apartment about 2 miles from school. The more he explained the better I felt about surprising him. Matt's his roommate at the apartment. I loved Matt like a brother, so that's perfectly good. He also explained that he tutored other students to make extra money, which makes no sense to me. He already makes enough money from him business. Then he elaborated that he did it mostly to help keep him busy.

That's when I decided on getting a tutor for my classes. One way or the other, I am going to find a way to surprise him and that might be the perfect way. The tutoring schedule listed the time slots open and listed the classes he could tutor in. The only bad thing is that it will be two more weeks before he has an opening. At least with his class schedule and the tutoring schedule, keeping tabs on him would be easy.

I examined his schedule for tutoring every day, but they all seemed to be girls. After about a month of trying to catch up and get a head a little I was going to adventure out. I went to the library and met up with a few girls from my class. Tammy, Sue, Rachel, and Bobby all sat closely together discussing something of interest to them all. I walked up and Sue pulled out a chair for me, "Oh, my god Jess, Rachel's telling us about this tutor she has. I am going to sign up just to have time with him; he sounds gorgeous."

My heart raced as I listened to them talk about him. Everything they described fit my Paul to a T. I sat listening and then observed Rachel getting up, "I am off to put the moves on him today."

I stood up and spoke before I realized what I was doing, "You don't want to do that." I didn't even glance around for him when I spoke out, but I saw him out of the corner of my eye walking into the library. They all stared at me surprised at my outburst, but if I didn't want him to know yet I had to hide. I grabbed my stuff walking away.

"Hey, what is going on with you?" Tammy yelled after me.

I just wanted to get out of there. I was trapped, so I found a home in a corner, but I had to see him. I peeked around the corner. Tammy found me and walked up to me with glaring eyes, "What are you doing? You're acting like a stalker."

I laughed and shook my head.

"Do you get nervous around cute guys?"

I looked up at her and then peeked around the corner, "Do you think he is that cute?"

"YES! Don't you, Jess? Or do you like girls?"

I shook my head as I stared at my Paul.

"Jess, you are seriously becoming one of those weird people sitting here staring like that. You should let me introduce you."

"NO!" I turned back to her, "I'm not good around cute guys. I freeze and get all sweaty, so it wouldn't be good. Can you just come get me when they are done?"

She smiled at me, "We need to get you out of your shell."

I shooed her away from me and peeked back at them. I found a spot on the floor where seeing him through legs of tables happen to be the best it would get. I gaze at him, while keeping an eye on Rachel, too. Time slowly ticked by, but when it had been 50 minutes I saw Matt walk in and up to Paul. Was I ever going to be released from this captivity?

Paul introduced Matt to all the girls sitting at the table with them. My breath escaped me with a huff of frustration; this could be awhile. Picturing myself walking up to them and what reaction each of them would have. Paul would get up moving to me, hug me, and maybe even kiss me. Rachel would rip my head off, and the rest of them would be stunned into silent mouth dropping awe. Not that I wouldn't like it, but I wanted to surprise him in a special way. Not just springing on him like it's no big deal going to school here with him.

Paul

"Matt, this is Rachel and her friend's Tammy, Sue, and Bobby."

Being polite he shook each of their hands. I only hoped that one of them sparked his interest. My ploy to find him a girlfriend didn't look promising, but Matt happened to be one of the greatest friends a person could have. I wanted to pay him back for all the bullshit I put him through over the last few years. The problem with Matt is that his shyness held him back. I had no problem with talking to girls I have no feelings for, my heart belonged to one girl and I am going to marry her someday. Tammy recognized his shyness, "Well, we would introduce you to our friend Jess, but she is a little shy."

Shy would be a good match for Matt, but Jess? My heart dropped to my stomach as my eyes stared at her. My mind drifted instantly to my sweet Jessica, how much I missed her.

Matt worked on his shyness and made an attempt to say, "I am shy too. I would love to meet her."

I am impressed with the change in Matt. He seemed to be trying a little harder, but to find a girl as shy as him would be interesting. Both of them being too shy would be really funny to witness, and to think we would both end up with a Jess. I started to wonder how 'many' Jessica's go by Jess. On a weird hunch I asked Rachel, "What is this Jess's last name?"

I saw Matt turned to me quickly giving me a scolding, but we were both relieved when she said, "Hanson or something like that."

I laughed and shook my head and turned to Matt smiling. He just stood there shaking his head at me. Yes, I'm still hung up on my, Jess. I am still in love with that little girl and I wanted to marry her with all my heart. "So where is this friend?"

She pointed to the back of the library, "So Matt, would you like to meet her now?" I suggested.

He grinned as I pointed in one direction for him to go and I walked the other way. We're going to meet this shy girl that would be perfect for Matt. It's my mission to supply him with the perfect girl. I only embarrassed myself three times saying the name Jess to see if any of the girls I found were her, but they just shook their heads at me.

I went back to the group of girls and set up another time for Rachel to help her with interpersonal communication class, and another later in the week for Math. Sue and Bobby wanted to set a tutor session. They had to go through the proper channels so I gave them my blog to register and sign up for a time. I try to help the students that come first. I took one last eyeing search around the room, and it seemed weird to me. I took one more deep breath and pulled Matt out with me.

We were heading to the truck, "Matt, what is the possibility that my Jess is here?"

"None. She broke up with you, Paul." His words hit a little more harshly than I expected.

"But we still talk and the last time she agreed to see me."

"Paul, no! She broke your heart and it's very unfair for her to do that. You should try dating one or some of these girls you tutor. That Rachel is a hottie."

I huffed, "She isn't Jess."

"No, she is not and that is why you will go on a date with her, and the next one and the next one. You need to get over Jess and even if you don't like any of them at least you're trying."

I got in my truck not happy with Matt, "I still love her."

He laughed, "Yeah, I know, but it wouldn't hurt you to test the waters."

"I don't like water."

"Yes, but what a variety."

I shook my head as we headed home.

Jessica

I worried if I would ever get out of the library and that bathroom. Why did they come searching for me? I went back to the table and sat down with the girls. Rachel asked, "So, what was that about?"

I laughed and raised my eyebrows, "Just a little shy, especially since they're so cute."

Rachel scrunched her nose, "Good, because the shy one wants to meet you."

I grimaced, "The shy one?"

"Yeah, his name is Matt."

I held back a grin as I remembered this guy wanting to join my family. My mom and dad were easy to talk to about anything, and he took advantage of that. My mind also wandered back to him Val all cuddled up together. Even if he is the best guy in the world he isn't the one for me. Besides I would never date a friend of Paul's even if I didn't still love him. I played along, "Well, maybe someday."

They all laughed at me as I sat back down to continue to work on homework again. From now on I needed to avoid meeting up with people when they were scheduled for a tutor session.

Telling myself to stay away from him when he is tutoring didn't last long. I found myself drawn to follow him, observe him, and study his every move. Pretty soon I would have to have him tutor me, because my obsession was hurting my school work. I needed to figure out the best way to surprise him, because if I didn't, surely I would go crazy. My stomach fluttered as I imagined walking up to him while he was tutoring Rachel. I would love for him to kiss me in front of her; being honest, I would love for him to kiss me in front of them all. It pleased me that his heart belonged to me.

In my private little cove in the library where I spied on him I waited for Paul and Rachel to show up for their appointment. I always arrived a half hour before and left a half hour after they were done. The problem with that, today they didn't show up for the appointment. Realizing it must be canceled I headed for my room pouting. On my way to the dorm I saw him setting up a blanket in the commons, and then Rachel sat down on it. He did the same while Rachel moved closer to him. My hands tightened into fists at my side, my heart raced with anger, and my face flushed with heat. Paul had every right to do this, but I still loved him. This is a little too cozy for tutoring.

Tammy walked up behind me, "Yes, she is making head way with that one."

I turned to her, "This was her idea?"

"Yes, but she said he agreed without persuasion."

I turned to walk around the other end of the building, "Jess, where are you going? You should let me introduce you. His friend seemed really interested in meeting you."

"I'm not feeling well; maybe another day."

I ran up to my room and straight to the window. Tears pricked at my eyes, while my stomach twisted to knots. Seeing Paul with someone else tore her to little pieces. Why had she decided to wait for a special moment? Now someone else had his attention. The pain in my heart felt like a knife had been shoved into it and then twisted back and forth to make sure the pain was excruciating. I should hurry up before he changes his mind about loving me.

What surprised me the most is the kiss. Not even realizing it my hands went to the window, and I must have screamed because it didn't last very long when they both looked up to my window. I fell back onto my bed to whimper, cry, and then sob some more. The only thing that repeated in my mind is *what have I done?*

That night I exhausted myself from crying so long and hard. I broke up with him to avoid the hurt and sadness and all I caused myself was more heart ache. Why did I decide not to tell him that I'm here? Oh, the surprise that I was planning, but had no idea of what it was yet. Great, I screwed this plan up.

My phone rang and I wasn't going to answer it, but I wanted to hear his voice, "Paul?"

"Hey."

"Can't sleep?"

"No."

I huffed. I was hoping it was from the guilt of kissing Rachel today, "Is there something wrong?"

"Yes… No… Jess?"

"What is it?"

"Nothing."

We fell asleep listening to each other breath. I knew what was wrong and he felt like I did when I kissed Greg. It wasn't what I thought it would be. Just like it wasn't Paul for me, that kiss with Rachel, it wasn't me.

2

Discussing my issues with my roommate Karlie hoping she would have suggestions for me, but she didn't have a clear opinion. She listened, nodded, and stared at me not saying much of anything. I guessed she didn't want to discuss my problems.

The weeks seemed to go a lot faster the closer we got to the end of the first quarter. I had to buckle down and really start to study to pass my classes. My classes are hard; the homework impossible, and my wandering mind lands on thinking school isn't for me. To distract myself from school work I follow Paul every day, but that drives me crazy. How many girls does he have to kiss? Kissing Rachel has broken my heart, but now it seems he gives each girl a kiss or two. Spying on him obsessively causes sadness to engulf my daily routine.

By the end of the quarter I stopped talking to my roommate especially after I saw her tutoring session with Paul. She disappointed me, but he wasn't mine anymore. I broke up with him.

Each painful kiss embedded in my phone to remind me that he had done this, and if the subject came up he wouldn't be able to deny it. Scanning through the pictures I noticed a trend. He would meet a new student a couple of times in the Library, then they would meet in a remote spot, kiss, and then all of it would end. No more kisses, no more remote spot, just the Library or they would not sign up with him any longer. Never more than one girl at a time to a remote location, but it would only happen once with each girl.

Either they didn't kiss very well or they didn't do it for him. I hoped and prayed the latter. Knowing him for so long before we were together I had watched him go through girl after girl never really having any kind of lasting relationship. He had good reason though, his last serious girlfriend before me died. They had snuck out late one night to make their first time special. As a teenager he thought, at the time, that sex was very important for their relationship. She changed her mind and they argued as he drove her home. Distracted by the argument they failed to notice the dump truck coming or when it ran into the passenger side of his car. When he told me she gasped his name just before she passed away he had tears in his eyes. With me he never pushed the issue of sex; in fact he loved me enough to wait as long as I needed. The sad part of it is; he promised my dad that I would have to agree to marry him before we took that step. I'm too young to get married, so we're still waiting.

The three years we had been together he had been so good, so why did he go back to girl after girl? He seems unsatisfied with the selection, or he didn't connect with any of them. As I realize that no one would do it for me like Paul, he would also realize the same.

To distract me from obsessively stalking my ex-boyfriend I joined a few clubs. My favorite of the clubs is: "Changing the World." The mission statement said "We will live a full and plentiful life, when we help others in need." This is where I met Iaesha. She's a beautiful girl with mocha colored skin that radiated a glow of perfection. She went on and on about the peace core and how she had plans after she graduated from college to go help somewhere in the world and make a difference. The more meetings I went to the more I distracted myself from Paul. Yes I loved him, and if he needed to move on I loved him enough to let go. Planning and helping others in need gave me a sense of pride. Someday I would make a difference in someone's life. Seriously considering joining a group heading to a remote country on a mission I weighed the pros and cons. My reasoning told me that it would be better than staying here to wallow in sadness.

I should have never said that in front of Iaesha. The next thing I knew she introduced me to a bunch of people who were talking to me like I was going with them on their excursion. Then everything happened so quickly. I had a passport, the flight booked, and my name on the list. So confused of how all this happened in no time at all. When I spied Paul kissing yet another girl my whirlwind brain told me to go through with it. Perhaps not getting phone calls from Paul as often made this more real to me.

As time passed quickly, I had to confirm my plans. Iaesha had everything worked out to a tee. If I joined them I could take my finals early due to the tour leaving late March. So torn on what to do I wanted to consult with the only person that had my best interest at hart. I wanted to be here with Paul, but that showed signs of impossibility. I really sucked at this school thing. Not knowing if it's because I wasn't ready for it or if it's my obsession for Paul watching.

Needing help and advice from someone whom I loved, not wanting to scare my mom and dad, and I didn't want to tell them that I failed at college.

Staring at my phone wondering if I dare call Paul; reasoning it out in my head I came up with needing his advice and his voice in my ear.

That's when I hit the button to call him.

"Jess!"

"Hey." That came out completely opposite of how I wanted it to.

"Are you okay?"

"I think I screwed up Paul."

"Why do you say that?"

"I think I ruined it for us."

"NO, Jess. What do you mean?"

"Have you kissed anyone, Paul?"

Silence filled the phone. At least he didn't lie to me.

His voice more determined, "I have one question for you?"

"Okay."

"Do you love me?"

"Yes."

The tears started to stream down my face. My roommate Karlie walked in and took one look at me then walked out.

"Jess, I have."

His confession didn't take away my misery like I expected it to, "Okay. I love you, bye."

"Jess, wait a minute. You kissed Greg."

Blame, what a mean defense. Covering the mouth piece to hide my sob I tried to get a grip on my emotions, but speaking without gasping or blubbering happened to be impossible at this moment.

"Jess, please. I didn't want to. Matt, just keeps hounding me. He doesn't want me to go back to the way I was when I lost Annie, and it's just..."

Grasping for a breath I bellowed, "What?"

"Shit Jess! I love you, but you didn't want me. Remember you broke up with me. I tried to kiss a few girls, but it's not the same."

Confused with what to say I took a deep breath and tried to get it out without letting him hear how devastating his kissing other girls had made me, "What do we do now?"

I covered it quickly as I lost it again.

"Where are you?"

I sniffled and took another deep breath, "School."

He laughed, "What school? Where?"

"You can't come now, Paul. It's been a really bad day and I just..."

"Okay, when and where?"

"When I am done with classes on Thursday, I had planned to go home. I'll tell mom and dad that I had to stay another day and...."

I took a break to breathe, still holding the tears at bay.

"And what, Jess, anything?"

"Meet me at the cabin."

"Okay, we get done the same day."

"You will be there, right?"

"Yes."

"Paul, I am serious. You have to promise me."

"Jess, I will be there. I promise you."

Scared that he would get side tracked, not show up, or worst of all just blow me off like he had done in the past. If he didn't show up it would be the end to the end, "Paul, I couldn't handle it if you..." I covered the mouth piece again.

"I swear to you; I will be there. I love you."

"Okay, but please don't..."

"Jess, I am going to be there. What time?"

"I will be there by 7 pm."

He laughed, "I will be there by 6:50 pm."

"Are you sure?"

"Oh, Jess. Yes, I am so sure. I have missed you so much."

With the phone on my ear I lie down on my bed listening to his breath heavy and fast against his end. Relaxing a little I took my finger off of the mouth piece and my breath trembled.

"Jess, was your day that bad?"

"Yes."

"Do you want me to stay on the phone?"

"Yes."

"Do you want me to sing to you?"

"No, it will make me sadder."

Listening to him moving around and humming to himself as I laid there listening to him helped me to drifted off slowly.

Pulling off passing my classes I got one A, three B's, and four C's. Not happy with my grades, but I passed. That is what matters the most, next to seeing Paul.

Lying to him about the time; I wanted to have time to set it up the cabin romantically. Chinese food, candles, and Rose petals, this would be a night to remember. My intentions to make love to Paul had other benefits too, like stop kissing other girls. The closer I got to the cabin the happier I became. So close to 6 pm I got busy right away putting the food in the oven to keep it warm. Placing the lit candles all over the cabin and then sprinkling the rose petals everywhere, this would be a night he wouldn't forget. Table is set for two, the dinner candles lit, now for the sexy silk camisole with five minutes to spare. Trying a bunch of different ways to stand to wait for him; I leaned against the counter, then the table. But it didn't seem right so I sat on the table, but it would send the message of desperate need. Next to the couch and lay down, but that said *take me now*. Indeed I wanted to make love to him, but he would have to work to get it. I had to be sure that he loves me more than anything.

After all my poses my nerves twisted my gut. Wondering how much time I had now I glanced at the clock that now read 7:15 pm and in that instant my heart broke. Obviously he's late, which told me that he broke his promise. I tried to convince myself otherwise, but after my persistence of how importance it had been to me. If he didn't show up I wouldn't be able to talk to him ever again. This was my final straw as others would say.

My phone rang so I picked it up.

"Jess, I am running late."

Anger bit out my reply, "I can tell."

"Jess, I will be there shortly."

"Okay." I didn't believe him but I had to know for sure, "Why are you late?"

"One of the kids called me with a problem. Tom hasn't dealt with this so I had to show them how to fix it. Now I am covered in grease and this stupid..." He grunted, "Thing won't budge, but Jess don't leave. I will be there as soon as I can."

"Bye, Paul."

"You're not leaving are you?"

"No, I will wait."

"I love you, Jess."

I don't think he understood that my decision to leave the country happen to be based on this one night. If he didn't show up I would agree to go. I grabbed a blanket and curled up on the couch heart broken. My will to live is gone, my heart is hurting, my mind is telling me awful things; and I have to get away. If I go to a place where people would need and appreciate what I have to offer maybe, I would find purpose in my life again.

Disappointment hit me when I woke finding myself still alone. The candles melted into blobs of wax, resembling my emotions. If it could hurt any more than last night, it did. I blew out the candles one by one and the last one went out when my tear dropped to it. This part of my life is over, the sobs seeped from me as I changed and gathered my stuff. Sitting behind the while unable to see I sat there for a short while trying to compose myself enough to call Iaesha.

My time to commit to a purpose, "I am going with you."

"Really?"

"Yes, I have nothing here that I need to stay for. Thanks Iaesha."

"Yes, I am so excited. We are going to a new world."

"Yeah, that's great. I will talk to you when I get back to school. You can tell me what I need to bring."

"That sounds great." She squealed, "I am so happy you are going."

I wasn't but I didn't tell her that.

I drove to Paul's house with a small bag of stuff. After his mother opened the door her happiness to see me lite her eyes, "Jess, what a lovely surprise. What are you doing here?"

Working myself up to handle this I took a deep breath and gave her a huge smile, "I brought a gift for Paul and wanted to drop it off for him on my way home from school. May I leave it in his room?"

"Sure dear. Help yourself."

After making my way down the stairs I went to work. First of all I pulled down the poster of pictures of us together that hung on his closet door, tucked it between his mattress and box spring. It would be too hard to get that out of the house without his mother noticing. I put up a poster of a girl in a bikini for him instead. Every guy likes the girl in a bikini poster. Next on my list is to erase his computer. There are files and files of photos, even ones that I hadn't seen before. I downloaded them to CD's. After verifying that they actually made it to the CD I deleted them from the hard drive. The wolf pictures were a gift to him so those could stay. Finally, the framed photos. Each one, I lay down after pulling the photo out of the frame. His room was empty of me so I went to the den where I found our prom pictures. One more search of both rooms proved that no more memories of me were left behind. I didn't want him to make a shrine like he did with Annie, his last girlfriend. God I loved him, and I didn't want to hurt him. I convinced myself that everything I did was for the best. Heading back up the stairs with my bag in hand, I hugged his mom. My throat swelled and my body shook. I had to get out of there fast before she figured it out I'm losing it. I kissed her cheek and smiled, but my eyes tiered up betraying me. I hurried out the door rushing to my car. Her voice yelled after me full of concern, "Jess, are you okay."

When I got in my car the tears spilled out, but I waved hoping she wouldn't stop me. Not being Paul's girlfriend meant that I wouldn't see them either. It seemed my life had ended. A loud rap on my window startled me enough to make me jump out of my skin. Slowly turning to face Paul, but relief hit me to see his father. A gasp escaped me as I put my car in reverse and slowly backed away. He spoke loudly as I moved away, "Jess, are you okay?"

I shook my head, and continued to back away waving my goodbyes.

I wasn't going very fast because the tears were obstructing my vision. My next stop, Annie's grave. I wanted to see Freedom and I didn't know how to find her. A whole story in itself it's hard to explain, but the jest of it is Annie came back as a wolf to protect Paul. I think she wanted to make sure Paul could be happy again one day. Too bad it wouldn't be me making him happy.

My phone rang and my heart sank as I picked it up not saying a word.

"Jess, where are you?"

Between the tears, and the swollen throat I couldn't talk to him. I would have to say goodbye to the man I love with all of my heart. The pain shot through my heart so I hung up without saying anything at all.

Pulling into the grave yard I found Freedom lying on the grave. I got out running to her and put my face to her fur hugging her. She licked every inch of my face as she trampled around me. Her excitement made me feel loved and wanted, which I needed at this moment. I took off the forever ring that Paul gave me and laid it on Annie's grave. Forever cocked her head hinting at a question. I huffed out, "He doesn't have much time for you either I see."

She shook her head like a dog would. Wondering if it's her answer or shaking out her fur from me patting it down while hugging her. Wanting to spill everything to her couldn't happen. If Paul could understand her like he thought he did, then he would know the whole truth of my plans. Leaving words unsaid; I just didn't want to take any chances of him trying to stop me. I went back to my car after saying my goodbyes to Freedom, telling her I wouldn't be back for more than a year. She followed me and sat in the way of me closing my door, "Girl, I have to leave now."

She didn't move at all. I yelled at her that Paul and I are over and that I had to leave now. I pushed her out of the way and closed my door completely bawling now. My phone rang and I answered it yelling, "WHAT!"

"Jess, where are you?"

"I can't do this anymore, Paul, not now not ever."

"What can't you do?" He sounded angry.

"Paul, you promised."

"I am here, where are you?"

"It's over this time, Paul." I yelled at him.

"Don't say that. I can't live without you."

"You have for the last two and half years, Paul, and I made it easy for you this time."

"This is not easy. I love you and we are going to get married. Remember that, Jess?"

"Not anymore, Paul. I love you, but this..." My voice cracked and sobbing took over. Anger and sadness overwhelming my inner core; I couldn't talk anymore. I sat there trying to wipe my eyes so I could drive, but the tears flowed out faster than I could wipe them.

"Come back, please."

"Paul, I made this as easy as I could. You won't hear from me, and I won't answer your phone calls anymore. I love you." After hanging up I didn't answer as it rang and rang. I started on my way home.

I made it to town and pulled over to cry some more. I must have looked stupid or something because people honked at me. I heard the phone buzz and in my confusion I opened it.

"Jess, please don't do this."

I sent a picture of him kissing one of the girls that he tutored. I got another buzz shortly after I sent it.

"Jess, I told you about it."

I sent him another one, and another one. I sent him all the pictures I had collected over the last few months before he text me again. His reply wasn't what I expected.

"Who sent those to you?"

I laughed to myself and didn't reply. Now maybe he understood why I had to get away from this.

Paul:

Who hated me this bad that they would send her pictures of me kissing someone else? Why would anyone do this? This had to be fixed, but how? Those kisses didn't mean the same thing to me that I felt when I kissed her. She had to see the difference. If I showed her pictures of us together, of us kissing it would be obvious that I loved her. All this would end once I send her photos of us happy together. Running into the house I headed straight to my room as my mom yelled after me, "Paul, did you see Jess?"

I stopped on the stairs and walked back up staring at her, "Jess, was here?"

"Yes, she brought you a gift on her way home from school."

"How long ago did she leave?"

"I don't know. A half hour or so."

Dad walked in full of concern, "Paul, she was crying when she left. She didn't talk to me at all."

Mom turned to him, "When did you see her?"

"When she was leaving I knocked on her window to say hi, but she was crying pretty bad and she pulled out without saying anything to me."

My body trembled with anger. Worried about what she left for me I headed straight to my room down the stairs. Searching my room I didn't notice anything that she had left me. This whole thing's a nightmare; so I called Theo.

"Paul, what's up kid?"

"Um, when Jess shows up there can you call me?"

"Okay, why what is going on?"

"We were supposed to meet last night at the cabin, but I got stuck working and now she is so mad at me that…"

"You were meeting her at the cabin?"

"Yes, but I think…"

"Paul, why would she meet you at the cabin?"

Really frustrated I yelled, "Because, we have been talking and she needed me. It is possible that we were going to get back together, no I KNOW we were going to get back together, but I think…"

He interrupted me again, "So, you haven't seen her?"

"No, and now she won't talk to me. Just, if she shows up there call me."

"Paul, what happened?"

"Nothing! I didn't meet her. When I showed up at the cabin she was gone, but now…" I noticed my picture frames were faced down. I crawled on the bed to look at them as I talked to Theo, "FUCK."

He yelled, "What?"

All my oxygen disappeared from my chest as my world collapsed. All of the photos of us are gone, "Theo, I have to find her, but if she shows up there call me. She was pretty upset… I am worried about her driving."

"What is going on?"

"She took all of my pictures of us. Theo, please call me when she gets there."

"Yeah."

"Bye."

After hanging up I walked to my closet. Taking a deep breath and closing my eyes I opened the door. Calming my nerves with another breath I opened my eyes. Once open my fears came true; all of them gone. I text her quickly, *"What did you do with my pictures?"*

So pissed at her right now that if I did find her I was going to, shit. She couldn't just erase our life together. Heading to my computer to find the pictures again; I could order more. Why would she be so stup…? Shit, they were gone too, but in the folder she left a note.

Paul, I have always loved you and I always will. It will be easier this way. You won't have to be reminded of our time together with our photos. It's time to move on for both of us, and I don't want you to live in the past.

Jess

My gut wrenched in a heaving movement as I rushed to the bathroom. Dry heaves filled the room as I thought, *what the hell is she doing to me?*

Why did she do this? We're supposed to be together right now. Not wanting to waste another minute I called her and let it ring, but this time she didn't answer.

3

I grabbed my bags out of the car with my room in my mind. If I could just make it there without interference then I could cry till the hurt subsided. There were two things between me and my wallowing, my dad and mom. Of course they were in the kitchen awaiting my arrival. I figured Paul would call my dad, but with us trying to sneak off alone I thought this time he'd avoid talking to my dad.

Dad came at me right away, "You planned to meet him at the cabin!"

"Now, Theo, give her a chance to get in the door."

Glancing back and forth between the two of them, I had nothing to explain. I swallowed and lost it screaming as I dropped my bags and stormed to my room. "Nothing Happened! He Didn't Show! You should be Happy!"

Not hesitating I fell to my bed and continued to cry. There should be nothing left after that long car ride home, but I had plenty left to last longer than I wanted. Mom did come in and check on me once in a while trying to coax me out, but I couldn't get out of bed. The ache in my body and the pain in my heart made it hard to move. Mom tried to comfort me with food but death would be easier than the pain of knowing it's over between Paul and me.

Dad came in one day and sat on the bed and rubbed my back, "Jessica, are you going back to school?"

I rolled to him with a slight smile, "Yes."

"Are you sure you want to do that?"

"I will finish this year. After that I will figure something else out."

"So, it's over this time, you're sure?"

I nodded, "I caught him kissing other girls."

He looked at me squinting his eyes in disbelief, so I continued, "I gave him one last chance to work this out. To explain why or how things should be between us, but he didn't show up."

"You did break up with him."

"Yeah, but I did that because he was too busy and he blew me off for two years dad. You know I love him, but that isn't enough for both of us. My surprise didn't work either. That's when I observed him kissing another girl."

His head tilled while his eyes search my face for truthfulness.

Confirming my actions, "It's not just one girl either, Dad."

With understanding he asked, "Are you sure you want to go back there then?"

"I will be okay now. I have to be."

He took my hand and pulled me up, "Well, if you are going back to school you better get your stuff together."

"Why? I still have time."

"Um... no you don't. You have to be back by Monday."

"What about Christmas?"

"Passed. You didn't even move on Christmas."

"New Years?"

"Yeah, you were crying that day, too."

He pulled me to the kitchen and made me breakfast. Mom went up and down the stairs doing the laundry, but smiled at me every time she passed by me. I had lost a month's worth of time. Mom placed my clean clothes on my bed while I packed my stuff in my bags. I had the rest of the day to watch a couple of movies with them and eat dinner. The depression made room for numbness. This is good considering how lost I am about my future.

Paul

I tried to call Jess, but every time I did I got her voice mail. It's better this way because I'm lost as to what I'd say. Sorry wouldn't cut it this time. When I called the house phone I talked to Theo. He gave me a hard time after seeing her so miserable because of me. Pleading and begging for a minute on the phone with her he still refused. The impression he gave me led me to understand she's in no shape to talk to me. Hell, I wasn't in any shape to talk to her either. If I could fix this by talking to her neither one of us would be this miserable. But if I didn't talk to her soon I'd lose her forever.

There was no hope for a future with my Jess any longer. From now on we'd go in different directions with no way to change that. At least when we called one another it kept us connected, but not anymore.

Matt came down the stairs asking, "You ready man?"

"For what?"

"School."

"We just got home."

"No, you have been sulking in your room for a month now."

"I missed Christmas and New Year's?"

"Yeah, I had to explain why you bailed on the gig."

Not sure how I lost so many days, my sulking had to stop. I grabbed my unpacked bags heading to the door.

Matt laughed, "You did pack?"

Miserably I glance at him replying, "Never unpacked."

"You need to stay away from serious relationships. They are not good for you."

He's right. I had to get back to school and forget girls all together. I pushed him out and up the steps. Finding my mom in the kitchen I kissed her on the cheek. Turning to me she reassured me, "This is temporary Paul. I know you and you will fix this if you can. I love you."

Wanting to agree with her I nodded, but this time it's going to be different. My focus geared to my music, school, and business.

My dad met us by the truck. He stood there not saying a word making this goodbye weird. He stood near the front of my truck with his elbows leaning on the hood. Making a point that he wanted to talk I moved to lean against the truck next to him. Both of my parents had put up with my depression over the years and I am sure he didn't want to see me like that again. Clearing his throat he spoke, "I liked seeing you happy again." His eyes scanned my face searching for that kid who lost his mind a few years back.

I gave him a slight grin, "Yeah. It was nice."

"I like that little girl. I especially like you with that girl." He hesitated while examining me, but then continued, "You smile when you're with her."

Hitting me where it hurt, a lump swelled in my throat preventing me from replying.

"Sometimes we have to do things we don't want to, but the reward is worth it."

This had to be my dad's way of telling me to find Jess and do whatever she needed me to do? Doesn't he realize that is exactly what I want to do, but I don't even know where she is.

Jessica

Back at school and thankful for the numbness. Numb is better than complete misery. Now that I stopped stalking Paul I've had a hard time avoiding running into him. It seemed that I dodged him at least once a day, glancing over my shoulder watching for him.

Sometimes I went to eat and sometimes I didn't. Not wanting to be around people much and Iaesha was badgering me that I should be preparing to go. No longer wanting to go, knowing I had no choice now, I hoped that the suffering I'd witness would pull me away from my own.

At the end of February the girls came to my room for a night out. All I wanted to do is get through this last part of school and then to leave this place forever, not go out for a night of fun. There's a huge festival in town called The Ice Gala. At the festival there would be ice sculptures, sled racing, and crowning of the ice king and queen. Later in this old warehouse there would be multiple bands where they could dance to all types of music. It's supposed to be a great place. Sure my roommates are tired of me moping, so they ganged up on me. I am being forced to go. Standing in the shower fully dressed I realized that they weren't giving me a choice. Giving in I washed my hair and body stripping my clothes as I went. Talking myself into it as I stood in front of the mirror I encouraged my nerves, *you deserve a night out. Go for it. It can't hurt you.*

When I got back to my room the girls had clothes laid out for me on the bed, "A mini skirt in this weather?" It is the end of February. They had to be crazy or mad.

Casey, a girl from my English lit class spoke up, "Jess, that is what the leggings are for, they'll keep your legs warm. I brought boots too. You have nice legs and you should show them off."

Rolling my eyes while I dressed didn't help with my attitude, but I did like the top. It was a sliming sweater that hung just down to my butt and had a dangerous V-neck. There wasn't much to show off here, even though I had developed very nice boobs, if you ask me. Next, Tammy worked on my hair, and Bobby did my makeup sitting on the desk in front of me. Afraid of what they had done to me I went to the mirror. More than anything I worried that they made me look slutty, but to my amazement I didn't resemble myself at all. I don't think my own father would have recognized me all mad up like this. It sounded odd to me that I chuckled as they pulled me from the dorm.

At least they didn't make me go to the day events. We were getting there by 7pm, eating, watching the crowning, and then dancing all night.

Finding that I enjoyed most everything filled me with strength that my life would go on after Paul. As much as I needed this I could use a break and find a bathroom. Having a few beers with the girls left me a little tipsy as I wandered from room to room in search of the little girl's room. When I found the bathroom the line stretched down the hall through the doorway and into one of the halls where a band was playing. They're good but the line moved quickly bringing me down the hall and to the restroom.

With everything back in place I put lip-gloss on and went out to search for our group of girls. Again moving from room to room I found smaller rooms where DJ played the music of their choice. Reaching the big rooms where the bands played I found Sue. She had wandered off herself, so we weren't in the clear yet. Taking her to back to the bathroom I waited down the hall. The band that played in the hall next to where I stood had ended their set. The large room filled with a hum of voices until they announced the next band that would play. Sue showed up in time to grab my arm and scream, "We are staying for this one. These are guys from our school and the lead singer is amazing."

She watched the stage while I looked for the rest of our group. The music started and we danced a little, but I never even glanced at the stage. I didn't care who they were because I wasn't going to be here much longer. When something familiar filled my ears my heart began to race, my hands shook, and my knees went weak. I turned to the boy who was singing my song on the stage. The song is the one that Paul wrote for me. I stood there in shock watching him play and sing.

"Jess, dance with me."

I didn't move, I couldn't move. Remembering how romantic it felt sitting in his truck staring into his eyes, as he sang the song to me. The song seemed to pull us together. His eyes searched the room, and then connected with mine. I froze not blinking, not running, or even breathing.

"Oh, my god, Jess. That is him, isn't...?"

Turning carefully to her, "He won't recognize me. Let's go."

He quit singing as we started to walk out. Over the speakers, everyone heard my name flowing from his mouth. I closed my eyes and continued to walk away. That's when he yelled my name again while people booed. We got out the door and I took off at a full run, "Get the others and meet me at the car."

"Jess, wait where are you...?"

Not waiting for her reply. He would never leave me alone to wallow in my sadness if he could prove that I'm here. I ran down halls and through big areas getting lost in people as I made my way through the crowds. He kept yelling, but that pinpointed how close he was behind me. I found a back door guarded by a very large man, and my name wasn't being bellowed out any longer. He put up his arm to hold me from going out the door. Panicking, I pleaded, "There's a crazy guy chasing me and I need to escape from him."

He squinted his eyes at me, "Will you come back another night?" This guy hinted at flirting.

I grinned and batted my eyes, "Maybe, if you're here."

He grinned and opened the door as Paul's voice rang out again. When the door opened I didn't hesitate, and the door slammed behind me as I ran for the car. Thank god, Rachel was waiting there for me.

"Where are the others?"

"I will come back for them. Jess, he must have it bad for you. He yelled so loud everyone in the building knew he wanted you."

"I know, just go. I can't see him... ever."

She drove fast to the dorm and dropped me off at the front door. I ran inside and went to my room sitting in front of the door. I should have never left my room in the first place.

Paul

That's my Jess I am sure of it. That girl had the same face, the same figure, but she had grown up into something more than I remembered. If I get closer, get a good look, I'm sure I can prove that it's her. Questions, so many questions running through my head as I chased her- What was she doing here? How is it that she would be here tonight? "J-e-s-s."

Chasing her through this crowd it's hard to keep her within sight. Getting a glimpse of the top of her head I hopped I followed the right girl. Matt chased me, scolding the entire time, "Paul, it's just your imagination."

I stopped for a second and searched the room for her head to appear again. Matt caught up to me, "Paul, no! You're not right about it being Jess."

More determined than ever, I didn't want him to think it's an illusion. I glared at him, "She is here!"

Getting a glimpse of her over his shoulder I took off again after her, "J-e-s-s."

"Paul, stop. She isn't here. You would have known."

I kept running until we got to a door I thought she ran out of. Gary, the big security guy here, stopped me, "Where do you think you are going?"

"After that girl. She is my girlfriend."

"No, she said a crazy guy was following her. I don't think she would be running from you if you were her boyfriend."

"Gary, that's my Jess."

"No way."

I gave him pleading eyes. He glanced at Matt for confirmation that I hadn't lost my mind again so I turned to Matt too, "Please, you have to believe me."

Matt nodded, "If he says it's her; it has to be."

Gary shook his head, "I can't do it. Girls got to have protection and she's running away from something."

Taking off toward the front doors with a growl, it had to be her. Running through room after room pushing my way through the crowds of people time seemed to stretch out in front of me. If I didn't hurry she would disappear from my life forever. This is my one and only chance to speak with her, to win her back. Shoving through the front doors I ran into the street to search in both directions. Matt came storming out the door behind me and bumped into me, "Do you see her?"

Shaking my head I started to jog in one direction and Matt followed, "Paul, why would she be here?"

It was like a light bulb went off in my brain. I stopped and turned on Matt, "Did you send pictures to Jess? Me kissing other girls?" If he did I would kill him right here and now.

"No! I wouldn't do that. You belong with Jess. Besides the kissing was my idea to stop you from being miserable."

"She sent me pictures of me kissing the girls that I tutored. How else did she get them if you didn't send them?"

He had this puzzled expression on his face.

"Matt, she has been here the whole time."

He shook his head, "That isn't possible."

"Well, then you explain how she got those pictures."

He shook his head more, "Are you sure that's her?"

I ignored his ignorance and headed for my truck. I was going to find her and there's one place to look.

Matt followed, "Paul, where are we going?"

"To the school dorm."

"Why?"

"It's her. I'd know her anywhere and where else would she stay."

We got to the truck but Matt stood in front of me with his hand out. I glared at him, "What are you doing?"

"Trust me. It'll be quicker if I drop you off and Then Park."

I handed him the keys and got in the passenger side. I tapped my foot the whole way because I would have gone faster than him. Driving me crazy with his old man driving we finally made it to school. Not waiting for him to stop I jumped out and ran up to the dorm. Asking the dorm manager where Jess lived.

She gave me a disapproving glare, "I can't tell you that."

I ran down the hall knocking on doors, "Jess... Jess... I know you are here... Jess... please."

All of a sudden I felt large arm restrain me pulling me back to the sitting area. I struggled but he had me at a disadvantage. My arms locked behind me and he lifted me off the floor.

"Now, Paul, you know better than this. Settle down."

"No, it's Jess. She is here. I saw her tonight. Kevin, please help me."

Matt came running in the door when Kevin tossed me to the couch. He pointed at me scolding, "Settle down or I'll call the police."

I put my head in my hands pleading, "She is here. Please help me?"

Matt sat down by me, "Hey, you have to calm down or you won't see her at all."

I leaned back with my arm over my eyes. Shit, I cannot believe I didn't figure this out a long time ago. I sat silently while Matt talked to Kevin. A group of girls came in acting odd. They looked at me and whispered to each other. Three out of the five girls happen to be girls I had kissed and my body ached with regret. Or were they hiding something. I watched as they walked down the hall and they kept glancing back at me, laughing. They knew something. I glanced over at Matt who was distracting Kevin. Getting up I followed them up the steps they took to the next floor. Following them I peeked to watch what rooms they went in. Matt must have been keeping Kevin distract; no one was coming for me. Listening at each door for Jess, she had to be here in one of these three rooms. I heard crying, sobbing, and then her voice and how frantic she sounded. I knocked, "Jess, baby, please talk to me."

Karlie opened the door, "Paul, what are you doing here?"

"Jess is in there. Please let me talk to her."

She tried to look confused, "Paul, I don't know what you are talking about."

"Don't play dumb with me. I heard her. Let me talk to her now."

Karlie closed the door and I knocked and started to yell to her. "Jess, please. Oh come on Jess. Please, I need to see you. Jess, you should have told me you were here. Jessica Jenson, answer me."

I felt those horrible muscles pull me back slamming me into the wall, "I told you, Paul."

I sat down and cried like I never have in my life. She's on the other side of this door. I was so close to her, but yet she was so out of reach. Kevin and Matt pulled me up and walked me down stairs. I didn't move after that. My mind raced through all those days; how I spent them and what she saw. I remembered one day in the library where I had this feeling like she was there and Matt helped me search the library. Giving up our search with me thinking I just missed her too much.

Matt gave up and went home. I wasn't moving from this dorm until I saw her. Kevin got another call and he was very reluctant about letting me stay, "If I have to come back here tonight you are going to jail."

I nodded, "I will behave."

He ran off and I walked back up the stairs. I sat down leaning against the wall across from her room. I didn't want to disturb anyone so that I would go to jail, but I wasn't leaving either.

4

Monday morning Kevin walked down the hall towards me. He pulled me to my feet, "Have you been here since Saturday?"

I nodded, but didn't have anything to say for myself. I didn't want to leave until I talked to Jess. Karlie walked out, and directed us down the stairs to the lounge area. Kevin led me to sit on the couch.

Karlie started, "We need to make an arrangement."

Excitement filled my inner core. Jess wanted to arrange a meeting with me. Kevin sat down by me. Not sure if Kevin intended on restraining me or to prevent any outburst on my side, but the support comforted me. Karlie paced back and forth in front of us as I watched her anticipating how this would go.

She stopped and directed all her attention to Kevin, "He can't stay in our hallway."

As Kevin peeked at me I wondered what this had to do with Jess and my reunion.

Karlie, a furry red, shouted, "Paul, she has to be able to go to class."

This is going to be easy. I leaned back, crossed my arms over my chest, and confirmed, "Fine. As soon as she sees me I'll leave."

"No, Paul, you can't be in charge. Kevin, tell him he is going to hurt her worse if she can't go to class."

Raising his eyebrows with a glance at me, "She is right. You don't want to hurt her, do you?"

That isn't my intention. I shook my head and stared down the hall, "So, what does she want?"

"She wants to go to class without worrying about trying to avoiding you."

She shouldn't be avoiding me at all, "Can you tell her I will go away, but after she sees me?"

Karlie shook her head no. No matter what I said Karlie didn't agree with me and neither did Kevin. Both of us missing classes wouldn't fix anything. Wanting her to stay here at this school happened to be a benefit for me, because I would have time to win her back. Letting them think that they won this argument. I reluctantly agreed with stipulations, "If she will give me her class schedules I will clear out before she needs to go to class and I will stay away until the class is over allowing enough time for her to make it home."

Kevin, more perceptive of my inner thoughts, established, "Paul, she needs to be able to eat, do her laundry, and go to the library. The girl needs her life back."

Not agreeing, I just wanted them to think I agreed, "Fine, I will give her space."

Karlie walked away going up the stairs. I looked at Kevin pulling out the box with the ring. I handed it to him, "She's supposed to marry me someday."

He took the box examining the ring. Handing it back to me, "So, what happened?"

My business had to come first for a couple of reasons, and both of them had to do with her. "I screwed up by not putting her needs first."

As if he understood he grinned, "Okay, we'll figure something out, but you can't make her see you if she doesn't want to."

We both watched Karlie coming back with a paper in her hand. She handed it to me, but waited my scrutiny out.

With careful planning she would have to run into me, but girls are smart. I had to make it sound like I wasn't giving up yet, "I will clear out an hour before she is supposed to go to class and I will be back an hour after she is done with class. I will also give her two hours for dinner, laundry, and whatever else she has to do. That is the best I can do unless she will just talk to me for 5 minutes, it's all I am asking. If she doesn't want anything to do with me after that, then I won't hang out in the hallway anymore."

Karlie glared, "You are incorrigible. What I saw in you baffles me. I guess that will have to do, because she isn't going to see you."

I got up and walked out. I went far enough that I wouldn't interfere with her going to class today, but I had to have one peek at her. I noticed when she came out from the dorm. My heart pounding harder than it ever has, my breathing uncontrollable, my feet moved me closer to her. Wanting to run to her, pull her into my arms, and never let her go again seemed extreme, but I missed her so much. She paused on the walkway scanning the area, making sure the coast was clear. Close enough to see her delicate beauty worn with pain. Her skin had paled, her eyes puffy, and yet her beauty radiated around her engulfing her in a heavenly glow. Okay, so maybe it was the sun coming up behind her, but it wrapped her with its stream of lights. Maybe if I groveled at her feet she would take my ring and be forever mine.

I jumped a mile when a hand gripped my shoulder.

"You promised, Paul." Kevin was standing next to me, holding me still while she escaped me. Holding back until Kevin let go, but then again the experience didn't seem to be enough and my feet moved once his hand let go.

Another grip, this one more firm than the last, stopped me, "No. You said you would let her go to class."

I nodded and observed her walk into the building.

Time to change tactics. I got flowers every day, and placed them by her door while she went for dinner. I tried to contact her every day with a text, but I kept it simple. Like: *"Jess, please talk to me," "I need five minutes," "I miss you," "look great,"* but the one that stopped her was *"will you marry me."*

Another tactic, I left notes on the door in the morning and would wait outside in case she decided to talk to me. I tried to go to class too, but found myself searching for a glimpse of her as I walked from room to room. I quit all tutoring, because all I wanted to do is win her back. The days went by so quickly that today happened to be her birthday.

My gift to her had to be extreme. I called Karlie and made arrangements to deliver flowers to her room. Why she agreed I am unsure, but I'm thankful none the less.

A time from our past, Jess's 18th birthday, came to mind. She had been so angry with me about not spending more time with her. Yeah, I blew that to shit. That day I had bought her flowers to represent our past, present, and future. It took me a while to get them all in her room. Karlie watched as I placed the bouquets of carnations on one have of the room. The biggest bouquet I placed a card with my word- *The carnations a symbol of how many days I have loved you.* On the other side of the room I filled with red and white tulips. This card said- *The tulips a symbol of how many days I will love you.* Ended the gross display of flowers with three bouquets of roses; putting the final card in the middle. Standing there a moment remembering everything about her as he placed the final card that read- *The roses a symbol of everything I love about you.*

With hope that she'd remember their love and forgive him enough to at least have a conversation with him. He'd win her back if she found it in her heart to open back up to him.

Karlie supervised my every move, but her face indicated that this weakened her defenses. I moved to the door, my heart ached with leaving. One last glance at Karlie showed her that I didn't do this to start trouble I only wanted a moment of Jess's time.

She stood there wrapped in her own arms, "You are in love with her?"

Nodding as I stared into her eyes pleading for help. I had to ask, "Is she coming around at all?"

The pains in my heart reflected on Karlie's face as she shook her head no. Leaving with no argument I went home to shower before heading back to sit by her door.

Matt's edginess made me nervous as he followed me around the apartment waiting for my melt down. Determined not to let that happen again, I put on my coat to head back when my phone buzzed. When I pulled it out Matt and I shared in the triumph that the flowers had somehow worked on Jess. My blood rushed through my body sending a tingling sensation to my extremities.

It was a single text from her, which happened to be better than nothing at all until I read it, *"Thanks for remembering this time."*

My knees hit the floor when the air escaped my lungs. She's gone and nothing I do will change that. I had neglected her needs for so long there's nothing left in her heart for me.

Lying in bed not realizing how it came to be that I never made it back to Jess's room. Confusion filled my head why I didn't have her here in my arms professing my last love. Matt barged in, "Paul, you either have to stop this or get her to see you. I can't watch this anymore. Why do you have to be so over the top about one girl?"

The text from last night filled my brain and that deep gut wrenching twist of lost ripped at my insides.

Matt pulled me to my feet, "I will not allow you to do this to yourself. Get up and do something Paul."

On my feet I followed him pleading, "Matt, can you talk to her. Tell her anything she wants to hear. I need your help!"

He walked out the door. If he talked to her it might help, but it seemed that I had to do this myself. If I heard her voice it might help me a little. I picked up the phone left on Jess's message from last night. Though I didn't break down like I had last night it still burned deep in my heart.

I decided that her recorded voice would have to be enough for now. I just needed to hear her voice.

Completely surprised that she picked up, but she didn't say hello either. What was she doing? Did she want me to beg?

"Jess?"

"Um, no. Is this Paul?"

"Yes, who is this?"

"It's Karlie. I thought you agreed to give her space."

"I am. I just expected to get the voice service. Why are you answering her phone?"

The line seemed eerie quiet. She wanted to tell me something but didn't want to at the same time.

"Paul she doesn't carry her phone anymore. The only time I see her with it is when she calls home, and last night."

All my questions came out in a rolling wave, because Karlie wanted to help me. "Is she okay? Did the flowers help? Is she going to see me now? I can't take this much longer."

"Um. That's the reason I answered the phone. I am a little worried; she has a meeting with the administrator this morning."

"When?"

"She just left."

"Is she having problems with classes?"

"I don't think so. All she does is study. I think she's doing better than the first quarter."

"Is it money?"

"Honestly Paul, she doesn't talk to anyone anymore. She hardly eats. And most of the times I can't even sleep in my room because I can't stand hearing her crying all time."

If she would just see me I'd take all the sadness away from her, "She cries a lot?"

"That would be an understatement. Last night she didn't sleep at all. She sat in the window cell and cried all night holding one tulip."

Trying to process her reaction in my head jumbled together. She's done with me forever, but I wasn't letting her go. I made it harder on her. I had no intention of hurting her further, but my protective side sent me to the Administrator's office. I called Theo on my way there.

"Hey, what's up kid?"

"You could have told me she was here."

"What?"

"She has been here all year and I just find out about it."

"Paul, she was planning a surprise and it didn't go well and then when she came home she was upset. I didn't see the point."

"The point is that I could have been spending time with her this whole year and now I just find out and she won't even talk to me."

"Hey, it was up to her."

"I know, but what is the problem now?"

"What do you mean?"

"She has a meeting with admissions this morning. Do you have any idea what it's about?"

"I have no idea. She hasn't said there were any problems."

"You know if it's money; I can take care of it."

"I don't think so. I paid for everything already and I checked the account last week."

"So, you don't know what is going on with her?"

"No."

"I am on my way there now."

"So, you two are talking?"

"No, but I want to help her."

"Paul, I don't think it's a good idea."

"Well, I guess it's not up to you. I am here and if she needs my help I have to try."

"Boy, I don't want her that upset again."

"I hate to tell you this but she has been this way for a long time now and it's not getting any better. I have to try."

"Fine, but call me. Please."

"Yes, of course. I will call you as soon as I find out what is going on."

"Okay. Love you boy."

I laughed, "Yeah, I love you too, dad."

It's like my second nature went into effect. Becoming the business person; knowing exactly what to do next. If there's a problem I always found a way to take care of it. Jess's problem might just be the thing we need to get us back together. Hell, we were already family. She had to see that we are destined to be together.

Running into the building I came to a halt when I saw her sitting in the office about the sixth cubical down the narrow passage of offices. The glass shielded me from hearing the discussion. I sat down outside the office on a bench with a view of her. Witnessing her aggravation, the gestures with her hands, the shuffling of papers, whatever her problem was it was a big one. After observing her for a half hour I got up and stretched, paced a little then sat back down on the bench. If she needed help she had to know I am here for her. Another forty-five minutes had gone by bringing me to my feet again. This time I went for a drink at the fountain. When I turned she came out the door. Her eyes showed how troubled her emotions were when they met mine. The stare lingered between us, both afraid to make a move. Trying to ease her pain my mouth opened to offer her my help, but nothing came out. I cleared my throat and tired again, but she was already heading to the door.

I ran and stood in front of her, "Is everything okay?"

Her gaze made it back to my eyes and she shook her head no as the tears filled them.

I caused her more pain, "Is there something I can do to help?"

She shook her head pushing forward to get past me, but passed my arms and into my chest with her face hard. Not expecting her to react this way I enveloped her into my arms. I wrapped my hand around her head to hold her to me and wrapped my other arm around her to hold her tight. Air filled my lungs to the fullest for the first time in months. As I took in the scent of her hair it filled my nose and I buried my face to her head whispering, "Jess, It's okay. I am here now."

Yes, that was the wrong thing to say. She was letting me hold her until I opened my mouth. She pushed me away and started to walk away. I grabbed her and pulled her back to me, "Jess, please tell me what is going on that has you this upset."

Her eyes came back to mine and I wanted to drop to my knees and beg her to forgive me. They were so green but the whites of her eyes red. I let go of her and stared into those eyes. She hit me full force with her body again wrapping her arms around my waist hugging and squeezing me so tight. So confused, so tell me why I'm in love with this crazy over emotional girl. Oh, yeah, I could breathe when she was around.

Lifting her into my embrace I carried her out. She wrapped her legs around my waist and held on to me like her life depended on my hold. When we passed Kevin he gave me nod of approval. I had my Jess back just like that. I whispered to her ear, "Do you want me to take you to your room?"

She shook her head no.

"Do you want me to bring you home?"

She shook her head again.

"Do you want to go home with me?"

She nodded. I was bringing my baby home with me.

"Do you need anything from your room?"

She shook her head no, so I headed straight for my truck. I opened the door and set her down on the driver's seat. She scooted over so I slid in next to her. She laid down right away with her head on my thigh and her face to my stomach. Tracing my fingers through her hair as I drove to my apartment brought me back to our past, our love, and our future together.

Sliding out of the truck I pulled her with me until I could take her into my arms again carrying her into the apartment. The further we got the tighter she held onto me. Finding a chair near the table I sat holding my love. Enjoying every minute of holding her I needed to understand this turn of events. I pressed my lips to her head asking, "Jess, are you going to tell me what is going on with you? I can't help you if I don't know what to do."

She shook her head tucked her face deeper into my neck. As much as I loved that she wanted to be this close I needed to know so I could help her.

"Jess, I need to know. I have to call your dad back."

Everything ended abruptly. She pushed away from me standing up yelling at me, "Why do you have to call him about everything. Shit, Paul."

Confused by this I stood too. If she tried to run I would stop her.

"Where is the bathroom?"

I pointed to a short hallway, directing her to use the one off my room. She stormed into it closing the door behind her. Standing by my bedroom door waiting for her to come out so we could talk, trying to clear my name, "Jess, I called him to see if he knew why you were in the admission's office. I wanted to help, but I promised I would call him back."

She opened the door and stood there glaring at me like I had done the worst thing in the world. Trying for the innocent stare, knowing that I screwed up again, I crossed my arms over my chest. Frustrated with everything to do with her I found myself being short with her, "Jess, what do you want from me? I want to make you happy and everything I do makes you miserable."

She moved to me wrapping her arms around my waist and resting her face to my chest, "This helps the most."

Such a simple gesture, worry filled my chest. With her in my arms I would do anything she asked of me right now.

She peeked over my shoulder, "Is this your room?"

I pulled her to the living room, "Yes, it is but that doesn't fix things, Jess."

She smiled up at me with light in her eyes. Her arms wrapped around my waist again as we headed to the living room. I sat down on the couch, while she climbed into my lap. We sat and held each other silently. I wondered what I should do to help her, but I was so happy to have her in my arms that I didn't push the subject of what's wrong. The silence between us left my mind wandering with a million unanswered questions. The main one being, what made her so miserable that she came to my open arms?

We did well just sitting there, but I lost it when she kissed my neck. I lifted her chin to me and kissed her mouth. Another mistake I had to make because when she kissed me back it released all of my control. I moved to her mouth consuming her. This wasn't a child's game anymore. We were both consenting adult, though I had agreed not to take her virginity until she agreed to marry me, the thought made my loins jump to attention. My hands held her face trembling with wanting to hold her harder to me. In one swift move I lifted her off my lap and lay her down moving next to her so I could feel her whole body against mine. The kisses a playful dance of lust, as I traced mine against hers, nibbled on each lip, and sucked her in for more. Her leg wrapped around my hips allowed a heated sensation against my erection. I felt my body press against hers even though my head was telling me no. If she wants to make love I am not turning her away, that's what I always did in the past to preserve her innocence. With any luck she would get pregnant the first time around and she would have to marry me. Her hand came up to mine and gently loosened my grip on her face. Her lips pressed to mine but then pulled away from me and tucked into my neck. Not sure of what would come next I scooted to my back while she draped her body against mine. Her leg coming up to rest on the over grown hard on in my pants, her mouth found my neck again, but this time she whispered, "I love you, Paul." I pulled her tight to my body pressing my lips to her head. My heart raced, my breath panting from the excitement of her affections. It took a while before I could calm myself taking sweet long breaths against her, holding her. My baby is home, now I had to find a way to keep her here.

When I felt the heat of her breath rhythm against my neck I knew she slept. I wanted to sleep too, but I was afraid this would all end.

Matt walked in and looked at us lying on the couch. He walked over glancing down, "Is that Jess?"

"Who else would it be?"

"I should have known better. I can see the difference in you already."

"What do you mean?"

"You look… happy."

I am happy. I have my Jess in my arms and I could breathe again.

Jess spoke, "Hi Matt."

"Hey, Jess. Glad you're back."

"I was never gone."

"Oh, yes you were to Paul."

She looked up at me and smiled, "I should go back to the dorm."

I shook my head, "You should stay here at least for the night. You can have my room and I will stay on the couch if you want."

She gave me that soft little smile and started to get up from our cuddling session. I held her hand to stop her from moving away from me.

"Paul, like you said this doesn't fix things. I need to go back to the dorm now."

I shook my head not looking at her. My hands trembled as I let go of hers. I put my head in my hands entangling my fingers in my hair to pull it out if she said she didn't love me, "I can't, Jess."

"What do you mean you can't? Are you going to keep me captive?"

I huffed, "If I have to… yes."

She turned to Matt for help, "Matt, will you please take me back to the dorm?"

He laughed falling down in the chair, "I can't either, Jess. I hate to say this but you two belong together."

Her hand brushed under my chin pulling my face upward. I shook my head until my eyes met hers. I would do anything she wants, but let go of her even for a minute.

"Paul, I shouldn't have let this happen. It will hurt more and I can't do that again. Why won't you take me back to the dorm?"

"I'm scared that I won't ever have this chance again."

Determined to keep her here I went to my room grabbing a large T-shirt and a pair of boxers setting them on the bed. When she peeked into the room I pointed, "There, you can sleep in that. You can have my room and my bed. I will take you back early enough to get to class."

She tilted her head, "This is going to hurt worse, Paul."

"I don't care. I am not letting you go."

Not wanting to hear her say no I stormed to the living room, sat down on the couch, and folding my arms on my chest.

Jessica

Picking up the T-shirt taking in the smell of him that lingered on it. My heart grew with comfort with his scent. It wasn't sweaty; more of a manly scent of working outside, but a hint of musk cologne. After changing into the T-shirt, I pulled back the covers and crawled across his big bed into its warmth. My reward for caving to Paul's open arms. Not a hard mattress that creaked of plastic every time you move. Tracing my hands over his sheets and up to the pillows, grabbing one I sat back up pulled it to my face and inhaled his scent again.

The guilt that overwhelmed me about Paul already hurting, how would he be able to handle me leaving for a year? I wanted to tell him, but I couldn't. He would never let me go, but I had to now that I agreed. Plus, maybe seeing others hurt and suffering would make mine seem foolish. At least that's what I hoped. This is my opportunity to find anything else that I had to get rid of. Not finding anything in his drawers or in the closet to remind him of me satisfied my curiosity until I turned on his lap top finding a huge picture of us together. Stopping at his house to get rid of our relationship didn't get rid of everything. This all had to go before I left. It would be easier if he didn't have to be reminded daily of me. I went back to the bed and heard a knock on the door. Covering up a little I answered, "Come in."

This amazing good looking man walked in with eyes on me. That crooked smile on his face as if he's up to something. His eyes so worn; I supposed that's my fault for not seeing him. He did sleep in the hallway for almost two weeks. He walked to his dresser and took out shorts and a muscle shirt, "Just grabbing clothes, Jess, and then I will leave you alone."

I sat there watching him search slowly to get things out. I knew he hoped I would ask him to stay, but if I did the pain would be so much worse when I left. It isn't about what I wanted or needed, it's about protecting him the same way I protected myself. I didn't want him to hurt deep down in his gut, like the world would be better without him, the way I do every day. The knowledge of me leaving and not seeing him killed me a little more each day. I thought about the meeting with the administrator. He advised me that I'd pass my classes based on my homework and I wouldn't have to take any finals due to volunteering to help a third world country. The whole time he had talked to me I focused on not seeing Paul, not hurting him, and no more pain and suffering for me.

While not paying attention to Paul, lost in my own world, I heard my name on his mouth, "Jess,"

Catching me off guard I jumped, "Yes,"

His eyes were so caring, as they stared at me, "Are you okay, really okay?"

Trying to hold it all in I nodded, but my eyes stung threating to tear up. All I thought about now days happen to be the man who stood in front of me now. How I wanted to give into letting him have my heart, but with me leaving the pain I would cause him. I had to protect him from hurting again.

He came to sit on the bed and traced his hand along my cheek, "Please let me help you. Tell me and I can help fix whatever it is that has upset you."

I reached up and touched his chest and gazed into his eye, "My sadness is from missing you, Paul." I didn't lie.

The slight grin washed from his face but his eye didn't leave mine, "Why didn't you tell me you're here? We could have had the whole year together."

"I planned on surprising you, but you didn't live on campus so I tried to spy on you to find out where you lived. Then school seemed to get harder and harder until I got side tracked, and then I witness you kissing someone else. I thought you moved on, and then when you didn't show up at the cabin I came to terms with that and I couldn't put myself through it anymore."

"I am not over you and I will never be over you. I love you and want to marry you." He got up and grabbed the white box and came to sit on the bed. "Jess, this will keep us together forever. All you have to do is say yes."

"I can't, Paul, not yet. I still have something I have to do."

"Can we do it together?"

"Not this, Paul. When you didn't meet me I agree to…" Choking on the words the crying took over and I couldn't finish what I needed to say. I fell back covering my face bawling. There's no way to change my future for the next year. I'm leaving him and my heart pounded to near explosion from the sadness that engulfed me.

He crawled over me, "Jess, what did you agree to do?"

I rolled away from him curling up to a pillow hugging it. He lay down beside me wrapping his arm around me.

5

I woke to Paul opening the curtains with the biggest grin on his face. He's so cute with his messy hair in the morning. He pulled back the covers and grabbed me by my ankles pulling me to the edge of the bed, "It's going to be a great day. Come on sleepy head." When he let go I rolled over and crawled back up to the pillows, "I'm not going. I like sleeping in a real bed."

Laughing and pulling my ankles till they dangled off the bed he dropped them, and grabbed my wrists to pull me to sit up on the edge of the bed. The next thing I knew I was flung over his shoulder. I pretended to be a limp rag. He moved around the room and walked out. I reached up grabbing the shirt to cover my butt. Paul held Matt's door closed as we went by it.

"You can put me down now."

He laughed walking into the bathroom.

He set me down in the tub and I glared at him. "I need to go to the dorm."

He opened the medicine cabinet and set my shampoo and conditioner on the toilet. He smiled and pulled out spritz spray and then he bent down and pulled out a blow dryer. I shook my head surprised that he has all my supplies here at his apartment.

He walked over to me smiling, "You need to wake up first."

He turned on the cold water making me screamed, "You jerk that is freezing." I reached for the hot water.

He backed out of the bathroom, "Remember, Matt is here and you…" He looked down at me, "are wearing a white T-shirt."

After he backed out closing the door I looked down to see what he meant. Yep, completely see threw. War of the Roses came to mind, how I would get back at him. I took the shirt off and then the underwear wondering what he was planning on me wearing to the dorm to get my clothes.

Paul

I want to keep her here so she'd see what it would be like to live with me. My hope for her to like it here replayed in my head over and over as I went to make breakfast. She had to be happy here to stay with me for the rest of our lives. Matt stumbled out, "You slept with her?"

I glared at him, "Yeah, we slept!"

"You're happy?"

"Yes, I am. Do you want breakfast?"

"You're cooking, yeah. What was with the screaming?"

"I put her in the shower and turned on the cold water."

He laughed, "She's the type of girl that will get revenge."

"Jess, no. She wouldn't do that."

He laughed out loud. I finished and made three plates. I ran to the bathroom, "You take longer than I remember."

She opened the door and I backed away. With only a towel on, she walked across the living room to the table. Matt's mouth hung open. I walked over to him and hit him in the back of the head to remind him he was staring. He choked, "I'll finish this in the living room."

He picked up his plate and moved to the couch. Jess looked down at the table so I asked, "Are you hungry?"

She smiled and walked towards me, "Are you?"

Confused, and a little irritated, "Jess, Matt is here. You should get dressed?"

She laughed, "Yeah, and what am I supposed to wear for underwear?"

I shook my head and laughed with the thought *Commando.*

She walked up to stand directly in front of me, "I bet you didn't think about that when you put me in the shower."

I smiled at her with the biggest grin shaking my head no.

"Besides, someone else may need a cold shower." She opened the towel in front of me making my heart pound so hard I heard it in my ears. With every intention of staying in control I concentrated on her eyes, but when she moved my attention move south. What a perfect body. Her breasts were the right size to fill my hands or my mouth, either fine by me. My eyes still wandered further south when she swished her hips. Her waist thin, milky, and smooth; I could play for a while with that belly button. A throbbing in my groin my eyes ventured further over her body almost to the sweet spot when she dropped the towel. I grabbed it quickly wrapping it back around her pulling her against my body.

It might sound like a growl when I yelled, "Matt!"

"Yep, I'll eat this in my room. I told you, Paul."

"Woman! What are you trying to do to me?"

Dancing with sparkle her eyes met mine. Her mouth parted just slightly when the corners of her mouth twitched to a smile. When her hand stroked against me I closed my eyes. If she wasn't careful I would do it right here on the table, take her like breakfast.

Her giggle; a painful delight, "Told you someone else needs a cold shower."

She took the towel from my hands and wrapped it around her and sat down across the table from me. She crossed her legs and sat there smug and took a bite of a piece of bacon. I walked over to her and leaned down to her ear, "You are cruel."

She laughed, "You're the one that wanted to see me in a wet t-shirt, Paul."

She's right I need a cold shower after that display. That's pure evil on her part. This is going to be fun. I have five weeks to win her over before school's done and it's going to be the best five weeks of our lives.

After a shower and dressing I worked on a wardrobe for her to leave the apartment in. As I set out a few things she strolled into the room.

Jessica

Oh my god he's gorgeous. Standing here in front of me in nothing but a pair of jeans hanging low on his hips tempted me to touch. A fine cut man he has grown into with ab muscles that rippled, oblique's that V, arms that bulged without flexing. No wonder they couldn't keep their hands off of him, he took my breath away.

"Jess, I hope this is okay. You'll have to go commando until you get to your dorm." The thought made me grin from ear to ear. Taking advantage of the situation he continued, "Maybe you should bring some of your things here?"

I grinned but I shook my head. This is all going to be over in two weeks when I had to leave for South America. How could I let this go on knowing that it will be so painful for both of us? Realizing that I'd hurt the man that I loved. I needed to behave and push him away gradually. Maybe I should be a pain in his ass so he wouldn't like me anymore. There are so many things that I loved about Paul, like the way he looks at me, the way he touches me, the way he holds me, and most of all the way he loves me no matter what I do.

He moved around me intending on leaving the room, so I turned to watch as he pulled a shirt over his head. He glanced back at me grinning, "You have to hurry or you are going to end up going to class without anything on under that."

With that grin of his, how am I going to push him away?

We walked up to my dorm room hand in hand. God I missed this so much. He waited in the living area while I went to my room to change. When I came back out he was helping Karlie with something in her school work, but stopped immediately when I came out. His face went white with fear that I was going to be angry and Karlie turned to me, "Jess, he is such a good tutor; you should let him tutor us still."

Laughing with a sigh when I replied, "I didn't make him quit. You have to ask him." Our eyes met with challenge.

I wanted to know if he'd choose me, or if he had to do more with his life. His challenge happened to be me or work.

He gave me the crooked little smile but spoke to Karlie, "No, I can't. I have neglected Jess way too much. I need to have more time to spend with her."

It put a smile on my face to hear him say that, because we only had about two weeks and then it would be over again.

He held out his hand for me to take, "Are you ready?"

I nodded and took his hand following him out of the room. We walked to class together, "Jess, I will be waiting right here for you when you are done."

"Don't you have class or something?"

He raised his eyebrows, "Yeah, something."

I rolled my eyes and shook my head as I let go of his hand to walk into class. He pulled me back, "Aren't you going to kiss me?"

I raised my eyebrows teasingly, "You think I want to kiss you in public, Paul? People might get the wrong idea."

"That's the idea. I am in love with you."

I smiled embarrassed as a few people walked pass me into the room. His hands came to my face and he kissed me passionately. He took my breath away and he gasped as I pulled away. Oh, my goodness, I am so in love with him all over again. I walked in backwards staring at him, "You'll wait for me?"

He nodded with the most pitiful face. Being apart for this hour and a half is going to be torture.

After the school day I went to my dorm. He was still in class but I put a bag together. Karlie walked in, "I thought you were lying to me about Paul, and you were fantasying about the guy."

I laughed, "We have been together for four years, except this year, but our hearts still belong to each other."

"So why did you break it off with him anyway. I'd never let that one go."

"He was too busy for me, and it made me sad all the time, but now I wish I didn't have to leave."

"Iaesha?"

I nodded.

"Does he know?"

I shook my head. "I gave her my answer when he promised me he'd meet me at the cabin and then he didn't show up so I said yes."

"He looks at you like he is in love with you."

"Yeah, I hope so, but he gets busy and I need more attention than what he gave me. It's always a competition with his business, his first love."

"Are you going to tell him?"

"Not now. He won't let me go and now I have to go."

"He is going to be heartbroken."

"Me too. I love him with my whole heart."

"Yeah, I noticed."

"Please don't tell him; let me when the time is right."

She nodded as he came storming in, "Jess!"

I held my bag up, "Just getting a few things in case I end up in the shower again."

Karlie laughed, "Getting right to it I see."

"No!" Paul said with disgust, "She needed to wake up, that is all."

He took my bag and my hand. My heart thud a little faster. I'm in heaven. On our way back to his apartment we stopped to picked up dinner for three, not leaving Matt out. Paul said if he didn't make Matt food the guy would never eat. He doesn't cook.

We ate dinner the three of us and I detected a funny grin on Matt's face all through dinner. I nudged him with my foot to get him to stop but he kept smiling and would giggle to himself a little now and then. Paul and I made plans for the whole week and our time together. I knew that all my free time would be here with him. Trying to push him away slowly wouldn't happen; I needed him so badly right now. We moved to the living room where we did our school work, but I finished first. Now with my school work done I stood up and put it away. Reaching over the back of the couch I tickled Paul's ear. He shooed me away, but I persisted on attention and whispered in his ear, "I need time." He grabbed me and pulled me over the couch to his lap. When his eyes met mine they were full of desire for me. He needed play time too. Gesturing to Matt still studying, Paul let me get up. Matt got the hint without us asking. He stood up sighing, "I guess I am going to finish in my room."

Crawling on the floor towards him I pulled on his leg, "Matt, please don't leave us alone."

He shook his leg, "Jess, stop it."

I stroked his leg leaning against him, "You shouldn't leave us alone."

Paul grabbed my legs pulling me back to him, "Yes, he should." Crawling over me he pinned me down as he hovered over me.

I reached again, "Matt, help me."

"No, I like when you two are together. Sorry, Jess, you will have to fend for yourself."

He walked into his room and closed the door.

Grinning from ear to ear, Paul is mine for the rest of the night.

His body pressed to mine the arousal evident. Possible this is the night we show each other how much love is there.

His fingers touched my cheek, "Do you like to torture me?"

A little nervous with the inclination of making love to Paul I shook my head no and pushed for him to get off me. He sat back watching me get up, "So am I on the couch tonight?"

Shrugging while walking away to the bed room I closed the door behind me. I needed a couple of minutes to compose myself. After changing into sleeping shorts, yes they were really short, and a camisole that sat just above my belly button I walked back out making my way around the couch to Paul. He sat on the floor with his legs stretched out in front of him crossed at the ankle just viewing the TV. Stepping over him to demand his attention he didn't hesitate letting his eyes trail up my body. His hands not able to stay off me traced my calves. I sat down on his lap facing him. Admiring his features I ran my fingers against his forehead, and then traced them down his cheek. He gazed deep into my eyes and gave me that great smile. My fingers found a dimple and I traced my fingers deep in it. A touch of embarrassment touched his face as his gaze dropped from mine, "Jess, are you going to marry me?"

I whispered, "Someday Paul."

His eyes came back to mine full of worry, "You still love me, right?"

I wanted to show him how much, "I have always loved you, Paul." More determined to make him understand I held his face to mine, "And I will always love you. Just sometimes we let other things get in the way."

He agreed, "Then you need a cold shower little girl."

Heaving my chest in front of him hoping he would notice how much I have changed, "Are you sure I am a little girl, Paul?"

His hand came to my chest and his finger slipped under the edge of the camisole tracing it down to the cleavage. He was shaking his head as his eyes followed his finger, "Your right; you're not a little girl anymore."

Taking his hand in mine entangling our fingers together. I laid my head to his shoulder with my nose along his neck so I'd smell him. He wrapped his arms around me, "Jess, what is it that you have to do?"

Nudging his neck before I pushed to get up, "I don't want to talk about it Paul. Can we do that later?"

He watched me as I put out my hand for his. He followed me to the bed room, but stopped at the door waiting for me to tell him what we were doing.

I pleaded as I noted the gaze on his face, "Can you sleep with me?"

He smiled and crawled onto the bed next to me. I curled into him tracing my hand up and down his chest watching him breath. He stroked my arm and kissed my head. He'd have night mares tonight. He always did when he worried.

6

The nightmare did come in a wave of whimpers and body twitching, but I soothed them by whispering in his ear, "I am here Paul."

Back before he and I ever had a relationship his girlfriend had died when a garbage truck ran into them. She had gasped his name as her last word. The guilt he carried haunted him for so long. My dad had given him hope by hiring him to help with our cabin, and then referred him to others. That is how he started his business. He would sometimes stay at the cabin with us. At first I would hear him in the other room, but after we got to know each other he would come to my room and fall asleep sitting up next to the bed with his fingers barely touching me.

After he figured out that I would wake when he came in he started sleeping on the bed with me. I would run my fingers through his hair to sooth him; sometimes I would just wrap my arms around him to hold him. It wasn't until we started dating that dad put a stop to that, but if he had a bad dream he would still show up and I would still do what I could to comfort him. He always told me he slept better when he could hear me breathing. Nothing ever happened when he would come into my room, except the need to sleep next to him.

I wanted to wake Paul the same way he woke me the other day. Sliding from the bed I snuck out and started breakfast. When I had a couple of pancakes done I knocked on Matt's door, "Time to eat."

"What?"

"Matt, it's time to eat."

As I heard him get up I went back to Paul's room opening the curtains. Not having to say get up to him, because he already pulled a pillow over his face. Yanking down on the covers my eyes took in every inch of his amazing body. Hearing me giggle to myself he peeked from the edge of the pillow, "What are you giggling about?"

I bit my lip, "You're not a little boy."

He rolled over covering his head more. I crawled over him and rubbed my hands up his back, "Did you need to stay in bed today?" I leaned down and kissed his back.

When he rolled to his back he took the pillow from his head and covered himself.

I giggled more witnessing his morning hard-on.

"You don't want to kiss me like that unless you're asking for it."

A rise my eyebrows with the biggest grin on my face I teased, "I am asking for it, but the stove is hot and ready."

Quickly I scooted to the end of the bed pulling him by the ankles; he didn't budge an inch. He laughed and threw the pillow at me, "Out, unless you plan on helping me with this."

I ran out of the room. Matt filled his plate as I came back to the kitchen moving to the stove I flipped the pancakes. He shoved a huge bite in his mouth, "Jess, are you moving in with us?"

"NO!"

"I don't mind. So far I've had breakfast every day that you've been here."

Finding his logic humorous I sighed, "But you had to study in your room."

With all joking aside he asked, "Are you happy here?" Not waiting for my response he continued, "Paul is happier with you here."

Not answer him the pain shot through my heart knowing I would be leaving soon and it's going to hurt him again. My stomach turned. I avoided answering him by finishing the pancakes on the stove, washing a few things in the sink, setting a plate in front of Paul. Then I escaped to the bathroom for a shower.

Paul

"Jess, aren't you eating?"

She yelled *no* from the other room. Matt avoided my questioning glance so I asked, "Did something happen, that I don't know about, that would piss her off?"

With eyes filled with apology Matt caved, "I asked her if she was moving in here. We were joking about her making breakfast. I like her here and I told her you are happy too." He leaned over the table towards me and lowered his voice, "It's like I pissed her off or something. Her mood changed in an instant and she got all quiet. Maybe I hurt her, but I didn't mean to upset her."

That's how it went with her. One minute playful and fun and the next she'd put up a brick wall. We had to be more careful around her. Leaning forward I filled him in, "She says she has to do something and she won't tell me what it is she's doing, but my intuition tells me she is leaving."

"Well, we all are. School is almost done."

"No, it's more like she is leaving for the summer, but she won't talk to me about it and she gets sad and defensive whenever I ask about her plans."

"I'm sorry, Paul. I just wanted her to know that I like her being here too."

He liked her here for one reason, "Yeah, you like being fed."

"Dam right."

"Dam right, what?"

When I glanced back up at her she tapped her foot and put her hands on her hips. She's adorable when she is angry. We didn't help the situation because we both cracked up laughing. Matt stood up and put his plate in the sink and jogged toward her, "Dam right I like when you're here with us. You both cook and feed me. What is there not to like about that." He passed her smiling, "My turn in the shower."

She watched him go in his room smiling. Her gaze came back to me questioning, "That's it?"

My voice hinted at laughter with my reply, "Yeah. He likes a full stomach."

She walked over to me and knelt on the chair across from me. She was smiling so she didn't stay mad for long. I grinned at her waiting for her to say something as I ate. I took a huge bite, but couldn't wipe the grin from my face as she stared at me.

"Do you want milk?"

She was going to wait on me, so of course I agreed that I wanted a glass of milk. I eyed her getting up and getting me a full glass of milk. When she walked over to me and sat on the table, she pushed my plate out of the way. This new forward girl sitting on the table made my groin pulse, "I guess I am done?"

She grinned handing me the glass of milk and scooted in front of me. I drank the glass of milk keeping my eyes on her, but traced my hand up her thigh.

Fingers traced through my hair. My eyes locked on hers to see what she's going to do. With her you had to expect the unexpected. Her face grew to a mischievous grin and then a full smile. She huffed with a little laugh as her eyes sparkled, and then she asked, "Do you want to skip and spend the day with me?"

Who wouldn't want to do that, "Yes."

She was giddy, but it hit me like a brick wall and I cringed as I continued, "Shit, I can't, not today. Can we do it tomorrow and make it a long weekend?"

Her smiled disappeared a lot faster than it had grown, "I can't. Not tomorrow."

She started to move away from me. I gripped her arm, "Just a minute, Jess, we can come up with something. Give me a minute to think about this."

She did stop moving away from me, but if I didn't come up with a great idea she would think something else came before her. It wasn't like that for me not any more. I just had things that needed to be done on someone else's time line. It's not a question of what I wanted to do. It's about what I had to do or I'd have done everything to fit around her, "Jess, stay here a minute. I am going to grab my schedule; I just need to look at one thing."

When her lip came out, my knees went week. Pressing her against the table, "Stay here I just need one minute."

Blinking away the tears that already started to well in her eyes she nodded. Darting to the bed room I collided with the chair stubbing my toe, yelled and danced off into my bedroom. In the other room I could hear her giggle. With a limp I hobbled back to the kitchen where she sat waiting with her hand over her mouth and eyes wide with surprise.

Her words came out muffled as she asked, "Are you alright?"

Sitting down in front of her I set my schedule in her lap, but glanced up at those wide questioning eyes. "Yeah, I'm alright." Grasping her legs I pulled her feet to rest on my thighs. Concentrating on the schedule I ran my finger down reading each entry. Her toes gripped at my legs distracting me. I peeked up at her grinning. She has no idea how bad I wanted to toss my schedule to the floor, lean her back on this table and finish my breakfast; Jessica with a cherry on top. Shaking off the temptation my eyes scanned the schedule again finding what I was looking for, one test in my 10 am class. Weighing my options, stay here with Jess or take a test. Regretting my discussion before I even mentioned it I took a deep calming breath. Not wanting to see the disappointment in her face, I confirmed, "I just have to go to my 10 am class." As tone as she is her leg muscles flared a gut sensation told me she didn't like my answer. Gripping her thighs once more I pulled myself between her legs. The scent of the sweetness that lingered between them gave me a full hard-on. If I didn't move soon I'd be toast. My eyes began to water from the pain of need. Taking a chance I peeked up at her, "Please tell me that's okay."

The smile crept back along with the pout. I couldn't help myself but chuckle a little she's so adorable.

My breath caught when she asked, "Should I go to my morning classes then?"

I shrugged my shoulders, "I guess whatever you want to do. We could meet for lunch and then what ever you want to do."

She took my schedule away setting it down on the table. She scooted forward and ran her hand through my hair pulling my head back, "I have issues with asking you to promise me something."

I didn't know how to take that and I didn't know what to say. She moved her feet off of me and slid down to my lap. She wrapped her arms around my neck and tucked her face into my neck whispering, "If I am going to class you need to get ready."

I picked her up as I stood and headed to the bathroom. She moved her face so I could see her smile. Resting my forehead to hers, "If I am going to get ready either you have to let me go, or you are coming into the shower with me."

She let go but I didn't. I'd be happy to have her company in the shower. Reaching for those sweet tasting lips I moaned while I nibbled them. Her hesitation as I let her go she inquired, "Why do you do that?"

With raised eyebrows, "Because you're sweet."

She glared at me and let go running into my room. I watched her grab something from her bag and put something on her lips on her way back to me, "Like this." She kissed me with her whole mouth as I licked her lips, but I shook my head. She released me confused, "That's not it?"

I shook my head and tipped her back sucking her neck and kissed her up to ear, "That's it. You entice me, your sweetness."

She giggled and pushed me away, "Go take a shower, and hurry. If I am going be on time for class we have to hurry."

I laughed and kissed her and then went into the bathroom. My mind drifted to her over and over again in the shower; the little pout, the taste of her lips, and the pulse in her neck. I had to shutter to shake off what I wanted to do to her. It didn't work because I thought about her legs and running my hands along them, tasting her stomach as I kissed her. Okay, she's definitely a woman now, so why are we waiting? Oh, that's right, I want her to marry me and I promised not to do that until she agreed to it.

We were heading to class and I pulled her to a stop outside the room, "I will see you in a few hours. Will you meet me at my truck?"

"No."

"No?"

"You have to pick me up like a date."

"From where?"

"My dorm room, and don't be late or I might not be there."

"You wouldn't!"

"Don't test me."

She walked away from me and leaning forward I almost fell over my own feet. She knew how to drive me crazy.

When I finished my class, I ran the whole way to the dorm and up the stairs to her door. I knocked and one of her roommates answered, "Jess, please." I huffed and gasped for air. She came to the door with another bag full of stuff, "Why are you panting like a dog?"

"I didn't want to be late."

She laughed, grabbed my shirt, and started walking pulling me behind her. We ran into Kevin, the security guy, on our way out. "Hey, how's it going with you two?"

Jess turned to me and gave me that disapproving look.

"Jess, he kept me from camping out 24/7 at your door."

She turned back to him, "Thank you. He is a little obsessive."

Kevin laughed as she pulled me out the door. I wrapped my arms around her waist and picked her up twirling her around, "So what are we doing?"

"You said we're going to have lunch."

"Okay, we'll have lunch. What do you want?"

She grinned at me crawling in the truck. She was going to drive me insane with her facial expressions. I had to shake it off once again and move on with our day.

We stopped after lunch and picked up movies and snacks. Next we headed to my apartment for a day of cuddling, movies, and whatever else we come up with. I hoped for the last. She's so playful watching the movies and eating our snacks. She tried to throw M&M's in my mouth. I fed her cotton candy on my fingers. We cuddled and had chips with dip together. She moved around a lot so I just observed her as she did different things. When she lay down on the opposite side of the couch I took her feet in my hands and started to message them. Touching any part of her pleased me. She leaned back closing her eyes and we heard Matt coming in the door. He took one glance at the room with disgust, "You two are cleaning the apartment."

Choking out a laugh, because I did all the cleaning anyway, I rolled my eyes. Not giving us any more thought he went to his room mumbling.

Jess asked, "Do you think he is irritated?"

"Yeah, probably."

Leaning over the back of the couch to see that sexy little body make its way to Matt's room, I ached with need. After she knocked and he opened the door she dragged him back to the living room, "You my friend, need relax time."

Enjoying the view of her I waited to experience her next move. Pushing him to sit on the couch she held up an M&M.

Matt quickly turned to me with a questioning stare. I shrugged as one came at his face ricocheting off his face. In her scolding voice to demanded, "Matt, you're supposed to catch it in your mouth."

He was shaking his head as she threw another one at him. I stood up and grabbed a handful. Tossing one at him made him yelled at us to stop.

"Jess, show him how to do it." When I tossed one up she caught it in her mouth with ease. His eagerness to be part of our little playtime he caught one in his mouth. We ended up feeding him everything trying to get him to catch it with his mouth. After pelting Matt over and over with M&M's we settled down for a few games of Rummy. As the night crept upon us Matt migrated back to his room leaving us alone again.

Being alone with Jess happened to be my treat for putting her first on my list. We sat down to enjoy another movie as I put my head in her lap to be as close to her as possible. Not that the movie's bad, but I am with Jess and all I wanted to do is take in every second I can. Delicate fingers ran through my hair relaxing me to a light nap. When the touch didn't fill my needs any longer I curled into her more to take in her scent of sweet vanilla, with a touch of spice. The sensation didn't resemble anything that I could remember, but my mouth watered anyway. Tugging her tank top up just a tad so that when my mouth made contact with her skin I could savor what lingered for hours. Her fingers tightening in my hair which made me aware of her tense body. Nuzzling to her core I traced her stomach with my face making her body ridged. Could she be nervous to let me touch her this way? She pushed me trying to get out from under me. Pressing her back down I crawled over her pinning her to the couch. Seducing her into telling me what she had to do might just work. She wanted me now, and wanted me badly, I could sense the need in her body.

Staring into those beautiful green eyes I traced my fingers along her cheek, "Are you going to tell me what you have to do?"

While pushing to get away from me she scolded, "Do you want to make me sad?"

Not wanting this to end I held her tighter preventing her from moving, "I just want to experience everything about you, baby."

"Yeah, and baby?" Her eyes pierced into mine with anger, but had stopped pushing away from me. Moving to my side letting her keep her secret I took what she would give me. I kissed her cheek, pulled her hand to my mouth to kiss that too. We spent the rest of the night, and most of the next day on the couch touching each other tenderly.

Friday I wanted to take her out, but she wanted to stay at the apartment. Matt was going on a date so we stayed home. She explained that she wanted to spend quality time with me and nothing else matter but the time we were getting together. Sunday night my body hurt with need, and from lying around doing hardly anything. A long shower to wash away my need is what I needed the most, but caved to her going first.

Like we had been doing this all our lives we seemed to move in unison. She went to the shower first while I picked up the living room, which took her forever. After my shower I noticed things were put away, but the best part of all Jess laid in my bed waiting for me. If that didn't make a man's dick hard I don't know what would. Avoiding giving her a full view of my needs I turned away from her to get dressed in boxers.

Crawling into bed next to her, "Jess, are you sleeping."

She turned and cuddled into me, "What do you think?"

Her leg slid between mine and traced upward. I gripped her thigh holding her from the surprise that waited if she went any further up, "No, you're not sleeping."

She rolled her eyes, "No! My legs are smooth, and silky."

This woman had no idea what she did to me all the time. I reached down pulling her leg to avoid my growing hard-on. My hand trailed along the softness of the now shaved legs, which caused a twitch in my groin. This put a smile on my face, "Very nice."

She took my hand and pulled it further up her leg.

This is her way of begging for it, "Jess?"

She grinned and nodded.

I glided my hand further to her as she moved closer to me. My heart was racing. How could I do this when it meant so much more to me than what it would be if we did it now? I love her too much.

Restraining her, hovering over her, and holding her down. My erection zeroing in on the warmth of her sweet spot I pleaded, "Jess, if we are going to do this I have conditions."

With a grin she replied, "I knew that was coming." She nibbled on my lip, "Please don't ask me what I have to do. It will ruin my mood."

Now throbbing with need I shook my head.

Untrusting she urged, "What do you want, then?"

"You."

Not getting it at all she questioned, "You said conditions?"

"Yes. Not tonight. Not for our first time together."

She was skeptical, "What are you thinking?"

I rolled to my back pulling her along with me. Raising both my hands to cup her face and stare into those eyes. She needed to understand what I wanted, "You are special, Jess."

Searching my face for understanding she waited for me to explain.

"I want our night to be as special as you are to me. Remember the night we planned to meet at the cabin?"

I could see the sadness coming to her face.

"You were planning on making love to me. I promised your dad that you would have to say you'd marry me. All those times when I stayed away when I should have given into your needs... I wanted to keep my word, but I also wanted to keep you. I want to make it up to you. I want to make it special, a night to remember for the rest of our lives."

Tears had welled up so much that one dropped out landing on my nose. So far so good now the next part, "After school is done I will get the cabin ready and we'll continue that night."

She shook her head and traced her mouth along my chin, "Sooner."

Not the reply I expected, "How soon?"

The grin on her lips pressed against mine as her teeth nibbled, "Now would work."

I shook my head and held her face to mine looking deep in her eyes, "Your two week vacation this summer."

Eyes glaring, another response I didn't expect, "Okay, fine." She kissed my lips quickly and rolled away from me.

Shit, it didn't work. She's supposed to tell me what she was up to, because this would interfere with what she had to do. She's not supposed to be okay with it. I traced my hand down her arm, "Jess?"

"No, you have your stipulations."

I traced my mouth along her shoulder, "Jess, be realistic... when?"

She turned to me and nuzzled in, "Can it be soon, please."

"Friday?"

She moved up to kiss me, "Make sure there's food and water."

Not understanding her logic, "What do we need that for?"

That sexy, seductive grin grew on her face, "I don't plan on letting you leave this room till Sunday morning."

If anything from tonight made me hard as rock it's a tossup if it's the look in her eye, or the suggestion of lasting three days. Trying to disperse the thought, "It doesn't last that long."

She bit her lip, her eyes lit up, and that smirk told me she would make it last that long. Having a hard on, thinking about having sex with Jess, and having her curled up to me with her lips pressing against my shoulder this would be a sleepless night. Her sleepless night would come Friday, because it would be a night to remember.

7

It's hard to believe this week went by so smooth. We went to classes, did homework, and cuddled at night. We ate breakfast, lunch, and dinner together. I loved every minute with her and things changed for the better. She's going to agree to marry me when I ask her, but it had to be on or before Friday night.

I had gotten almost everything except for the flowers, so after class on Friday I stopped at her dorm. She didn't let me in and I found that odd, "Jess, what are you doing?"

"Surprise, why what are you doing?"

"Well, there are a few more things I have to get on my way home and I hoped you'd meet me there about 8 pm."

Her eagerness to go along with this set off alarms in my head, but it had to be my nerves. She pushed out of her room to walk with me to my truck. All touchy feely she wrapped herself to my side, running her hand against my abs, her lips pressing under my chin. So turned on, that I'm worried about lasting even 3 minutes alone with her, but I'd try my hardest to make this special.

I left her looking out my rear view mirror. Standing there watching me leave, her eyes so content on me. She'd say yes tonight for sure.

Rushing home I put candles everywhere. The rose petals sprinkled all over the bedroom. As special occasion required a special dress for Jess, so I laid out the one I bought for this night. With her eyes as green as they were I went for the black evening gown. Wondering how she would look in it would be answered tonight. Not wanting to waste time cooking, I had picked up our dinner. Trying to keep Matt away from the apartment didn't work out. He agreed to stay in his room. Tonight it's Jess and me with no interruptions, no distractions, and nothing to stop us from taking that next step. I set the table and put on music. After a shower I put on dress slacks and a dress shirt. I walked through the apartment nervous as all hell and looked out the window to see if she's here yet. Pleased to see her pull in and park. My instincts told me to rush out and meet her, but going for the seductive controlled personality I waited patiently. Uneasy and nervous I opened the door for her. She is too because she wouldn't even meet my gaze. I stopped her, "At any time, Jess, if you change your mind just talk to me."

Her eyes rose to meet mine full of tears. Assuming they were happy tears it filled my heart. It's finally going to happen, Jess would be all mine after tonight. I directed her to the bathroom, "Your dress is on the bed; meet me at the table."

She walked away glancing back to me as she entered the bathroom.

Jessica

I griped the sink to steady myself as my stomach rolled. Saying good bye to my roommates and packing my car turned out to be harder than I thought it would be. I would be on a plane in 36 hours and it kill me, and what it will do to him I had a good idea. Confused about what I wanted more, to give him a night to remember, or just run leaving him without heartache. The mirror showed a pathetic needy girl who didn't understand how that beautiful pure hearted man could love her. Would he love me through this? That's when I decided I would tell him tonight. If he still wanted to be with me than it would be, if not then I had to let him go. Only doing what he wanted I did my hair, make up, and then snuck to the bedroom. He already set it up for our encounter tonight. Rose petals everywhere, candles arranged around the room perfectly, the sheets and bed spread clean and folded back ready to consume us. At the end of the bed a beautiful black dress laid waiting.

I put fancy underwear I picked up for this night but the dress required no bra. I shook my head with disbelief that he got me one like this.

When I walked out he turned to me with his hand on his chest as he gasped. Not waiting at all I walked over to him and into his open arms he whispered into my ear, "You take my breath away."

Guilt washed over me, "Paul, I have to tell you something."

Not wanting to hear me out, he redirected my attention, "Let's have dinner first."

I swallowed and nodded following his lead to the table. He pulled out the chair for me as I looked back at him. I choked up already, how am I going to tell him the emptiness he had nightmares about is going to come back. In less than 36 hours the sadness is going to engulf us. Tears welled in my eyes so I turned to the table. Tonight is going to be the hardest night in my life. He served me food and sat down to eat with me.

There's hardly anything on his plate so I asked, "You're not hungry?"

A lopsided grin grew on his face showcasing that dimple as he replied, "I'm somewhat nervous."

I reached for his hand, "At any time, Paul, if you change your mind just tell me."

He laughed and scooted closer, "I will never change my mind about you."

I sighed and swallowed to keep the lump coming to my throat.

Silence fell over our dinner as we slowly ate. Scenarios ran through my mind of how I'd tell him. So wrapped in my head I didn't notice how quiet he is. Glancing over to see him dazed and off in his own world. I guess we both were.

He took my hand leading me to the living room where we danced slowly body to body. Reaching my arms around his neck I pulled him closer to stare into his eyes. He took me away from the sadness so easily. I forgot what I wanted to tell him because he helped me to believe that we'd stay this way forever. I didn't have a choice about going, but this was unbelievable and perfect. My fingers slid down his shirt to the first button. Searching his eyes for disapproval I undid the first one, then the second continuing until his shirt opened freely. After letting me trail my hands around him and place that kiss to his chest he made his move slowly walking backwards toward the bedroom. We closed the door when we were in his room. He searched my face wondering if I would change my mind. When you enjoy the tender touch of someone you love the only thing you want to do is take things further. He had been good for long enough and I loved him with my whole heart. We made our way to the bed but stopped at the side. His hands moved to unzip me bit by bit with an antagonizing leisureliness. I sighed with a laugh that's when he stopped to gaze into my eyes. Without the smile his dimples gouged his cheeks. After pulling the strap from my shoulder he kissed there with delicacy that sent shivers down my back. Wanting more of this tingling sensation I held his face to me turning my head to give him room on my neck. His hesitation seemed to stop him from continuing. It's the expression that played on his face left me wondering if he's changing his mind. Watching his eyes search the room my stomach did a flip. Tonight, our last chance to be together and he's changing his mind now? As his eyes came back to meet mine they sparkled bright from the light through the window. Or it could be the thought of consummating our love that made them shine like that. With raised eyebrows he confessed, "Candles."

Relief washed over me as my knees went week. Wanting to fall to the bed I refused to let my body cave so easily. When he let go of me I laughed and observed him lighting each candle as he made his way around the room. Taking each other's hands when we met at the side of his bed he confessed, "I really don't know how to make this perfect."

"You just did, Paul." I put my arms around his neck and kissed him in a way that should have curled his toes. His arms wrapped around my waist and held me tight while returning my kisses. When we both stopped kissing we held tight to each other not knowing how to take the next step. Planning it out like this made it uncomfortable and nervous for both of us.

If we're going to get through this tonight something had to change, "Paul, turn around first."

Brown Puppy dog eyes popped out of his head when he pulled away to see my face. That questioning, doubtful face stared at me as his body went rigid.

My voice a little shaky I pleaded, "I am so nervous. Can we crawl in the bed and explore first?"

Though his lips curved into a smile he only kissed my nose before turning around as I asked. I slid the dress off and crawled into the bed covering myself.

"I'm ready, Paul."

Laughing with anticipation he turned but motioned for me to turn away, "Your turn."

The bed caved under his weight, and the heat of his body warmed me as he crawled in next to me. Not wanting to wait a minute longer to be next to him I curled my body to his. Entwining my legs in his, I ran my hand along his chest, and kissed him over and over along his neck.

He kissed me carefully, but his hand trace up my leg. When his hand reached my core he stopped kissing me, "Did you change your mind?"

I shook my head grinning from ear to ear, "I have never gone to bed completely naked. It's weird."

Again he kissed my nose, but disappeared beneath the covers. Just to witness him in play I lifted the covers. Those eyes came back to meet mine filled with delight. The flick of his tongue against his lips caused a heat reaction between my legs. We would have no problem if he slid into me right now the moisture between my legs told me this. With the sexiest smile on his lips he made contact with my stomach. Instinctively my hand moved to his head running my fingers through his messy hair. A whimper came from deep within me; the sensation too good to refuse. Abruptly it came to an end when he slid my underpants from my body moving away from me further into the depths of the covers. It wasn't in me to complain, but I groaned with disappointment. Crawling back up the bed to me he hovered gazing into my eyes. His stare as innocent as a new born, guilt washed over me for what I have planned.

Voice gruff with restraint he demanded, "Jess, touch me."

Letting my fingers trail up his arms and biceps my attention on how dark his eyes seemed to be getting. Shaking his head he growled out, "Not there Jess."

This is my play time too. Stubborn to give into him I ran my hands up over his shoulders down to his chest only to brush his nipples with the palm of my hands.

Strain filled Paul's face when he closed his eyes and groaned, "Are you teasing me?"

Reaching up I nipped one of his nipples with my teeth.

The warmth of him as he ground his hips against mine sent a thrilling shiver up my spine. Gasping at the sensation only to have it end when he moved to lie down next to me. He propped his head on his hand so that he can look down at me. Hoping it's not over, my eyes wide with wonder why he stopped.

Paul

To keep her legs parted I laid mine between hers. The last thing I wanted her to do is change her mind, but I almost blew when she tried to take a bite out of me. If she wanted to play I would give her what she wanted. After tonight she won't want anyone else for the rest of her life, she's going to be all mine.

Her wide eye stare made me smile, her innocence written on every inch of her face. How she didn't see it on mine I have no idea, but we're going to experience this together

Trailing my fingers against her waist I asked, "Are you afraid to touch me?"

Shock is the only word to explain the expression on her face.

"NO!"

Not the response I expected her to give me.

"Then touch me."

Really trying hard to hold back the grin spreading across my face it's impossible she lit my whole world. When she finally reached to touch me she placed her hand on my face. Her finger traced my dimple as always.

Shaking my head, even chuckling a little I took her hand and brought it to my mouth, kissing her open palm. Taking each finger in my mouth one by one, sucking, licking, and kissing each of them. Coming up with a way to experience this together she had to get over her fear of touching me right now. That is something I would want her to do on a regular basis. Her chest rose and fell rapidly, and all I wanted to do is dive deep into her, but I also wanted her to be completely comfortable with our sexuality together. Leaning away from her, taking her hand down to me, I wrapped her fingers around me. Her lip twitched nervously as I stroked myself with her hand. Releasing her hand from my grip I hoped she would take over handling me.

Her whisper came, "It's hard and soft at the same time."

Moving as close as possible to let her explore my penis, I decided to explore her. She has never been heavily endowed in the breast area, but seeing them now. How perfectly round they are, how fare the skin on her breast is, and the way her nipples puckered there right in front of me. Perfection is what I saw in her. As I ran my finger against the areola she stroked her hand against me. Gently squeezing her nipple between my fingers and then rolling it, she squeezed and stroked harder. The more pleasure she experienced the more she gave me the pleasure of her hand. When her finger rubbed against the tip to find moisture she gasped. Consuming her gasp I took advantage of her mouth. If kissing her wasn't heavenly enough her hand continued to touch, stroke, and message my membrane. If I didn't stop her soon it would be over before it begins. I pulled gently away from her grasp moving down to take each breast in my mouth. I wanted to touch and taste every inch of her. Her protest will come eventually, but for now she let me do what I wanted. Taking her breast in my mouth licking, sucking and nibbling, my reward her hand cupped my head against her. After moving to the other her lips pressed to my forehead with a moan, "Oh Paul!"

To me that's permission to continue, which I had every intention of doing. The end goal to have the warmth wetness of her stroking against me while screaming my name helped me to control the eagerness. I definitely had this in the bag if she already called out my name. Now it's time to get serious. I pulled myself from her grip and slowly kissed her down the middle as I made my way south. Only pausing at her belly button to drive her a little mad as I devoured her there. Both of her hands gripped my hair. Not wanting to wait another second to see her next reaction I made my way to the sweetness of her core and planted a full open mouth kiss.

Pushing up to her elbows looking down at me with an uncertain expressing showing her disbelief of what I just did she scolded, "What are you doing?"

Acting like the devil himself I dipped down only to run my tongue from her opening all the way to her clit keeping my eyes on her for the reaction. Dropping her head back, falling to her back, her hands fisted the sheets when I licked up her clit to suck her flavors. Naturally her legs opened to me as she raised her knees placing her feet to the bed she bucked upward at the sensation. Needing to control her I wrapped my arms around her legs pressing her stomach down as I devoured her into ecstasy. Her whimpers, her cry's, and her moans all came out with my name on the end.

"Paul, I need you now."

Not yet baby, which I didn't take time to tell her. I continue my assault of the wet folds, her clit, and the core of her until her legs shook from pleasure. Slowly I crawled up her as the rest of her body trembled against mine. She's mine all mine, all she has to do is say it.

My own pain of throbbing needed to be satisfied, but I had to hear the words. "Are you sure you want to do this?"

Her word came out breathy, "Yes."

Spreading her wide beneath me I rubbed against her core, "Tell me."

The need in her voice came out pleading, "Please Paul. I need you in me."

I wanted to stay true to my promise to her father. Still not the words I wanted to hear from her I asked, "Are you going to marry me?"

Jessica

Why did he have to make me come if he didn't intend on finishing the job without telling him I would marry him?

He reached between us stroking me with his penis held in his hand. He knew what he was doing and it drove me crazy. Wanting him to fill me with his love before I explained the bomb I intended on dropping on him. Reaching my arms around him to pull him tighter, hoping he wouldn't be able to resist. Taking the tip his penis and placed it against my opening without inserting he drove me mad.

That crazy devil grin came to his face as the pressure of him told me he is there and willing if I said the words. If I told him no, would he stop making love to me? Finally breaking the silence he pushed, "Jessica, you have to tell me you will marry me."

I bit my lip and dug my fingers into his butt pulling him to me, "Not yet, Paul, please."

He took my hand and sucked on my ring finger searching for something with his other hand. When he found what he reached for he slid his mouth from my finger. He gazed at me with pleading eyes as he pushed a little further into me, driving me to want to beg him to do it. I wanted to tell him I'm leaving and that he had to hurry, our time was limited. He slid the ring on my finger, "Please tell me you will marry me?" He pushed into me a little more and I gasp, "A year."

He pushed harder almost in me.

"We can plan on a year?"

"Start planning in a year."

He pushed into me as the tears escaped my eyes and trickled down the side of my face. Waiting to see if it hurt being the first time for me his hands came to hold my face, "Does it hurt?"

I shook my head because it didn't hurt, but my heart did. He pushed to me again as his mouth came to mine deeply. His tongue taunted me as he pushed to me again driving deeper with each stroke. He moaned as he moved to and from me. When he would pull away I wanted to beg him to push into me again, but by the time I would open my mouth he'd dive back into me. Words escaped from him with his mouth on mine, "So warm."

Yes, it's warm, filling, and oddly good to me. His movements became faster as he moaned more. The tingling started in my toes and I gripped him tightly, but his release filled me as his body fell onto mine resting there. His face came to my neck as he kissed, licked, and sucked. I laid there realizing he's done. I traced my hands up and down his back wanting him to move to me more. His lips came to my ear, "You didn't come again did you?"

I smiled and turned my face to kiss him, "It's good."

He laughed with a sigh, "It's not supposed to be good."

I grinned as his face came to mine and he moved a little. I raised my eyebrows as he slipped away from me. We both giggled and kissed more as his body move to mine again. His kisses still filled with need as our mouths moved together. The tingling came back as he swelled inside of me. I had to quit kissing him to breath and his hands came to my face to hold me to look at him as he stroked deeper and deeper. The slower and deeper he went the tingling sensation increased. I gasped and moaned a little. The sound surprised me that it came from me and I closed my eyes with embarrassment. His lips pressed against mine, "There, Jess." diving deep hitting an area inside me that ignited with each stroke. His rhythm easy to follow only increased my longing to have him in every way. I nodded and gasped again. Oh shit that noise escaped from chest this time. His smile grazed my face as he concentrated more on moving the way that was making me moan in ecstasy. Seeing the creases in his forehead grew with his concentration as he moved to me more determined.

It became too intense, "Paul, stop."

He stopped pushing so hard but didn't stop moving that way and I held my breath.

Gasping in between long torturous thrusts he blurted, "Are you okay?"

Something seemed to be happening to my body which I couldn't stop so I nodded and shivered. He went back to moving to me smiling as he stared into my eyes, "Jess, it's supposed to be like this."

When he pushed into me so slowly my body took over rising to meet him, tilting in a way that gave him deeper access to my core. Each movement we made complimented each other as if our bodies took over craving more. The mixed emotions over whelmed us as the tingling moved up my body and festered in my stomach. It's like swinging when you close your eyes and tip back to get that rush of tingling but only better because you had someone to share it with.

Not being able to handle the pleasure tears filled my eyes his voice came deep and careful, "Jess, let it happen, please."

I closed my eyes allowing myself to love him without all the clutter. It became a different world to me as we moved together as one. My movements complimented his as I dug my fingers into his skin. I heard him moan and his body tensed even more. He gasped with every movement into me and I made noises that didn't sound like me at all. He pushed hard to me and this amazing rush filled me causing me to erupt inside and scream out his name. I gasped for air as his movement slowed the pleasure complete. I came with him in me and it was better than I could ever imagine. It wasn't that way the first time, but he didn't stop until I shared that experience with him. I could do that every minute of every day if my body could handle it, only now I'm exhausted and my body limp and weary. If I tried to move it would tremble everywhere. His face rested next to mine his cheek caressing mine. The sensation of his smile glided against my face while whispering, "That is how you make love."

I moaned a yes and kissed his cheek. His mouth came back to mine as we kissed softly, playfully, and loving. His nose nudged mine while our lips consumed each other's. This urge to cry took over causing me to lose it. I couldn't stop the tears from coming and then a sob escaped me. After making love to the man I am madly in love with why would I cry like this? Our love is amazing and wonderful; I never imagined it could be so perfect. I put my arm over my face to hide my embarrassment. I didn't want him to see me this way because I'm not sad at this moment. I am so happy that it filled my heart with everlasting joy.

"Jess, why are you crying?"

I yelled with my squeaky voice, "I don't know."

He laughed slightly but then asked in a serious tone, "Did I hurt you?"

I shook my head and gasped for more air. He moved to hover and I grabbed a hold of him to keep him here.

"What do you want me to do?"

I yelled again this time my voice cracked, "I don't know."

He moved to my side a little and traced his fingers over my face, "You know I love you?"

Still not being able to look at him I nodded.

"Tell me what you are feeling?"

Trembling with my tears I slowly got out, "Scared... Wonderful... Amazing... Happy... Confused."

"Confused?"

"Yeah."

"About me?"

Bellowing, "NO! Why I'm crying."

He laughed and pressed his lips to mine gently, "I heard this could happen."

I lowered my arm to peek at him pleadingly.

"The first time; sometimes it's so emotional when you love someone."

"Great, you could have warned me."

He laughed and kissed my face everywhere, "I love that you are like this. You love me almost as much as I love you."

Pushing him away I tried to roll away from him, but nodded to tell him I did love him as much as he loved me.

Holding me preventing me from escaping his embrace he whispered in my ear, "I have to tell you something."

Pain seared my heart with fear. Did this turn him off? His hand gently pulled my face back to his gazing at me with the softest eyes, "Jess, remember when you wanted me to kiss you?"

Regaining my sanity I nodded, but I sniffled trying to control my tears.

"How you wanted me to be your first for everything?"

I nodded again taking a huge gasp of air and but it came out with quick breaths in, "Yes?"

"You are my first."

Staring into his eyes I couldn't quite get what he said.

"I have never been with anyone but you."

"But, you had lots of girlfriends?"

He grinned, "Because I never wanted to do anything with any of them. You are my first for everything..." He shrugged his shoulders, "Except for kissing."

Still wondering what exactly did he mean, "So, you never did this before with anyone?"

He shook his head as he pressed his lips to mine again. I wrapped my arms around his neck and then my legs. He pulled me close and rolled to his back with me laying on him. I moved down and laid my head on his chest. His kiss came to my head and the trace of his hand down my back comforted me.

We must have laid there for a long time and I rolled from him grabbing the sheet to pull around me. He pulled back on them, "Hey."

I pulled harder and ran to the door.

Reminding me he blurted out, "Matt is out there."

I laughed but still snuck into the bathroom. Pulling the sheet up to use the toilet the surprise came when I stood realizing the toilet filled with redness. With hands trembling I cleaning myself with toilet paper and water, trying to rid myself from the blood that came from me. I had no idea there would be so much from the first time. In a daze moving from the bathroom to his bedroom not knowing how or what I would say to him. As I got closer to him lying there naked, every part of his body ripped in muscles proving how perfect he is. I definitely did not compare. I sat down on the bed not saying a word. His arm wrapped around me and pulled me back to him. He traced his hand down my back lowering the sheet from me, "I wish you wouldn't cover your body. You are the most beautiful person I know."

Not feeling very pretty right now I pushed him away. Evaluating the situation he scooted up against the headboard and reached to pull me to him. He cradled me against his chest, and I couldn't refuse how amazing it felt to have his arms around me. Wrapping my arm around his waist and rested my head to his chest completely curled into him.

His chest rose slowly and sank as air escaped his chest when he asked, "What's wrong?"

A little embarrassed for yelling at him about this very thing a long time ago, it's going to be a hard one to explain.

"Remember that time in your truck when we were messing around."

The squeeze of his embrace came with a laugh as he said, "I remember lots of times when we messed around in my truck."

Frustrated I huffed, "The time I yelled at you because you fingered me."

He pressed his lips to the top of my head, "Yes. You thought I broke your cherry and you didn't want to lose it to fingers." Laughter escaped him as he remembered the scene.

This didn't make me happy, so I reached up pulling his face to look at me, "I didn't"

Laughter still filled his eyes, "Of course you didn't"

Raising my eyebrows hinting at the situation.

"Oh…" He breathed out as the realization came to him. He pushed me forward, rearranged the pillows, gently laid me down on the bed. When I was all tucked in he laid next to me propping his head in his hand to gaze at me. His hand gently rubbed my stomach, "Are you in any pain?"

More embarrassed than experiencing any pain I shook my head no. Closing my eyes his hand left my stomach only to touch my face gently as he traced the contours of it.

Relaxing with his soft touch luring me into sleep I closed my eyes to enjoy the intimacy of his tenderness.

8

I woke to the most amazing sensation of a large tender hand tracing down my back and a warm breeze on my neck with the faintest touch to my ear. I didn't move so that he would continue to touch me this way. The curve of his body against mine burned my skin. His chest pressed against my shoulder when he leaned over to kiss my back gently. Flipping his hand over; he ran his fingers down the middle of my back slowly. Once he got to my lower back his thumb moved back and forth across my lower back. Easing his touch I barely felt his hand against my skin as it skimmed over my butt causing a great big grin to fill my face. The hardness of his erection rubbed against me and a moan of need escaped his chest. As he touched me, running his hand down my leg, he pulled it up a little while his breathe became heavy. He moved to hover over me lowering himself so his shaft rubbed against my wet folds enticing me to wake from this perfect dream. When his mouth came to my shoulder blades he kept his mouth open as he traced my back gently gliding his lips over my skin. He rubbed against me again and my craving to have him in me increased. Caving to that need I rolled over facing him. The grin on his face grew showing those dimples that lured me to his face. Reaching for him when he decided to move away from me I gave him the pout. Scooping up the rose petals he tossed them in the air allowing them to fall all over. As his eyes roamed over my body his thoughts showed on his face with that crooked mischievous grin appearing on his perfect mouth. Working his way up my body slowly blowing the petals away from my skin he placed butterfly kisses to my body inch by inch. Twisting, turning, curving, and arching, my body craved the attention. It was the tip of his tongue to my abdomen that made me squeak out my pleasure. My toes tingled, my core wet and ready, all he had to do would be to slide into me, but he didn't. He sat back on his heals admiring the sight laid out in front of him. I am putty in his hands.

His fingers and hands wrapped around my wrists as he pulled me up into his lap, until his arm wrapped around my waist holding me to him. Lost in the depths of his eyes as they lingered on mine I'd agree to do anything he wanted right now all he'd have to do is ask. My legs wrapped around his waist as I waited for the new experience he'd bring me.

Pressing his forehead to mine he breathed in deeply let out the words with the release of his lungs, "I have never wanted anyone or anything more than you at this very moment." Reaching around his neck to pull him closer to me even one inch between us is too far apart. Holding me away from his body long enough to allow the hardness of his erection to easily penetrate my sweet spot, diving deep into my soul. Wetness of his mouth attacked my breasts licking sucking and nipping himself into a frenzy as his body rocked into mine. His thrust came deeper, harder than I expected. When his eyes fell on mine I wasn't surprised how dark they had become. Possession of greed filled him as his body rocked eagerly to me. Too fast for me or my liking I whispered, "Slower."

Instant conflict filled his face. My needs verse his. Gliding my hands down his back I noticed every muscle tensed at my touch as he slowed down his movements for me. The strength in his arms held me while the slowness of his invasion reached the spot of sensation I needed and wanted. Allowing myself to get lost a deep moan came from deep within me without my control. The intensity of his thrusts increased again, but it caused the loss of the pleasure I'm so close to having. This time I ordered him, "Slower!"

A growl escaped him, "Jess, I can't." His body moved faster again. I kissed everywhere and mouthed to him, "Oh, Paul. Please slower."

I tried to kiss him he turned his head to concentrate on his movements, every thrust straining his body beyond any pleasure. So close to release, another gasping moan came from me, and he moved even slower. Pulling almost all the way out and slowly inserting until he hit my inner core. After the fifth or sixth time he spoke into my ear, "Come on baby. I need you to come, NOW!"

His demand triggered my body to respond gasping out, "Yes, Paul. Oh yes. Oh Paul. Yes." Craving this new pleasure I wanted more. Releasing Paul from agony I begged, "Paul, harder!"

Holding me tighter to his body every muscle bulging he gasped into my ear, "You sure?"

I wanted him hard and fast my need out weighting my thoughts, "Yes."

His smile pressed against my cheek still not giving me what I wanted he replied, "You're positive?"

"YES."

My body already in motion to be pressed against the bed before I got the full word out, and yes is a short word. My legs propped over his biceps tipping my body up to him. The position a little uncomfortable until he circled his hips with each trust causing his hardness to stroke things within me I had no idea they existed. Yelling out in bliss, "Yes baby!" seemed to encourage him more. In with a swerve of his hips, and retreat that left me wanting more, the deep dive into me and the speed all too much at one time. Fisting my hands in the sheets was all I could do to hold on to my sanity. Lost in the intensity of it all; Paul glorious in his demands, "That's it baby. Come for me again. Come for me hard!" When I opened my eyes again the triumph showed on his face; the proudness of giving me pleasure evident as he ground into me deeply and thoroughly. Leaning down to kiss me he spoke into my mouth, "That's it baby. Tell me how much you like it."

Heat sprayed into me as I screamed out Paul's name over and over again until I had nothing left to say. He's a god in bed and he is mine to have.

When he rolled over so fast I thought something was wrong. He released his hold on my legs and my body rested on his with the warmth of him still lodged between my legs. I was afraid to move, because if he wasn't in me I would be empty. We fell back to sleep in each other's arms.

I woke and kissed him where my mouth had been resting on him. His chest so beautifully cut and I loved to touch every curve of his body. He sighed, "I am starving."

Laughing I reminded him, "I told you to bring food."

"I didn't think we would stay in here this long."

I crawled over top of him, "We have been waiting a long time for this."

He smiled and traced his hands up my sides pulling me to him, "Was it worth the wait?"

Kissing him softly, and then I rolled my eyes gesturing that I had to think about it. His irritation that I didn't reply right away boiled over as he grabbed me and rolled over on top of me, "Are you teasing me?"

"Yes, Paul. You were worth the wait." I kissed his cheek, "Am I?"

His kiss came hard and passionate as he mouthed to me, "Oh, yes...yes...yes."

I laughed and pushed him away, "Food, Paul. I am hungry."

He laughed and traced his hand against me, "You want more?"

"No, and I am sore so no more of that today."

He frowned at me, "Really?"

Nodding with my response, "Yeah, really sore now."

He laughed, "Wow. I didn't realize you'd get sore."

I touched his penis, "You're not?"

He pulled away, "Yeah, but that is because I do all the work."

I pushed him away and he grabbed his boxers trying to slide them on and almost fell over but grabbed the bed just in time. I laughed at him grabbing the sheets pulling them over me. He crawled back up to me, "Jess, one thing."

"What's that?"

He grinned and bit my lip, "Don't freak out but we are getting married."

I put my hand on his face and pushed him away. He laughed and went out of the room but taking one last glimpse at me.

I rolled over curling up with a pillow and admiring the ring that's on my finger, torn between smiling and the sadness. Would he understand that I have no choice, and would he wait for me? I do love him and I want to marry this beautiful, hunky, muscular man.

Would it be easier if he thought I didn't love him? Would he be able to breathe if I convinced him it's completely over this time? No matter what I would do he's going to get hurt and I love him so much.

"Jess, are you sleeping?"

Turning to watch him walk back into the bedroom, his face full of concern; I must have let the sadness take over. He moved to the bed with a tray of food, but stared at my eyes with wonder. It took everything in me to give him a little smile as I thought about being away from him in less than 18 hours. He set the tray down on the night stand and crawled over to me, "Jess, don't do this. Don't be scared. Please, just trust that I love you and we won't plan anything for a year."

I touched his face as the tears in my eyes leaked out. I gave him a better smile this time, but his loss of understanding left him speechless.

He grabbed the food and gave me a forkful of scrambled eggs. We devoured the whole plate and he fed me grapes as I curled up in his arms and rested on his chest.

We only ventured out for the bathroom use. I brushed my teeth and took a shower, but went back to him as quickly as possible. He took a turn but his showers took too long for me. He didn't understand that we didn't have much time left. I walked in and tried to hurry him. He just laughed at me and took his time.

"If you miss me this much come in here."

I peeked in and shook my head, "Still sore."

He laughed and continued. I gave up and went back to bed to wait for him. When he finally returned I curled into him again and traced my hands over his body. I wanted to get my fill so that I'd survive this journey I had to take. Just holding him next to me gave me too much time to think about leaving. Fear kept me from telling him even though I wanted to spill everything. After all this time we finally connected and he'd refuse to let me go.

As the time ran out I tried to plot out how I'd do this, but every time I try to get up he wakes. Asking myself, *"How am I going to get out of here?"* I needed to get rid of the pictures on his computer so he wouldn't have to be reminded of me during my absence. With the intention of keep the pain to a minimum; I would leave a note. What should I say? I love you but goodbye? No, I wanted him to wait for me. Torn between leaving the pictures and telling him I had to leave for a year, or leaving them so he'd remember me.

He was distracting me with his hands as they glided over my skin. He brought me back to this moment and I gazed up at him. The smile on his face was completely adorable. I nuzzled back into him and he sighed with pleasure.

When it was getting late and the sun was going down my heart filled with pain as it thudded against my chest. He took it the wrong way and decided to be playful again.

I insisted, "No! More food."

He grunted as he moved from the bed and went to the kitchen. This time I followed wrapped in the sheet. He peeked back at me concerned, "Jess, I'll bring it to you."

I walked over to him and wrapped my arms and the sheet around him resting my head to his back. His hand reached around me holding my lower back to pull me closer. I kissed him and kissed him. He finally turned around and put something in my mouth; it tasted amazing.

He pulled me to the table and I sat on the table facing him in the chair as we ate. They were little sandwiches but in a flower tortilla all rolled together. We laughed and giggled as we ate the whole plateful. Matt walked in, "What are you two doing out of the room? I didn't think you'd surface until Monday."

We both laughed but Paul answered, "Yeah, we do have to eat."

"You guys are having sex and she is sitting on our table. I eat there."

I giggled, "But I have a sheet wrapped around me."

He shook his head, "Yeah, in the sheets you had sex in. Jess, that is disgusting."

"Matt, settle. The table can be washed."

Paul pulled me to him, "We should go back to the room so we don't gross Matt out anymore."

He lifted me and headed for the room. I made him stop for brushing again. We stood there together as his body grazed mine. We giggled and watched each other in the mirror until we finished. As we went from the bathroom to the bedroom we heard Matt yell, "You didn't do it in there; did you?"

We laughed moving into his room but Paul answered, "No, you're safe to use the bathroom."

In a rush to get back in bed he pulled his boxers off and laid down gesturing me to come lay with him. I wanted him to be so tired that he wouldn't wake when I left. It would hurt too much to see his face. I crawled over him pulling up the sheet as I sat on him. He looked up at me his eyebrows up with wonder. I rubbed against him.

"What are you doing?"

"You do all the work!" I gave him a look that would challenge him to not move at all.

He grinned, "Okay I won't do anything. It's all you this time."

Winning the argument I grinned and rubbed against him more. It wasn't long before he closed his eyes allowing the sensation take over, growing long, hard, and willing under me. Maneuvering my body to find the right spot his hands came to my thighs gripping.

"Paul!"

He moved his hands away from me putting them behind his head. That crooked smile stayed on his face even though his eyes closed. When I pushed to him a little the smile went away and his face changed from happy to pain.

"Does it hurt?"

He shook his head as the smile came back. I pushed a little more and he slid into me easily. His eyebrows furrowed and a grimace came back to his face. Forcing himself to stay calm and relaxed with long slow breathes. Using his abs as leverage I push away from him all the way to the tip of his erection only to slowly consume him again. His mouth opened and a sound from deep in his chest came out in a low moan. Continuing the agonizing slowness the agony came and went from his face. When his hands came back to grip my thighs he growled, "Oh, shit Jess."

Controlling him I scolded once again, "Paul!" Easing up a little I allowed his hands to stay on me but shifted my hips as my body consumed him again. Explaining the movement, "This is how to go slow."

His hands moved away from me but gripped the head board and his hips raised to thrust into me prematurely. Happiness filled my heart that he wanted me badly and this drove him mad. Reminding him once again I deepened my voice, "Paul!"

He moaned with dislike but lowered as I pushed harder to him.

"Oh, Jess." His eyes opened full of need, only to close again as I gave him what he needed with a harder faster rock against him. When his eyes scrunched in the effort to control the release his body so badly needed the moans and verbal pleas became constant. Giving in to him I gave everything I had moving faster and harder until surly he couldn't stop himself, and then I slowed back to a snail's pace.

"No... no... no... please... no."

When I pushed to him he released the head board sitting up pulling me to him. The need of our bodies took over enhancing every movement, every breath, and every heartbeat. Starting where we connected our bodies enveloped each other.

Even after the heat of his release scorched my inside bursting my release, he continued to move in me. Hard and full in length his coming didn't satisfy his craving. Leaning back bracing myself as he worked hard to get himself off, but nothing seemed to be enough.

As he slid away from me I worried that he had given up on the second release of the moment. That the intensity of this too much to handle.

When I felt his arms link under my legs I understood. He pinned me to a better angle for his rough thrust. No matter how many times I came, he always had more for me if I wanted.

The pleasure of us together unexplainable, but not enough to satisfy the hunger of more, and I wanted more of him. The slight kisses to every part of our bodies as we made love. It didn't matter where our mouths were because we kissed whatever part of the body that's there for the taking. The exploration of our touching of our hands enhanced the desires we experienced. I wanted him to know I loved every part of him and every part of us being together.

He finally rolled to his back completely exhausted, "I don't know where you came from, but oh my god do I love this." I reached back and propped up the pillows and moved to lean back. He rolled to me resting his head on my stomach. His hands and arms reached around me to hold me. I could watch him for eternity never getting tired of watching him fall to sleep. The pain in my heart came back at the thought of my departure. Running my fingers through his hair while my mind ran wild with worry for what this would do to him.

Hoping exhaustion would keep him sleeping, I tucked a pillow under his head as I inched my way from him. When his arm wrapped around me tighter I rubbed his back until the tension in his arm relaxed again.

After getting out from under him I whispered his name, "Paul?" to see if he'd answer. With no response I made my way to the computer where I inserted the disk to download the pictures on it. Tears pricked in my eyes when I deleted them from his computer. Knowing I'd hurt him when I left, this would hurt him even more. The only reason I had to do this was to keep it from reminding him of me. He had to live his life while I'm away. Not look at me on a daily basis to only feel that pain over and over again.

"Jess, what are you doing?"

Jumping at the sound I went into panic mode, "I have to start a new job in the morning. Just checking what time I have to be there."

He held out his hand for me and I got up taking it and crawling back in with him. I traced my fingers through his hair and rubbed his back.

"Is this part of the thing that you have to do but don't want to talk about?"

I whispered, "Yes."

"If it's a new job are you staying up here for summer, because we could live here? You could move your stuff in and I could stay here with you and wait for you to get done. I could feed you and you know. We could be together."

I wanted to stay here with him so badly, but that wasn't going to happen. I rubbed his back more, "I would love that Paul."

He kissed my stomach and put his head back down on my belly. I waited for him to sleep again and then I moved out from under him yet again. I went to his desk to write the note, but had no idea of what to say to him.

Dear Paul:

I cannot explain the love I feel for you. This has been the best days of my life and I will cherish them forever.

What I am regretting is the months ahead. You see when I was miserable I agreed to do something that would take me away from you. I didn't know how to tell you or what to tell you. I tried to stay away, but you are so darn cute. Your persistence caught me unprepared to keep you away and now that we have had our moment I don't want to leave. But the choice and the commitment already made.

Glancing back at him the tears began to fall. No matter what I agreed to in my heart I didn't want to leave him. Not now or ever. Letting my eyes fall to the ring on my hand as the tears streamed down my face. This pain will be unbearable for both of us. I wiped my face and tried to continue.

I tried to figure a way to cause less pain, but the pain will come. I deleted the pictures of me so that you would not have to be reminded of me every day. I am leaving your ring with hopes that someday you will forgive me and place it on my finger again. I am not allowed to bring things of value so the phone is yours too.

If you find it in your heart to forgive me someday I would love another chance to spend my life with you. Until then I don't have a choice.

I'll be gone one year, but I tried to make it easy for you. There is nothing left of us together except for the memory in our brains. The initial pain last about six months Paul and if you can survive that the pain will lessen.

As far as where I am going. Well, at the time I needed to find a place where the pain was greater than my own from missing you. I found it! And now the pain of being away from you will engulf me once again

My tears dripped on the paper and I wiped them away but it smeared the paper a little. Taking my last fill I looked back at him and gasped from my pain.

> *I am sorry, Paul. For leaving, for not being able to face you and most of all for the pain that is to come. I think you feel the same as me and I know I will walk in darkness for the next year.*
>
> *I love you!!!!!!!!*
>
> *Jessica*

Getting up I folded the note grabbed my stuff, and stood over him regretting having to leave. I wanted so much to touch him and hold him one last time but the pain would be too much. If he woke up I wouldn't be able to conceal the pain in my heart. I went to the bathroom to get dressed and washed my face to compose myself.

I walked out putting the note, ring, and cell phone on the table.

"Jess, what are you doing?"

My heart dropped when I heard Matt. I closed my eyes not turning to him and I tried to get the words out with a normal tone but I knew my voice was going to betray me.

"Um, I start a new job this morning and I have to go."

He was walking towards me, "Why are those things on the table?"

Caught in the act of hurting Paul again I didn't want to face him I turned and sprinted to hug him tight.

"Jess, you are scaring me. You should let me wake Paul."

Not letting that happen I shook my head and looked up at him full of tears. Nothing I did could hold in the hurt I already felt. Not only having trouble breathing but to swallow, impossible due to the lump in it. Gasping I blubbered, "Matt, you don't want to do that. Um, I left him a note and it will be okay. Just make sure that he knows I love him with my whole heart. And you need to be there for him. Don't let him do anything harmful to himself."

"Jess, tell me what is going on?"

"Promise me right now! You won't let him hurt himself. I need him."

"Of course not, Jess, but what are you doing?"

Convincing myself this would be the best way for Paul I forced a smile on my face and kissed his cheek. I knew he would wake Paul as soon as I made it out of the door.

He held me tight not letting go, "Jess, where are you going?"

Not giving a true answer I replied, "Where the pain is greater than Paul's and mine."

When I pushed myself from him I put my hand on the note, "Make sure he gets this, will you?"

"Jess, tell me what is happening here?"

Having the best and worst day in my life all wrapped into one day I headed for the door. There's one thing that Matt needed to understand so Paul would; that I would be back. Letting the tears fall I glanced back with only one thing left to say, "Take care of him until I come back please. I love him."

Closing the door I ran to my car. It would have to be a quick getaway. Driving away with my eyes on the rear view mirror seeing Paul run out of the door with his hands entangled in his hair retched at my heart. He didn't understand why I would do this, and he would never understand that I didn't have a choice.

9

Paul

I woke to Matt having a panic attack, "Paul, get up Jess is leaving."

"Yeah, she is starting a new job this morning."

He tossed me my boxers and pulled me off the bed, "No, it's more than that."

Confused with his frantic voice and his determination to get me up, "What are you talking about?"

"You better hurry or you won't be able to stop her from leaving."

"I need to stop her?"

"She left the ring, her cell phone, and a note."

I jumped up, "She left the ring?"

He moved to the window allowing me to get dressed, "Yes, damn it. Hurry up. Shit, she started her car, Paul."

I got up and ran out to watch her drive away. I ran back inside going up the steps two at a time. Storming in the apartment and advancing on Matt, "What did she say?"

"She was crying, Paul, and mumbling something about pain being worse than yours and hers."

Not registering everything that just happened I picked up the ring and slid it on my pinky and opened the note.

Dear Paul:

> *I cannot explain the love that fills my heart when you're in it. This has been the best days of my life and I will cherish them forever.*

My voice firm and angry I let out my comment, "Then why the fuck did you leave the ring?"

> *What I am regretting is the months ahead. When I was miserable I agreed to do something that would take me away from you.*

Shaking my head I realized I should have been more insistent on finding out what she had to do, especially if we had to be apart for it.

I didn't know how to tell you or what to tell you. I tried to stay away, but you are so darn cute. Your persistence caught me unprepared to keep you away and now that we had our moment I don't want to leave.

Glancing up at Matt for answers only to see him wipe his face with his hands; he is as upset by this as me. So I'm not over reacting because this confuses me. I closed my eyes voicing my opinion, "If you didn't want to leave, why didn't you tell me? Fuck Jessica!"

But the choice and the commitment had already taken place.

Shaking my head not believing this happened. She had to at least tell me where she's going. I continued to read.

I tried to figure a way to cause less pain, but the pain will come. I deleted the pictures of me so that you wouldn't be reminded every day. Also I am leaving your ring with hopes that someday you will forgive me and place it on my finger again. Valuables are not allowed so the phone is yours too.

Broken is a better word for what this did to me. Walking in my room going to my computer I clicked on my photos, but they're gone just like she said.

Matt followed, "What? Did she leave you the address, a map, WHAT?"

Choking back the bile that worked its way up from my stomach the only thing I could get out, "My pictures of her..." The emptiness filled me from the inside out. Grabbing the desk to hold myself up I raised the letter to continue to read.

If you find it in your heart to forgive me someday I'd love another chance to spend my life with you. Until then I don't have a choice.

Blinking away the tears in my eyes I argued with the letter, "Yes, you did have a choice! Damn it! I'd done anything to help you to help keep you here. Why didn't you see that?"

Matt walked over to me staring at me. Not able to take my eyes from the letter I continued to read.

I'll be gone one year, but I tried to make it easy for you. There is nothing left of us together except for the memory in our brains. The initial pain last six months Paul and if you can survive that the pain will lessen.

The sound of my sorrow came out in a groan, "No Jess. This can't be happening, you didn't need to leave. A fucking year!"

Matt voice cracked, "A Year?"

Completely devastated I held up the letter yelling at Matt, "That's what it says!"

He shook his head in disbelief as I continued to read.

As far as where I am going? Well, at the time I needed to find a place where the pain was greater than my own from missing you. I found it! And now the pain of being away from you will engulf me once again

I fell to my knees to pray that this wasn't happening. My body grew numb: it felt the same as the day Anne died right in front of me.

I am sorry, Paul. For leaving, for not being able to face you and most of all for the pain that is to come. Understanding what we mean to each other I am sure I will not be the only one walking in darkness for the next year.

A sob escaped me when I realized that she's right I will walk in total darkness for the next year. Going into autopilot I got up even though my entire body shook from the adrenaline trying to pump life back into my veins. I had to stop her, there had to be a clue, a way to stop her, a way prevent this torture.

Glancing at Matt for answers, but his face filled with pity. The day my parents brought me to the psychiatrists Matt had that hopeless look on his face. He put out his hand for the note so I handed it over to him with hope that he would find a clue of how to stop her from leaving.

Rushing around my room I grabbed a few things shoving them into a bag then headed towards the door. Matt yelled from my room, "Oh my god, Paul. What happened?"

I had no idea what happened. Why she'd leave after agreeing to marry me. I ran out the door, "I need to stop her."

He followed right out the door, stopping for a second to check that the doors locked, "How? We don't know where she is going."

Starting with the most obvious I confirmed, "Her dorm."

This time I didn't argue that he wanted to drive. Lost in my own head with the idea of not seeing her for a year I couldn't see the road threw the tears. He drove fast to the dorm making me thankful. I ran up to her room and knocked frantically. Karlie answered the door sleepily, "Paul, Matt, what are you doing here?"

"Is Jess here?"

"No, she packed all her stuff on Friday and didn't plan on coming back. She's supposed to be with you."

I shook my head, "Did she say where she's going?"

"No. She had personal issues and that's when I noticed her hanging out with Iaesha."

"Who is Iaesha?"

"This strange girl that's into volunteering to help people in troubled countries."

A cool sensation moved through my body as I realized she's leaving, leaving. More like far away from me. If I wanted to change this outcome I had to get to her before she left, "Where is Iaesha's dorm?"

Karlie grabbed a robe and joined my pursuit down the stairs. We knocked and knocked and finally someone came to the door, "What is it?"

Karlie addressed her, "What are you doing here?"

"What do you mean? I go to school here."

"Where is Jessica?"

"She has to be on a flight this morning."

This nightmare got worse and worse. Blood rushed to my hands, which grew into fists. I wanted to hit this girl in the face but Karlie prodded more, "I thought you were going with Jess."

"No, I'm not going. I help from here. I get recruits and sign them up to go help."

Anger pounded hard against my head. Moving closer to her, "Where is she going?"

"South America!"

My blood pumped hard in my veins. So close to losing it completely I forced myself to hold it together so I could pry for more info, "Where in South America?"

The glare I got triggered my anger. My hands fisted, but the only movement was my eyebrow with a questioning rise.

She shrugged, "How am I supposed to know? They don't tell me those things."

Having to get away from her before I punched her in the face I took off at a full run. I had to stop her; I had to get to her first.

Karlie yelled after me, "Paul, I'm sorry."

Getting in the truck I ordered Matt, "Go to Jess's house."

"What?"

"Head to her house."

"But... She's not here?"

How do I explain this one, "She thinks she has to go to South America. She signed up for something and she is heading to the airport but I bet she won't leave without saying goodbye to her mom and dad. We'd catch her there."

Thankfully he took off and headed to the cities. Two and a half hour drive of misery, wondering how he would cope without her for a full year. Repeatedly he wished she'd told me about this situation. She says she loves me and she didn't want to leave, but felt helpless. Remembering how I had asked about this without knowing and her avoidance on telling me. After my process of the way things had progressed I yelled out, "Damn it!"

"What?"

I closed my eyes as the pain poured out. The words fell from my mouth, "I sensed she had a problem, but every time I brought it up she'd cry. I didn't want to upset her so I dropped it. I should have..."

"Don't blame yourself, Paul. She has always done things the wrong way. I don't want to sound mean, but she drives you crazy with her ways of manipulating it so that what she thinks is best for you."

"No! I'm wrong. What I did to her over the last few years, wrong. Did she say anything else?"

"Yeah, I am supposed to make sure you don't do anything stupid to yourself. I'm also supposed to take care of you so when she comes back you will still be here."

I shook my head, and held it in my hands, "Please go faster."

He laughed, "Call her dad. Do they know what she is doing?"

"I don't think so." When I pulled out my phone I noticed the ring still on my pinky. With a promise to Jess I kissed it and then dialed Theo.

"Hey kid. It's way too early in the day, so what's up with you?"

"Jess, left."

"What?"

"She is going to South America. Don't let her leave."

"What?"

"If she shows up there don't let her leave."

"Slow down. Explain this to me."

"I'd explain if I..." I started to cry and handed my phone to Matt. Explaining this to Theo I'd have to admit she left me.

I listened to Matt explain everything we learned while I collected myself. When he finished explaining I got on the phone in time to hear him take a deep breath, "Okay son. Just hurry."

I hung up the phone and stared out the window going through everything in my mind. Her face kept reappearing as I watched her smile, her pleasure, and her eyes as the sparkled in the candle light. Everything I researched to make sure she'd never want anyone else to touch her the way I did, and it didn't compare to the real thing. We're perfect together with the pleasure the desires and fitting so right. Why didn't she just tell me right away? I could have stopped this from happening. We're supposed to be planning our future not time apart.

Jessica

As I drove home the tears continued to stream down my face. Short on time I wouldn't be able to argue with mom and dad, so I had to find a ride to the airport to avoid a long explanation. Also if Paul showed up they wouldn't be able to lead him to me

"Jess?"

"Hey, Greg, I need a favor."

"What is up?"

"I need a ride to the airport. Can you meet me at my house at 5:45?"

"Am or pm?"

"Like in a half hour."

"Where are you going?"

"Um, remember how isolated I had been when I broke up with Paul?"

He answered with caution, "Yes."

"Well I decided that I would go somewhere the pain is deeper than my own. I signed up for it last November, but I need a ride to the airport. Can you do it?"

"Yeah, I'll just throw on some clothes. Pick you up in a few."

"Thanks."

I pulled into the driveway and ran inside with my bags. Dad stopped me in the kitchen, "What are you doing home?"

Still full of tears I demanded, "I have to go dad."

As I pushed by him mom stood second in line, "You need to explain what you're doing."

"If only I had time. I'm supposed to be there by 6 am." I pushed by them and they followed. I dug for summer clothes and stuffed them in my bag.

Dad sounded concerned, "Where are you going?"

Stopping for a second I turned to him, "I had to go where the pain is worse than mine, dad. When Paul didn't show up at the cabin I agreed to go and it's like the military. Once you sign up you don't change your mind."

Mom asked, "So you tried to change your mind?"

"Yes. I went to the administration office and talked to someone but they essentially told me I had to go. Because I signed a document before they purchased the airfare it's final. I'm going." Everything that I hoped for lost to this commitment I lost it entirely as the tears streamed out now. Mom and dad eased up on the lecture. In fact they tried to console me but there isn't time for this. I hugged and kissed them both.

Mom cried, "You agreed to marry Paul?"

I nodded while trying to stop crying. Wiping my face swiftly but the tears came faster and harder. I pushed pass them with my bag in hand barking my orders, "I won't be able to call or get in touch with you for the first month. After that I'm not sure how it will work, but I will try as soon as I can. I hugged each of them again and kissed them saying my goodbyes, but looking out the front window I didn't see Greg yet.

The phone rang and dad went to answer it. "Yeah, kid she is here... No, we can't stop her... She tried and it's not possible... Of course I believe her... yes, of course." He held the phone out for me. I shook my head as the tears were flowing harder, "Please, dad I can't."

He held the phone out for me, "You said you would marry him. He deserves an explanation."

Refusing didn't work. Dad raised his eyebrows, "I know what happened between you two."

I grabbed the phone sobbing, "What?"

"Jess, why are you leaving?"

"I don't have... a choice... the day at the admin's... office I asked... you were waiting... I gave into you... I love you..."

"But why did you agree to go?"

"Because you didn't show up at the cabin."

With anger in his voice, "Is this a payback?"

I screamed at him, "No. I love you! There is no choice I'm going. I agreed a long time ago, because my heart hurt."

"Jess, just don't go. We can figure this out."

"Paul, we have to let go now."

I handed the phone back to dad and hastily kissed his cheek again. Moving to mom I hugged and kissed her cheek, "I will get a hold of you as soon as I can."

Dad put the phone to his face again to talk to Paul. Regret and pain filled every part of my body so hearing his voice dug the pain deeper. Letting my dad know I whispered, "I do love him."

I ran out the door to Greg's truck. I through my bags in the truck and got in the front seat. He looked at me and put out his hand for me. I took his hand in mine clasping it tightly and cried my eyes out all the way to the airport. He didn't say a word, because he understood how much I loved Paul.

Paul

"Theo, don't let her go. Please don't let her leave. I am almost there. I need to understand."

"Paul, she said she tried and they wouldn't let her back out. She is going out the door."

"No, please don't let..."

Grasping for anything I begged, "I'm afraid she won't come back."

"Paul, calm down. Just get here."

I hung up the phone pleading with Matt to go faster. Unlike Matt he drove like a mad man, but she's slipping through my fingers and there's nothing to stop it from happening.

Jumping out of the car as he pulled into the driveway I ran in the house grabbing Theo's shirt begging, "Where did she go?"

"South America."

"No, what airport? I need to stop her."

He grabbed my arms, "You can't stop her. She has to go."

"NO! She is mine now. I'm going to stop her from leaving. She is going to marry me. Theo she said yes!"

Tears blurred my eyesight but I made a mad dash to her room. Digging through her drawers pulling things out letting them clutter the floor, but nothing. Her desk as neat as always only disrupted with my panic shuffling of the papers searching for a clue. The contents of her bag from school dumped on her bed I grabbed and tossed items looking for information. Nothing to be found I made my way outside to her car. Under her seat, in her glove box, and her trunk but not a thing with what airport she's scheduled to depart. She must have left something that would tell me what her flight number is. There was nothing. I ran back in the house but stopped as they waited for my return. The sympathy in their eyes is too hard for me to see, so made my way to her room again. Believing that my efforts are a lost cause, I stared at her room in bewilderment. How did I let this happen, let her lose her control to where she assumed this is her only route? She should have told me what was going on, there had to be a loophole in the document that she signed. My hand found her sweat shirt so I pulled it to my face falling to my knees. Falling to the floor I leaned against her bed putting the sweet shirt to my face. As if smelling her would bring her back to me. The memory of making love to her repeated in my mind. How our love had been so perfect.

"Paul, son, what are you doing?"

I lowered her sweatshirt enough to look at him, "She destroyed everything, all my pictures of us together. She left the ring that I put on her finger last night, and the phone. I can't even call her."

"You gave her a ring?"

"Yes! Damn it. She said yes. She agreed to marry me." I shook my head and put the sweatshirt over my face again.

He came and sat down on the bed putting his hand on my shoulder.

"I waited for her and she waited to be with me. She is the only girl I have ever... We were going to get married."

He put his hand on my shoulder and walked out leaving me here to sulk in my misery. I got a rush of excitement and ran out, "Matt, take me to the airport. I have to find her."

The phone rang and we all turned to it at the same time knowing it would be her. Theo walked over and picked it up saying hello. He looked right at me and held the phone out to me.

Cradling the phone into my neck like it was her I pleaded, "Jess, oh my god. Please tell me where you are, I will come get you?"

"No, Paul, not this time."

"Jess, tell me what I am supposed to do?"

"You need to let me go."

"No! I love you."

"Paul, I've always loved you and I always will. Bye Paul."

"No, please don't hang up, Jess. Just tell me where you are. Why are you doing this?"

"So it will be easier."

"What will be easier? Revenge Jess, for all the times I stood you up?" Lowering my voice I continued to plead, "I told you that I waited for you too. What we shared." What I wanted to talk about couldn't be said aloud with her dad right behind me.

"No. So it will be easier to get through this, because no matter how bad I want to stay with you I can't. I did try Paul, I truly did. You need to let me go now even though I don't want to go."

"Jess, please don't do this."

"Paul, the pain will last six months and then it will fade and you will forget."

"I will never forget you, Jess. I am in love with you and after this weekend how come you didn't tell me about this?"

"Paul, I couldn't stand to see the pain on your face. It would have been harder for me, because I experienced it too, and now it will burn a whole in my heart being away from you."

"I already lost one person that I loved; please don't do this to me."

"I am not doing this to you, Paul. Don't you see I am trying to make it easier for you? I only got rid of the pictures so that you wouldn't be reminded of me over and over again as you viewed them. That's what made it hard for me. I am so sorry for this Paul. I love you."

"Then don't go. I will take care of it."

"You can't. Not this time, Paul. The decision was made back in November."

"When I didn't show up at the cabin on time?"

"Yes."

"Oh, Jess, why didn't you tell me? I would've dropped everything for you."

"But you didn't, Paul. Like always you'd expect me to understand and that is why I expect you to understand this."

"Jess, I had no idea that it was so painful for you. Please tell me where you are going?"

"You are kidding me. You didn't know I was miserable. I begged and pleaded with you to spend time with me. I was dying inside and you continued to keep doing it. I loved you, Paul, more than anything in this world and I still do."

"Jess, please. I am begging. You understand that? I am begging you to stay."

"That choice was taken away from me. Just remember that I tried to break the contract. Please forgive me, Paul. This is it Paul they are boarding."

"No, Jess. I promise I will never hurt you again."

"It's not an option anymore."

"Yes, you have a choice. Don't you dare hang up that phone, Jess, or... or I will never forgive you."

She started to cry and I knew I hurt her more than I ever had in the past. I begged, "Please, Jess."

"Paul?"

"Yes."

"Please tell me you didn't mean that."

"Jess, NO! I'm desperate; please tell me where you are going? I will follow you."

I heard the dial tone. She hung up on me and left me to the empty darkness where there's no air, no light, and no Jessica. The blankness engulfed me as I gasped for air. She's gone from my life and this deep gut wrenching told me I'd never see her again.

When everything went black my body convulsed in reaction to the abandonment. A hand came around me to pull me back to reality, but I didn't want to come back without Jess. I stared into the empty space that was now my life without her. I didn't understand any of this because my world had ended. It would be easier not to live than go one day without her face to brighten my day.

10

Everything left me in a daze, numb to the world. Theo's hand gripped the back of my neck as his eyes pierced into mine. His lips moved like words should be coming at me but there's nothing. Not grasping anything the air escaped my lungs while I stood there in limbo.

Jessica

He would never forgive me for this. I hurt the one person that I loved more than myself. My tears continued to stream down my cheeks as I made my way down the single isle to the very last seat taking the one by the window. The idea of not seeing Paul for a full year is bad enough, but the pain in his voice told me what this did to him. Lost in my misery startled by a man standing over me when he asked, "Do you mind?"

Avoiding eye contact I nodded without looking up to show him my misery. He sat down and I heard him sniffle. A guy with a heart sitting down next to me, that's how lucky I am. He spoke to me, "What is his name?"

Not wanting to talk about my miserable life I gave him a one word answer, "Paul." My eyes wandered over to get a glimpse him. My guess is correct. He's as miserable as I am so I asked, "What is her name?"

He gave me a slight grin amongst his misery, "Alison."

Giving him an approving smile and then went back to looking out the window. The plane's engines roared and the sadness is over bearing the tears a full stream now. Leaving Paul this way had to be the worst day of my entire life.

As a gesture of comfort this guy put his hand out with his pinky in the air. Not deserving this at all I still wrapped my pinky around his. The gasp that came from him filled me with relief. We shared the same pain, the same torment, and the same comfort. We didn't need to talk to understand each other.

Paul

Stung with a heated sensation across my face shocked me into breathing again. Tears filled my eyes when I realized Theo slapped me to my senses. Pleading with hope that he'd understand, "I love her. I kept to my promise."

He gave me a small smile while asking me, "What did she say to you before she left?"

I gasped for air, "She didn't."

Matt handed him the note. As he read it his forearm pressed against my chest holding me up against the wall. A smile grew on his face, "Paul, this tells me she loves you."

That's something I already know, "But you let her go."

"No, she tried to get out of this. She didn't want to go but she signed a contract. You understand contracts."

"No, she's gone and..." Squeezing my eyes shut, not wanting to see the reality of her loving me and then just like nothing at all she's gone from my life.

A strong sting against my face again caused the reality to come back and fill my lungs with air. Not only did I not want to come back to this nightmare I didn't want to go one day without her. Words escaped my mouth without my brain working, "shit, that hurts."

Theo laughed at me, "Are you back with us now?"

My heart bleeding, my face throbbing, and my eyes burning I nodded staring into his eyes wishing for an answer.

Theo gripped my shoulders firmly as he stated, "She wants you to wait for her if you can handle that. Boy, can you handle that?"

All I got from his determined voice is *wait for her* and *handle that.* Men aren't supposed to cry at least that's how society molds us, but losing two people I love in less than one decade. It's enough to put any man in the loony bin. So what am I supposed to do while I wait? My eyes searched Theo's eyes for answers.

The warmth of his smile, the steady gaze he gave me brought calmness to my hysteria. As if reading my mind, "Now, if you love her and you can wait for her there are things that you may want to get worked out in your life."

Lost in wonder I asked, "Like what?"

"You need to stay busy. Treat this situation like she is here at home and you just can't see her for a while."

I nodded but confused about what he said.

"You need to go back to school and finish your degree. Try to fill your days with classes, studying, and whatever else you can do to take up all your time. You don't want to ponder about where Jess is. For all you know she is at school a hundred miles from you, and she needs time to grow into a woman. Can you do this for her, for me, and for yourself, Paul? I love you like my own son and she said yes to marry you. It would be my honor to make it official. You need to handle this like a man and get your life straight."

Everything he said made sense, but cluttered into a mumble of words that rolled together. Jess is at school? Part of their family? Life straight? What is this man trying to tell me?

He turned to Matt, "I need you to make sure he does this."

Not knowing what Matt said or did because my brain numbed to the world.

Theo held my neck tighter, "How is the business, Paul?"

I shrugged, "handed it over to Tom. I wanted to be with Jess and she needed more time together."

He grinned and hugged me, "I am so happy you love my daughter." He released me and looked into my eyes, "You will handle this because she needs you in her life. Someone that cares this much about her will be rare and I believe in you."

Air entered my lungs again but the tears came to my eyes which made it impossible to see his face anymore.

Someone tossed him something but he lifted it to my face. Recognizing the softness of terrycloth I wiped my eyes so I'd see him clearly. I didn't understand why he smiled at me. It's the end of my happiness so why did he have to be happy about that.

He took a deep breath, "The house, how is it coming?"

I searched my brain for an answer, but what did this have to do with Jess? My only grasp came out, "It's not done yet."

"Well, if you two are going to get married in a year don't you suppose you should get it done?"

None of this made sense. She couldn't marry me if she's gone.

"Paul, she wants to marry you when she gets back if you will forgive her for leaving. Think about it. She didn't want to leave. She tried to get out of it. She said yes to marry you. She asked you to forgive her, and wait for her. Is that something you can do?"

I nodded as he explained this to me.

"Then you need to have a place for the both of you to live."

Finally I understood as he went over the high points. Nodding with comprehension I need him to tell me the next step.

"Go finish the school year. Go home and work on the house. Get everything in order, prepare for the future, and be ready when she comes home. I would love to see my daughter in a white gown standing next to you, son." He pulled me into the biggest bear hug, which shouldn't come from my future father in law. He took me in when no one trusted me after losing Anne.

I nodded realizing that this man has given me more support than I ever deserved and I loved him and his daughter more than my own life.

"I need you to not do anything stupid, because my daughter loves you so much that you would be cheating her of a great life with you. This is not final like Anne's death. Jessica is coming back!"

I nodded agreeing with him even though this seemed strange that he would be talking this way.

He gave me a smile and turned to Matt, "Did you get all of this, because you need to make sure he stays on track. You will call me if you need help with... call me if Paul needs help."

"Yes sir."

"I mean no time alone for a while, can you handle that?"

"Yes, sir."

"Take him back to school and make sure he stays on track. I will be up the first weekend you are at home. We will meet at the house. Paul, we are going to get started on the house."

I nodded as he let go of my neck and walked me out to the car. I got in but something didn't seem right.

Lying in my bed seemed so empty without Jess. This is the worst dream I have ever had in my life, worse than those of losing Anne. Tossing and turning couldn't push them away this horrible ache in my chest wouldn't subside. When I rolled over again I opened my eyes finding Jess there offering me comfort. Her fingers threaded through my hair relaxed me. She didn't ask me the usual question, which made things seem out of place, but she's here with me now and it's all that mattered. I pushed the painful nightmare aside when she crawled over me rubbing against me with that cute little luring smile that begged me to kiss her. Reaching up I traced my hands along her sides pulling her to me. I didn't want to hurt her or scare her off with that fear from the dream that took her away for a year. Her mouth came to mine and pressed hard and needy. She made me happy and took my breath away. She rubbed against me again and I forced myself to not close my eyes. Not wanting to get so absorbed in the moment that I might lose her. Every enticing move caused my hunger to grow. When she leaned down to nibble on my bottom lip I gave into the pleasure closing my eyes to enjoy every sensation.

Just like that she's gone. My eyes flew open in search of Jess through the emptiness that engulfed me. Reaching into the air in search of her body, and her face gasping for air as I realized I let her escape me again. I rolled over and put my face to the pillow where her head had been. The scent she left behind filled my head with her essence.

This dream came again and again, each time being a little different, but each time being more real than the last. This dream I had filled my broken heart only to have it shattered again. The hardest part was waking from it to find her gone.

I wanted to see her more so I decided to be creative. There were nights I sprinkled the drying rose petals over my bed. Other nights I lit the candles and waited for her to come to me. It's amazing to get this little time with her. To see the brightness of her eyes, the smile on her face. She's so playful and cute that I wanted to hold her forever, but every time I thought it was real I woke to her not being there.

After weeks of this I decided that I wanted to make her stay. Finding the perfect rose I went to bed with it in my hands. While I waited for her to come I planned out my persuasion to keep her here this time. It seemed like I waited forever but she did show up, only after I fell asleep. Her warmth caressed me as her hands wandered up my back massaging every tense muscle in my torso. Pleased that she made it I rolled over swiftly not only to feel her, I also needed to see her.

To my delight her grin sparkled with sin. I grabbed her thighs pulling her to me and she giggles without a sound. Confused how she could laugh without any sound worried me, but it didn't matter. She is here with me, and had every intention of keeping her. I gasped for air as I pulled her warm moist core against me again. She leaned over kissing my chest while her hips ground into my rock hard dick. The pleasure too much to endure to wait a moment longer but I had to make this last all night. Refusing to close my eyes I, willed myself to hold on to this, I bit my lip to remember the pain that would come. When she scooted down further away from me I wanted to demand that she come back here and never leave me again, but she wasn't leaving. Her hands roamed my abs, her eyes bright with mischief, and her mouth drooling, all while her intentions came clear. Her mouth dipped to the hardness she caused. Keeping my eyes on her became challenging when her tongue started at the base of my cock and trailed up to the very tip of me. I whimpered because if she put her mouth around me I wouldn't be able to hold back my release. I grabbed her wrist holding her there so she'd have to stay here with me. It's bad enough that I dreamt about her mouth wrapped around my dick but when her lips wrapped around the tip of me, not only did I close my eyes, but they rolled back in my head. Reminding myself that I shouldn't have closed my eyes I hastily opened them again searching for Jess.

My hands held only sheets, I am hard as a rock, and Jess disappeared from my life again. My glorious night with Jess had ended leaving me wanting. I got up, blew out the candles, and fell to my knees by the side of my bed. I begged god to give this one back to me. I wouldn't live through losing another love.

Night after night I prepare for my evening with Jess. I brought food one night, because if we didn't go out we would need food. Another night I stocked bottles of water. Not sure what I did wrong that made it impossible to keep her here with me? I tried everything but she wouldn't stay with me.

Matt came storming in, "That is it! I promised Mr. Jenson that I would make sure you stayed on track. You are going to class today if I have to get you in the shower myself."

He pulled me from my bed dragging me with the sheets.

"No Matt, she comes here to be with me. I need to stay here. Not sure when she is going to come back. I don't want to miss her."

"You are delusional. That is it! You are getting back to your life now. I know it's painful, but you have to be prepared. Remember what Theo said... when she comes back you'll need to be ready to marry her. If you are delusional you won't be ready."

He pulled and pushed me into the bathroom but when I flatly refused the shock of severe pain against my cheek. I grabbed my face staring at him, "What the hell did you do that for?"

"Paul, do you love her?"

"Yes, of course I do that is why I need to wait here for her to come back."

"No! Do you want her to come back?"

"Yes, but if I wait for her she comes every night. I just have to wait in the..."

"No! Is this helping you? I'll answer that. No, it's not! You need to go to school and finish the school year. We only have two and a half weeks left and you need to finish this."

I had to agree with him. I decided to get in the shower, but he continued to talk to me.

"You need to show her that you've grown up and you appreciate the time you have together, and that you will be able to support her. Besides, it doesn't help you to feel sorry for yourself."

I got out of the shower. He did leave the bathroom, but he left the door open. I walked out glaring at him, "Fine, I am going."

He grabbed his stuff and waited for me when I walked out. He laughed and I turned around in a circle wondering what he was laughing for.

"Paul, it's not final like Annie. You can change this and you have a year to get your shit together."

"Fine, I said I was going."

"Yeah, well you might want to put pants on before we go."

Taking notice that I forgot to put those on I walked back in my room and put pants on my body.

It's Not Over

By

Melissa M Marlow

Preface:

The night an endless darkness you cannot escape. It's so empty and lonely it takes my breath away. If I close my eyes I feel you here holding me, linking our fingers together, and sharing the sight before us without one word. It's you that grounds me and keeps me here, for without you I am lost. I force myself to breath hoping that each breath will force time to move forward bringing you closer to me if not by distance, but by time. It will be our time again, and I will never let you feel so lost, alone, or let you feel pain in your heart.

Paul: Remember when...

Jessica: you had night mares.

Paul: You didn't ask...

Jessica: questions of you.

Paul: You held...

Jessica: your hands in mine.

Paul: You believed...

Jessica: in you.

Paul: I will not...

Jessica: let you down.

Paul: Say you will...

Jessica: wait for me.

Paul & Jessica: Because our lives together... It's Not Over.

1

Even though I went to class daily I remained numb day after day while finishing the school year. Calling Theo daily became the norm; if not for encouragement, then for the chance to check if Jess contacted them yet. He always reminded me that she said it could be more than a month before she'd be able to contact them, but it still didn't help with the absence of her from my life.

After arriving home I continue to sulk daily. What can I say, I am in love and hate that she left me. Matt didn't allow me to continue this for very long he just showed up today and pulled me from my parent's house. We headed somewhere, but I didn't want to go anywhere or do anything. All I wanted was for Jessica to come home, marry me, and spend the rest of our lives together. Why is that so wrong? I have been planning this, and working my ass off so that we'd have a comfortable life together. This is the thanks she gives me? She agrees to run off to another country because I was too busy for her. Not good enough and if she showed up right now I'd... I'd... I'd pull her into my arms and never let her go again. I don't know if I'm madder about being a pansy, or if I am mad that she didn't let me take care of getting her out of this agreement.

I sat staring out the side window, stewing in all my anger while Matt drove. It's bad enough that all this has happen, but now that I am no longer at school my nightly visits from Jess are few and far between, and if she does show up at all she seems so far away. Watching her do simple things like changing clothes, doing homework, getting lost in the TV, or just smiling at me from across the room. This emptiness is killing me.

Matt has good intentions. He brought me to the house that Jess and I would live in forever. We walked around the place evaluating what still needed to be done, but I didn't get excited until Matt started to ask me questions of my plans. He took notes as we went through the entire place. The plans already designed, the foundation already laid, but truthfully it had only been a distant dream of mine.

The next stop Matt made brought us to the lumber yard. We met with a consultant who scanned the plans and invoiced each item we would need to complete the house. Matt's excitement helped me to overcome my deep depression and set a new goal. The most important goal is to have a home for Jess and I when she got back.

The guys that worked for me called me more and more. My days and nights filled with working my business, and working on my home. The business grew more now that I'm home to run it. I found myself getting more accounts, and more employees to handle the work load. I set up shop in the basement so when I didn't run the business I'd work on the house.

Nick showed up with Matt one day and started to help with the house. We didn't talk at all, but he knew a few things I didn't; especially with installing the windows. The story behind Nick is a long one, but to make it short he's Anne's brother. For a while he blamed me for her death. To tell you the truth I blamed myself, which drove me to the psych ward for a few months. After that no one talked to me except Matt, Theo, and my parents. I didn't blame anyone else for what happen to me I did it to myself. As a teenager that is something I'd have to live with for a very long time. Jessica is the only one that made the nightmares, that I endured, go away, and that's when I forgave myself and gave my heart to her.

Getting account after account my business grew like the wild flowers out in front of the house. Jess would complain about all the time I spent on business if she'd been here, but she's not and I couldn't turn it away. This happens to be my way of coping with her absence. I need to get a handle on all this before she comes home or she'd really give me the one two for not having any time for her.

Not only did my employees work for me, but they also volunteered their free time to help with the house. One night when everyone came to help I asked them to help me find more employees to cover all the work. I promoted Nick to a crew manager and walked him through everything about running the business. We had an understanding now about Anne and he became one of my best friends. Even after working the long days helping the crews out, he still came to give a little time to help me build my home. We had the frame up in no time and I took the night off to call Theo.

"Hey son, what is going on with you?"

"Just wondering if Jess contacted you yet?"

"Actually she did e-mail us a few times. I will send them to you, but please don't try to contact her. This is just to keep you posted."

"Thank you. I will take what I can get. When will I get the e-mail?"

"I just sent it. How are things going?"

"Great, but not the way I want them to be. My business has grown and the house is framed."

"Wow, I can't wait to see it. I will be by this weekend."

"Great, plan on working though. I want it done before I go back to school."

He laughed at me, "I am impressed, Paul, and Jess will be too."

When we finished talking I went to the computer to read her email. I wanted her to say she's miserable without me and that she needed to see me. I set myself up for a fall because she only mentioned me once.

Hi mom and dad, I miss you terribly. I found what I expected. The people are miserable with hunger and poverty. I'm not getting to eat much and I have been sick a lot lately. There is a little girl that I have fallen in love with so I share my food with her. Please don't tell Paul I am sick he will worry. I love you
Jess

She's worried about me worrying about her. That's all I needed to put me on cloud nine. She's sick though... maybe she would come home sooner, but I really didn't want her sick. Not getting to eat did not make me happy either because she's already so perfect in size this wouldn't be good for her. A little girl, what does she have to do with Jess?

I started the day with an upbeat in my step. I set up a stereo to play music while we worked. Nick showed up later and noticed the positive in me. We got the roof on and shingled in no time at all, but the house still just a frame. Nick joked with me about how many rooms we would need but I didn't have an answer for him. We only had plans for the basement and first floor, but I wanted bigger to impress Jess. I wanted a dozen kids if Jess would give them to me, so I wanted to plan ahead for whatever she decided.

She sent weekly emails to her parents, and Theo forwards them all to me. Each one I read filled me with happiness. Her description of the place she stayed had no real foundation, only a tent for privacy. The other thing that brought me comfort was her unhappiness of not feeling like they accomplished much. Her partner found good hiding places if danger got too close. Reading that one four times to decipher what she meant about danger, but needing a hiding place worried me. She made reference to the little girl again. How big and innocent her eyes were and how the guilt of eating in front of this little girl tore her heart to pieces. That worried me a little because Jess probably gave her the food without thinking about staying strong. The more emails I got the less she visited my dreams. I tried to encourage it by staying there in the house waiting at night for her to come. Gathering wild flowers by day; intending to beg her to stay one full night. I only needed one night to get me through, but she never came close enough to let me hold her.

As Jess pointed out before she left, seeing her at night made my mornings unbearable. Not wanting to move from the bed, finding it hard to breathe, never wanting to open my eyes again, and most of all to continue to press on with my life.

My business thrived with new crew managers and over ninety employees. The best part is that we needed to add more jobs to cover all the work. Nick wanted to do both jobs, because he was saving up for a place of his own. He joked with me that he's going to buy the land next door so he could keep me in line with Jess. We all had a good time working together. The bathrooms were the first thing we finished on all three floors. I took it as a hint that I needed to shower more regularly, but the best part is we could use the indoor facilities while working on the house.

Weeks and months passed and the emails faded a little, but still maintained one every other week. She sounded weak, depressed, and wanting to come home. When we had the first floor done I ordered furniture. It's my first living room set along with a TV and sound system that would rock into the next county. The table and chairs would come with all the appliances for the laundry room and the kitchen. Having two bedrooms on the first floor I ordered two bedroom sets. I also treated myself to a desk and a new computer in my office. Matt talked me into workout equipment for the basement and I had a home to live in. The only we had to finish happened to be the upstairs rooms, but I could finish them later on when we decided what we'd need.

The next email I got didn't sound good:

Mom and dad,
Don't worry, but I have been getting sicker this last month and they can't figure out what I have. I am going to the hospital in another city. It will take us awhile to get there, so I won't be able to write to you for a while. Please don't worry. I will email you as soon as I can to give you an update. Please don't tell Paul. Love you, Jess

I called Theo.
"Hey son, what is going on with you?"
"She is sick. Is there another email? Am I missing something?"
"No, that is all we got."
"But we should go get her. Did she ever tell you where in South America she is?"
"No, Paul I send you everything we get."
"She is sick... how bad is she?"
"I send you everything. We have to wait to hear."

Worried beyond explanation I pushed the guys to get the up stair rooms done. If she's coming home sick I wouldn't have much time to work on them. I enrolled in school again, but I didn't know if I would even go for sure. It all depended on my Jess coming home.

I added 5 more crew leaders and 50 more guys to my list and took on a lot more accounts. Unorganized and frantic explained how I am most of the time. If someone called in sick the crew managers took on the jobs.

I got the phone call that I was waiting for , "Theo?" My heart beat so hard the pounding muffled the sound in my ears.

"Hey, son, you are going to want to check your email."

"Why? What's going on?"

I ran to my computer and turned it on clicking as fast as my fingers could go on a computer that took its time to boot up and become responsive to my demands finally linking into my email.

"Paul, give me a call after you read it. Please don't take it the wrong way."

"Why?"

"Paul, I am not supposed to share these with you so you need to promise me that you are not going to over react."

"Okay, I'll call you back."

Mom Dad,
I am sick, very sick to be more specific. They have no choice but to send me home. I am weak and need to rest a lot, so I won't be able to do anything for a while. I'm sorry this will be hard but I can get better with time.
Dad, I understand that you love Paul, but please don't tell him. I need a little time to myself before I have to deal with him and it hasn't been a year.
Jess

What the hell did that mean? Deal with Paul. Don't tell him. Fuck that! I've been working my ass off just to build her this effing house and if she's coming home she's going to deal with me like it or not. We're getting married. Putting up with this crap of not wanting to see me, its complete bull shit. Anger boiled my blood to the point of not calling Theo back. I didn't want to take it out on him.

Keeping myself busy didn't distract me from the words dancing in my head. Shit, she didn't want to see me after five months of being apart. What the hell is that? I never kept her waiting this long. And then every fight we had about her waiting for me time after time I realized something so horrible I didn't want to admit it. Shit, I did make her wait for me, but she didn't understand I did that for her. Not liking the conclusion I came up with I still had to honor her wishes. It's only temporarily until Theo told me I could see her. Having another argument with myself I decided that if she's going to be my wife then I should take care of her not them.

Worry and confusion filled not only my days but also my nights making it impossible to sleep. Waiting for her arrival became torture as I called Theo only to be told they hadn't heard anything yet. What if she's so sick she couldn't come home after all, and if she dies none of us would ever have closure? Wondering what beam I would hang myself from as I stared at the ceiling in my bedroom.

The dreams started again with her coming to my bed taunting me with her lips and eyes. Caving to her needs I gave her every pleasure imaginable to keep her here. When her body crawled over mine, grinding against me it told me we'd be together again. Our reunion would be sweet, and she'd be all mine for at least a week. We had to make up for lost time.

I cancelled my classes and stayed at the house. Matt left for school, but advised me to call him when I got word of her arrival. Nick spent the nights with me until my eyes fell shut. What ran through my head if she didn't come back gave good reason to have everyone worried about leaving me alone to dwell on the possibility.

Every day, I bothered Theo and Marie for information but the same reply came day after day. No word yet and they would contact me as soon as they had more information.

Jess:

I didn't realize I shouldn't have written my mom and dad yet, because this process is taking a lot longer than I thought it would. It didn't help the hospital didn't release me for two more week saying they had to stabilize my medication.

Because returning home early special arrangements had to be made in order to get me home. Going from one aircraft to another, and sometimes staying for several hours on layovers until the next flight would take me to the next stop. The closer I got to home the more tired got, but I took my medicine as directed. All I needed to heal happened to be my bed at home. It had been a month since I talked to my mom and dad. They must be worried sick, and yet not as worried as they will be when I get home. It's bad enough that I am sick, but I'm bringing them a gift that they are not ready for any more than me.

I called from the airport, but no one answered at home so I took a cab. As I walked in I dragged my bags with me to my room. My room a complete mess with my bags from school emptied all over my bed and floor. That must have been Paul, and they didn't even try to straighten it up for me. I tried to organize the room, but exhaustion hit me full force. Ignoring the mess in the room; I pushed the rest of my stuff to the floor creating enough room for me to sleep. I don't even remember feeling the pillow under my head when the sleep overcame me.

The loud voices and the banging of kitchen cabinets woke me. I tried to get up but struggled with my condition. I yelled at the top of my lungs but it came out dry and weak, "Hey, I am sleeping in here."

The noise still erupting from the kitchen it's obvious that my weak voice didn't clue them in that I am home. Getting up and stumbling my way through the living room and into the kitchen, "Are you guys celebrating being kid-less or what?"

Mom dropped the bowl she had been holding splattering it all over the floor. Dad came at me with open arms. I held my stomach, "Easy does it dad I am weak and tired."

He looked me up and down noticing my frail state, but didn't reference my stomach at all. He hugged me tightly and kissed my head everywhere, "We have missed you so much and Paul can't wait to see you."

I pushed him away stroking my stomach as mom made her way in hugging me tightly. Their attention welcomed me home, but my illness made me weak and dizzy so I grabbed the chair to stead myself.

My mom gushed, "Oh, dear are you alright?"

A little irritated I grumbled, "NO! I am sick. That is why they sent me home."

Dad's face flashed with anger, "Not only sick. You look a little something else too."

Smiling more to myself then about the situation remembering the exact night I conceived my little one, "Yeah, about that…"

Mom pulled a chair in front of me asking me more excited than I expected, "Are you sick at all or just pregnant?"

"Mom, I have malaria and I am pregnant. It's dangerous for the baby. That is why they sent me home."

Dad pulled up a chair, "So, the father is…?"

Cutting him off before he mentioned Paul again, "Not with me, if that is what you are asking."

"Does he know?"

"No, and it's going to stay that way."

This time his words came out hostel, "He has the right to know."

I shook my head, "Dad what about me? Aren't you worried about my welfare, god, I just get back and you are lecturing me."

His anger deflated, "Your right." He stood up and kissed my forehead and hugged me tightly again. The only thing he couldn't do is leave Paul out of the picture, "Paul is going to be happy to hear that you are home anyway."

I shook my head, "Under the circumstances we should wait to tell him I am home. Don't you agree?"

"Oh, yeah. I guess so, but he calls every day."

"Just tell him no word yet, please."

Mom hoped up, "Can I get you something to eat?"

"No, I need sleep." I got up supporting my belly with my hand heading back to bed, but looked back them both, "I missed you, and dad promise you won't tell Paul yet. I will take care of it when I have more strength."

With a stern face he replied, "I promise, but don't make him wait. That boy is still in love with you!"

I walked away knowing he would tell Paul I'm home, but I hoped he would tell him to stay away.

As I suspected when I got up dad had Paul on the phone. I knew he couldn't keep his promise. He loved Paul as much as I did.

"Yeah, she is safe here at home."

"NO!"

"Um, she needs to rest and shouldn't be around people yet."

"No! I said no boy."

"Paul, she threatened to leave again if you show up here. She said she would talk to you when she is doing better."

"No, I will have to lock you out. I can't lose her again. You are not the only one that loves her so give her time to get her strength back."

"She is thin mostly skin and bone. The illness has taken a lot out of her."

"You will be the first to see her. As soon as she can have visitors I will call you."

"I love you too, kid."

Pleased beyond words on how he handled Paul. I walked out and hugged him with everything I had. He offered to get me food or water or anything. I took out a piece of plain bread and ate that while I drank the water. Not happy with my choice of food but he still consoled me.

"Jess, honey. Can I ask about the father?"

"Not yet. I'll tell you everything in a few days, but I need sleep right now."

He nodded and I headed back to my room.

2

I caught dad talking to Paul a lot. When I would walk into the room he would quiet down and turn away from me. In disgust I rolled my eyes grabbing a piece of bread and some water and headed back to the room. Instead of going to my room I decided I needed to listen to what he told Paul about me not wanting visitors. Even though I wasn't ready to tell him about the baby I didn't want dad to tell him either. Paul didn't need to marry me because of the baby. He still has to be in love me enough to want to spend the rest of his life with me not knowing anything about the baby.

I leaned my ear against the door and listened to dad's side.

"No, you still can't come down here."

"Because she is… yeah, that is the perfect word for her."

I am what? That is not fair. If I am going to spy I should at least get the whole story.

"She still needs to get her strength back; all she does is sleep."

"No, all she eats is bread and water. I tried but she doesn't want anything else. She's probably still getting morn… more sick."

"No, I mean she needs to eat meat, potatoes, veggies, and some fruit. She isn't looking healthy."

"I really appreciate you wanting to help, but Paul I don't want her to leave again and she isn't ready."

"I'm not sure. It may be that she doesn't look like herself and she doesn't want you to see her this way?"

"I know, son. Yeah, of course we understand that you love her, but right now it doesn't matter. It's not up to me."

"How is the house?"

"Almost done! Wow, I am impressed. What did you decided to do with the upstairs?"

"You finished one room in case we wanted to stay. You think of everything."

"Yeah, who can understand a woman's mind any way, you will have to ask her yourself."

"No, not now!"

"Yeah, Kid. It's a good idea and stay busy. It shouldn't be much longer."

"Let's just say it's a hunch."

Pushing my way through the door into the kitchen I glared at my father. He needed to keep his mouth shut and he almost blew it with the morning sickness.

"Paul, I have to go. Yeah, we'll stop by in a couple of weeks."

"Okay... Okay... Yeah, I will tell her. Haft to go. Yes, she is."

My dad smiled at me with his reply to Paul, "Yeah, I remember she said she would marry you. This doesn't make any sense, but it will with time, Paul. Love you, son. Bye."

He hung up the phone still smiling at me, "So, why won't you see him?"
"I don't want him to marry me because of Mason."
"Mason... who is Mason."
Rubbing my tummy indicating it's a baby boy. The tears filled his eyes as he walked over to me and touched my stomach, "I am having a grandson?"
I nodded, "But dad we need to do this my way, okay?"
The enjoyment filled his heart and his face. He didn't care how I handled it after finding out it's a boy. He's having a grandson and he is ecstatic about it.

Dad became much more pleasant about everything after that. He didn't mention Paul or that I should be telling him about it. He did however tell mom that it's a boy and she came home with something new every day. She washed everything at the end of the week only to start a new week getting more things that he may need. My eating improved with keeping down rice and soup now. Mason grew inside me every day. Because of my frail body I had to hold my stomach more and more to balance him with the rest of my body. Going to doctor appointments every week to check my illness and make sure Mason continued to grow healthy.

By the end of September I had extremely bad back pain and the nausea continued all day and every day. Wanting to give Paul's parents the same opportunity as my own parents I wanted to call and talk to his mom. When I finally braved it out and called her the excitement in her voice satisfied my need. The best part of telling her about the baby she planned on being there the day Mason entered the world. It's still hard for her to understand that I didn't want Paul there. After explaining that I wouldn't trap him into marrying me we came to an agreement that I would tell Paul before delivery. To me I still thought it should be a year apart. He had to understand how hard it had been for me, and that he wanted this relationship for the rest of his life.

Even though I did everything they told me to do my illness didn't improve so being sleepy and weak continued well into this pregnancy. Seven months along and I had cramps every day. Mom worried about it being too early for me to be having this much pain. I drank lots of water like the doctor told me to. She said my body needed more hydration, but I could only drink so much and then I would have to go to the bathroom causing me to cramp again. What a cruel cycle.

I will never forget this day of Nov 3. The pain in my back so unbearable it woke me up. When I got up to go to the bathroom the cramping came. Grabbing my stomach to support the weight I still leaned over to endure the extreme pain. Making my way to the bathroom thinking if I could just go pee everything will lighten up.

When I finally got to the bathroom I got more than I bargained for. A full gush of watery fluid poured out, but the scary part followed with a pain that knocked the wind out of me. It lasted only a couple of minutes. Thankful for the break I didn't take my time heading to mom and dad's room waking them, "Um, I think we have a problem."

Dad sat up blinking his eyes, mom got up coming to me right away, "Jessica, it's okay to get a little cramping. Drink some more water and lie back down. It gets better when you put your feet up."

I started to cry while I walked away to get dressed, "I don't think he's going to wait; my water just broke." Not sure what made me cry but the emotions wavered out of control. Paul doesn't even know yet.

Getting mine and Mason's bags I made my way to the kitchen waiting on mom and dad. Currently they were in panic mode so I made the call to Paul's mom. She'd head out very soon but before she hung up she asked, "Do you want him to come with me?"

I have never been so confused in my life, "I can't. Not yet."

"Okay, I am on my way."

Thankfully she understood where I came from even though I wasn't sure my self anymore. Scared might be the better word to describe what's going on in my head.

Two hours passed like nothing as Paul's mom walked into the room. Mom and dad greeted her like family, but dad of course glancing out the door, "So, Paul is parking the car?" dad asked.

Rachel, Paul's mom, looked at them confused. I grinned guiltily and then grimaced in pain, "He's... not... coming!"

Dad moved around the bed closer to me taking my hand, "You didn't talk to him, Jess?"

"No, was planning on it, but Mason decided to come early."

"I am calling him." Dad stormed away from me, but Rachel stood up walking in front of my dad.

"She's your daughter so give her a break today. She explained it to me and though I don't agree it's up to her if he's here or not." She didn't waist another minute as she stepped around him coming to my side. Thankfully she understood my point. She traced her hand across my forehead, "Jess, your father is right. None of this matters because he is in love with you and this will hurt him."

The pain in my heart out weighed the pain in my stomach. Give me death it would be easier than making these decisions, and dealing with this pain.

When the doctor finally walked in to deliver Mason my dad escaped before he had to witness anything disgusting. This is the most humiliated thing in my life. Both my mom and Rachel got to witness this doctor shoving his fingers into me feeling god knows what. When he pulled his fingers out of me he smiled, "You are almost ready to push."

That is not what I wanted to hear. Panic stricken I searched my mom's and Rachel's faces to see if it's true that I hadn't even started yet. After all that pain I thought he would be here by now, but we haven't even been getting him out. Scared shitless, quite literally, I asked, "Can't you just cut him out?"

Mom stood up coming close to comfort me, but I didn't want to do this anymore. I shook my head, "Mom, I can't do this. The pain is too much for m... e..." Oh my god the pain is progressively getting worse. The doctor did something as Rachel stood up with a video camera and I shook my head no. She smiled at me, "What if you want him to see this Jess. It will be okay; this is his son."

I couldn't breathe the pain excruciating now as I felt pressure where the doctor was.

Glancing up at me with a calming smile, "You have to breathe and not push. Come on help me out, no more pushing."

I'm not pushing my body is doing that on its own. I grabbed Rachel's arm begging, "I changed my mind. I want him here. Please call him."

She set down the camera and held my hand, "Jessica, you made your decision and now it is too late. He could get hurt trying to get here to you so now you have to deal with this on your own. Your mother and I have both done this and you can do it too. Just focus on what the doctor tells you."

Doing everything the doctor told me to do, if my body didn't follow my direction it's not my fault. Mason pushed his way out as my body shoved him out. It's like a collaboration to cause the mother as much pain as she can stand so that this doesn't ever happen again. This is all Paul's fault! I wouldn't have had sex with him at all if I had any idea the outcome would be so painful. Forget wanting him here. I never want to see the man again no matter how much I thought I loved him. Noticing Rachel with the camera I screeched, "Make sure you get the pain he c... oh shit... f-ing this hurts."

Holding my breath I pushed with everything I had left like the doctor directed me to do. This is never going to end.

The doctor finally told me to stop pushing again, but my body didn't agree. His eyes met mine as he explained, "Stop pushing. His head is out, but I need to make sure its fine to continue. Look at me right now and just breathe through it. Understand?"

Glancing at my mother hoping to share the excitement but one hand covered her mouth while the other stared in shock.

"What! What's wrong?"

His voice demanded my attention "Look at me Jessica!"

There were those calming smiling eyes staring at me, "it's okay now. You can push now and give me one more good one. Give it everything you have."

I gripped my legs pushing as if my life depended on it. The relief when he entered this world had more satisfaction than making him with Paul. Glancing down I saw the doctor place him on my stomach. Mason seemed too small, but from what I could tell he had little hands, and feet. Watching the doctor do something to my poor little man, but laughed when it made him scream. I reached for him and my head twirled a little making me queasy. My eyes drifted back to the doctor not understanding this odd sense of losing myself. Darkness enclosed my sight while bells and whistles went off. Shaking my head to rid this sensation, it's like slow motion when you're about to lose it. The darkness created a tunnel for me as I watched the doctor take Mason from me Rachel set the camera down moving closer, and my mom...

3

I blinked confused and wanting to see my baby. Feeling around for that stupid button to get a nurse while trying to yell wasn't doing me any good, because I had no voice, and I felt a panic attack coming on. I barely got a chance to see him. What if something happened to him? I would never forgive myself. Why didn't I tell Paul? He would have never left Mason the way that I did.

Mom walked in, "Oh my god Jess. You had us all so worried."

"Mason?"

"He is beautiful, but a little early. He is in the ICU."

Needing to see him I shook my head trying to get up. Dad walked in and pushed me back down, "No, you don't. You have been out for three days. Take it easy! If you want to see him that bad we will get a wheel chair."

Dizziness filled my head and made my stomach flip. A nurse came running in and put something in my arm. My eyes roll back in my head as I screamed *NO,* but the darkness won that argument.

The next time I woke my mom and dad sat off to the side of the room in cushioned chairs. Rachel bounced her arms as she walked with a little bundle. Noticing my alertness she walked over to me and tears flowed down my face. Three days of his life I missed how many more did they put me out for? She laid him down in my arms and stared at my beautiful little man. Missing those days hurt in my heart. I'd never get that time back and it made me think of Paul and how unfair I have been. Wanting to tell him more than ever, but the question still remains. Is he really sure he can make the commitment that he is purposing with two of us to love. Rachel's tears filled her eyes as she sat down next to me commenting on Mason and I, "Jess, you are beautiful, but you will be happy to know that this little guy resembles his daddy, especially when he was a baby. I can't wait to show you the pictures."

In search of every little part of him I unraveled him. I had to count the toes and fingers making sure that I hadn't caused him any deformities with my volunteer work. So satisfied in my presence his eyes stayed wide open as if he watched me. So pure, innocent, and uninfluenced by the world or the pain in which we cause each other. Bundling him back up I brought him back to my body. The body craved what now lay in my arms, so I rested my nose and lips on his face to show him his mother's love. When his little mouth puckered and then his little tongue came out I gasped with delight.

I whispered to him, "You are too perfect to keep to myself."

Rachel stood up, "I can call him now?"

Shaking my head no but I had the biggest smile on my face, "My way."

She leaned down to kiss his forehead, "Jess, make it soon. You don't want him to miss this stage, he is too perfect."

I nodded, "When can I go home?"

She turned to my mom and dad. Mom stood up and walked over, "Three days. You have to gain some strength."

Not wanting to take my eyes off of Mason I didn't protest.

It wasn't long before Mason and I headed to the cabin. Dad packed two bins full of stuff to last us a few weeks and then they would be up to bring more supplies. I took and extra-long nap before the drive. I needed time alone with my baby to figure a way to share him with Paul.

Paul:

"Theo, I heard Jess had to go to the hospital. Is she okay?"

"Yes, but I called for a reason."

"She is agreeing to see me?"

"No, but it might be sooner than you expect."

"Really?"

"I need you to do me a favor."

"What is that?"

"I need you to get the cabin ready for us. I want extra wood inside and the fridge stocked."

"When are you coming?"

"Tomorrow, but you can't be there when we get there."

"Jess is coming with?"

With no argument either way; she'd be with them.

He coughed, "She needs to rest Paul and she wants to be alone. Please leave her be for a while. She will come to her senses fairly quickly."

"Her senses?"

"Yes, she is going to need help and I'm sure she will ask you. Please, Paul, if she had any idea I talked to you about this she'd disown me and in her condition she can't be on her own."

"I will, I promise."

No matter what I said to Theo, this is one promise I didn't intend to keep. She's mine and she needs me. I would give her a day or two, but that's it.

I went to set up the cabin bringing extra wood inside the cabin and I stocked the fridge with food. Theo advised me to make it all soft food like Yogurt, apple sauce, rice, and lots of soups. She needed substance and I should be getting her real food. Steak, potatoes, and vegetables like Theo had said to begin with. This is ridiculous and I should just stay until she gets here.

Jess:

Dad called the Watson's and arranged for Katelin and Seth to come help Mason and me get moved in. Thankfully dad didn't mention anything about Mason directly. He only told them that I'm weak from malaria. Mom and dad got me a phone so I wouldn't be stranded at the cabin with no communication so when I got close I called Katelin. She headed over and met me at the car. I took Mason out from the car seat as Katelin watched me, "So, who is this?"

"This is Mason."

"Your parents said you wanted to be alone. Why would you bring a…"

I grinned, "Yes, he is my baby. Don't be so shocked. I haven't seen you in over a year."

We walked in together and she asked too many questions, but I put him back in his seat not taking his warm blankets off of him. I went to start a fire. I waited to take him out but he complained which probably means he's hungry or needs to be changed. Those sweet little innocent coos gave me comfort. After it warmed up a little I went into the bedroom to feed him. I heard Seth and Nick as they brought in the totes of supplies. A little nervous to see them, but I had to face facts. I am a mother and it didn't matter what they thought.

I walked out with Mason in my arms, but after the long drive I really needed a nap. Seth, Katelin's annoying brother, dug into a bin, "Jess, where do you want this one? It's full of baby stuff."

He didn't get it yet so I grinned with my reply, "By the couch."

When his eyes rose to meet mine his face took a dive into a frown. Nick, Annie's brother and one of my first love interests, stood motionless staring at me. Seth walked out without saying a word. I watched him leave confused why he was upset. Katelin took over and told Nick where to put things, so I went to lay down on the couch with Mason. Katelin walked over and sat on the couch next to me, "Can I get you anything?"

"No. I am good. I am getting tired already."

"Okay," she peeked at Mason and smiled, "He is so little."

My tone took defense, "He's a little early."

"Well, he is sleeping so close your eyes and I will stay awhile."

I did what she told me. When the couch sagged by my feet I opened my eyes to Nick staring at me again. Ignoring the questioning stare I closed my eyes avoiding his eyes.

He nudged me awake, "Jess, you look like hell."

"Yeah, malaria will do that and then on top of it I had a baby."

"Obviously, Paul has no clue?"

He worked for Paul so of course Paul didn't have a clue.

Forcefully I opened my eyes glaring at him, "You know he doesn't and I would like to keep it that way for now. I need some time alone with my baby."

No matter what I said I wanted he didn't intend on listening to me. He's going to blab.

"Can I ask whose it is?"

"No."

"It's his?"

"I said you couldn't ask."

"But you shouldn't be alone. Look at you."

"Usually I'm better than this. I am just tired from the drive."

Beyond tired now I closed my eyes for a second, but they're so heavy I couldn't open them again.

Next thing I knew Matt stormed into the cabin. At this rate I'd never get any rest. He came and squatted in front of me his face full of worry, "Jess, what the hell did you do to yourself?"

Not thinking it would happen this fast it freaked me out that he's already aware that I'm here. Cringing I asked, "Does he know I'm here?" My only thought... Dad!

"Yes, Jess, but he's respecting your wishes and sent me to check on you."

I sat up wrapping my arms around his neck, but Mason squawked.

Katelin walked over to us handing him to me, "Jess, I think he is hungry again."

Matt stood up backing away and staring, "Jess?"

I pleaded with him as I held Mason tight to me bouncing him a little, "Matt, I need some time alone."

"Jess?"

"I am not ready to see him. It supposed to be a year."

"Jess, he didn't let you go."

"Well, I have someone else to think about now."

"You've found someone else?"

"No, but I have a baby now."

"It's yours?"

Holding back the tears I spoke more firmly, "Yes, he is."

He already knew the answer before he asked, "The father is?"

Avoiding his eyes I lied, "A one night stand. I tried to forget, Paul."

There's no excuse as to why I lied. I wanted to tell Paul first, and now it's all a lie.

He glared at me while Katelin walked over, "I thought he was Paul's baby."

Matt turned to her and so did I.

A little put off she huffed, "What? He looks like Paul."

Matt leaned over and pulled a little on Mason's blanket. I tried to pull him away but Matt moved over me more, "Jess, he does."

I tried to sound light and nonchalant, "You two are losing it. He does not."

Matt moved closer again and put his face so close to Mason's, "Yes, he does, Jess."

Covering Mason up to prevent Matt from getting any other ideas about Paul being his father and then I demanded, "Out Matt. I have to feed him."

"I can't leave. He said I'm supposed to watch over you until you will see him."

I touched his face, "Matt, I am so tired and I need to feed Mason. My body is weak and I don't have the strength to deal with this right now. Let me feed him and get some rest then you can come back and we'll talk."

He closed his eyes and shook his head, "I'm not telling him."

"I don't want you to. I will when the time is right."

He got up and Katelin took him by the arm leading him out the door. Hopefully, he wouldn't tell Paul. It's my only chance of figuring out how I'd tell him. I did promise his mom that I wouldn't keep Mason away from his father. If we were going to be together he had to do it with his whole heart not because of Mason.

Figuring Katelin and Matt discussed how much Mason looked like Paul, because it took her a long time to come back. Closing my eyes while I fed Mason I dozed sitting straight up. It hurt every time I fed him now, making me not like this breast feeding thing.

When Katelin came back in she went back to putting stuff away. I enjoyed my peaceful moments and relaxed into sleep. I didn't know how long she'd stay until she touched my arm gently, "Jess, you look so tired."

Nodding I tried to open my eyes, but they didn't want to cooperate.

"Jess, I have an idea. I'll take Mason to my house just for a little while. I'll show him off to my mom and we'd rock him and cuddle him for a little while so you can sleep."

Her hands lifted him from my arms. I tried to protest, "No, he's my responsibility."

"I know, Jess. But you need rest and this is just a little while."

"You're not going to show Paul are you?"

"No, I would be afraid to tell him. You get to do that on your own."

As if I could stop myself from sleeping, my eyes closed peacefully and I drifted back to sleep. I didn't have time to worry if they would bring Mason to Paul for inspection. My only thought as I drifted off was if Katelin had taken enough supplies for Mason.

4

Paul:

I paced at the house waiting to hear from Matt. Nick wouldn't tell me what upset him. Over the months we have worked together and he understood how much I loved Jess. So why he'd keep something from me I'm not sure, but he wouldn't even look at me tonight? Is she that bad that I'd shove everything a side and go to her even though she wants time alone. Maybe that's what I should do anyway. I could force her to listen to me, to let me take care of her. I could lock her up in the new house and keep her to myself until she listened to me and agreed that this time she would stick around and marry me. Not really sure what to do I continued to pace the floor. If it had been dirt I'm sure it would have been two feet deep. Giving up on waiting I decided to hit the punching bag to work on the aggression that was building minute by minute. If someone didn't call me or tell me what the hell is going on soon I'd head to the cabin and not let anyone get in my way.

It didn't matter how hard I jabbed and punched to get rid of my anger, Nick's worried face came back to my mind. Did she tell him that she would never see me again? No, her dad made it sound like she would ask for me in a few days. What the hell...

My phone rang and I picked it up, "MATT!"

"Yeah."

"So what is going on there?"

"Um, she's pretty frail, and ruff around the edges."

"Okay, she's sick. I already knew that."

"Yeah."

"Is that it?"

"Not exactly."

"Okay, what?"

"This one you are going to have to see for yourself to believe."

"What do you mean? She agreed to let me go over there?"

"Um, that isn't what she said. I think she said something about waiting a year, but... um... I don't think you want to wait a year."

"She doesn't want to see me. I can't go there. I'll wait a little while."

"No... Paul... I wouldn't wait a day on this one."

"Really?"

"Yeah."

"I will be right there."

"I can't stay for this, Paul. You are going to have to deal with this one on your own."

Already in my truck and on my way to the cabin, "Is she that bad?"

He chuckled but said, "Yes. But there's something else that..."

"That what?"

"Paul you have to calm down. You have to keep your mind about you when you get there."

"What? What are you trying to tell me?"

"I really can't say. Call me if you need me, but after your visit."

"Okay."

He hung up without saying goodbye. What's wrong with him?

I pulled into the driveway and walked up to the door. My heart pounded against my chest, my hands shook, and I can hardly breathe so I turned around and walked back to my truck. No, Matt said I had to see this for myself so I had to stay and I have to see her for myself. Working to encouraging myself I confirmed it in my head that she loves me, and this will be okay. She may not think she wants me here; but I am in love with her and it's my job to take care of her. She's just being stubborn and stupid, especially if she needs me.

Taking a deep cleansing breath, shaking my hands to get rid of any nervousness I'm feeling. I turned the handle and pushed the door open waiting for her to yell at me for showing up. The cabin stood dark and a little on the cool side. With the intention of just checking on her I moved into the cabin. If she's okay I'll give her the space and time she needs, but if she needs help I am not leaving her no matter how much she protests. I noticed the fire dying out so she must have went to bed. Making my way to her bedroom I noticed a lot of extra bins and luggage. She plans on staying a long time so I know she is here to be with me. Why is she making me wait then? I should just pull her into my arms force her to give in to me! But the way Nick reacted it's obvious that she is more frail than what I am imagining.

She's not in her room or the bathroom so I made my way to her parents room telling myself to take is nice and slow. Make her beg for your attention, play a little hard to get because she is the one that left you. No Jess there either. I huff my disappointment. The frantic way Matt talked about her made me think she was too weak to go wandering off, or maybe she went to say hi to Katelin. That has to be it. I'll just get the fire going a little better so when she gets back I can get a good look at her. Then I'd decide if I am staying or going.

After getting the fire to a roaring blaze I stood and wondered how I would get her to come back from Katelin's. I needed to see her, and this waiting drove my mind even crazier thinking she got disoriented and wandered out of the cabin. That's it. I am just going to go over there and demand to see her. I turned heading toward the door, but there she laid covered up to her nose in blankets. A grin grew on my face over joyed that my baby is home and there she is right in front of me. The only part of her visible happened to be the top of her head and her eyes. She looked so sweet and peaceful I didn't want to disturb her. Everyone told me how weak she looked. I walked closer to try to get a better idea of how bad off she is but her face hidden under the covers. Her eyes looked deep with dark circles and her skin is shallow. As I moved closer observing her cheeks. They were so thin my heart started to ache as I moved even closer to her. Kneeling down by the couch wanting to wrap my arms around her, but she still didn't want to see me. Trying to preserve her innocence I caused this. I caused this destruction of my perfect girl. My heart hurt from all the pain I forced on her. Between my heart pounding against my chest and the heavy sigh I thought the sound alone would wake her, but she did not move an inch. Not able to resist her I traced the back of my hand along her cheek. Focusing on her face I watched for her reaction which came as a smile. Relief raced through my body all because of the smile that grew with my touch. It's my touch that made her happy. When I did it again she replied, "Paul."

My eyes closed as my chest heaved and my heart jumped a beat. Leaning over to her ear I whispered, "Yes."

Her slight smile grew to a grin but she never opened those beautiful luring eyes to gaze upon me, "You're not supposed to be here for a year."

The pain of her being this close to me and not able to see her tore me to pieces. Not allowing her to push me away ever again, "Matt said I had to come. That I wouldn't believe him even if he tried to explain."

I slid my hand under the covers searching for hers'. I found it all skin and bones. No meat on it at all. There's nothing left to my bodacious baby, "Jess, what did you do to yourself?"

She slid her hand away from mine, "I'm sick."

Removing her hand from me told me I upset her. All I wanted to do is stay with her and take care of her. I had to try something so that she would allow me to stay with her. My heart ached for her and I wanted to touch her more or to hold her. Settling for tracing my fingers across her forehead I smoothed away the worry lines, while watching for any sign of acceptance from her. It worked fairly well as the grin on her face came back. The blood pumped through my veins bringing the adrenaline to every part of my body making my hands shake.

I noticed her hand trying to escape the blankets and I moved them to help her free her hand. It reached for my face, "Can I touch your dimples, Paul. I have missed your face."

I wanted to jump up and down saying yes, yes, and yes, but I didn't want to move away from her either. Quickly I took her hand in mine guiding it to my face. Closing my eyes as her delicate hand moved up and down my face, but when she presses her pointer finger in my dimple I grinned just for her. It's that simple touch, so much like making love the first time. Her finger moved up and down pressing against my face. I was holding my breath waiting for the rush when she spoke to me.

"Breathe, Paul. Is Mason here?"

Who the f---ing is Mason? I didn't like that she touched me this way and asking about someone else. She has nerve. Is that what Matt tried to hint at? The shock of someone else here with her is that why he couldn't tell me? "Mason who?"

Her face stayed sweet and calm. She didn't worry about how I took it that she asked for another man.

"My little man, Paul."

I stared at her without breathing. My worries had come true. She found someone new, but in such a short time and while she was sick? I moved closer to her and whispered in her ear, "Jess, I hoped we'd try again. Start all over, and spend a lot of time together."

"Paul, you should go. He will be back soon and I need to sleep."

"I am not afraid of him. I will fight for you, Jess."

The grin on her face brought me to a new level of happiness. She wanted me to fight for her. Letting myself breathe again when she spoke, "He doesn't compare to you. He can't do to me what you can do."

She loves me more than him and he will never satisfy her the way I do. I knew she still loved me but I wanted to hear it, "How is that, Jess?"

Not wanting to over react by jumping up and down, or yelling at this guy she brought home to get out, so I moved closer to her. The smiles still there but the tears leaked out of her closed eyes. Hoping they were happy tears I tried to wipe them away when she answered me, "Break my heart."

In three words she shattered my heart. Searching my head for answers, a response, but I had nothing. The only thing that made any sense to me is that he couldn't break her heart because she didn't love him. She loved me and that's why it hurt to be apart. Oh, Jess, what am I going to do to make you understand that I have changed, or did I hurt you so bad that we don't have a chance?

In desperation I begged, "Jess, do you love me?"

She stated quite clear, "Always have and always will."

All of this didn't make sense to me. I lost it and tears filled my eyes, "If you love me why did you bring him home with you?"

Her face saddened, "Because I am the mommy."

Shocked I asked, "What do you mean?"

The slight grin came back to her face, "Paul, go home. Mommy needs to sleep now."

Mommy? "Jess, please talk to me?"

Her voice came weaker and slurred, "Paul, I need sleep. Come back when it has been a year."

Now she pissed me off, "No. I am not leaving."

The slight grin came to her face and a tear dripped out from her closed eyes again, "Okay." She nuzzled into the covers and tucked her hands back beneath the blankets. Begging and pleading for her to speak to me. Even trying what already worked once by tracing my hand against her cheek and forehead but there's no response to my coaxing. No matter what it did to me I wanted more time with her. Even if we held hands it would be something. If she wouldn't speak to me, and I didn't want to be away from her I compromised by resting my head on the couch by hers admiring her in sleep. That is until my legs went numb. I finally gave up watching her. Obviously she needed her rest. Giving up I sat against the couch in front of her and leaned my head back closing my eyes to wait for her to wake again. I thought about this Mason person and how he'd react to me being here with her, but I am going to fight for Jess. She's mine in the first place and he should go back where he came from because I'm the man in her life. Well at least until she left because I broke her heart. It all seemed so long ago and so many things are more important than the hurt. Its more about the love we shared and the ultimate desire to share our lives together. We were like magnets that couldn't be separated by time or space.

5

When the door opened my heart pounded hard beneath my chest. Instinct told me to get up and charge this guy, but he might not be aware of the love we shared. No, I am not going to move and he can catch me here with Jess. He'd have to back off because I'm not going to let her go.

"Hey Jess, are you awake?"

Katelin's voice came out careful and soft. Thank God it's her. Jess would be glad that she came back to check on her almost as much as I am. Katelin carried a baby that decided to make a lot of noise, and I didn't want her to wake Jess if it's rest she needs. I got up quickly encouraging her to quiet the baby. "Shhhh, she is sleeping. You might not want to bring that baby in here. Jess is sick."

Startling Katelin as I made my way closer she side stepped me, "Paul! You're here?"

She went around me to Jess. I followed quickly, "You shouldn't be bringing that baby by Jess."

She laughed, "Wake Jess up. Now, Paul."

Moving between them I tried to prevent her from waking Jess. If Jess woke up I wanted her attention. Katelin can take that baby and leave. Forcefully I insisted, "No, she needs to sleep. Can you quiet him down?"

She pushed me aside as Jess sat up holding her hands out for the baby. Katelin asked, "Jess, did you get some sleep?"

"Yeah. There is my little man." She cradled him in her arms bouncing and cooing at him to settle him down, but glanced back at Katelin, "How was he?"

This whole situation confused me. That's her little man? But that's a baby. Making my way around the couch I watched as they discussed Katelin's mom reacting to a new baby.

Katelin explained further, "He's a happy baby. He did really well until about a half hour ago. Then he started to complain and cry. We tried everything but he wouldn't stop."

He wasn't crying anymore in Jess's arms. When Jess's eyes rose to meet mine it looked like she had no idea that I was here, "Paul, you're here?"

I nodded watching her cradle this bundle in her arms. Katelin carried on without acknowledging me, "Sorry, we tried to keep him longer so you'd have more time to sleep but Mason is a hungry little guy."

The word escaped me without thought, "Mason?"

When both of them turned to me they shared a look of disapproval. Not only did the glares make me uncomfortable and stupid, but they told me to leave without saying a word. At this very moment I am stupid.

Dumbfounded would be a better word to describe the empty thoughts. Not understanding why Jess took this bundle in her arms so calmly, calling him Mason, and her little man. What the hell is going on?

They continued to talk to each other about him getting the good stuff first. About him not taking the bottle no matter what they did. This baby, Mason, seemed awfully little, but I am a guy and how would I know about the size of a baby. He made little noises, not quite cries it sounded more like whimpers. Fascinated by this perfect little person I moved closer. Jess cradling him in her arms it made me forget about fighting Mason.

"Baby?" Hearing myself say it surprised them and me.

They both turned to me again. Now I saw a little fiery in her eyes when Jess stared at me, while I stood there stunned. Matt's right about this; I'm having a hard time believing my eyes.

Katelin stared at me but asked Jess, "Is everything okay here?"

Jess's attention came back to me again, "Yeah, I think Paul's leaving anyway."

I'm not leaving. In fact I didn't say anything at all that would indicate that I am leaving. Not knowing what I am supposed to do, so I tried to get it straight in my head before opening my mouth again. That is a baby and from what I can tell it's Jess's baby. But she has only been gone... In my head I counted the months. She left at the end of March, 1... 2... 3,4,5,6,7,8. But that isn't enough time if it's... Holly shit, he is my son. When I moved closer I peered down at him but spoke firmly, "I am not leaving."

Jess ignored me but I stayed there observing her kiss him, hold him so carefully, and love him. Just to be certain I went through the numbers in my head again and found myself sitting down next to her watching them together.

Jess spoke again which gave me a little startle, but her words were directed to Katelin, "Tell your mom thanks. The sleep helped a lot and I should be good for a while now."

Memorized by the way Jess held him. It's probably a good thing he's so small, because her arms appeared to have no meat on them. He squawked and I laughed. His mouth was going to town searching for something that his little hands weren't satisfying, "Jess, is he hungry?"

Katelin told Jess she would be back to check on her tomorrow but my eyes stayed focused on him. Did he resemble me? No, he looks like every other baby I have seen, but much smaller than I would expect. I went to reach for his hand, but Jess pulled him away from me scolding, "Did you wash your hands?"

She brought me back to the real world with one sentence. I stared into her eyes wondering what to say or what to do.

"Paul, I have to feed him, you should go."

Matt's right with this being something I had to see for myself. There is no way to explain this, but I'm not leaving. I shook my head no, but didn't say a word. She scared me a little when she glared at me, but I wasn't leaving. If he's mine then I... why wouldn't she tell me?

Her eyebrows rose as she looked into my eyes, "I am not comfortable feeding him in front of people."

I got up quickly and moved to the kitchen and paced glancing back at her when I wanted to ask a question but didn't say anything. Trying to slow my heart rate I breathe in with my mouth and out through my nose, or should I be doing that the other way around. Light headed from breathing all wrong until I heard Jess moaned in discomfort like she's in pain. I ran back to the couch peeking over the back of it, "Are you okay?"

"No, this hurts."

"Jess, why does it hurt?"

"Because he sucks like a vacuum, and it makes my stomach contract and it hurts."

Whispering in her ear, "How old is he?"

The pain on her face eased as she turned to face me. Oh, how I wanted to kiss her. Her mouth was like a red juicy apple for me and I wanted a bite to see if they were still as sweet as I remembered.

"He is three weeks old."

She laid her head on the back of the couch and I didn't move. As thin as she was her neck tempted me. Wanting to touch it maybe trace my fingers down it or my mouth. Whatever she would let me do. I heard the kid squawk again. Peeking over at Mason I laughed, "He is demanding like you, Jess."

On defense she scolded, "No, Paul he is not like me. I just don't make enough to feed him."

With how thin she's gotten I'm not surprised. Glancing around the room searching for something that I could do to help her, "Do you want me to make a bottle for him?"

"Yeah, just put it in the microwave. Oh shit this hurts."

"Jess, you should let me take a look at it. If they are chapped there is stuff to help with that. It's perfectly normal and I'd run get what you need if you want me to."

I pulled out a pan and put water in it, "Jess, I am not going to use the microwave. They say it is bad for the baby."

I wanted her to believe I'd be a good dad if she would just tell me he's mine.

"Jess, how is it going?"

She wasn't talking to me so I walked back over. His little arms and legs were just a moving and Jess sat peacefully sleeping. I put the blanket over her and took him. It's my chance to check him out, but she woke up clinging him tighter to her, "Paul, don't."

Reassuring her with a smile, "It's okay. I will feed him his bottle." She pushed me away and I stood back wondering what her intentions were. As she moved to get up she peeked at me quickly and then her attention went back to *him.* Carefully she placed him in my arms cradling his head into my arm. The way she touched me moving my hands where she wanted them to be. My heart raced as I observed her adoration for this little guy. She moved her hand over his head and kissed him carefully and then her eyes came back to meet mine. Not comfortable in letting him out of her embrace I waited for her to make it okay for me to take him. I tried to breathe slowly, so my emotions wouldn't come out, but I gazed at her searching for a hint that she still loved me to. All of her attention and love directed at the baby in the way she adored him in my arms. If she paid any attention to me she would recognize that I stare at her the same way she does at him.

"Please be careful."

Wanting to get comfortable to feed him I backed up a little but she held my arms to keep me in front of her. Her eyes searched my face and for a split second I thought she'd kiss me. My hands shook as I held Mason, but not because he's there, it's the way she gazed into my eyes so deeply. Every part of me missed her. If I didn't glance at her mouth I would never have seen the slight grin before she let me go and crawled back into her cocoon on the couch. Being able to check her out the only thing noticeable about her is how skinny she's become. There's nothing left of her which made her look anorexic. Well I suppose after not eating much that is exactly what happened to her. It made me sad to see her this skinny, "Jess, do you want me to make you something to eat?"

"No, just feed him. I am fine."

"Jess, he is little."

"Yes, he was early."

My heart was racing because I wanted to know for sure, "How early?"

She closed her eyes and put her head down, "Five or six weeks, maybe seven tops. It didn't help that I got malaria."

"Is he okay?"

"Yes, Paul. You should feed him."

I walked over to the chair with him to cuddle while I fed him. When I sat down she leaned over the arm of the couch watching me.

"Jess, you should really let me feed you."

Her eyes didn't fall on me they stared at him. Jealousy is a horrible thing but it's there and the worst part of it is I'm jealous of this innocent child that is probably my kid. I started to feed him like she wanted. He settled down right away and went to work. He must have been hungry because he sucked it right down. His little eyes stared up at me blank from emotion. Memorized by the way they looked so empty, pure, and untouched. Not able to take my eyes off of him memorized by how much of Jess there is in him, and the little noises he made captivated me. We stared at each other for so long he finally blinked, and then again, and yet again each time they stayed closed a little longer. Wanting to laugh when he gave into sleep; it won over his curiosity of me. Pulling the bottle from his mouth only to witness his mouth still working to suck from it. Not able to contain my laughter I kept it to a breathy chuckle.

Jess pulled my attention back to her as she laughed out loud.

"What Jess?"

She rolled over and covered up, "You are a goner like me. Just remember to burp him."

"Wait, Jess. How do I do that?"

"Put him to your chest and pat his back very lightly until he burps."

I watched her nuzzle into the couch and waited for her to sleep. The little guy needed to burp so carefully and awkwardly I brought him to my chest. His little hands touched me so softly that my heart raced. Why wouldn't she tell me he's mine? I did what she told me and he did finally burp. I chuckled to myself as I sat here holding my son. He had to be mine with the time frame she's giving me. I knew she wasn't with anyone before me unless she did something right away while she… shit. Not believing it for one minute I'm absolutely sure he's my son, but I needed to find out. The first place that came to mind happened to be Mason himself. First things first so I laid him on my lap pulling the blanket from him. Inspecting his little hands, small hands little fingers, all there, but no hint of me. Pulling the bottoms off next to see his feet I found little bitty feet, but those toes were definitely Jess's. As I played with them he jerked his foot away. He's ticklish and the temptation too great, so I ran my fingers up his body to his waist and he squirmed. He is ticklish like me. I put his clothes back on as he moved his arms and legs around in the air. Giving up on the search I pulled him back to me and held him there. His hands traced against my chest as he squirmed in my arms. Enjoying his innocence I found myself holding his head kissing him and taking in his scent. He smelled like Jess so much that my love for this little guy already grew to a new level for me.

Holding this little guy for so long we both dozed off. Waking to a faint beeping noise I determined it came from the kitchen. When I got up too quickly I startled the little guy. He stuck out his bottom lip and I almost fell to pieces. That pout is the spitting image of Jess when she tried to get her way about something. I held him tight as I walked to the kitchen searching for the noise. I listened and walked around searching for it and it seemed to be coming from his diaper bag. Digging with one hand in the bag I found a little square clock so I pulled it out. If she had it set for a reason it might be important enough to wake her. With Mason in my arm we headed back to the living room where Jess slept. As I sat down on the edge of the couch I ran my free hand against her back, "Jess, hun, there's an alarm going off."

She bolted up and pushed me out of the way. Following her to the kitchen to see what's so important that she set an alarm for. Frantically she searched the bag as I put Mason in his seat tucking a blanket around him to keep him warm. Her hands shook while her body trembled.

"Jess, what are you doing?"

"Medicine."

"Does he need medicine?"

"It's for me."

She continued to dig and finally pull stuff out of the bag frustrated.

"Jess, how much does Mason weigh?"

"Almost six pounds."

"Is his dad small, short?"

"No, Paul. He's just early. He'll catch up."

"How long is he?"

She took the medicines out of their bottles but dropped a bottle, "Paul, stop asking me questions!"

Wanting to help I moved to grab the bottle off the floor, but stepped closer to her. She held onto the counter to support what weigh she had left. So close to her I inhaled the scent of her shampoo, but only reached around her holding the bottle out in front of her. If she'd lean back into me it would be like old times. In my imagination she leans back into my body, but reality her body stayed rigid. Whispering in her ear I told her, "Jess it's okay. I am here now."

She started to cry but her tone stayed firm, "Please don't do that."

I didn't understand, "Do what?"

Anger filled her words, "Be nice to me."

I closed my eyes and pleaded, "Jess?"

She turned to me, her eyes meeting mine. Tears filled them to the rim as she spoke, "Paul, all this: me, the baby, everything... it's a lot to take in and you have to be really sure."

"Sure of what?"

"It's not about you and me anymore. You would have to be there, and you would have to be a daddy, Paul. Is that what you want? It has to be what you really want or it stops here and now."

I didn't know what to say. All I knew is I wanted her in my life.

She turned away from me crying harder than before. "Paul, you need to go and really think about what you want and don't come back unless you are really sure. I couldn't live through another heart break."

I didn't want to do this to her. How can I screw this up? I wanted to make her better and now she's crying. This is her way of telling me to back off and I didn't want to hurt her ever again. The one thing she didn't understand that I would eventually show her is that none of this matters if I have her in my life. Wrapping my arms around her I spoke softly, "Jess, I didn't mean to make you cry. If it will make it better for now I will leave, but only if you want me to, but I can't promise to stay away. As for everything else we will have to take it one day at a time. I will learn how to do the rest."

Reaching to kiss her cheek wanting to turn her to me and kiss those luscious lips, but she's definitely not ready for that. I asked, "Can I bring you food?"

She nodded so I released her and walked toward the door. Stopping in front of Mason in the seat I leaned over him. If she told me he is my son I'd want to kiss him too but I just inhaled deeply closing my eyes. Her scent remained on him.

"Paul, what are you doing?"

I glanced back at her with a huge grin "He smells new."

She laughed trying to wipe her tears from her face, "Your weird, Paul."

Bending down to pear into those eyes again, I wanted him to recognize me. Shaking his hand I spoke to him directly, "Later little man."

I walked to the door not wanting to walk out. Afraid she wouldn't be here when I got back, but my guess is that she's too week to go anywhere. What I hoped she'd do is beg me to stay, but she didn't so I glanced back at her pausing in the door. If she'd just let me kiss her she would understand that I am completely in love with her.

"Paul, you were leaving." Her giggle filled me enough to get out the door.

6

I headed to the job-sight where one of the new employees needed help. Craig's there to put his two cents in on how to do things, so I hoped he didn't scare the kid. It's not safe to drive stunned and dazed. All I could think about is how sure I am of wanting to be with Jess. I know I love her with all of my heart. My heart ached for her at this very moment. Not only did I want her in my life I needed her. Being a daddy? This is going to take a little more time to adjust to. If he's mine I am already his Dad, and I would want to be part of his life even if I didn't have Jess. What am I saying? His is mine; he has to be. But what if he isn't... would I love him enough to be his father, and if we have children together I'd have to treat Mason as my own. This isn't a question if I wanted to be a dad or not, if I want Jess in my life then I am one already.

The only troubling thing about this whole picture is if he isn't mine and Jess didn't want any more kids would I be okay with that?

Yes. My answer is still yes, because if I want to have Jess in my life then it's all worth it. Right? Why I still have doubt about anything of this then? I guess I'm a little more shocked than I ever would have guessed.

A rap came to my window bringing me back to the here and now. Somehow I ended up at the job site where Jeremy had trouble. Not remembering how I got her scared me a little. Getting out Jeremy started to run through everything that they tried, however I didn't see Craig.

"Where is Craig?"

"He went to get supplies."

Jeremy's young and talkative and he carried on the conversation without me. Trying to focus on the task I explained what I did to fix the problem step by step even making him do the work for the experience. My mind drifted back to Jess and processing what I wanted. I kept coming up with her. All I wanted in life is this beautiful amazing girl that took my heart and filled it with emotions. Remembering the way her body trembled as I put my arms around her to help her with the medicine, about the sweet smell of her hair.

"Paul, you seem to be somewhere else today."

I looked up at Jeremy and I felt myself blush. My mind is somewhere else it wrapped up in a small thin package, "Yes, um... you're right, sorry."

"Is everything okay?"

"No, confused about life that is all."

"A girl?"

Not wanting to admit that he hit it right on I grinned and confessed, "Yeah."

"Do you love her?"

That question made me laugh, "More than life itself."

"So what is the problem?"

It hit me like a brick that nothing else mattered. I loved Jess enough to deal with all of it. She's worth it and I didn't want to go one day without her. I looked back at Jeremy, "You're right. There's no problem at all. Can you get the rest of this?"

"Yeah, why?"

"I need to tell her I love her."

Already missing her smile I raced to get back to my precious Jess. One thing I did have to stop for is food. She needed meat on those bones so I didn't break her when I hug her.

Mackley's happen to be our favorite spot for dinner so I stopped there ordering two of the biggest steaks they had, waffle fries, and a Caesar Salad. She needed substance to put meat on those bones. Abby asked questions but I didn't want to waste any time getting back to my Jess.

Everything moved in a blur as I made my way back to her. It came to abrupt stop when I entered the cabin, food in hand, to Mason screaming frenziedly. Letting the bags of food drop I snatched him into my arms wrapping another blanket around him. His body temperature cold against my body and that's when I realized the whole cabin is cold. Yelling out as I searched for her, "Jess. Jess, where are you?" The cabin is small but time slowed as I checked the bedrooms. The only door that remained close is where she had to be. Knocking to avoid an embarrassing situation, but she didn't reply. Twisting the door knob, pushing the door open, and finding her there lying on the floor reminding me of the day I lost Anne.

The way she laid there motionless my heart sank. Is it that easy to end a life? Two in my single life was too heart wrenching to accept. Getting a better handle on Mason I reached down taking her wrist in my hand. My breath stalled while I searched for a pulse. Though her skin is cool to touch I gasped when I felt a faint beat. Only having one reason to ever let her go and this is that one reason; to call Doc Ferriday. He lived a few doors down from the cabin.

"Hey, Doc, I have an emergency at the Jenson's can you come over." I was starting to lose it, "Something is wrong with my Jess."

"I will be right there."

Not wanting to let him go, but Jess needed me so I put Mason in his seat, "I am sorry buddy but your mommy needs me. Hang on little buddy, I'll be right back." With the intentions of keeping him warm I covered him with a blanket, and then I grabbed a few more running them to Jess. Engulfing her in the blankets I pulled her to me as I sat on the floor, "Jess, please don't leave me now."

"Sleep, Paul."

Oh my god she spoke to me and my heart beat harder for her. Friction is a good thing for circulation so I rubbed her body everywhere trying to warm her.

"I do love you, Paul."

The most wonderful words in the world, the tears flooded my eye. This is her good bye, to leave with the most amazing last words. Cherishing them I traced my fingers against her blue lips. It might be the color blue that scared me so much so I put my lips to her open mouth to warm them. Everything ignited in that moment, her lips pressed harder against mine more than I thought possible from her. If she's saying her goodbyes than it's the last time I'd kiss her, so I let it continue. Taking her face in my hands I made sure she knew I wanted to kiss her forever. Her body came alive rising to meet me as we sucked, licked, and nibbled our last moments together.

She moaned her disappointment when I stopped kissing her but I heard the door.

"Shh, Jess, it will be okay now. Hold on for me Jess."

With the kiss over she relaxed in my arms. Never opening her eyes she still cuddled there with a grin on her face. Wanting her to hold on I yelled for the Doctor, "Doc we're in here."

He found us in the bathroom with Jess cradled in my arms. Everyone in town walked on egg shells around me for years, because I had lost it when Anne died. They called me the ticking time bomb, but Jess made all that go away. The sad part of that is Doc Ferriday gazed at me with that same look that everybody used to give me. When he squatted down in front of me he wiped back the hair from her face, held her eye open, and then grabbed her wrist. He stayed there for about a minute and then he tried to take her from me. I wasn't ready to let her go yet so I held her firmly in my arms.

Doc's eyes softened, "Paul if I'm going to help her you need to let me take her."

My throat constricted, my eyes watered, and my heartbeat did double time, but let her go I couldn't do.

This time he decided to be firmer, "Paul! Let me help her. She's got a good pulse, but you need to let me take her." My attention moved to him and I grudgingly let her go into his arms. I slipped and stumbled to get up to follow him. He went to one of the bedrooms and almost ran into me as he came back out. I moved to let him by as he walked into the next room.

He scolded me, "Paul, it's cold in here."

She needed me and I left, "I know. I shouldn't have left. The fire is almost out and there's not much heat coming from it."

He walked to the couch and laid her down while I hovered for answers.

"Paul, I noticed the baby. You need to make sure he is warm enough. Put him to your skin it will warm him better."

I moved away and pulled off my shirt then pulled the blankets off of Mason. Picking him up gently cuddling him into my body and cupped his little head to my chest. I walked back to the doctor and he stood taking a blanket to wrap around us, "Yours?"

With confusion I stumbled trying to explain, "No. I'm not sure. If he is mine she would have told me."

He grinned, "Really?"

I didn't know what to say. He went back to working on Jess. Mason complained so I paced with him. I put my lips and nose to him and he smelt so much like *her*. I wrapped my hand around his little head kissing him. My love for her directed to him. Still sniffling but the screaming had stopped. My efforts well rewarded because I satisfied his needs for now.

The Dr. Ferriday glanced at me, "Paul, I need to take blood. She is thin."

"She contracted Malaria in South America before she had this little guy."

"Well that does explain a few things, but she shouldn't be staying here by herself, Paul. Not with a new baby and being this weak."

Excited to offer, "I will bring her home with me."

He chuckled, "Well, first things first. Who can take care of the baby if I admit her?"

"Admit her where?"

"Paul, I'd like to observe her at the hospital for a couple of days. Is she breast-feeding?"

The image of her pain came to mind, "Yes." My eyes drifted to her once again. Her body laid there limp and motionless.

"Paul!"

Not worrying about all the details I asked, "Is she going to be okay?"

"Yes, but I need to run a few tests and what about the baby?"

Fumbling again, "I will take him home with me. Maybe my mom and dad... shit, her parents?"

"Hey, calm yourself. See if you can get him to eat and give me a little time to take care of her."

I moved to the kitchen and put Mason in his seat. Those big eyes stared at me, but when his bottom lip came out it quivered. Standing here all I wanted to do is watch him for hours with all the little quirky faces he makes. This little pout will captivate me. When he let out a small short cry I chuckled. It's obvious he's complaining about something, "Okay, okay little man. I'm on it."

I put my shirt back on, started the water, and put the bottle in the pan. Glancing over to see what he decided to do with Jess, but he's on the phone. All the while he talked he did things to Jess. When he made his way to me he hung up the phone. He stood in front of Mason with a great big grin on his face and baby talk coming out of his mouth. Chuckling I checked the bottle.

"Paul, can you take a few days off to take care of them?"

"Yeah, I guess."

"Good. I have stuff being delivered to your house. She is breast-feeding so I don't want to take her away from him. You will have your hands full. Are you sure you can handle this?"

"Nope." But I nodded as the blood raced through my veins with excitement. She's coming home with me. After hearing that I got lost in my own world and how this would play out. Her being so thankful that she would throw her arms around me kissing me over and over to thank me for rescuing her.

Nothing could take me out of my psyche except for the Doc's next comment, "He resembles you."

That surprised me that someone else saw it too. I thought it's me being hopeful, "You think so?"

He chuckled, "Is it a possibility?"

My mind wandered off thinking about the time frame and it's *very* possible. I closed my eyes wishing she would have given me more exacts. I nodded.

He put his hand on my shoulder, "Do you want this?"

When I glanced over at Mason I decided then that I wanted him to be mine more than anything except for spending my life with Jess.

Doc sighed, "I have to do blood work to make sure he is fine so Paul, if you would like there is a blood test to make sure."

My attention went back to the doctor with aghast. That would be deceitful, but if he's mine and Jess didn't tell me that's deceitful too. So torn on saying yes or no, but I wanted to know.

"Okay, it's done."

He moved to Mason and checked him out. Lights flashing threw the window when the ambulance pulled up to the front of the cabin. Panic ran through my body with the fear that Doc didn't tell me something important. He's going to take her away from me, but I had to keep her. He said she's going home with me. "I thought you were going to let her come home with me."

He stopped me, "Paul, we needed some help moving her to your place. They will get all the blood work done in the ambulance and we will take the baby with us so they can make sure he is okay. Why don't you go get set up at the house. We'll be there in about an hour and a half. Can you get everything ready by then?"

Not wanting to ever be apart again I shook my head, "You want me to leave?"

"Yes, Paul. Everything is fine now and we will make sure it's okay to leave her with you. Are you sure you want to do this?"

I wanted nothing more than have her come home with me for the rest of our lives. Maybe if she's comfortable there she would never leave me again. I glanced up at the doctor, "Yes."

I called my mom and asked her about baby stuff like a crib, blankets, and diapers.

She stopped me and asked what was going on. After I told her about Jess needing help and that she and her baby were coming home with me she had one thing to say, "Paul, honey, are you sure this is what you want?"

She caught me off guard so I went into defense mode, "It doesn't matter what I want, and I love her."

"Okay, honey, I will bring everything I kept. We'll be there in an hour."

Relieved and confused wondering if all of this is something I wanted? How do I know if I can handle all of this? That is right, it just doesn't matter... I love her.

7

When mom and dad arrived they helped me move everything in to the house. We put the crib and changing table up in my bedroom. Mom stocked it with everything that I needed. Then she put a bunch of bottles and cleaning stuff by the sink for me. Though she stayed busy getting everything set up to make it easy on me she still took worried glances at me. Following her from room to room she explained everything to me. If only she understood that I wouldn't remember a thing. My mind remained on Jess coming home to the house I built for us together. No matter how I evaluated the situation, to me it's my one chance to convince her to stay. Hoping that, *I love you Jess*, would work.

My dad lingered in the shadows of the rooms just to taunt me with his chuckling. If he had something to say I wish he'd say it and not annoy me when I am stressed out like this.

She stopped and turned on me, "Paul, don't you think you should be taking notes. It's a lot to remember."

Writing it down would have been a good idea, because as soon as the ambulance pulled in everything she had said evaporated. Rushing out to meet them I reached for Mason in his seat and followed the Doc Ferriday into my home. Not really sure what's right and wrong I placed him on the table for my mom to see. Immediately she pulled him from the seat and cuddled him to her, "There's my grandbaby."

Frozen in a mid-turn I glanced back at her. Her eyes wide with shock as they met mine, but then they pierced at me, "You said you wanted this!"

Scaring the hell out of me after a night like this didn't seem right, but I did say I wanted this. Directing Doc Ferriday down the hall to where Jess and Mason would be staying, I followed along in case he needed something more from me. When I came back to the living room I glanced out to see they had Jess out of the ambulance, then I hesitantly glanced at my mom still holding Mason. Sometimes I'm a control freak and being this unprepared through me for a loop I needed something to ground me. Mom glanced up at me with worried eyes. She must read that I'm on the edge of losing it. Her eyes left mine for Mason's but she spoke to me, "Paul, you need to talk to him. Tell him stories, read to him, sing to him, and love him. He will need attention from someone who can love him and right now that is you."

As my mother directed me my father walked over to her taking Mason from her. In awe I observed him talking to Mason, bounce him a little in his arms, and then he kissed Mason's little forehead. My mom and dad took to this Grandparent naturally and treated Mason as they're own. The tears welled in my eyes as I saw their interaction with each other and with Mason.

They stood together like they were dancing, but held Mason between them giving him all of their attention. Confusion flooded every part of my brain about their understanding, compassion, and unbiased opinion of the situation, so unbelievable that they did this for me, because I loved Jess.

My attention went to the gurney Jess laid on while they moved her inside the house. Doc barked orders on what they were to do, but glanced up at me, "You seem to have everything set up good. We'll just get her settled in and then I'll come get you."

With everything settled and organized the ambulance people left. Doc Ferriday reassured me that she's going to be okay. We discussed a few things and he agreed to check on us every day at noon.

After the Doctor left mom and dad stuck around for a little while. They took turns holding Mason. I wanted them to leave so I'd have my little family to myself, but thankful because the fear settled in my stomach. Running a business I could handle, but this I had no idea how to handle it. Not only did I agree to take care of Jess I also agreed to take care of Mason. Chuckling with a sigh when I realized I am screwed.

Mom and dad left late, but only after mom gave me a lecture about being responsible and strong. We went over making a bottle, changing a diaper, a challenge when it came to boys. Most importantly they made sure I would be comfortable with Mason alone.

After they walked out the door I held Mason to my chest as we walked back and forth from the living room to the bedroom to check on Jess. His little head rested against my chest making gurgling noises. After the hundredth time of checking on Jess I decided to sit down in the rocker recliner. When I put my nose down to Mason's head I enjoyed that he smelled like Jess; it made me smile with delight. I laid him back on my legs to gaze at him again. Waiting for him to do something, but he didn't do much of anything. I gazed into his eyes searching for something, anything that would tell me if he's mine. The empty stare left me needy. It's a wonder how anything can be so pure and innocent on this earth. I traced my fingers against his and then checked out his feet again. He's utterly perfect in every way, but so little that I worried about hurting him without knowing it. Holding up my hand to his chest, which happen to be the same size as him.

As his face change to that little pout that he does I chuckled. So much of him came from Jess. My enjoyment ended when he let out a screech I stopped laughing and stared at him. Shit, what does that mean? Waiting for what I don't know but I didn't have to wait long because that little pouty bottom lip pushed out again. The bad part is this time the screech came quicker than the last time. Not waiting for another ear piercing screech I pulled him to my body getting up to do something for him. We, as in me, decided that maybe he needed food. It isn't easy to make a bottle while holding him but I managed. We paced and I bounced him a little while it warmed in the pan. His little hands rested on my chest, gripped, and the moved against my chest causing a heaviness to fill me. Right now I am all he has to take care of him.

Humor filled me when the little man tooted in my hand reminding me that if Jess didn't get better soon then I'd be changing diapers. Not looking forward to that experience. As soon as the bottle was ready I headed to the recliner to get comfortable with him while he ate. Every time I tried to give him the bottle he'd take one gulp and let out a complaining cry. After several attempts to feed him and his refusal meant that it was time to try the other horrible thing that I didn't want to do at all.

Mom did bring me a changing table so at least everything I needed was in one place. Thank goodness for moms. Changing the diaper hadn't been a horrible experience it went rather smooth. As soon as I got him all wrapped up again that little pout came out followed by the screech. His complaining more persistent I tried the bottle again, but found that he didn't want that either. Nothing worked when this little guy made up his mind on what he wanted the only problem is I didn't have a clue what he's insisting on having. His body quivered, and twitched in my arms till his cries became sever. Jess needed to wake up and help me.

No matter what I did to wake her once in the room she didn't budge an inch. I knew he wanted food or Jess, but how can I do this without touching her without her consent? Almost losing control I raised my voice at Mason, "Kid, stop screaming so I can think."

To hell with touching or not touching he'd get his way even if I had to cup her breast in my hand to make him stop crying. It surprised me that his near hyperventilation didn't make Jess respond to him in any way. The thought that she should have gone to the hospital if this didn't faze her. After lying Mason down next to her on the one side I rushed to the other and crawled next to her leaning against the headboard. Next I pulled her in front of me to hold her in a sitting position. She did moan and complain, "Paul, what are you doing?"

I pleaded, "Mason's hungry. I am just helping you feed him."

She turned her face to me and she had a half smile or smirk on her face. If she's testing my abilities I am going to be so pissed at her. My heart raced from the adrenaline pumping through my veins for what I was about to do. Collecting all rational thought I breathed slowly to calm my nerves because this had to work. As I pulled Mason to the front of her he already showed signs that he understood what this meant. His little mouth searched for her breast. My hands trembled as I unbuttoned her shirt but his face turned to her like the force of nature. The awkwardness of the way we sat made it difficult for him to latch on to her. My whole body shook as I cupped her breast in my hand holding it out for him. Naturally I would never offer Jess to another man, but this little guy needed her more than I did at the moment, even though my needs were becoming evident in my pants. His little head bobbed and prodded but couldn't quiet take her, so I took her nipple between my fingers squeezing it into his mouth. That's all it took for him to latch on and suck her further into his mouth. Removing my fingers he engulfed her into his mouth while her body went ridged against mine. A thrill of excited washed over me that we had success, but not wanting to risk the happy dance at the moment it may interrupt his eating.

When Jess's body pushed back against mine and she moaned worry filled me. She had said it hurt to feed him last time.

"Jess, are you okay?"

She moaned with pain, so I peaked at her other breast and it did look chapped and sore. My heart sank because this had to hurt. I would have to ask the doctor about getting her something for that. I tried to comfort her and whispered to her ear, "Shh, Jess, I'm here. Everything is going to be alright now."

Her body nuzzled into me filling my heart completely. From the bottom of my heart I loved this girl. Taking advantage of her in this condition didn't seem right but my need won out. Cherishing the softness of her skin on my lips I ran them against her face. My privates jumped at the purr that came from her chest. Kissing the corner of her mouth when she turned to me might have been a little pushing, but I'd take anything she'd give me at this point. Getting lost in her scent, her soft skin, and her whimpers of pleasure I almost forgot that I'm holding Mason to her. That's until he squirmed and gave a faint disapproving whimper. Bringing me back from the fantasy where I'd been I glanced down to find the issue he had. A very lopsided breast exposed that he had taken everything from the one side of her. Reaching around her I moved him to the other side of her. Already a professional at latching him on, I held her nipple first for him and took advantage of her neck. Either Mason's sucking, or mine caused Jess to tense again. This time she planted her feet on the bed and pushed back into my body turning her face away from me. I felt bad that what he needed hurt her. I traced my mouth along her neck hoping it would ease her pain.

Startled when she spoke, "Paul, I love you."

Not hyperventilating but close to it my chest rose and fell in response to her. Deep down to the bottom of my heart I've always known that she loved me, but to hear it come from her beautiful plump lips took my breath away. In a husky breathy voice I reply, "I love you too, Jess."

She tilted her head more making room for my face to trace along her neck breathing in her essence. Pressing little kisses everywhere my lips grazed.

Words slipped from her lips, "This is going to hurt."

Hesitant to continue I wondered what she meant. What part of this did she mean? Is it Mason's eating habit or me kissing her? My lips nipped at her ear while asking, "What will hurt?"

Lost in the dream world she sighed, "When I wake."

Did that mean it hurt to love me? No, it had to be that she thought she dreamt about us together. With the need to make understand how real this is I explained, "Oh, Jess, it's okay. I am here now and we will be together forever."

She didn't reply but relaxed in my arms, but then the little guy squirmed again letting me know he's done with her. Regretting the thought of being away from her I still had a job to do and that meant I had to let her rest while I took care of our son. His persistence had won my attention. It took maneuvering to get out from behind her, but when I did Mason and I headed back out to the rocking chair with his bottle. Now he took it just fine. It humored me that he's that picky already. Holding him in the rocking recliner gave me time to cherish what just occurred with Jess in the bedroom, and anticipate the next time he needed to be fed. There's hope for us to be together for the rest of our lives. We just had to move forward carefully.

The next two days went somewhat uneventful. Mason and I fell into a routine. As long as I gave him my full attention he didn't cause a fit when he ate and I held Jess. My love for him grew more and more each time he ate, because it became a very intimate experience between the three of us. Even if it lasted a short while it happened several times a day.

Jess remained silent during the feedings but cuddlier with each time. The doctor stopped by at 12 noon both days and he brought me ointment for her breasts. My plan is to help her with putting the ointment on her nipples the next time we feed Mason. Every day consumed with holding Mason, feeding him, and changing him. The poopy diapers were the worst, but we had an agreement that he wouldn't pea on me if I kept him clean. Amazed how boys have that much force behind going pea. It's a learning experience, and now I have to clean my new carpet in the living room, bed room, and the couch. Now I understood why my mom persisted on changing him at the changing table.

Afraid I wouldn't wake up with him so I lay next to him on the floor to sleep or I held him in the chair. It's a quiet day and my eyes kept closing even though I resisted until Mason decided he needed another feeding. Excitement rushed through my veins I didn't even mess with fixing a bottle I just sat it out on the counter and headed for the bedroom. This is my intimate time with Jess and I loved every minute of it. Crawling in behind her and holding her up grew easier each time we did this. He latched on to her with ease now that we had it down. Thankful for his skills on the matter of breast feeding, it allowed me to trace my lips along her neck taking in as much of her as time would allow. She grabbed my leg with discomfort, and it through me off for a minute, but when I realized that she was still in pain from having chapped nipples, "Shh, Jess. I have something that will help, and I'll put it on after he's done eating."

I choked when she said, "Okay, Paul."

Consumed with excitement at the sound of her voice I let a smile fill my face as my heart started to race. Mason took a little longer than usual. She must be getting enough rest for her body to produce more.

I whispered, "Jess, hun, are you awake?"

She was shaking in my arms and making sounds like she was whimpering, or maybe crying. I held her tighter and whispered, "Why are you crying?"

She was trying to hold the crying back but I saw one tear escape down her cheek as she spoke, "This is going to hurt so bad when you're not here."

Mason started to fuss at the worst time. I moved him over and she cringed as he started to eat on the other side. I grabbed the ointment and put a little on my finger, "Jess, I am going to put something on you to help heal where Mason is sucking, okay?"

She didn't say anything, but she did nod. Glancing down at a weird angle I tried to make sure I got the ointment where it's needed. She turned her head to me. Her lips presented to me like an offer that I am unable to resist. I touched my lips to hers to see what she'd do. When her mouth opened to mine my heart raced while I tried to decide what to do next. My breath brushed against her lips while I waited, wished, and wanted to stay here for the rest of the day. A faint little moan came from her chest giving me the permission I needed. Brushing my lips against her I waited for her eyes to open only that didn't happen. Her mouth did open against mine inviting me to taunt her top lip and then her bottom lip with sensuous nips from me. The growing need for her attention I released her breast only to cup her face holding her where I could continue to steel soft kisses from her. Lost in my own head I let the moment take me to another place and whispered to her lips, "Will you marry me?"

The kissing stopped on her side. Wrinkles formed on her forehead while her eyes scrunched as she replied, "I don't care if this is going to hurt, yes."

Torn on how to handle this sadness that keeps sweeping over her, somehow this isn't real for her. Leaning my face to hers I continued to kiss her softly as Mason nodded off and allowed me more time with her. I do believe I loved this little guy more and more each day. If they stayed, no if's about it. They will stay and Mason will never have known that I questioned if he's mine or not. He will know me as his father no matter what because I wanted her, I want to be his father, and I want to be a family with every ounce of my heart and soul. The best part of this ordeal is I will have a fishing partner. Removing Mason from Jess's breast I laid him next to us on the bed and gently put her clothing back together. When he didn't wake I held her tightly in my arms never wanting to let her go again.

When my eyes got heavy I decided that it wouldn't be a good idea to stay like this, because I may forget about Mason being here in the bed with us. Forcing myself out of the bed I scooped Mason up, but with him in a deep sleep I took advantage of placing him in the crib and then crawled back into bed with Jess. I took her hands in mine pulling them up to my lips where I kiss them until my eyes got too heavy. Leaning in for one last kiss I whispered to her, "I will be here when you wake up Jess. I promise you this."

She did give me that half sleepy smile. I had to ask one last thing, "Jess, is Mason mine?"

Her smile evaporated with her reply, "Does it matter?"

Already gone over in my head I knew it didn't matter, "No, I am hoping he is mine."

She smiled but her breath indicated that she held back tears. I didn't get it. Is she happy or sad with my answer?

"Oh, this is going to hurt so badly."

I pulled her hand to my mouth kissing it again, "I love you, Jess, more than anything. Sleep, I will be here when you wake up."

She sighed deeply.

8

Only sleeping a few hours before Mason cried again, finding comfort that my worries of not waking to him weren't needed. His cries woke me with a startle that made me move from the bed very quickly.

This morning feeding Jess didn't respond to me, but she did let me kiss her. She gave me hum's and awe's of happiness. The best part is she didn't cringe quiet as bad when Mason latched onto her. Bright eyes and ready for the day Mason and I headed to the kitchen for a bottle. We cuddled in the chair while I had the news on the TV. When he started to fuss again I turned off the TV, put music on, and walked around bouncing him to the music as I talked to him. He seemed to be happier when I spoke to him. Now seeing the pattern when he's tired; it starts with his eyes blinking more frequent, then the blink lasting a little longer, until they are too heavy to lift any longer. Continuing the boring dialog of how the weather will be tomorrow until he slept in my arms. Before heading down stairs I placed Mason in his seat and took the whole bundle with me. A little business while things are quiet wouldn't hurt. Running through my business emails I saw a few more requests for bids. Then I went over the schedules to make sure everything's covered, and to see where I'd place the new client if need be. One by one I called all foremen to make sure everything's being taken care of and see if they needed anything. Everything seemed to be running well enough without me.

I called Theo next. I waited to call them in case they would want to come get them. Now that I've taken care of them for a couple of days it obvious that they'd stay with me now. Plus I have the means to stay home and take care of them. The phone call with Theo went well. Neither one of them had the ability to take time off from work so Theo thanked me for handling this. I did promise to keep them updated on how Jess is doing. Happy that Jess and Mason are here with me in the house that I built for us to share, rather than the cabin with how cold it'd get in there without a fire going all the time.

We moved out to the workout area with Mason in his seat. Those deep dark eyes stared at me while I prepared to workout. A scratch came to the door alerting me to Freedom's presence. After letting her in I filled her in on Jess being back and the little package she brought with her. Freedom went to check him out sniffing every part of him until her nose rested on his belly. He had a quick twitch of a smile. My heart raced with happiness that they would be friends.

Freedoms eyes questioned me. Freedom is the incarnation of Anne and her thoughts came to me like words. No one but Jess believed me that it's Anne. Telepathic she asked me, *"is Mason yours."* Dumfounded I sat on the floor next to both of them to explain the situation, "I thought about the time frame Jess gave me and he probably is. She won't tell me anything confirming it or denying it. Matt said she told him that she had a one night stand with someone so she'd forget me, but that doesn't sound like Jess."

She tilted her head in question, *"he looks like you."*

Agreeing with her analogy I grinned and agreed, "Yeah, he does."

She stuck her nose to his belly again making him grin. I hugged her knowing he likes her. She gave me another confirmation; *"he smells like you."*

Giving her a realistic view I explained that, "I've been holding him almost nonstop for the last few days."

Her response floated into my head, *"you should find out for sure. Can I stay?"*

Moving slowly she pressed her head to my chest. Of course I caved, "Yes, of course, but why?"

Her head nuzzled into me, *"I'm getting too old for the cold. It would be nice to come to a home and this little one will need someone to watch over him. Keep him away from the lake and other wolves."*

Pleased that we'd be a family. Most people would be afraid of a wild wolf, but this is my Anne and she would protect my family if need be. She curled up by Mason's seat so I went back to working out. It didn't take long before she wanted out again. It must be too warm for her yet so I let her go, but told her to come back whenever she wanted a warm place to stay.

Taking a seat on the workout bench Mason's eyes came up to meet mine again. His eyes so dark brown that the iris and pupil blended to form one big black question. Deciding that we needed to agree about his mother I went into a full argument.

"Mason, I love your mommy."

He didn't do anything. Good he didn't have a problem with that. We argued, no I argued with myself on Mason's behalf which parts of his mom I got, and which parts he gets. Too bad that his empty stare didn't carry much of an argument so I caved and let him win every part of it. All of this is going to suck when Jess wakes up because he'd get all of her. Thinking about it caused me pain so I confessed, "You can win every time."

Startled by the most beautiful sound in the world Jess's voice came out a little raspy, but clear as she walked towards us, "What can he win?"

My eyes found her face, but traveled down over her body as she stood there in my button up shirt and nothing on her legs. She also held up the IV bags still attached to her.

Not able to contain my excitement I blurted out, "Jess, you're awake!"

I stood up and walked towards her right away, but she passed me going for Mason. Disappoint filled my heart when she went to him first picking him up, after all I have done for her. She pulled him to her body and kissed him everywhere touching and feeling every inch of him searching for something.

She directed her voice to me, "How long did sleep?"

My heart sank, but only because I wanted her to come to me. Did she not remember telling me she would marry me? "A few days."

Sadness touched her eyes as they filled with tears, "He must be starving?"

I grinned, "No, I fed him, Jess."

She looked up at me and she wasn't smiling. Glaring would be a better word for what she aimed my way, "How? He only takes a bottle after he breasts feeds."

Embarrassed I dropped my eyes to the floor. The lure of her didn't keep me from peeking at her through my eyelashes, "Yeah, I know." That came out a little harsh, "I..." Shit, how do I explain this? "I... um... I helped." That came out smooth. "You talked to me. You don't remember?"

Now not a good time to explain that I held her nipple in my fingers and shoved it in his mouth. Thankfully her attention went back to Mason, but she still spoke to me, "No. We talked?"

The high I had been on from seeing her up and about now crushed by her not remembering that she agreed to marry me, "Yeah, it's not important. Can I get you something to eat?"

Her disregard for me so easy for her she walked toward the stairs with him in her arms. She stopped next to me making my heart race with anticipation. My eyes stayed glued to her the whole time.

Eyes squinting with unbelievable distrust, "You took care of him the whole time?"

Why is it so hard to believe that I did this? We were intimate during the feedings so why didn't she remember? The stare sadden me and I didn't want to see that in her eyes so I looked away. Now if my heart would stop beating so hard, and dam it Paul breathe. Not wanting to scare her I didn't mention that she said she loves me, but that made my stomach flip around on me. If she let me kiss her it might come back to her. What is my problem? Oh, yeah she is up and capable of walking out the door plus she didn't remember telling me she loved me.

Thinking about my time with Mason brought a grin to my face, "Yeah, he's pretty mellow. I talked to him and when we argue he always wins."

She tried to lift my chin with the hand that held the IV in it. When my eyes reached hers I hoped that I didn't appear as pitiful as I felt.

Her green eyes penetrated mine melting me to mere putty as her lips parted. I wished for them to touch me anywhere would be great. No kiss as my reward, but a simple smile as she said, "Thank you, Paul."

I had to tell myself, get a grip but I spoke to her, "Jess, I'll be right there. I'll get his seat."

She started up the steps and I stared after her until she moved from my sight. Her legs were thin and bony reminding me of how frail she is. Not at all like they were when we made love. I walked back to the bench and sat down. I had to take a few breaths to try and calm my heart, because it's over reacting from seeing those eyes staring into mine. After taking a few deep breaths I force myself up grabbing Mason's seat and heading up the stairs two at a time hurrying to be next to her. She sat at the table talking to him. I went straight to the fridge after putting the seat on the table in case she wanted to put him in it.

"Scrambled eggs okay, Jess?"

"Anything is fine, I am starving."

"Yeah, I noticed."

She got self-conscious and fidgeted trying to cover herself up, "I didn't do this on purpose, Paul."

Not intentionally but I did hurt her feelings, "No, Jess I just mean you haven't eaten in three days and you're thin." Shit, I did it again.

She moved her legs under the table and pulled the blanket over her arms holding Mason, "Well, you look good, Paul. Do you work out a lot?"

Great way to change the subject of her being thin, "I had a lot of time on my hands, Jess." Oops, I might have used a little too much sarcasm.

She turned her attention away from me and back to Mason putting him in his seat and talking to him. Open mouth and insert foot now. If she would just tell me she loves me and she'll stay here with me forever we'd have half a chance at normalcies. It'd happen but it's going to be harder than I originally thought.

Before the eggs were ready I put bread in the toaster. I made both her and I a plate of food. Bringing the plates to the table I set one in front of her. The other one next to her so I'd be close to her, "Jess, would you like milk or juice?"

"Oh my god, milk! I'd love to have milk."

That's a little weird. A little over reacting but it's possible that she needs milk really bad. I poured us both a glass when she spoke to me again, "All this food is more than I eat in a week, Paul."

Shit, I hurt her again. I walked back over to the table and leaned over to put her glass in front of her, "Jess, eat what you want. We'll give the rest to Freedom."

"She is here?" Jess got up to go see her. I grabbed her arm and gave her a pleading glance, "Jess, eat first, please."

Surprise rose on her face when her eyes met mine. She sat back down and took a bite talking to Mason. I glanced at her out of the corner of my eye waiting for anything from her. When she spoke again she caught me off guard, "You need to understand that I didn't do this on purpose."

Giving her my attention I glanced over at her interested in what she had to say but only because she'd be talking to me.

"They fed us first and there's this little girl, about four years old. Anyway, I couldn't eat while she went hungry so I gave her most of my food."

My heart sank. She did find a place where the pain we went through was nothing in comparison to the pain and suffering they went through each day.

Jess continued, "We called her Masey and that is where I got the name Mason. She called me Jessup because she couldn't say Jessica."

Her attention stayed on Mason, playing with his feet. Almost as if a light came on she brightened from within and then she turned to me, "Paul, do you have internet here?"

The excitement in her face improved my world, "Yes."

"May I email someone to check on her?"

My heart raced seeing her excitement and I choked out, "Jess, whatever you want. What's mine, is also yours."

Her attention went back to Mason. Did I over step the grounds again? Shit, I just want her to be comfortable here and stay with me for eternity.

"Masey is going to be so happy to see Jessup's baby."

Then she spoke to me again, "Do you have a web cam?"

I didn't have something she wanted deflating my bubble she created, "No."

"Can I use your truck to go get one?"

I didn't want her leaving ever for fear she wouldn't come back and then it hit me, "The doctor is going to be here at noon. How about I go get one while he is here? After that if you would like to go somewhere I will take you wherever you want to go."

Her smile enhanced the sparkle in her eyes. "That's perfect. Right Mason? I told you he is perfect, didn't I?"

No I am not perfect. I just want to make her happy. Did she mean that in a good way or bad? Glancing at her plate where a few bites went missing my eyes moved back to gazing at her.

She got a funny grin on her face before she spoke again, "If you stare at me it's going to make me nervous."

Letting my eyes travel over the room only to make their way back to her I apologies, "Sorry. I just can't believe you are here and not running out the door."

She turned to me her playfulness gone. Her face hard and stern is letting me know that she didn't like what I said. I screwed up, yet, again.

"There are two parts to that, Paul, but if we discuss this it will be over and done. Okay?"

My body tensed with the coldness in her voice so I sat up in my chair giving her the attention she demanded at this moment. Scared that this might be the end of our relationship wishing I had waited to bring it up, because I needed more time with her.

"First, I gave you one last chance to be with me. Remember when I asked you to meet me at the cabin."

A sucker punch to my gut is what that was, "Yes." I already understood this part, maybe not all of it.

"I had to give them my final decision Sunday by 8am. You didn't show up on time and that is when I agreed to go to South America."

Whinnying I begged, "But Jess, if I'd known I would have..."

She put up her hand to stop me from explaining, "It doesn't matter how or why, but that's when I made the decision. That is all I meant by it. Second, remember when I asked you to be my first for everything?"

Shit. This is going to hit me in the gut even harder. Not wanting her to continue to the second part, but I agreed, "Yes, Jess."

Holding my breath for the impact only the impact she enforced upon me pushed my limits. She reached for my hand taking it in hers. My knees when soft, my stomach turned, and I held my breath. Her fingers messages mine until I glanced up finding the love in her eyes and a beautiful smile when she continued, "Everything that has happened to us I still wanted you to be my first. So when you stopped me from leaving school that day I tried to find a way out of what I agreed to do, I caved. The only thing I thought about is you. What it would do to you when I left, how sad you would become, and how I'd break your heart for leaving. Wanting to keep you for myself I wanted to share that with you with hope that someday it'd all work out. Paul, you are my first and it was..." Her eyes danced across my face searching for understanding, "... amazing, wonderful, and perfect. I couldn't have asked for anything better, but I had to go anyway. Because of that I wanted to let you go so that it wouldn't be as hard for you."

Everything swirled in my brain. Is this her way of telling me she let go with her heart? Not wanting to listen to the truth I still had to find out, "Did it work?"

Her expression empty as she studied me. Her answer came out breathy, "No, it didn't, Paul. I am here now, but you have to be sure."

All the blood must have drained my face because I shivered with the cold that washed over me. Men don't cry so I held it in with the last bit of strength I had, though my eyes did fill with tears. She did still love me. We just needed time to adjust and I could handle that. Warmth and caring now took over her face. It's not like I'd blurt out I love you Jessica and none of this matters so I just replied, "Okay."

She let go of my hand, "Can I be done now?"

Without her telling me she loved me and that she would stay, she helped me to understand that if I wanted her here then she'd be here. We needed to lighten the mood. Standing up I grabbed for her hands pulling her up, "Yes, of course. Do you want to see Freedom now?"

She giggled scrunching her shoulders like I gave her a gift, "Yes,"

When I went to grab Mason she stopped me with that scolding motherly stare. Worry explained the look on her face. Reassuring her I grinned with my reply, "He likes her. He even smiled at her."

The sad puppy dog eyes and that pout won me over every time when she said, "You showed her already?"

Chuckling and leading her to the living room I explained, "Yes. He smiles when she sticks her nose on his belly."

She had tears in her eyes, "He smiled? I missed his first smile?"

There I go again making her tear up; I really suck at this. Extending my hand for her to take she wiped her tears away and then took my hand. Setting the carrier on the floor I let go of her hand and went to the door. Whistling as I opened the door, but Freedom laid there on the porch. She came running in and hit Jess full force. Jess must have braced herself for it, because she didn't fall over form the impact. The excited exchange between the two calmed my nerves. She moved to sit as Freedom sat in her lap.

"You must have forgiven him too?"

Freedom licked her face over and over again. Wanting to be a part of the happiness I moved closer to enjoy their interaction. Freedom jumped up keeping an eye on Jess as she moved closer to Mason. Jess smiled, "Yeah, Paul told me you already saw him."

She stuck her nose on him and he smiled again. Jess looked up at me with tears over filling her eyes again. Not wanting to see the tears again I moved even closer to her and pulled her head to rest on my leg. If she'd let me I'd pick her up and hug her, but we needed slow and steady so I contained my urges. I love her and I didn't want to lose her by being stupid. Jess looked up at me, "What does she think of him?"

Not wanting to tell her the complete truth so I told her, "She thinks he is beautiful."

Freedom turned on me and started towards me growling.

Jess figured out there's something else I didn't say, "Paul, what else?"

I can't win today, "Okay, okay. She thinks he looks and smells like me, but Jess, I have held him for the last three days. Don't read into it. Please, don't get mad."

She didn't get mad. She put her arm around my leg resting her head on it, "She's not the first one that says he looks like you, Paul. It's okay."

Relief flooded into my chest. Oh, my god did I want to pick her up and hug her tight. I needed to move away from her before I dropped to my knees and pulled her to me to kiss her for days, "Jess, if I am going to the store I need a shower. The computer is down stairs in my office behind the work out area. The password is…" Shit, she is going to find out I am hung up on her but I gave it to her anyway, "… Jess."

She glanced up at me smiling.

I tried to ease the situation and I shrugged, "I couldn't help myself. Anyway, help yourself. Are you okay getting down there with Mason?"

The condescending glare she gave me told me she'd get down there on her own.

After letting Freedom out I headed to the shower. My mind stayed focused on Jess the whole time, driving me crazy for being away from her for even a minute. It turned into a seven minute shower because of my rushing. With only a towel on I headed to my room, but when I walked out she came down the hall towards me. As if frozen I stood still and waited for her to come to me. Only after she stood in front of me did I step back to let her by me. A moment of tense desire, lust, or love all rolled into one perfect package named Jessica. My eye lingered on her as she moved into my room where I put her belongings. Living in the guest room for a while is my gesture of respect for her privacy. She stopped and turned back to me, "Isn't this your room?"

She is sharp, "Yeah, but I thought you might need the privacy for a while and the crib fits better in there, so I took the guest room."

My heart skipped a beat when she floated back to me like my dream angle. Needing to settle my breathing, and the hard on she flares with that gleam in her eye I held my breath. In my head the one with a brain I told myself *don't kiss her, don't kiss her unless she kisses you first*. Standing directly in front of me her hand came up to caress my chest with butterfly fingertips. I'd drop to my knees right now and beg her to be mine for now and forever until the end of time.

As all these thoughts flooded my brain her sweet voice filled my ears, "You did this for me?"

Tongue tied, and branded the only reply I had in me, a nod. Her arm wrapped around my waist skimming her fingers along my back. If my towel fell right now she would see what she does to me. When her cheek found a place to rest against my chest a gust of air escaped my lungs. If Mason didn't obstruct our connection she would surely understand what she did to my heart.

Her voice came as a soft whisper, "Thank you."

Already releasing me and moving into the room before I finished saying, "Your welcome."

Stumbling I found my way into the guest bedroom falling on to the bed. My hand covered my chest with an attempt to slowing my pounding heart. We had to take this one step at a time, but it'll be difficult not to confess that I am totally in love with everything about Jess.

When I finally got myself together enough to leave the room her door remained closed. She must have been feeding Mason. As I walked to the living room I saw Doc pull up in front of the house. I went out to greet him, "Jess is awake!"

He grinned, "and this makes you happy I see. You didn't even say hello."

Laughing with my reply, "Sorry, Doc. How is your day going?"

Doc had the strangest smirk on his face as he informed me, "I got the results back. Did you decide if you want to hear the truth?"

I closed my eyes because I did want to know, but it didn't matter because I would raise him as my own either way if Jess married me. I opened my eyes staring directly into his, "Nope, don't need a test to tell me I'm going to be his father."

He gave me the biggest grin, "You are in love with that girl."

I grabbed his bag for him, "Yes, I am."

He walked away from me mumbling, "Well than you would be pleased with the results."

I stopped and stood there stunned. Did he just tell me I am Mason's father? Why hasn't she told me? Maybe she just thinks it's someone else's? But she has to realize the possibility. Shit, how am I going to tell her? But did he really tell me I am?

"Paul, are you coming?"

I looked up and realized I still stood there frozen. He grinned at me and walked in as I ran up behind him. I lead him down the hall and knocked on the door, "Jess, Doc Ferriday is here. Can we come in?"

"Just a minute, please."

Glancing at Doc I shrugged my shoulders, but had to ask him, "So, all the tests you ran... is he okay. I mean he's not sick like Jess, is he?"

"No, he is amazingly well considering what she has been through."

"And Jess, is she going to be okay?"

"Yes, she is doing okay. She needs rest, fluids, and of course food to get her strength back."

I took a deep breath of relief. She would be staying awhile so I'd get to help her. I put my head down to take a deep breath. The Doc put his hand on my shoulder. A touch of endearment but happiness that I'd get to keep her happened to be enough for me.

We heard her, "You can come in now."

I opened the door and let the doctor walk in first of course I followed him into the room. The doctor asked a couple of questions and she answered them shortly, but glanced at me. She twitched nervously, and kept peaking at me until she finally spoke up, "Paul, would mind leaving us alone. You said you'd go get something for me."

I stumbled because I really didn't want to leave now but I did say I'd go get the web cam, "Oh yeah. Okay. Are you sure you'll be okay?"

"I will be fine, besides the Doc is here and I still have your phone number if you still have your cell phone."

I couldn't help but grin. Not only did I have my phone, but I still had hers. The Doc coughed a little to remind me that he's still in the room and so am I, but I'd have to quit looking at her long enough to go. Her car wasn't here yet so she couldn't leave even if she wanted to so why did I find it hard to leave? I guess I am still in shock that she is here with me.

"Paul, is there something else?" She gave me a wondrous smile.

"Your phone is in the night stand, Jess."

I turned and quickly escaped from the room before she'd refuse.

9

Looking at all the options I had to ask for help to get the best one, because it's for my Jess. My intent to show her she'd have everything she wanted or needed with me. Next the flea market where I picked up fresh fruit and a bouquet of flowers, also a squeaky toy for Mason. Only after I made sure it's for babies and not a dog. The lady did laugh at me but assured me it's a baby toy. When I left I forgot to ask if we needed anything else for Mason so if we do I'd have to go out tomorrow too. Maybe she and Mason would like to go with on an outing. My outing took forever with not wanting to be away from Jess one minute. Pulling up the drive I noticed the doc had left already. It irritated me that he left her alone.

Coming to a complete halt after rushing in I stood there in awe. Mason sat in his seat on the counter while she moved from the stove back to him, stopping for a second to touch him each time. The music played in the back ground as she danced a little with each step. Fascinated by her I stood watching. Her hair hung down her back wet, she hid her body with a pair of my sweets that dragged the floor, but her feet were bare. Her pink toes peeked out from under all the material. The t-shirt she's wearing had to be tied at the side of her waist in a big ball because of its size. That must be mine too. Why would she want to wear those big old baggy clothes? Not saying how long I stood here watching but when she turned and jumped out of her skin with a scream did I come back to reality. She is here in our home, with my son, and I'd love her till the end of my life.

Mason's screeched loader than Jess so I hurried to settle both of them, "Jess, I am so sorry. I didn't mean to startle you."

"Shit, Paul, you scared the crap out of me. You shouldn't sneak up on a girl like that, especially after she spent time in South America."

I set the flowers, and the bags on the table reaching for Mason, "Sorry buddy, hey it's alright. Mommy is having a heart attack." I pulled him to my body holding his head to me and walked bouncing him a little.

"Jess, are you okay?"

"Yeah, but next time say something when you come in."

Holding back my chuckle I asked, "Why are you wearing those clothes?"

She eased a little staring at me, "I didn't bring much with me."

I turned away with Mason so she wouldn't witness my disappointment. She didn't plan on staying, and this is a sign. I have got to do something to keep her here, "Jess, do we need to get you clothes?"

"No."

Did she plan on leaving soon? Shit, this is not good, "Jess, I didn't know if we needed anything for Mason, so I thought…, if you want…, we could go to town tomorrow. We can get what we need for him and if you want we could get you clothes that fit." Please say yes, please. I want you to stay.

"Paul, did you get flowers?"

I had forgotten to give them to her, shit, I just keep blowing it, "Yeah, they're for you."

Wanting to see her expression I turned. Her attention focused on the flowers as she displayed them in a glass. I have vases, but this made it homier. I walked back out to the kitchen. She still hadn't answered me about the clothes and that made me worry. Trying to peak at what she's cooking, but she grabbed my arms and directed me away from the stove, "Not when you're holding him please."

"What are you making?"

"Soup. I'm not sure what kind but you had a bunch in the freezer and it's easier on my stomach. Out now!"

"That's why I made them."

I moved to the table to sit with Mason, "Jess, he is a really good baby."

She stopped and turned to me with surprise, and then a grin came to her face, "Yes, he is."

She went back to being busy.

"Jess, you didn't answer me about the clothes?"

This time when she turned to me tears filled her eyes again. I cannot win today.

"Paul. I wanted to wait awhile. I hate to buy it and then grow out of it in a month. You understand."

I felt so bad. I got up and walked closer to her, "Jess, that's fine, whatever you want. Your mom and dad should bring stuff up for you."

She stared at me with those beautiful sad eyes, "I wasn't planning on calling them for a while."

Now I am confused because that meant she did plan on staying longer, but I talked to Theo already so another bad move. I had to tell her, "Jess, I have been giving them updates on how you and Mason are doing."

"So..., what am I doing?"

I laughed with a sigh, "sleeping."

A flash of a grin appeared and disappeared so fast that if I hadn't been staring at her I would have missed it. This made her happy. Finally I did something right by her.

"Can we let them assume that I am still sleeping? I don't want to go back. It's a little weird, at least till I can figure out what I am going to do to support him." She placed her hand on his little head. My heart was racing again, and I'd pass out if I didn't take a breath soon. Containing my excitement I walked away from her, "Anything you want, Jess, but we should get you a few things."

"I don't want to be this way, Paul."

Here is another stumper and if I say the wrong thing she might not want to stay with me longer. Entirely aware that she didn't do this to herself on purpose I went for light, "Jess, don't stress about it. You are hot no matter what."

Shit, did I say that out loud? Crap, I did. Cursing myself for being forward I had to watch that, because we needed to take this slow.

Her hands wrapped around my waist and her forehead rest on my back. She was touching me. Do I turn around and hug her; would that be too much?

"Paul, that's what the web cam is for. You will get to see my little angle and you will see why I couldn't eat looking into her eyes."

I did turn around and carefully pulled her in next to Mason. She touched his little hand, "Jess, not only were you feeding her, you were feeding him, and you got sick. You are home now and you can get better."

I did kiss her forehead as we stood there in silence. I lowered my face to trace hers with hope that she would respond to me, which she did. She leaned into my face to mimic what I did to her. The buzzer went off on the stove and she moved away from me. In an instant I lost the ground we made. I sat down to eat with Jess at the table. Memorized by the way her mouth opened, how her lips closed over the spoon, and then when she pulled it back out, pure torture. Mason did a good job distracting me by squirming and complaining in my arms, but then Jess got up to take him. I pulled him away, "Not till you are done, Jess. It won't hurt him to wait a little until you are done." And I have a bone to pick with this little guy for taking me away from the most beautiful sight I have ever seen.

I stood up and paced around the kitchen. I could tell it bothered her that he isn't happy, but he isn't crying either. A screech here and there to tell me he wanted something and then the pout. I chuckled as I watched the little lip quiver with his bottom lip out, "Jess, this is when he resembles you the most."

Furry blushed her face as she stood up to take him from me, "That's not funny."

She went down the hall toward the bedrooms and I followed trying to explain, "Jess, I meant that he is so adorable when he does that. It makes me want to give him anything he wants. Like you, Jess."

She stopped and turned to me glaring. I almost ran into her. Less than an inch from me and my heart beat faster. I took a slow deep breath to try to contain the pulse rushing through me. Raising her face to mine she softened her gaze. I must look like a lost puppy dog lowering my head to her. She spoke to me with a soft whisper, "So if I did that you would set up the web cam right away?"

She stuck out her bottom lip. My knees went weak. I'd drop to them if she said or did one more thing to me. Oh god, that is exactly what I meant by the pout. Closing my eyes to control my urge to touch those lips with my mouth instead I placed my fingers on her lips, "You don't need to do that to get what you want, Jess. I will go do it now."

Her hand touched my face. I opened my eyes to see if this was the moment she would kiss me. Her face held a smile, but she didn't kiss me she just said, "Thank you."

She turned to walk in the room, but continued to talk to me so I followed her to the changing table. "I don't want to miss my video date with Eric."

Fuck, who is Eric? And I just agreed to set it up assisting her to see someone else. What the hell, am I that much of a sucker? I had to ask, "Eric is Mason's father?"

Busy with changing Mason's diaper she didn't even glance up, "NO! He's my partner from down there. He's going to make sure I get to see Masey."

Not the guy that I thought, but partner. Did that mean she and him were together now? "Partner?"

"Yeah, it's funny how we ended up together. When I left here it was the worst day of my life, when he got on the plane he chose to sit by me because I looked sadder than him. Plus he knew I wouldn't bug him for answers. He sat down and asked me, 'what's his name?' It surprised me so I glanced up at him. He looked worse than me. We exchanged the names of the people we loved and left behind. He put out his pinky so I wrapped my pinky with his."

"So you two are together?"

"No, Paul! They made us have partners down there and we paired up because we were both in love with other people."

"So by partner you mean?"

Irritation danced on her words but she gave me a warm smile, "Work partners. Look over each other's back partners. It gets a little rough down there."

That's a total relief so why do I still get this gut twist when I think about her and him spending time together. They could have been together in comfort alone. It is possible.

"So did you two... have a relationship too?"

As soon as I said it I wanted to take it back. None of it matter if she's home to stay.

"Paul, I have only been with..."

She stopped talking as her eyes rose to meet mine. Jess, please just say it. Tell me I am the only one. It doesn't matter, but it would make me so happy right now. Please tell me I am Mason's father.

"Paul, would you mind, I am going to feed him."

Rolling my eyes at the diversion, "I have seen you feed him. In fact I helped you."

She gave me a mischievous grin, "So, you felt me up when I was sleeping?"

Embarrassed I blurted back, "No! Well sort of, but it wasn't like that. I was just helping you. I mean him. It wasn't like that."

Her eyes danced with delight, she's going to laugh at my expense and I'm getting frustrated with her. Heading toward the door with the intention to walk out, and not letting her play with my emotions I stopped at the door, "You were very cuddly and you talk in your sleep."

If I hit the right never she'd be stunned so I glanced back as I closed the door.

Her mouth hung open. Yep, I got the reaction I wanted, Ha!

Heading down stairs to hook everything up my heart felt lighter than it has been for a while. Only after setting the camera up in my office did I let myself be distracted with anger. The more time it took to set it up the more time I had to ponder why I'd set it up for her to speak with another man. By the time I finished the blood pumped through my veins heating me to the core. What am I doing? I am such a sucker. Needing to get rid of the anger before seeing Jess again I stayed in the basement to work out harder and longer hoping to ease the rage going on in my head and body. One problem with this video date, it's with *"Eric"* of course that came out with a snotty smirk. After an hour of sweeting I gave up and headed back upstairs. Hopefully she'd be napping so I wouldn't need to hide my anger.

She wasn't sleeping, but it's a little odd to find her sitting in the rocker recliner staring out the window. No TV, no music, but just sitting there. Sadness not only filled the air it filled her face again. How could I be angry with her? Really I wasn't. More like angry at myself. If I would have met her at the cabin that one day none of this would have ever happened. Oh, my sweet, Jess. How am I ever going to get you to trust that I will never do anything to hurt you again?

"Jess?"

She turned to face me and a slight smile came to her face.

"What are you doing?" Please don't tell me you are contemplating leaving.

"Just thinking. Are you hungry I could make you something?"

"No, Jess, I'm fine."

Shit, I should have said yes, she might be hungry and not want to eat alone, "Are you hungry, Jess?"

Her face scrunched with thought searching for the feeling, but unclear she replied, "No, I don't think so."

She didn't even know what the difference of being hungry or not anymore. From this day forward if she brought up food we would eat at least something. Standing there a little loss on what to do or say I opted for avoidance, "Jess, if you're okay, I am going to take a shower. I worked out."

Please let me leave the room; I can't stand seeing you sad. I wanted to scream at her for her to stop this and let me love her. Instead I turned to head for the bathroom.

"Paul?"

I stopped. Why do you pull me and push me? It's tearing me up Jess, "Yes."

"What did I say when I was sleeping?"

Okay, Paul. Avoid the pain. Taking a deep breath I turned to her. I wanted to see her face, "That you love me!"

A slight grin came to her face. Could this be the moment that I get to kiss her? I took a step toward her.

"But you already knew that. I've always loved you, Paul, and I always will, but all of this? You said one day at a time."

I took another step towards her, "Jess, none of that matters at all. I love you."

She smiled more, "Okay."

She leaned back and closed her eyes. What does that mean? The pain of uncertainty crept into my heart again. Do I go to her, grab her, pull her to me, hold her, and never let her go again?

Still needing that shower for many reasons, that's what I decided to do instead of pushing Jess.

Showering didn't wash the ache in my heart away. She said okay, but okay to what? That I love her or that she loves me, but I still can't hold her. What the hell am I supposed to do with "okay"?

Heading to my room to get dressed I glanced down the hall toward the living room where I left her in a chair. Only she's not sitting there any longer, so I'll have to search for her when I got my barring's back.

10

The pounding on my door brought me to, while Jess's frantic voice pulled me out of bed, "Paul, Paul, hurry up."

I opened the door to watch her heading down the hall towards the living room glowing with excitement, "Paul, grab Mason for me. It's time. Hurry up."

"What Jess?"

"The video date. Please grab Mason and hurry."

She took off again heading down the hallway, but stopped and came running back touching my chest. The urge to grab her, pull her to me, beg her to not go to him, and to love me.

"Paul, please this is really important to me. Please come down and bring Mason."

That's when she left me standing there in shock. Okay, let me get this straight, because I am confused now. She's excited for a date with another man. It's important to her. She wants to show off Mason, but she wants me to be part of it? Shit this sucks. Wanting to give her everything she asks for I went to get Mason. Finding it hard on my heart to wake him when he lay there so peacefully, but it's important to Jess so I didn't give myself a choice. When I brought him to my chest it took him no time at all to close his eyes again. His face nuzzled into my chest and his little hand kneaded where my heart beat for him. Not being able to stop myself I asked him, "Mason can you show your mommy how to do this?" I laughed as I headed down to be part of Jess's video date with another man. Shit, this really sucks.

Jess's voice escaped my office as I got near. It's impolite to eavesdrop, but I needed to distinguish if she loved *'him'* or me. Not proud of myself for doing it but protecting my heart is my first priority especially with Jess here. Secondly, I wanted to be sure that my efforts will be noticed one day, and I'd get to keep her. Yes, she's here and I am going to fight to keep her, but being a true fighter I had to understand what I am up against.

I heard him say, "Oh Jess, you look so much better."

"But you don't."

"Forget that. You are home and it is agreeing with you."

"Yes, it is."

"Have you told him?"

"Eric don't push."

"You need to tell him."

Oh shit, she did love him. Fuck I am not going in there. They wanted to be together when they told me. How sick is this.

"Not yet. I have to be sure."

You have to be sure you can use me to the fullest, you have to be sure that Mason isn't mine? Come on, this totally sucks.

"You're at his house and he is taking care of you and Mason."

"Yes, but I..."

"No butts Jess. It's obvious that he still loves you, and it will be enough Jess."

"Enough for what Eric? I can't go through getting hurt again. It's just too hard."

"Jess, you love him more than anything in this world."

"Yes I do and you love Alison. Does that make everything okay?"

"He has a right to know Jess."

Yes I do. Wait no I want her. He has no right to tell her she has to end this.

"If he loves me Eric, as much as I need him to then there is always time to make sure."

"Have you two made love since you got back?"

"No, it's none of your business."

"Jess, you need to let your guard down so he can show you how much he still loves you. You are difficult to deal with when you have your mind set. Besides how long will you let him go worrying if you are going to leave?"

"I don't want to go, but this is a lot for any person to take on. I need him to be sure he loves me enough to accept everything."

"You need to show him, Jess. I plan on showing Alison how much I love her when I get home. Remember the one thing down here..."

"What's that?"

"Time is short and if you want to be with him quit wasting time."

"I am afraid."

"We're all afraid of getting hurt. Don't you think he is scared to love you too?"

If I waited anymore I may have to walk away. Tears filled my eyes because she is afraid to love me. Afraid that I will hurt her again, but it's time for all that to end so I knocked, "Jess, can we come in?"

Before getting the door open I listen to her scold him, "He's here. Behave. I love him."

My whole idea of her telling me they are together had been backwards. She confessed her love for me to him causing the pounding of my heart to echo in my ears.

"Paul, come here."

As I entered the room she made her way to me. She took Mason from me, but as she turned away from me she took my hand in hers pulling me with. She pushed me to sit in the chair and moved to sit in my lap. Her hand grabbed mine pulling it around her. In a way she made it okay for me to hold her. She glanced back with the biggest smile, "Paul this is Eric; Eric this is Paul, and here is Mason."

"Oh my goodness, Jess, he is beautiful." He leaned into the monitor a little looking at him. This guy is very good looking. I guess Jess does have the attraction to get his attention.

He smiled, "Paul, I do believe Mason looks a little like you."

I laughed as Jess scolded him, "Eric!"

Is he telling me that Mason is mine without telling me?

"Where is Masey?"

We waited while he called her. He glanced back at the screen, "She is coming with me, Jess."

"Did her mom die?"

"Yes."

"What about her dad?"

"Cross fire."

Did he just say crossfire? Am I hearing this right? Jess started to sniffle. Noticing her sudden sadness I worried about her being upset by this and the crossfire thing. What the hell did that mean?

"Paul, I'm not sure if Jess told you, but she saved my little darling by giving her food to her."

Eric pulled Macey in front of him while he hugged her tightly.

He spoke pointing to the screen, "Look baby... Jessup."

She screeched, "Jessup. Where Jessup baby?"

Jess pushed Mason up more so they'd see him on the screen, "Masey how did I do?"

"Perface Jessup."

Jess laughed and whispered to me, "She said I did perfect."

I laughed a little with Jess. Masey happened to be precious, but all over the place not being able to sit still. Jess cried with happiness, "Eric, she still gets to eat?"

"Yeah, I am still getting your food. She eats every day."

Jess leaned back to me sobbing. I traced my nose along her face adoring her.

"Masey, you are so beautiful. I miss you."

"Yep."

Jess laughed again, "Eric, when you bring her home can I see her?"

"Yes, of course." Then he looked out of the picture and talked with urgency, "Jess, we have to go same time next week?"

"No, not yet."

"Jess, it's bad."

Gun shots echoed in the distance as the monitor when black. Jess turned her face to me to cry more. Her body trembled against mine and I didn't understand what had just happen, "Crossfire?"

She nuzzled her face into my neck and her breath breezed over my skin, and yet I couldn't get that word out of my head, "Jess, you were shot at?"

She shook her head, "Not at, sometimes we were in the way."

Her mouth rested on my skin and it's so distracting, but I needed to understand. My heart began to pound hard, the blood flowed through my veins with heat, and I grew angrier than I could endure, "You are not going back there!"

Her lips pressed and then moved against my skin. The distraction would have been welcomed if the blood didn't pierce every part of my body with heat. She tried to distract me and it almost worked, but my body filled with anger and fear at the same time, "Please tell me you will never go back there?"

What would have happened to me if she'd been killed? Why did she have to go there? In a way I'd take the blame for her going, but I could have lost her forever. Her mouth traced up my neck reaching my ear calming my anger, "Not if you don't want me to."

I wish I wasn't so angry right now. I'd kiss her right now and she would probably let me, but shot at...killed? No, I am not okay with this and with my son. Is he mine to get this emotional over? I took a deep breath, "Jess tell me... is Mason mine?"

Jess didn't answer me either I am too angry or she's that upset with how they said goodbye. She held tighter to me and I never want to let her go again. I wrapped my arms around her and Mason holding them tighter. Things ran through my mind because there were so many thoughts that I couldn't sort out. I tried to focus on the moment here and now with them both in my arms. It wasn't until Mason decided he had enough cuddle time and didn't like being smashed between us.

She hugged and kissed him multiple times as we went up the stairs. Guiding her with my hand at the small of her back they still shook from the adrenaline pumping through my system. Stopping short for a moment to shake them as if that would release some of the toxin in my veins, but nothing would help me at this moment. She headed to the chair in the living room, while I went to the kitchen to warm a bottle. I turned and leaned against the counter staring at her. Her attention stayed focused on Mason, but as shocked as I am my eyes stayed on her in disbelief.

The fiery must have radiated from me because she said, "I know this is a lot, Paul. I am sorry. I should have insisted on the year thing."

That didn't help the anger filling every inch of my body. In fact I wanted to scream at her, *'don't you dare push me away now and not ever Jessica.*

Dam it.' I couldn't say what I thought so I turned away. I decided to make her something to eat.

Not wanting to take my eyes off of her ever again I glanced back at her only to find her tears flowing again. The information of her being shot at shocked the shit out of me, but if she thinks I can't handle it she'd run from me and that I could not handle. Shit, what the hell should I do now? I cut up some fruit and brought the bowl out to her. I knelt in front of her as I watched her wipe the tears from her cheeks.

I demanded, "You promised me you wouldn't go back, right?"

When her eyes met mine she nodded and the calm finally worked its way back into my body. Forcing myself to smile I continued, "It's okay, Jess. I am right here."

Then the tears really started to fall, but she nodded again. Taking her hand in mine I kissed it before putting her hand to the bowl of fruit I placed in her lap. The South America situation is too much for me to handle. But she is here now and there is no way I will let her leave me again for any reason. Not wanting to be away from her I turned around finding a spot on the floor next to them and leaned my head against her leg. Her hand traced my face and I closed my eyes to take in her touch, but she needed food.

"Jess, it's okay. Eat please."

She pulled her hand from me to nibble on the fruit. After a little while her finger traced my cheek again. I closed my eyes, her soft touch could make me sleep because it was so comforting.

"Paul, can you take this please?"

Needing to confess everything I turned getting up on my knees. We needed to talk about her staying here forever, about missing the feel of her next to me, and to explain that I will never ever hurt her again.

Mason was squirming and I caved into his needs rather than my own. When I got up to fix a bottle for him she took her turn feeding him. Waiting for my turn I stood towering over the both of them while she patted his back for burping. Realizing how much I missed holding him now that I had to share him. When she handed him to me I pulled him to my body moving to the couch. We lay down so I could watch him eat while his little hands touched my face. Jess went to the kitchen doing her own thing. I wanted her, but this... holding my, I think, son in my arms was simply satisfying.

She has to have a good reason to not tell me, but in my heart I loved this little guy as much as I loved her.

I glanced over to her in the kitchen making something, "Jess, what are you doing?"

"Making something to eat."

"Are you hungry?"

"Nope."

She didn't want to be this way and wanted to make that change. I never want to hurt her again and it's time for me to make that change that made me happy.

11

Jess:

As I made food I'd glance back to observe Paul talking with Mason. He's getting the hang of this daddy thing so good. Is he figuring it out, or does it really not matter to him. Oh, how I wish he would play with me like that. Paul, just forgive me so we can get back to loving each other. I miss your touch, your kiss, and I need you so badly.

"Paul, do you want soup?"

"No thanks."

I walked back over and sat in front of the couch so I'd be close to my baby and Paul. Paul reached to touch my face, "Is the soup easier for you to eat?"

Grinning with my mouth full I mumbled, "Yes."

"We should make more so you have a ready supply."

Eating like this made him happy.

The days go by slowly. We did go to town and he insisted on getting me a few things. I hated spending his money, especially if I gained weight and nothing would fit again. Preferring to wear his clothes and smell him all the time is what I wanted.

Trying to get his attention I'd walk to my room in a towel after showering. If he wasn't around I made it a point to walk to the kitchen for a glass of water before going to my room. He either didn't pay attention to me, or he would be down stairs working on his business.

I hated when he'd work out because those muscles are so defined when he comes up after working out that my mouth waters and my eyes fixated on him. The urge to walk up to him and run my hands against his sweaty chest seemed gross, but it glistened from the sweat. Why couldn't he just take me in his arms and tell me he loves me and wants to make love to me over and over again.

At night we'd put in a movie. Usually we'd sit apart, but today I needed to be close. He's going to have to tell me soon if he wants me to stay here and if he could handle everything I dropped on him. Wanting to get Paul's attention I put on a slinky tank top and little short shorts. I grabbed a blanket to cuddle with, but if he didn't touch me after seeing me like this, well, then it might not work out for us. I walked out to the living room where Paul carried on a conversation with Mason. It ended as I approach making me wonder what Paul says to him. I would ask him to stop, but Paul gets the most adorable look on his face when he's talking to Mason. After moving to the couch I sat down and put the blanket in my lap while sneaking a glance at Paul to see if he noticed. He didn't even peek at me. Shit, this is not a good sign. Perhaps he isn't attracted to me anymore now that I hurt him. He says he loves me so why won't he show me? Giving up on trying to get him to notice me I leaned back when he pulled Mason to his chest.

"I think he is tired, Jess."

I leaned my head to Paul's shoulder to keep my eyes on Mason as the movie started. He made it through about half way, but his little eyes slowly closed and then he would force them open. I chuckled a little.

Paul whispered, "What Jess?"

Turning to whisper into Paul's ear, "He's fighting it. He doesn't want to go to sleep."

"I should go lay him down in his crib."

Not wanting to be left alone without the comfort of Paul's body next to mine I made up a good excuse, "No, I like watching him sleep."

Paul turned to me and kissed my forehead. I loved when he does this. Kiss me Paul, on the lips please.

"Okay."

No kiss, but he agreed to stay this way longer. At least I got to be close to him. Mason's eyes finally stayed shut and then I closed mine. Paul took my hand and turned it over tracing his fingers over my palm. I relaxed right into sleep.

Paul pushed me up waking me, "Jess, baby, if you're sleeping you should go to bed."

Not wanting this to end I cuddled in more forgetting that we weren't here yet.

"Jess, bed time."

Not wanting to give in I sat up slowly as he stood up and put out his free hand for me to take. I grabbed his hand and he pulled me to my feet. The blanket fell to the floor.

"Shit," the expressed word coming from Paul.

Wonder washed over me as I glanced up at him. Why did he say that? He turned away from me right away. I let my eyes wander down my body to see if my boobs were hanging out, but I had forgotten that I dress skimpy trying to get his attention. I couldn't have been more pleased that I did get a reaction. It wasn't the one I wanted at least not yet. I followed him down the hall without a word as he took me to bed. He went to lay Mason in the crib and I followed. Resting my head on his back while I waited for him to turn to me. This is our night to be together.

He turned taking my hands in his. He walked backwards pulling me with him, but he made his way to the door. Sadness came quickly as I realized that he isn't ready, maybe this is still too much for him. He stopped outside the bedroom door, "So this is good night."

My eyes wandered over his body working their way up to his face, but his head bowed down to the floor. He's avoiding eye contact. Did I hurt him so bad that he'll never get over my leaving like I did? I pulled his face up finding sadness consuming him as much as it did me. All I wanted from him is his love, his devotion, and him for the rest of my life. If he didn't seem so sad I would have asked him to make love to me, but after seeing the pain there on his face telling me he wasn't ready for all this. Trying to think of a way to make everything better a thought came to mind. A smile grew over my face as I stared at him.

"What, Jess?"

Letting go of his hands I rushed to Mason's diaper bag and grabbed a CD out. Holding it in my hands wondering what he will think of this, "You know how I said I destroyed everything that would remind you of me?"

A gleam came to his eyes, "Yes."

"I couldn't do it. That's everything from your lap top at school."

Tears came to his eyes as he took it, staring at it full of doubt. Every emotion filled his face before he turned and walked away without another word. That didn't go as I'd hoped. My heart shattered into a million pieces while I raked my brain on what to do. The sadness that filled his face told me that everything I have done to him had been too much. If seeing those pictures made this worse than he shouldn't look at them. Knocking on his door I got no response, so I opened it to find it empty. On a mission to stop him from feeling any worse about this I headed to the living room, but with no one there either I headed to the basement. The light in his office glowed under the door, and through the one inch opening. When I got close to grabbing the handle I heard him say, "Oh Jess. I miss you so much."

I am right here and he still missed me. No, he missed how it used to be. How we were then. I am different now, things are different now. It is too much for him. My heart pounded so hard against my chest that I thought it wanted to leave me too. It will never be like it was, so now I did have to let him go. He can never love me like that again. I covered my mouth to hold in the crying, but the gasps of my bawling couldn't be contained. Rushing to get out of there I had to decide what I'd do next.

His voice caught me before I got to the stairs, "Jess, don't go."

It's hard to let him see how much this hurt but I understand now. Wanting to explain, "I hurt you again, and I am so sorry. It's just that I wanted to..." not being able to finish seeing the pain on his face I took off up the stairs and into my room. With not wanting to wake Mason I tried to cry quietly, but it took the pillow over my face to contain my sobs.

Paul:

Shit, I screwed up again. How can I make her understand that I miss holding and kissing her? I can't let her go and now she is going to run. Would she do it tonight? No, we didn't go get her car, but my truck is here. Just to be safe I went out to my truck and disconnected a few wires. Even if she'd figure out one she wouldn't be able to figure out all of them. More determined than ever she is not leaving me again, and I will do anything and everything to stop her. After going to bed I still found it difficult to sleep distracted by the muffled sobbing.

As I woke I went over my new plan to keep her that had replayed in my mind all night. She has to see that this is her home and this is where her and Mason belong.

I went to make breakfast thinking that I should go get Mason. It has been a long night and I can't believe he isn't awake yet, or maybe she isn't coming out of the room because I upset her so badly. Okay, enough is enough. I need her in my life and I wanted her to know this. I went and knocked on the door, "Jess, breakfast is ready."

She didn't answer so I peeked in to find her still sleeping, but my little guy let me know he's awake. He's soaked from head to toe, so I undressed him completely, wrapped a blanket around him, and went to the bed sitting down next to Jess.

"Jess, it's time to get up. A new day, let's go."

She peeked out from under the covers at me. The green in her eyes pierced me because the redness made them look even greener. Not letting the sadness engulf us again I leaned over her and kissed her forehead, "Come on sleepy head food is ready."

I walked out and put the baby tub in the sink for Mason. I ran the water as she stumbled to the table watching me, "What are you doing?"

"Did he sleep through the night?"

"Yeah, I guess so."

My attention went back to Mason as he moved his arms and legs when I washed him off, "This little guy was soaked so we are getting all cleaned up for mommy." I rinsed him, wrapped in a towel and brought him over to where Jess was, handing him to her, "Hi mommy. I am all wet."

She glanced up at me and grinned. Oh yeah, that is what I missed the most. Her grin a mixture of sweet, soft, and embarrassment. Kneeling down in front of her I found her so irresistible. She turned to me more and then our eyes met, "Jess, you do like it here, don't you?"

She nodded at the same time she said, "Yes."

That is all I needed to hear, "And I don't want you to leave."

She swallowed deeply, "Okay."

Okay she's not going to leave because she does like it here. We need more time to work out all the kinks. I stood up kissed her forehead and went to get the food for her, "We should do something today."

She grabbed my hand to stop me from moving away from her. I glanced down, hoping she didn't change her mind.

"I didn't want to hurt you last night."

This I can handle. I knelt back down in front of her, "Jess, I love you. You made me very happy, so happy that I got emotional. You loved me enough to not destroy all the pictures of our past together. It felt really good and I just realized how much I missed you. That's all, Jess."

She caressed my cheek with her hand but I wanted more. I slowly got up a little reaching for her lips. Please let me kiss you. I lightly placed my lips to hers. The warmth against mine satisfying enough, and she wasn't pulling away. I pressed harder and my lips filled with my heart beat which made my need for her become strong. I had to let go because I may go a little crazy and attack her if I stay here any longer.

12

We're definitely starting over. We went on dates twice a week. One day a week my mom and dad would come sit with Mason and the second day we would drop him off with them. My dad is really good about being a grandpa, but we didn't discuss it much. We called her mom and dad regularly and they came up at Christmas time and spent three days with us. It's easier for them to stay with us than at the cabin. Jess is tenser with them around, but for the most part we do okay. Our nights at home consisted of making dinners together, lying on the floor with Mason to play with him.

He is laughing all the time now and we both loved to torture him with tickling just to hear him giggle. The business is really slow now with it being winter and I only had to do a few driveways when it's a lot of snow and my guys needed sleep. I really only spent an hour or two a day on my business.

Jess is letting me kiss her once in a while, but I only tried once in a while. I didn't want to push any issues that might cause her to run. I did get to hold her hand on a regular basis now and touch her waist as we cooked together. We bought a scale so she could keep track of how much she gained.

She still had weekly dates with Eric, but she made me attend everyone with her. I liked this time as much as I hated it. She would pull my arms around her and god did that feel good. The last Sunday before March he told us he's coming home. In the presence of her excitement I offered for him, his girlfriend, and Masey to come up for a weekend. In Jess's excitement she made sure it would be the first weekend he was back. I wanted to kick myself for this, but it made her happy. After that web date she threw herself into my arms. Holding her tight as I melted in her arms, "Paul, you are the best."

My hand wrapped behind her neck and leaned to whisper in her ear, "I love you, Jess." Then I slowly let her go keeping my face down not wanting to know her reaction especially if it's bad.

Her face leaned against mine as she said, "And everything else?"

I wanted her to kiss me so bad, "Doesn't matter."

She moved her lips slowly against my face pressing little kisses as she made her way closer to my lips. My heart raced a million miles a second, "Are you sure, Paul?"

Oh yes, yes, I am so sure please kiss me, "As long as I get to see you every day of my life, I am sure."

Her mouth came to mine, soft at first but when her mouth moved to mine opening slightly I floated to another world. Slowly moving my arms around her I pressed to her lips harder. I knew grabbing at her and pulling her hard to my body would be a mistake even though my body burned with need to have her against me. Greedily I captured her mouth keeping with the intensity of how much I needed her, only stopping for split second to gasp for air before diving in for more.

Shit, it was over when Mason yelped and we both stopped. Staring at each other seemed like a lifetime, so when I smiled she returned one for me. I moved away from her grabbing him from his seat holding him up to look at me as we walked away. "You are supposed to be helping me little man, not interrupt us. I have a few things to teach you."

I didn't pay attention to Jess. She would have to decide if she would follow or not. We moved to a blanket on the floor in the living room and I laid with my face at his belly. When I kissed him there he'd laughed. Playfully I scolded him about getting all of our attention, especially when his mommy gave me sweet sexy attention in the way of kisses. Jess finally came up and laid down next to us observing us at play. Wanting to pull her in for a family threesome I reached for her hand. Though all of my attention is directed to Mason my heart soared when she took my hand in hers running her fingers along my knuckles. She held back from join in, but eventually got in on the playing with him too.

I finally had to get up to make something to eat.

She seemed worried about my absence, "Paul, did you want me to make something?"

"Nope, I got this."

She got up taking Mason with her I assume she went to change him. Knowing how good Carb's are for her I decided to make Spaghetti. She came back out with a blanket sitting in the chair to feed him.

The one thing that irritates me the most is when she feels the need to cover herself in front of me, "You don't have to do that, Jess."

A gentle smile danced on her lips, "I like cuddling with him and he seems tired."

At least she had a good explanation for it and I went back to work on dinner.

When it was almost ready I turned back to them finding her asleep with Mason. Remembering how cuddly she is when she sleeps I wondered; *should I even try?*

Determined I answered my own question with a yes, because the kiss went extremely well earlier. As I suspected Mason is sleeping. I leaned over her to take him, but I nudged her cheek with my nose, "Jess, baby, I am taking Mason to bed."

Sleepy eyes glanced up at me as I wrapped my hands around him to pull him to me. Her breast still exposed so I took her shirt and lightly placed it over her. She watched me but didn't say or do anything. Temptation lingered but I moved away from her with a smile on my face heading for the room.

Completely asleep again by the time I got back out I had to wake so she'd eat something. She complained, "sleep is good, Paul. Let me sleep."

"Nope, its food, then sleep."

She complained more as I pulled her to her feet, "I'm not even hungry."

"I know, but just a little Jess."

She rested her head on my chest as I dragged her to the table lowering her to a chair. I'd rather have kissed her when she is like this. She would be very responsive to me when she's this tired and I'd probably be able to kiss her for an hour.

No, self-control, she needs food. I hovered over her as those sweet eyes stared into mine, but I slowly moved away from her. My urges to kiss her are so strong right now I had to keep telling myself *stay in control.*

I put a small amount of noodles on her plate, sauce, a bread stick, and then put the same amount of food on my plate.

Her inquisitive expression encouraged me to explain, "If I eat the same amount of food as you I will be able to tell when you are hungry."

She gave me a very disapproving scowl.

I continued with a smirk on my face, "And I get to eat with you every time and I won't get fat this way."

Her face turned into the cutest grin, "You wouldn't want that. You would have to work out all the time."

I laughed, "Yeah."

She took her fork and grabbed a huge pile of noodles and put them on my plate. Her grin turned to a guilty smile.

I shook my head. Did that mean she likes when I work out? I would like my work outs to be in a different form, but it's still a little early to move to that already. She ate with that quirky smile on her face which drove me crazy the whole time. She didn't have to do much to get me going but I reminded myself if we went too fast she would take off. It only helped a little because then I would see that quirky grin on her face again.

When she finished I quit eating. Eating when she does, and the same amounts I will be able to tell when she should be hungry. I took the plates to the sink and she got up heading back to the bed rooms. My heart sank thinking this evening has come to an end. Leaning over the counter I put my head in my hands wondering if I pushed too hard tonight, but with that grin of hers I got my hopes up that we'd be kissing more today. Shit, what am I doing? I forced myself to do the dishes and clean everything up in the kitchen. Going to bed is inevitable. As I walked back to the rooms I prayed she would give me something anything before I got to my room.

She came out of the master bedroom and we both stopped where we were. Startled not only by her coming back out of the room, but also by what she's wearing. Standing there in front of me with a little tank top and those really small shorts that made her legs seem amazing long and shit... Paul hold it together.

Her eyes pleaded with me, "You're going to bed?"

Not sure I could speak so I shrugged but then got out, "I thought you were going to bed so..."

She gave me that smirk smile again, "Could we watch a movie together. Mason will have to eat again to sleep through the night, but it'll be awhile."

"Yeah," okay that almost came out with too much enthusiasm. Needing to contain my excitement calmly I continued, "That's a great idea. I'll be right out."

She floated down the hallway towards the living room while I stood there watching her go; my mouth hanging open, my eyes popping out of their sockets, and my heart pounding out of my chest. A shower to calm my nerves is what I intended on doing before joining her.

Jess:

He's going to cuddle with me alone. Making a cuddle spot on the couch for the two of us with a blanket and pillow I waited for him to join me. Disappointment filled me when the shower started. Shit, he's going to take his time. I curled up lying on the couch fighting the sleep off, but my eyes closed a little longer with each blink. When the door opened to the bathroom I perked up with eagerness. Oh yeah, hurry up Paul or Mason is going to wake up and we won't have any time alone. My heart raced with the anticipation of having Paul to myself. After our kiss today I wanted a lot more. His kisses took me away from any reality that I had left.

Patience is not one of my better virtues making it hard to not want to yell at him for making me wait. My eyes stayed glued to the hallway for a glimpse of him. What did any guy have to do to make himself presentable. If Paul walked out here nude that would be perfectly fine by me. When he appeared I almost gasped at how amazing he looks. He had lounge pants on that lay so low that you could see the muscle shirt etched with his muscles down past his waist. My body burned for his to touch me. Checking out his chest that is larger than I remembered and how those muscles bulged in all the right places. Powerful arms, wide chest, etched stomach, and oblique's that accented his waist; all of them perfect in my eyes. Every inch of them will be next to me in seconds. If I wouldn't resemble a girl in need I would have reached both arms out to him begging him to come to me faster.

If it's not enough torture to flaunt his body at a distance, but now he stood over me by the couch. Flinching when he asked, "Can I lay with you on the couch?"

The smile on my face hurt it's so big right now that I bit my lip to stifle it. I moved forward making room for him to lie behind me, because I have every intention of have his hands and arms wrapped around me. "Of course you can."

He crawled over me and it took us some adjusting before we found a comfortable position. After getting all settled in I pushed play for the movie to begin.

"What are we watching?"

Giggling about my choice, "A mushy love story."

He sounded quite disappointed, "Great."

Turning to him so I could see his face I asked, "Would you rather I put in an action movie?"

He's so sweet that he grinned at me, "No Jess, whatever you want."

With every intention I'd planned on getting into the movie blocking out how perfectly our bodies fit together; starting where my head rested below his chin all the way down to our feet. Our breathing is another thing that synced together, and with each breath his chest rose and fell gentle caressing my back. When his arm wrapped around me and his hand landed on my stomach I held back a whimper. My body tensed when his fingers traced against my stomach. He had to know what he's doing to me. And if having his body against mine wasn't enough his breath kept brushing against my neck and ear making the goose bumps appear on my skin. Giving in to those needs I repositioned myself to my back, but when I did I found him staring at me not the TV, "Are you even watching the movie?"

A burning desire in them gave me the answer without a word, but he replied anyway, "No."

Not sure how to get this started I asked him, "What are you doing?"

Eyes sparkling, mouth twitching to a sexy grin, and his fingers came up to touch my cheek while he said, "I am watching you."

I gasped as his fingers trailed to my lips where he ran his finger along the outside of it. Wanting to encourage him I laid there waiting for what came next, but his touch continued to be gentle and innocent. His body leaned into my side so I wrapped my free leg around him running my foot along the inside of his leg. His eyes squeezed shut as a deep groan came from him. It's when he opened his eyes I saw the need this time. Not just the desire but the burning need of wanting me to be his now and forever. His lips finally found mine as he gently nipped at my mouth and his body lifted from mine so I moved beneath his wrapping both legs around him. As he lowered back down to rub against me his mouth devoured mine, his tongue dove deep to tangle with mine. A small squeak came from me in excitement when his bulging membrane pressed against my core driving me to frenzy. He pulled away only to nip and suck down my neck to my collar bone. He pulled my strap off my shoulder trailing his face with it. His tongue licked, his mouth sucked, and this breath danced against my skin. When he exposed my breast he glanced up at me. Embarrassed by my size I said, "Still not that big."

He grinned sinfully, "Still bigger than I saw last time." His head dipped to me, but I didn't want him to release any milk, "Be careful, don't suck hard…" but before I finished my thought his tongue lapped against my nipple. His eyes met mine before his mouth covered me in the most intimate caress. My body responded to him instantly arching my back pressing my core against him harder. That's when Mason's first waking squeak pulled me back to reality. I grabbed Paul's head by his hair to stop him, but he took it as I wanted more right now. Quickly he moved to the other breast exposing it and diving into it.

"Paul."

"Aah ha. Me too Jess."

The way he twirled his tongue against my flesh I forgot about Mason's squeak. All I wanted was Paul to keep touching me.

His hand traced down to my leg pulling it up higher against his waist as he ground into me harder growling with hunger

This time Paul must have heard Mason too, because he let my leg go and came back up for a deep kiss. Mason didn't cry, he squeaked, or gurgled, even whined, but that didn't mean he's awake. Needing to be with Paul this way had been a long wait so letting it end isn't easy.

Mason now continued the whining with a crying tone. We both stopped and stared at each other. I didn't want to stop this and the needy grimace on Paul's face told me he has the same needs. Neither of us would make Mason suffer because of our wants and needs. Huffing disappointment I said, "Guess I should go get him?"

Paul pushed himself up a little to allow me to ease out from under him, but he bent down capturing my lips with his. Giving into him again I wrapped my arms around his neck pulling him back.

Mason really let us know he's awake with a full out crying fit. Pain struck my heart for ignoring him, and the trembling took over my body from wanting Paul so badly.

Paul pulled away again, leaned back in kissed my nose, and pushed away again to get up, "I'll get him Jess. You can collect yourself." He glanced back before jogging down the hall to answer Mason's fit.

He came back with Mason, but whispered to him. I'm sure he's scolding him for interrupting us again, but I sat up quickly to take him. His breath hitched as his crying subsided and turned to giggles and play time as we both gave him all our attention. The more time I spent with Paul the more I realized Mason resembles his father.

"Jess, are you sure he's not mine?"

My heart skipped a beat. The timing of his question freaked me out because of what my mind had been on. I swallowed to calm myself before turning to Paul inquisitively.

He grinned, "With his great timing, he's a lot like me."

We scooted closer together to play with Mason, but he didn't last long before the complaining started; still tired, and now hungry. If I hurried to feed him maybe we'd resume where we left off.

Accomplishing two things at one time I set up to feed Mason. Paul put his arm around me and traced his mouth along my neck. The warmth of his breath made me want to kiss him again. His lips glided along my skin working their way up to my ear, "Jess, I really do love you."

I cracked a little smile and turned to him. His hand cupped my face as his lips were back to mine. It's weird to be feeding Mason and kissing Paul at the same time, so I pulled away.

Cringing in agony he asked, "Is there something wrong?"

"Kind of. It seems weird to have him sucking my boob and you kissing me. That's all."

His pain stricken face rose to amusement as he chuckled out, "Yeah, I guess that would be weird."

Paul traced his hand along my face gently until I cringed in pain, "Ouch."

Paul had fear in his eyes, "What?"

"He bit me."

Paul tried to hold back a laugh, "He doesn't even have teeth, Jess."

"You let him bite your nipple and tell me it shouldn't hurt."

He was laughing, "Okay, Jess, you probably have to switch sides. I'll go make a bottle."

When Paul walked to the kitchen I moved Mason to the other side scolding him, "You shouldn't bite mommy like that. It hurts."

I cuddled him now a happy baby that he had all of my attention. His hand traced against my chest like he was kneading it. Not fully recovered I still didn't have enough milk for him so he started to fuss. He couldn't get comfortable and fought the sleepiness. Paul took him patting his back until he burped then cuddled him in his arms to feed him the bottle. I curled up to Paul wrapping my arms around his and leaned my head to his shoulder. Completely at home here in Paul's arms I relaxed into slumber.

Waking to a soft trace of Paul's lips against my cheek he whispered, "Jess, let's get you two to bed."

Through groggy eyes I witnessed the perfect man staring at me. He still had Mason in his arms, but able to get up and pull me at the same time. The thought of another day gone it would be Friday soon, and Eric, Amelia, and Masey would all be here. After introducing him to Paul he would understand why I loved him so much. Not only is he amazingly good looking, but he is also thoughtful and caring for Mason and me. Taking Paul's hand as he led me down the hall to the bedroom only letting go long enough to ease Mason into his crib. The warmth of his hands took mine again as he led me to bed, eased me into it, and tucked me in. I closed my eyes immediately but heard him say, "I love you."

I grinned with my reply, "I love you too, Paul. Always have and always will."

I thought for sure he would crawl in next to me to hold me but his absence filled me when the door closed. The bed remained empty next to me. Not wanting the night to end I jumped up, ran to the door, and opened it. Startled I found him standing with his forehead pressed against the door of the linen closet.

"Paul?"

He slowly turned his face my way with the biggest grin.

"Are you okay, Paul?"

Worry rushed into my brain that he's having doubts and I witness them. Shit, now what do I do?

"Yes, I am fine. Did you need something?"

Panicked now that I've witnessed his doubt I stammered, "No, I just…" think fast. Say something, "I wanted to say thank you."

He moved closer and stood in front of me. He took my hand in his starting with the fingers again, "Are you sure that's all?"

No, I want you to come to bed with me and kiss me you big jerk, but now that I know you're having doubts, "Yeah, I guess that's all."

Less than an inch in front of me he cupped my face in his hands, eyes locked with mine. My body burned for him making me miserable about him having doubts now. I love you and this hurts.

"If you're sure, Jess. Good night."

He kissed my forehead, turned away from me, walked into his room, and closed the door. Yep, this really hurt. Dam him. He says he loves me and he has me here, so why is he having doubts now?

There's so many good things between us it's hard to understand the doubts that Paul feels. Eric is going to be here on Friday. I hope he will have some words of wisdom for me.

13

The next morning I got up early to feed Mason. Luckily he went back down right away. My dad called and he didn't help me with the Paul situation. He wanted me to come home and start taking care of Mason on my own. If the relationship wasn't going to work out then it's time I get working on something to support him. Forcefully he pointed out that Paul had been supporting Mason and me for long enough and Paul didn't know how to say no, because of his feelings for me. Paul and my father talk all the time. I hoped that he would talk to him for me. My dad insisted that I am taking advantage of Paul, which made me cry.

He needs a break to figure it out? Is exactly what he said. I didn't want to leave, but if Paul still has doubts then giving him space would be a good thing. I grabbed a blanket and went outside to be sad by myself. Everything my father said ran through my mind, so I tried to convince myself he wanted us here, and then came up with what my dad said. Not really sure of what they talked about I wondered if Paul told him these things? Yep, that idea hurt more. My chest hurt so bad breathing became difficult and when I did my breath it came out as gasps due to trying to hold the tears back.

When the door opened I quickly wiped the tears and covered my face a little.

"Jess, are you out here?"

I didn't want him to worry about me crying, "Yep."

Making his way out to me he stopped when he had a full view. Now I hurt him, I saw the color drain from his face.

"One of the guys called and he needs some help today with some pipes so I have to work for a while."

He moved closer to me as his eyes searching my face. He stopped at the foot of the chair, "Are you crying?"

I nodded as the tears seeped out all on their own.

"Jess, what is wrong?"

Taking a deep breath before bellowing, "Dad called me this morning."

"Is everything okay?"

As if whipping the tears away I'd wipe the pain away, "When was the last time you talked to him?"

"At Christmas time."

Slightly relieved and half not believing that this is all my dad's idea not Paul's.

"Okay, so what are you upset about?"

"He said keeping Mason is my choice." The tears streamed down my face so I covered it with my hands to hide my insecurities.

Paul moved to sit at my feet rubbing my legs, "But he is amazing, Jess. Aren't you glad you did?"

Nodding I struggled to get the next part out, "He said that I needed to quit playing house and sucking you dry. He wants Mason and me to come home so I can get a job and start taking care of Mason on my own."

It's like the blood washed from his face making him pale white. He spoke desperately, "Jess, do you like it here?"

Of course I liked it here so I nodded.

"Do we get what Mason needs, and what you need?"

Agreeing again I nodded more.

Some of the color came back to his face, "Do you want to leave?"

He didn't want to ask the question; it's like he quit breathing to get it out. I shook my head so he'd resume breathing again, "But I don't provide for him."

He smiled sweetly, "If money was a problem Jess, I wouldn't have been able to stay home and take care of you. It's not an issue. I have enough money tucked away so if I lost all of my accounts today I'd survive... I mean we could live like this for more than a year. Remember, I neglected you so that I would be ready when you'd marry me."

Gaining some control I sniffled, "But last night you had doubts and I saw it in you."

He grinned, "The only doubts I had last night are in my self-control."

With wonder I glanced up at him not sure that he meant what he said. He wanted me so bad but pushed himself away, "So, you weren't having doubts about all this?"

"The only thing I doubt is that I'd make it through one day without you here."

Relief, excitement, and completely in love with him I tried to organize everything that he said. He leaned into me, "Jess, you should marry me. No one will tell you what to do if you say yes. You can stay home and be a mom, you can go to school, or you can even work if you want to."

It's not a real proposal. It has never been a real proposal. He has never got down on his knees and professed his love for me in a way that I'd say yes without hesitation. I smiled slightly because I wasn't turning him down. I wanted to be with him for the rest of our lives like we planned, but he would have to do a little better than this. So he needed an answer; I gave him the only one that did say yes or no, "I will stay."

He stared at me but finally words came to him, "Jess, I have to go to work. Promise me that you will stay. At least until I get back."

Not wanting to go anywhere I replied, "I promise."

"I mean it, Jess. You need to be here when I get back."

"Paul, I don't want to go."

He moved closer putting his face close to mine, our mouths almost touching, "If you decided you have to go." He paused, closed his eyes, and squeezed them shut like he's in pain to say his next words, "Talk to me about it before you leave."

His lips moved to caress mine, but I needed more. I wrapped my arms around his neck pulling him to me. Needing him to make me feel wanted I moved my lips against his provoking more. He pushed up hovering over me until I leaned back pulling him with me as our kissing turned into the tongue tango. Me being the needy one aroused a growl from Paul, "I have to go, Jess. You promised. You will be here when I get back!"

Full of regret myself I let go as he stood. His hesitated as his gaze wandered over to the lake, "Jess, you see that island?"

My eyes wandered to the lake in search of the island. After finding it I glanced up at him waiting for him to explain why he pointed it out.

He grinned as he turned back to me, "It's ours; I'll tell you my idea when I get back."

He went inside but came out in a rush and jogged to his truck. Before he got in he stopped to stare at me, "Jess, you promised, right?"

Excited I practically yelled my answer, "I promise you!"

I tried to let what my dad had said go by focusing on the kiss from Paul. Eric will be here Friday, he'll help me make sense of everything. Now that I didn't have to worry about leaving I headed in to spend the day with my baby. We played and hung out all day. I danced with him, crawled on the floor with him, and cuddled. He finally went to sleep around noon so I laid him down in his crib. Once my hands were free I dusted, cleaned, and did laundry. I even grabbed Paul's clothes hoping he wouldn't mind if I did them. After cleaning everything, Mason continued to sleep; I wondered what to do next. The only that came to mind is kissing Paul.

Holding the phone in my hand I stared at it trying to be brave enough to bother him at work. When the silence of the house got to be too much I pushed the call button, even though I worried he'd be irritated with me.

"Jess?"

"Yes."

"Are you okay?"

"Yeah."

"You're not leaving are you?"

"No, I'm not leaving." Disappointed that he's going to be worry all the time now; my words might have come out a little short.

"What's wrong?"

"Nothing is wrong. I'm just wondering if you're still busy, or between jobs?"

"No, I'm still busy. Did you need something?"

I sighed, "Nope, it's nothing. I'll let you go."

"Jess, please don't leave."

"I'm not leaving, but I am hanging up now."

"Jess, are you sure you don't need anything?"

He's so worried about me and leaving that I had to make this okay, "No, really, I'm fine, and I'll be here when you get back. I promised."

"I love you, Jess."

"I love you too, Paul. Always have, always will." I hung up quickly so he couldn't say anything else.

Paul:

I found her phone call disturbing after this morning. Did she really believe her dad is right about this? She did say she would marry me the same night she took off for another country. Making my way down the pipes to make sure there is no other leaks my mind stayed on Jess. This morning kept playing in my head, with my main concern is her leaving. She's not going to take Mason away from me now. Deep in my gut he is mine no matter what she says or doesn't say.

"PAUL!!!"

When I came back to reality Jeremy the kid that I was helping stared at me.

"The girl again?"

Jess did turn my world upside down so I smiled with her on my mind, "Sorry I'm a little distracted."

"Still having problems?"

"Not sure, but we have to get this done."

Going through the motions trying to hurry; I needed to get back to Jess as soon as possible. I kept going, but Jeremy yelled again, "PAUL!!"

Startled out of my head I glanced up at him.

"You're not help anymore."

"No, I can do this, Jeremy, it's alright."

"No, I mean I know how to wrap the pipes. The leaks are what I needed help with and their done. Go."

"Really?"

"Yes, some things are more important."

Jeremy understood life better than most. Making my way out from under the trailer I stopped long enough to tell him, "Remind me to give you a raise."

Hastily I wiped my hands off as I headed for the truck, but he yelled after me, "I will be expecting a good one."

Jeremy definitely played this to his advantage.

I drove like a mad man trying to get home to my sweet Jess, hoping she would still be there. She better still be there or I'm going to go ballistic. When I pulled up to the house relief filled me when her car still sat there. Taking a moment to put my worries aside I rested my forehead on the steering wheel. My body had been trembling this whole time, which I didn't realize until it had stopped.

One last controlling deep breath I headed in. As I walked through the front door she danced in the kitchen making something, but she didn't hear me over the music. Again my heart pounded hard in my chest, and my throat went dry thou my mouth watered all at the same time. She is the woman I want to come home to every day of my life. Making my way to her on tiptoes placing my hands on her hips and whispered in her ear, "Did you need something, Jess?"

She jumped turning around gasping, "What are you doing here?"

Surrounding her with my body I leaned to her, "Your phone call freaked me a little." My head dipped to her giving her all the power of our relationship.

She took my chin pushing up with her fingers so my eyes would meet hers, "I told you I would be here."

Trying to justify my behavior I explained, "I didn't want to take any chances. I just can't stand the thought of you not being here."

She smiled and traced her hand down my chest. It must have been obvious that I'm a mess from the thought of her leaving.

"I told you that I didn't want to leave."

I closed my eyes to take in the way she smelled of a flower, "Did you need something?"

"No, Mason is sleeping and I'm bored. If you are between jobs I hoped we could..."

All I wanted to do right now is to make sure she understood how much I needed her here in my life. Raising my hands to cup her face I took the one step that's separated us. When I opened my eyes I found her staring right back at me full of excitement. You didn't have to tell me twice, so I leaned down taking the kiss I had to have. The feel of how soft her lips are made me groan with pleasure. Her mouth opened enough to let me suck, nip, and dive into her deeply. The gasp did not come from me this time, so when her hands gripped at my sides my wild side came unleased, "How long do we have?"

She smiled as she kissed me but mouthed, "A half hour or so."

Not long enough to really show her how much I loved her, but long enough to enjoy her kisses. Diving deeper into her mouth with my tongue, the sweetness of watermelon or honeydew enticed my taste buds. Pulling away just enough to scold her, "You should have called me sooner."

We both laughed as we dove into kissing again. We used to kiss like this when her parents were going to be home soon and we had little time to enjoy so we hit is hard and heavy. Taking it step by step I walked backwards towards the living room with the couch in mind. The back of my legs hit the couch and I tumbled down trying to pull her with me, but she didn't follow, so our lips broke apart. Hoping this didn't have to end I stared at her as she grinned a devilish smile. What surprised me the most is when she crawled on to my lap straddling me. As she hovered over me she kissed just under my eyes at the top of my cheeks, my forehead, my nose, and then over to my ear. Her body ground against me while whispering in my ear, "I love you, Paul." Still using self-control I ran my hands up her back. When her breath penetrated my ear, and her lip wrapped around my earlobe I hissed at the pleasure of it. When I couldn't take it anymore I grabbed her around her waist flipping her to her back. Hovering over her staring down into those beautiful green eyes I wanted so much more than just playing and kissing her. For now kissing is what I had to be satisfied with. Reaching down to her lips I skimmed mine against hers teasing her for more. Her hands trailed my sides working their way under my shirt causing the blood in my system to pump harder through my body. Hungrily I captured her mouth diving deep tangling our tongues in a rhythm that only we shared. As her hands slid down to my ass pulling me closer her warm core rubbed against the bulge she caused me. If she is trying to drive me crazy she is very good at it.

I tried to talk to myself; *slow down, Paul, just enjoy what she is giving right now. It's just kissing, don't get carried away.*

Her hands gripped and massaged my ass grinding me into her. *No, too much, kissing is so good; please don't egg me on anymore.* Grabbing one arm I pulled it up over her head pinning it there, while I grabbed the other one bringing it up to join the other above her head. If I let her grind into me like that it is possible to spill my load while still clothed. Instead I wanted to kiss her, taste her, and just see the hunger in her eyes for me.

She stopped pulling away from me. Shit too fast. I kissed her lips softly, "No, Jess, I like the kissing."

She smiled and kissed me again, but then she stopped again.

I begged, "Please Jess?"

"Paul, Mason."

Ignoring her comment about Mason I just wanted to keep kissing her, and when she kisses me back like this. Oh how I loved the way she moved her mouth with mine, and then he squealed again. I stopped kissing her in defeat. Mason won this one.

She laughed as I laid my face against hers, "Times up."

Pushing myself up allowing her to remove herself, so she could go to the little shit of bad timing.

She did glance back at me, "Sorry, Paul."

Not wanting it to end like this I caved with a grin on my face and shook my head in defeat. She ran back to me and kissed my cheek, but ran to get him. So that's it, it is over for now so I sat up putting my head in my hands. There is only one thing that is wrong with this picture and its very noticeable as I glanced down at myself. I didn't realize how turned on I am. I hurried to the bathroom before she came out with him to take care of this before she knew how carried away we had gotten.

Jess:

When I came back out Paul wasn't on the couch anymore. When the toilet flushed I knew he hadn't left yet. Paul came straight to us and kissed Mason's head and then me softly. Mason squawked so Paul kissed him again, "Sorry little man, but I like mommy too."

His eyes came back to mine full of regret, "I have to go back to work, Jess, but I will hurry. I promise."

"Okay."

Nothing is better than what she gave to me; a half hour of bliss.

14

It wasn't long at all before Paul came back. Having dinner ready for him when he got home made it seem like we are a real family. After dinner we went to the living room to play with Mason on the floor. He's sitting up now so Paul lay at an angle in front of him and I leaned against his stomach. We played with Mason for hours. He likes to make noises that make us laugh and then he giggles. I am so glad Paul is here to see his son grow. I still didn't know how or when I'd tell him, but we are here with him so he can be part of Mason's life. When Mason grew tired I picked him up to cuddle in the chair, but Paul came over with his arms out. Sharing Mason is difficult but Paul is amazing with him. He turned music on and swayed Mason in his arms all over the living room.

Taking advantage of this free time I took a shower getting ready for bed. Meeting Paul in the hallway I turned to follow him into the bedroom where he laid Mason down in his crib. We both stood there staring at him. Is this a good time to tell him? He seems more than eager to help with Mason. Does he already love him?

Paul turned to me, "he is beautiful Jess."

This would be the perfect time to tell him, but his hands cupped my face and his lips pressed light little kisses against mine. Lost in his touch I had one thing on my mind. Using my tongue against his lips I lured him in for more kissing. Pulling me into his arms he moaned into my mouth, but I stepped into him. Not even realizing that we moved until we stood at the bedroom door again. The way he stared at me told me he wanted me as bad as I wanted him. "Jess, you can't kiss me like that it's too...." His eyes closed so I moved closer to him wanting every part of him touching me.

"I am trying to behave and we need to take this slow."

It's been months sense we made love, so why do we have to take it slow? See he still had doubts.

He kissed my forehead, "Good-night, Jess." He turned to walk away so I slammed the door standing there disappointed. Not wanting him to leave me I opened the door to stop him. I almost ran into him because he stood there with his hand out to grab the doorknob.

"Paul?"

He shook his head trying to explain, "I don't want to be away from you anymore."

My heart raced, "I didn't want you to go."

"So I can stay in here with you?"

"Yes."

Stomach turning, pulse pounding, and breathe a little short; I am nervous about wanting him to stay.

He walked back in as I backed up. We stood there gazing at each other not knowing what to do now both afraid to kiss now that he's staying in the same room.

He turned to the bed, "What side do you want?"

I shrugged, "I suppose the side that Mason is on."

We both walked to our sides of the bed and crawled in. I tucked the pillow under my head facing Paul and he did the same. We laid there looking at each other not saying a word.

He leaned forward and kissed me briefly, pulled away, and stared into my eyes. I liked it so I did the same to him, but when I reached his lips he moved his to mine. That's when I caved to my needs so I stayed there continuing to kiss him. I wasn't comfortable so I moved my pillow close to him and resumed kissing him.

He drifted off before me. With temptation lying before me I traced my hands over his chest; this is bigger than I remembered. Skimming my hand down further letting my fingers take in the muscles cut into his stomach. He moved a little so I moved my hand back to his face running the back of my hand against his cheek. How could this man love me after everything I did to him? I drifted to sleep kissing his face, chin, and jaw line.

Waking to Mason's little coo's of complaining are still pleasant to me, but lying in Paul's arms with my head on his shoulder is even better. So happy that he stayed with me I reached up pressing my lips to his chin.

A smile stretched on his face, "You heard him?"

"Yeah."

"Do you want me to get him?"

"No, I will get him in a minute. He's not quite awake yet and I like it right here."

A laugh in his breathe escaped him before his lips pressed against my forehead. It wasn't long before Mason was a little more demanding. Pushing myself up to go get Mason I hovered over Paul for a few seconds and then kissed him. I kissed him hard and playful, but then I moved away from him. Not letting me get away with it he pulled me back to lay on his body as he devoured my mouth and running his hands up my back. When Mason protested louder I pushed away as Paul complained, "You shouldn't kiss me like that when you have to get him."

As I picked Mason up and carried him to the changing table his tears turned to giggles. Paul crawled to the end of the bed and off to come say good morning to Mason. The screeching scream Mason gave when he saw

Paul filled my heart. Paul held his hands and talked to him while I did the changing. Their play put a great big grin on my face.

Paul asked, "Do you want to see how I fed him while you slept?"

Suspicious of Paul's motive I'm not sure I want to know this, but he is excited to show me. He moved to the bed and propped pillows up against the headboard. Leaning against the headboard he sat up holding his arms out for Mason. The biggest grin grew on his face as he watched me, "This is actually easier because you were dead to the world when I did this before. First I had to lay Mason next to you and then pull you up so I could squeeze behind you." Reaching for me he held his hand out for me to take. This is weird, but I moved to sit in front of him. His arms wrapped around me holding Mason to me. Mason did not approve of this long process causing my uneasiness to heighten.

Supporting Mason with his arms around me he whispering, "Don't think this is weird. You were out of it."

That is when he pulled my shirt up to expose me, but he didn't have to help Mason once he saw food waiting.

"He didn't grab a hold that easy, but you get the idea."

Relaxing back into Paul, "So you had to take his little head and probe my boob so he'd latch on?"

Paul's head lowered until his mouth rested on my shoulder. He spoke softly, "Yes."

I laughed on the inside, because I pretty much pushed him away, so he had no idea I was still in love with him at that time. I had to tease him a little, "Was it weird touching me like that not knowing how I felt about you?"

Kissing my neck while he replied, "Yes," he continued to trace his nose along my neck up to my ear breathing in.

Liking the attention he is giving me I asked, "Did you do that too?"

His breathe brushed against my ear. Strangely enough this turned me on, but as his breath moved to my ear he said, "Yes, you said you loved me."

Fear coursed through me. How much does he know? "What else did I say?"

He leaned his head to mine with sadness, "It would hurt you when you woke up and realized it isn't real."

I reached up to place my hand on his face and turned to him, "So you knew all along that I'm in love with you?"

His mouth twitched a little like he wanted to smile, "I hoped and prayed that you did and that it's still true, Jess. The only thing I don't understand is how we had the best night of our lives, and you still left me."

I reached for his mouth to quiet his question with the tip of my fingers press to his lips. Wanting him to understand I tried to explain again, "I didn't want to go. Honestly Paul, they wouldn't let me out of the commitment. And then you were there to pick up the pieces. Remember I tried to push you away, but there you were taking care of me again. It hurt to think I would be gone for a year, but the last thing I wanted to do is hurt you too. Then when we made love you filled my dream of you being my first for everything."

Tears filled my eyes as I rambled on and on until Paul pulled my face to the side. His lips grazed mine as he mouthed, "I am still scared you will leave."

I moved to his lips, but paused, "I'm scared this is too much to ask from you."

His eyes lowered and he shook his head no, "It doesn't matter. I love you."

Totally in love with him I moved my lips to his again and again. Getting carried away with Paul turned me on. That is until Mason bit me again, "Shit."

Pushing Mason away from me so I can see what he is doing. His little lip came out right before his screamed. I did regret yelling but it hurt.

"Jess, what?"

"He bit me again."

"Jess, he is hungry. He doesn't do it intentionally."

Glaring at Paul I scolded, "I'm beginning to wonder about that. Also I should show you what it feels like and then you can tell me how it's not supposed to hurt."

Paul laughed at me taking Mason in his arms trying to calm him down. Huffing at him not kidding about showing him how bad it hurt. Turning around I leaned my head down to suck on his nipple peeking up at him.

"I don't think you should do that, Jess. Mason is upset."

Taking his nipple in my mouth swirling my tongue around it first to show him how relaxing it can be. Then I licked the tip of it before I wrapped my lips over my teeth and bit down testing how hard I should bite.

"Um, Jess, you *really* don't want to do that."

I moved closer biting a little harder but kept it between my lips.

"Ouch."

When he experienced the pain I let go and raised my eyebrows questioning him.

He laughed, "Okay so it hurts, but now you have a bigger problem."

What is the bigger problem? "What do you mean?"

He lifted Mason off of him, laying him down next to me, "You better take him."

Paul moved off of the bed and walked away. He must be mad that I bit him. Shaking it off I took Mason to the kitchen to make him a bottle. We met back in the room and I placed Mason between us but kept my eyes on Paul. He didn't seem mad so what is his problem?

He was smiling and playing with Mason making him laugh and giggle. I joined in but I kept eyeing Paul, "So what, are you mad at me?"

He laughed, "Nope."

Placing his mouth on Mason's belly and gave him a zerbert, which is when you blow bubbles on someone else's skin. Mason pushed Paul's face away just giggling. It had to be the cutest thing I had ever seen. He laughed hysterically making the both of us crack up with laughter too. Paul leaned over him to kiss me, but Mason kicked at our faces. We both grabbed his legs but he continued to giggle.

"I think I am done breast feeding him, because I don't like that he does that."

Paul gave me that quirky little grin, "I liked it."

Wondering what he liked about it I asked, "You like it when he bites me?"

"No, I liked when you did it to me."

Shaking my head I asked, "That turned you on?"

He laughed picking up Mason holding him over his body. I laid down resting my head on my hand to watch the two of them.

"Jess, you have done better than most. If you want to be done with breast feeding I understand, and it will give me more time with him." Paul lowered Mason to his chest and Mason laid his head down and wrapped his arms around Paul the best that he could. I felt tears come to my eyes, "Paul, he loves you."

Paul looked over at me, "Does that make you sad?"

"No, really happy."

Paul handed Mason to me, "I'll go get the bottle."

I nodded watching him get up, and Mason screeched. I tried to reassure him, "Daddy will be right back."

Paul stopped and turned to me. The look on his face was incredible. He had this glossed over gleam in his eyes, "Daddy?"

"You did want that, right?"

A glimmer hit his eyes in a way that surprised me before he walked out. As fast as he left he came back with Mason's bottle. Crawling in next to us he held the bottle for Mason, but kept his teary eyes on me.

15

The week went quickly after that morning. Paul worked a lot this week due to the nice weather, and people wanting their cabins opened up. I didn't mind now that we established that I am staying.

It's finally Friday and Paul promised to be home by 2 pm. Eric, Masey, and Alison are going to be here at 4 pm. I cleaned everything, even though it didn't need it. Paul came home by 2 pm just like he promised. So pleased I met him at the door and jumped into his arms thanking him for being on time. Taking advantage of my actions he kissed me moving toward the couch. We fell to it and made out for a short while. We kiss, nibbled, tickled, and discussed the food we'd serve them. It's fun and playful like it had been when we use to be boyfriend and girlfriend.

The rumble of an old car in need of a new muffler pulled up in front of the house. Staring at Paul for a moment savoring how happy he made me. Paul didn't look so happy but he pushed me up anyway and pointed to the door for me to go. Glancing back at him before heading out the door he took a container from the freezer. I ran back to him and wrapped my arms around his waist hugging him so tight, "Remember, I love you more than anything."

He turned in my arms with a very confused expression. I reached up and kissed him deeply, but cut it short to run out to greet them. I yelled back, "Paul, will you get Mason?"

Paul:

What have I gotten myself into if she needs to say that to me? I picked up Mason and walked out to greet her best guy friend. This is going to really suck.

I stayed on the porch holding Mason as she ran to him. They hugged and she kissed him on the lips. My girl kissed another guy on the lips. I'm right it sucks already. He introduced his girlfriend Alison, while Jess picked the little girl up into her arms. Jess hugged her, and kissed her cheeks, but Masey's too busy turning her head this way and that taking in everything. When Masey grabbed Jess's face I laughed out loud, but then she asked, "Where Jessup baby?"

Jess set her down and turned her until she saw me, "That is Paul and he has Mason, my baby."

She came running at me so I moved to the bench to sit down so she could get close to him. I didn't want to be distracted by her, because I wanted to keep my eyes on Jess and how she acts around this guy. In my mind I wondered if he is the one night stand she had? Masey came to us and touched Mason's hands, feet, and stomach. When her eyes came up to meet mine they were huge, full of life, deep rich brown eyes camouflaged by extremely long black eyelashes. The way she glanced back and forth from Mason to me encouraged a smile from me. She tilted her head with a question, "You daddy?"

Liking her already I chuckled, "Yes, I'm the daddy."

We couldn't go into all the complications of the situation with a little girl.

Not very clear in her speech she stated, "Same as daddy."

She just made my day. Jess is right I am taken with her. Now that we got her to the bench next to me I got a chance to check on Jess. The three of them carried bags and headed my way. Eric had his arm around his girlfriend but he and Jess linked their pinkies together as they walked towards me. Jess introduced everyone. I stood out of place until he shook my hand and said to me, "Jess always said how great you are but this is so unbelievable. Thank you!

Pleased to make her happy I grinned, "Jess's friends are always welcome." There's nothing else to say about that.

We all walked in and Jess took them up stairs to find a room for them. When they all came back down, I stood in the kitchen getting dinner ready, but still holding Mason while juggling everything.

Mason didn't like the visitors much and he clung to me every time someone tried to touch or talk to him. I loved that he held on to me wanting me to protect him. I held him close as much as possible.

Jess came out to me wrapping her arms around my waist, "Can I help you?"

Whenever she touches me like this I'm in heaven. Turning to her I encouraged her to hang with her friend, "You have guests. Go catch up. I've got this."

She tried to take Mason from me but I stopped her. I leaned down to whisper, "Jess, he's a little scared. Give him some time to warm up to them."

She looked at him with his head on my chest and smiled. She kissed him then looked up at me. I wondered what that pretty little head of hers had going on inside. Keeping my eyes connected with hers while she stood there staring back at me I gave her a reassuring grin. That's when I felt the warmth of her hand trace up my back. If she has any clue what she does to me when she touches me then she has some explaining to do because it's driving me wild. Her eyes squinted and her forehead creased with thought but finally that pretty little smile of hers appeared as she said, "You do know you are the only man I have ever loved."

I kissed those soft moist lips but wondered if she meant with her heart or body, but I'll assume both. I tried to put it out of my mind as fast as it seeped in but it didn't work as I watched her walk away to be with him. I wanted to yell after her to come back to me, but I bit my tongue and allowed her time with him. After getting the soup to a simmer I paced with Mason. He's fighting his sleepiness. He finally knocked out after 100 passes by the front door while I tried to see what they were doing. After laying Mason down in his crib I headed out to be uncomfortable again with her and her friend Eric. As I walked through the front door I noticed Alison down on the dock with Masey. To my disappointment Jess and Eric sat very close to each other with their pinkies lock together again. Instantly my blood pressure peaked causing heat to pulse through my body now that I am pissed off that she's holding hands with him. Tamping my anger down I moved to sit in the oversized chair across from them my eyes lingering on their hands. When she squeezed his pinky once more a protest started to rumble in my gut, but she got up and moved to me. When she crawled into my lap she covered us with a blanket. Every ounce of anger drain from my body when she pulled my arms around her, this simple act filled my heart beyond words. I traced my lips along her cheek while they continued to talk, but she leaned into my touch. Eric laughed out loud making me want to punch his lights out. When I glared at him he just smiled smugly and said, "You do love her as much as she loves you."

Turning two shades of red with anger all because he had to point that out to her. Wait, he pointed that out to her. This could actually work in my favor. Trailing my fingers up and down her arms trying to give her the reassurance that I'm here with her while she continued to ask about people in South America. She pulled my hands around her and squeezed and traced my hands with hers as she talked to him. She brought a touch of heaven to my world with the cuddling. We didn't stay on the porch for long, because dinner had been simmering for a while. Jess had Masey sit between us, which I didn't like. With him here I wanted Jess next to me every second, but he gave his girlfriend most of his attention so it's alright for now. Though Jess tried her motherly ways with Masey on using a spoon, she just couldn't get it right. Thinking like a kid I scooted closer to her and nudged her. Those sparkly little eyes came up to meet mine filled with worry. Picking up my bread stick I dipped it in the bowl swirling it around. When I lifted it to my mouth I blew on it to cool it and then took a bite. She giggled and did the same, but when she blew on it the steam still bellowed from it. Holding her hand away from her mouth I helped her blow on it a few more times with her and then she took a small bite.

After getting that down I picked up my bowl and lifted it to my mouth blowing again, until I could take a sip. While I enjoyed her laughter I glanced around the table and everyone laughed out loud. Not understanding why everyone's laughing at me I looked to Jess for an answer. Maybe this is something that she already does. Little Masey waved her arms to get my attention then curled her finger for me to come closer to her. Leaning over to find out what she so drastically needed to tell me when she took her napkin and wiped my nose off. Humiliated I glanced up while everyone laughed again, but when my eyes fell on Eric he mouthed a thank you. Well, at least he thought I did it on purpose. We continued to eat, but Jess reached and traced her hand over to my shoulder. Glancing over at her I found her eyes full of happy tears and they glimmered at me. I guess doing something stupid sometimes makes everyone feel better.

After dinner Jess went to feed Mason. Alison kicked us guys out of the kitchen so we took Masey with us downstairs to entertain her. She liked the exercise ball the best. She rolled around as we stood there watching.

"You have a great place here."

"Thanks. I built it for Jess."

I saw him crack a smile, which embarrassed me once again.

"So, it has been going good?"

I looked down, "Really slow."

I heard him say, "The way she talked about you I wouldn't have guessed that."

That didn't make sense to me. Shrugging I said, "She found someone down there."

"No, she didn't."

"Yeah, she had a one night stand. That's what she told me."

He laughed even louder, "I lived with her. I would have known if she did. I'm telling you she didn't."

I turned away from him and played with Masey a little not wanting him to see my excitement. Mason is one hundred percent mine.

When he spoke again he asked, "You didn't know?"

If we're both in love why wouldn't she just tell me Mason is mine? When I turned to him he smiled ruefully, "Jess is going to kill me for telling you."

"Deep down I suspected, but I don't understand why she won't tell me."

For some reason my feelings were turning from jealousy to friendship like he wanted to be truthful with me.

"If I tell you, you have to promise not to tell her I told you."

Straightening my back preparing myself for another blow to my gut I waited for it. His smile irritated me with the secret he held. It's not that I didn't like him, it's that I didn't like that he had more information about Jess then me.

He finally replied, "She didn't want you to marry her because you had too." He raised his eyebrows like he was hinting at something a little deeper than what he said.

Never have I said we had to get married, but we did talk about it all the time. She agreed to it before she left, "I begged her not to go. She agreed to marry me before she left me without any idea what she had planned. I'll always love her."

"She wants the fairytale."

"A Fairytale?"

"She wants the idea of a Knight, in white shining armor, by the way that is you. To save her, and confess his ultimate desire to be together eternally."

"I have asked her a million times, she always says yes, but then it gets blown off like I didn't."

"So you know her answer, did you get down on one knee?"

While running my fingers through my hair my thought ran through my mind remembering each and every time we agreed to get married. Not once did I ask her properly making my gut turn and twist into knots. I felt like shit. That is the only reason we are waiting to get married? At least I knew what she wants now.

He grinned, "I asked Alison the day we got back."

Finally Eric said something that made my day, "And?"

"Yes, we are actually going to the court house next weekend."

Truly happy I shook his hand, "Congratulations."

I picked Masey up and brought her to the kicking bag. I explained that this is Jess's favorite and I showed her how to use it. She laughed and giggled the whole time. So many tragedies in her life and she is still so happy. I looked up at Eric and he held a smile also. I had to know for sure, "Did you and Jess ever...?"

"NO!" He said this like I insulted him, but he explained further, "Don't get me wrong. Sharing our living space and all our time together you would think that I might have tried to kiss her out of convince, but no we never did. I am in love with Alison and she has always loved you."

I wanted to go upstairs and kiss her till she told me everything in her brain. He must have read something on my face, "You're jealous of me?"

I didn't know what to say, but he was right. I glanced up and the grin on his face made me want to punch it out of him.

"That's good, you know. That means there is still passion for her."

What the hell is he talking about?

"You would still fight for her. She needs to see that side of you."

I was confused and hurt by this. She didn't need to see me become violent for her, "No, that's not true. She would get scared and run from me. I pushed her hard before and we fought all the time. That's why I stayed away from her when she needed me. I couldn't bear the fighting when all I wanted to do is love her."

"No, you are a regular guy that wanted sex from his girlfriend."

I was getting steamed again, "No, I wanted to share that with her so she would be mine forever."

"Yeah, keep telling yourself that because it has worked so well for you in the past."

This guy is a complete jerk. How could she be friends with him?

"Look, I'm not trying to piss you off. It's obvious you love her as much as she loves you, but you need to face facts. You were a jerk, like we all are when we want sex and you hurt her because of it. If you can look at the past and learn from it then you can change things."

He walked over picking up Masey watching me, "Down there things are different. Life is more precious than anything because you never know how long you actually have. Jess got lucky, but only because I recognized the morning sickness. I think I knew before she did, but when the malaria hit her I knew not to wait till the temp came. I rushed her to the hospital and we caught it before she lost the baby and her life. It is a privilege to see my Alison again and everything else just doesn't matter. If I had to go one more day without seeing her smile life would have no meaning for me.

I could see the tears in his eyes and found him very confusing. Masey took his face in her hands, "You have me."

He gave her the biggest smile and kissed her cheeks, "Yes, I do."

He looked back at me, "For Jess life is different now. All of this..." he gestured to the house, "...it just doesn't matter to her. Everything you can give her means nothing if you can't love her the way she needs to be loved."

My attitude changed in an instant. I wanted to know what she wanted, "How does she need to be loved?"

He smiled and sat down on the bench letting Masey go back to playing, "When we were on the porch and she came to sit with you..."

"Yeah?"

"...You looked at her."

I smiled remembering that happiness filled my chest because she pulled my arms around her.

"Yeah, that *look* right there. That is it. She wants to feel that all the time. She wants to know that nothing else in the world compares to her in your eyes."

I can handle that. I know exactly how I felt at that moment.

He chuckled a little, "And I do believe you love her enough, but does she see it?"

The way he twists things has me very confused, again.

He laughed out loud this time, "I did tell her that as a general guide for men that we suck at that. I hoped she would pay more attention to your attention because she missed your look when she sat with you. She also missed your stares when she talked to me over the web cam."

I smiled embarrassed.

"I see it and I told her I see it. I do want to see her happy, and I can tell that you are that person that will make all her dreams come true."

I stood up walking over to him and extended my hand to him. It's my turn to confused him, but he extended his hand.

Shaking his hand I said, "Thank you."

He stood up and wrapped his arms around me in a hug and patted me on the shoulder, "She loves you more than you can imagine."

This is weird but I felt relieved to hear something so final coming from him.

He let go, "Masey deer, let's go see what the girls are up too."

She ran to him jumping in his arms. He hugged her so tight but glanced to me, "This... right here... is worth a million bucks."

He started up the stairs and I followed with every intention to go straight to Jess and apologize for being a total jerk for all those years. We got to the top of the steps and I excused myself, "If it's alright with the two of you I will go check on Jess."

Eric gave me an approving nod as he wrapped his arms around Alison, and told her that he loved her so much. She giggles shyly. Why can't it be that simple with my Jess?

16

I knocked on the bedroom door, "Jess, can I come in?"

"Yeah."

I walked in to find her in the rocking chair with Mason feeding him. I knelt in front of her putting my face in her lap.

"Paul?"

"Jess, I have been a jerk for so long how can you even love me?"

Her hand traced my face leaving a trail of warmth allowing me to grin. She pushed her pointer finger into my dimple as she replied, "Do you really want an answer?"

I glanced up at her to see her eyes as green as they have ever been. The only time I've seen them this green is when she is... Oh shit she is horny. She wants me right now? But we have company, why now when it wouldn't be right?

Jess:

How do you explain how you love someone? I guess the best way is to show them.

"Paul, sit up."

He moved back sitting on his knees as I pulled Mason from me wiping his face. He reached for Paul so he took Mason from me hugging him and pulling his little head to his chest. "I love you too little man."

I reached for his hand pulling it to my mouth and kissed his palm and then I placed it on my heart. My heart pounded hard against the surface where his hand rested. I closed my eyes, "This is when I see you, hear you, or think about you."

I opened my eyes to see how that went with him. Eyes wide with excitement, his grin different in a mischievous way, and then he then took my hand and placed it on his chest. I found his heart beat as fast as mine did at this very moment. This is a huge step for us and I didn't want it to stop. I wanted his hands on me, the weight of his body pressing against mine, and to have him deep inside me. Shaking my head to clear it from all the ways I'd like to show him that my love ran deep and hard. I settled by pressing my lips against his forehead. Sighing with regret, "We should see what they want to do."

"Jess?"

"It's okay Paul. We have a lifetime to spend together."

He closed his eyes regretfully as he got up, and followed me out with Mason in his arms.

We decided on movies. Paul made popcorn and sat at my feet. He remained playful tickling my feet with Masey's help. In my attempts to stop them I glanced over to Eric and Alison finding them in a heated moment. I tapped Paul and gestured for him to follow my gaze. He gave Masey a bear hug but spoke to them, "Hey guys, you must be tired. Masey can stay with us tonight."

He glanced back at me, "Right Jess?"

I don't know what he's thinking because I pictured this a lot different than having Masey in our room with us. I pulled his head back to find his expression. He grinned, "So you can spend more time with Masey."

That is the reason they were here in the first place, so I'd get to spend some time with her, but I honestly thought that tonight would be the night Paul would make love to me again. Alison headed up the stairs with Eric on her heels, but he stopped halfway up, leaned over the rail, and asked, "You're sure?"

Pleased that Paul did this to make me happy, "Yes, of course."

Not hesitating he ran up after her. Giggling from the expression Eric gave as he went after Alison showed how much they are in love.

We sat there for a while watching a movie but Masey being a little girl decided she needed play time. We maneuvered sitting cross legged in front of each other doing the hand slap game as we sang our song together. She sang it in Spanish and I sang in English as we moved our hands together. Paul held Mason, but got up moving to the couch to watch us playing. He tried to entertain Mason, but he's taken by Masey's singing, "Jess, that's beautiful. Do you know how to sing it in Spanish too?"

It's a child lullaby originating in Spain that parents sang to their children so they'd fall asleep. I turned to Masey, and we sang it in Spanish together:

Masey smiled at me and then she grabbed my face, "Jessup beautiful."

"No, Masey beautiful."

Paul got up handing Mason to me. He picked her up, "Masey is going to teach Paul to sing the song."

Full of smiles as she sang a little and waited for him to mock her. When Paul glanced at me I sang it in English.

They continued to work on it until Paul got it down. They sang it together in its entirety. It's amazing the way his voice came across gentle but with that raspy song voice. I sang along as they continued, and I rocked my baby.

This is real family time, and we shared it with Masey until noises erupted from up-stairs. I had to wonder if this is real. Enormously uncomfortable with the situation I turned to Paul, and he's already on the move grabbing Masey, "Jess, our room?"

We virtually ran to our room where Paul turned on the discovery channel and kept Masey entertained as they continued singing her little song. While they sang I rocked Mason and fed him. Masey giggle a lot while glancing back and forth between us making Paul laugh too.

I scolded, "You two need to settle down now. Mason is sleeping so you have to be very quiet." I laid him down and moved to the bed to be with them.

Masey curled up to Paul but his eyes stayed on me. Tracing my fingers over Paul's arm, that held Masey, I returned the stare. When he finally cracked a smile it released me from the trance and that is when I closed my eyes in comfort. Not another peep from Masey as she drifted off to sleep with me.

"Jess?"

As I opened my eyes they connected to Paul's directly, but his gaze pleaded in their own way. Raising my eyebrows with question waiting for him to tell me what he needed.

"I've gotten use to sleeping next to you. Can I..."

"Yes!" came out of my mouth stopping his question before he finished asking. He moved away from Masey, but pulled her over a little. I moved to the middle as he came around and crawl in behind me, spooning his body to mine. His arm came around my waist so I entangled my fingers with his. His face caressed my neck awakening every nerve in my body. An electric spark radiated to my toes when he traced his mouth along my ear, just behind it, and then along my neck. Children in the room helped to stay in control as my heart beat so load I thought he'd hear it. The funny thing is we had slept like this, excluding the lips, so many times when we were younger before there was an 'us' that it's home to me.

When he stopped I peeked over my shoulder at him and that's when he kissed the corner of my mouth softly. Wanting more kisses I turned to him a little meeting his lips with mine. In perfect timing Paul inched back as I rolled to my back for a better connection. His kisses remained soft, his body pressed against my side, his leg moved between mine, and I wrapped my leg back around his. Begging for something deeper I opened my mouth nipping at his lips, running my tongue along his bulging bottom lip causing a moan deep in his gut, "Ummmm..."

He liked that and his hands came to my face. Touching me tenderly he traced his fingers against my face and through my hair, while his mouth devoured mine. I traced my hands up along his back and he made that sound again, "Ummmm…"

We continued to kiss until he whispered to me, "Do you want to go to the other bedroom?"

His kiss came deeper again. I didn't want to say no, and I did want this to progress. I am completely turned on with him rubbing against me. The only thing that came from my mouth is, "Kids."

His smile alone made the teasing more delightful. He finally replied, "Okay," and his kiss pressed hard and deep. He seemed satisfied to be here right now, even though his body didn't press to mine. Wanting to make him so hot we'd need to go to the other room anyway. It didn't help that the moaning floated into our room as Eric and Alison took advantage of the alone time. The kissing moved from passion to playful when he put his head down continuing to kiss me. He would kiss and nibble and then I would bite and claw at him. I did want him to understand how much I want him. Neither of us wanted it to end. We fell asleep like this and I slept the best I have slept in a long time.

Mason woke up early this morning. Paul moved to the kitchen to make his bottle while I fed him what I had. Paul brought the bottle right away, "Jess, I put baby cereal in there. If you want to quit breast feeding him you should start cutting back.

I agreed and switched him to the other side. Mason wasn't happy about the switch already but got back to eating right away and I continued for five minutes. Paul sat on the bed watching us talking to Mason to quiet him. Mason was too tired and hungry to care.

"Okay, Jess, that's enough it's my turn."

I handed Paul Mason and got up. Paul moved to the rocking chair and gave him the bottle. Mason didn't mind at all. I think he was too tired to care at this point. He didn't even finish the bottle before he was sleeping again. Paul glanced up at me, "Told you."

I shook my head at him. He got up to lay Mason down in his crib. I stood up moving behind him, wrapping my arms around his waist, and gliding my hands up his front. I rested my forehead to his back and kissed him there. He turned around wrapping his arms around me. I pressed my head to his chest, and we both stood there looking at Mason.

"Jess, he is so innocent and pure. Do you ever just watch him sleep?"

"Yes, I do."

"Do you want anymore?"

I didn't want to tell him no, so I didn't say anything. I think he was afraid of my answer so he didn't press the issue. I knew he would want one of his own, but maybe once he knows that Mason is his he'll be satisfied and be okay with just him, our beautiful perfect son.

Paul kissed the top of my head, "Jess, let's go back to bed."

I released him so he took my hand as we moved to the bed. I laid down facing Masey. I looked at that sweet little face with amazement that she ever survived that world we were once in. I felt him move in behind me moving close so that every part of him pressed against me. I felt his leg move between mine rubbing our feet together. His hand gently wrapped around my waist and he rapped his fingers against my stomach. I reached down to entangle my fingers with his pulling his hand to my mouth. I kissed his knuckles as he nuzzled his face to my neck as his breath grazed my neck.

"Paul?"

His whisper came to my ear so comforting, "Yes."

"I like it here."

His whole body raised with a deep breath. When he released the air he replied, "Good. I built it for you."

I grinned but wanted him to know it wasn't the house I was talking about, "I do like the house, but I meant here," pulling his arms tighter.

His body expanded with another deep breath as his chest pressed against my back. His mouth traced my neck mouthing to me, "I like it here, too."

We lay silently, but he continued to trace his nose along my neck. His thumb of the hand I kissed moved back and forth over my lips. I wanted to ask him to the other room so I could show him how much I loved him. My heart raced as I wondered if I should ask or if I should tell him about Mason.

"I'm scared."

His mouth quit tracing my neck, but came to my ear. He was very sweet and gentle, "Of what?"

This might just end it right her and right now if I am not careful. I held my breath, "To have another one." I let the air out cautiously so he wouldn't figure out that I'm nervous.

His touch still sweetly gentle, so when his hand released mine my heart sank. Was he moving away from me? His hand lowered to my chest and stayed there but he moved to hover over me tracing his lips along my cheek while whispering, "Why Jess?"

Pressing my lips against his, "It hurts. The pain is unexplainable."

His lips glided over mine tenderly moving back and forth, "I wish I'd been there with you."

I shook my head, "You wouldn't have been able to stop the pain."

"No, but I would have held your hand and told you that I love you."

Wanting the serenity of his eyes I leaned back into him glancing up. This is it the perfect opportunity to tell him about Mason. His hand cupped my face while his thumb glided against my jaw line, but his lip lethal to my lack of confession. Tenderness, loving, and needy distracted me again on what I want to tell him. When we gasped for air I whispered, "I asked for you."

As if I hit him the pain showed in his eyes, "You did? Why?"

Getting closer to the real reason, "I wanted you there. I didn't want to do it alone."

He swallowed hard and his eyes filled with tears, "You were alone?"

Shaking my head no not wanting him to feel bad, "Not exactly, but I certainly needed you."

He gave me the, "it's okay; I'm here now," saying as he traced his face along mine again, "Why didn't they call me?"

Reached up I brushed a kiss under his eye, "They said you would have risked your life to get there in time and it wouldn't have been safe for you." As I took a deep breath to finish he pulled me tighter. "I waited too long to ask for you."

He moved his face back and forth across mine in agony, "Why, Jess. I wanted to come to you when you got home. Why did you push me away?" His lips glided over mine.

"I was scared."

He stopped seducing me with his soft lips to find my eyes. Only when they fell on mine did I see the tears I caused, "I'd love you no matter what Jess."

The warmth of his body pressed against every inch of mine closing the connection with his lips pressed against mine. Heat flooded in all the right areas of my body needing to share everything including my soul with Paul. Breathing into each other exchanging our souls right there. Wanting to complete the exchange I ran my hands up against his back tracing every etched muscle that seemed to rise to the surface meeting my hand. The hardness pressing against my core sent tingles in my belly. If he wanted to make me beg forgiveness I would, "Paul I am..."

Impatiently his lips found mine not letting me apologies for my behavior, not letting me confess that he is the only man that I have ever loved. Not certain if he intended to make me forget the pain, or entice the needs swelling in places that I have forgotten about. Wanting to share everything with him in ways that needed more privacy I ran my foot along the inside of his thy. His body ground against my needy core while pleading, "We should go..."

Already nodding in agreement and that's when Masey's little voice rang out. "Jessup?"

Paul stopped on a dime. Taking a second to calm his need he moved so I could roll to her, "Hey baby, what's wrong?"

She reached for me so I took her into my arms.

"Paul sad?"

Sitting up I pulled her to my lap, "A little. Do you need a drink of water?"

She nodded holding her hand out to Paul. "It okay. Jessup take care of you.

He laughed with a sigh. I got up with her and walked towards the door to take her to the kitchen. I stopped and glanced back at Paul with sadness, "Paul, I wasn't sure how you'd take it."

When we came back, Masey wanted to be in the middle again. She curled up to Paul and took his hand, "You sing to me. Make you happy."

His grin went all the way into his eyes while they sang themselves to sleep.

17

We're up early this morning with Mason. I gave him a good feeding while Paul held Masey who's still curled up in his arms. He laid there staring at me and I tried to not pay attention to the way his eyes penetrated into me. Playing with Mason's toes making him giggle preoccupied my attention, but I'd glanced at Paul when Mason giggled. His face would lighten up each time the joyful noises came from Mason. Something is on his mind; it shows in his eyes, but he not saying anything yet. Waiting for him to spill the beans about what is going on in his brain I watched his eye movements as if he is explaining without a word. Eyes wandering down to Masey, then up to me, and then over to Mason. Seriously wondering if he had doubts now; I kept my thoughts to myself as his eyes continued to make the rounds again until he finally landed on me again. His face ignited with happiness when he said, "Are you sure you don't want just one more?"

"Give me time to forget, Paul."

"It should be a girl."

His happiness is spilling over so I asked, "Why?"

"Because I already have my little man to do guy things with you will need a girl to do woman things with."

I gave him a smirk of disapproval.

He chuckled quietly, "You're considering it, Jess. I can see it." He raised his eyebrows a few times with that silly grin.

Too much pressure right now, so I straightened my face and shook my head no. It didn't get the response I expected. His eyes now gleamed with the thought and his grin got even bigger than it had been. He laughed at me and eased Masey from his arms so he'd be free to get up. She clung to him waking up, "Paul, not sad anymore?"

He picked her up, "Nope, your right Jessup took care of it."

He gave me a quirky smile as he started walking out of the room with Masey in his arms, "We're going to make breakfast. How does that sound?"

She's full of giggles this morning, "Good."

Staying in the bedroom to finish feeding Mason I hoped Paul would drop the having another kid for a while. A very long while. He's already over protective because of what I went through with the Milaria I can imagine what he'd be like if I got pregnant? Huh... Maybe having another one wouldn't be so bad. Needing to get the idea out of my brain I put on a robe and headed to the kitchen to hand off Mason with hopes of a shower. When I walked into the kitchen Masey sat on the counter putting stuff in a bowl while trying to mix it. The counter filled and over flowed to the floor with flower. Paul turned to me taking Mason from me kissing his little face saying good morning. Mason loved his daddy and I love that we are going to be a family. Paul had Mason's chair ready on the counter and gave him a bottle while he kept one hand on Masey.

I wrapped my arms around his waist and kissed his back; I did love him so much, "Do you want some help?"

"No, go take a shower. We have plans today."

"We do?"

"Yep."

"Are you sure?"

"Yes, I have to prove to you that I can handle this."

I chuckled while walking away but stood my ground, "That's not going to make me change my mind anytime soon."

Planning and doing are two different things. Hot water to ease every muscle only lasted ten minutes or so when there's a loud crash in the kitchen. It's amazing how fast a shower can take when you picture your baby trapped under his overturned car seat on the floor after falling from the counter. Still sopping wet with only the robe wrapped around me I rushed back to the kitchen finding that the bowl of mix is what hit the floor. Paul glanced back at me, "That was quick."

Shaking my head I walked away. My heart pounded in my chest and my hands shook as the adrenaline eased.

After getting dressed, drying my hair, and dabbing on a little color I headed back out to the kitchen, which is a little out of control if you ask me. Eric and Alison came down the stairs standing next to me as we watched Paul juggle helping Masey with the mixture, and keeping one hand on Mason. Eric nudged me, "That is cruel."

Shoving my elbow into his gut I scolded, "He wanted to."

The gleam in his eyes flared, "It's cruel to dress dumpy too. Put on something that makes you totally hot."

Giving him a full shove and talking to Alison, "How do you put up with him?"

When she laughed out loud Paul glanced back at us, "Okay. Okay I need help."

Though we all laughed at his expense we moved to rescue him.

Alison grabbed Masey now covered from head to toe in flour. I wiped Paul's face with a towel removing all the flour on his cheeks and nose, "One more, hum?"

"Come on, Jess. It's my first time."

Leaning in I kissed his cheek whispering to him, "And it won't be the last."

Arms making their way around me for a hug I pushed him away, "Not like that you don't. It's in the shower for you."

Paul's plan is to go to town. They were having sidewalk sales at the mall, a corn feed and hay rides at the fairgrounds. As we headed out of the house Paul stopped me, "Jess, in case we get separated."

Although he had good intentions giving me money didn't feel right, "Paul, no."

"Jess, what if you want something? You don't want to have to find me."

The gesture is grand, but he's already taking care of Mason and me, "I can't."

He gave me a reassuring smile, "What is mine is yours too, Jess. Please."

Understanding his point I still didn't want the money, "No! Paul."

"What if you want to get Mason and Masey something, even like an Ice Cream cone? Please, Jess."

Puffing out my cheeks in frustration I huffed at him and took the money. Not really sure if I am mad or happy that he'd insisted. Once the money made it into my hand he tried for a quick escape in case I changed my mind, but I grabbed his hand. Turning back to me ready to argue another point until his eyes met mine all emotionally watery. Stepping closer he asked, "Did I forget something?"

How do I tell him that this small act hit me right dab in the heart. Clearly he loved me. Reaching out I traced my hand down his chest and nodded.

"What am I forgetting?"

I glanced up at him trying to give him a *look*. I wanted a kiss.

"Jess?"

When he didn't get my little seduction show I gave up, "it's nothing."

He took a step towards me leaning down to my ear, "it's okay, Jess, I am right here."

I turned quickly into his lean and kissed his neck. I caught him off guard so he moved away from me with his eyes closed. His hands came to cup my face and those wonderful soft lips pressed to mine and I got the kiss I wanted as he wrapped his arms around me to pull me close.

Eric walked by, "We'd get going if these two would stop making out."

Embarrassed we stopped immediately, parted, and went to grab the rest of what we'd need for the day.

We took two vehicles because of needing the extra room with the kids. Starting with shopping wouldn't have been my first choice. One, its spending money, two I'd be reminded of my weight, and third the guys were heading off on their own. Having separation issues when Paul took Mason with him my day didn't seem that great. As Alison dragged me from shop to shop I got a little more into by purchasing Masey and Mason outfits. Lastly we made our way into a lingerie shop. Alison talked me into a sexy little outfit. Only after trying on about twenty, her lecture that life is short, and it being time to move to the next step. As far as I'm concerned we passed the next step into unexplored territory. That's why we're both so uneasy about it. Not comfortable in sexy lingerie, but for Paul anything is possible.

We met up with the guys and headed to the hayride and corn feed. Masey eyes wide as can be when her eyes fell on the horses. Paul and I got a kick out of watching her. Paul even took Mason and Masey to pet the horses nose.

After that we headed to the race track were little kids raced mini-bikes. We walked over to the stands in search of seats. Abby walked up after Paul left to grab blankets. If I saw her coming I would have hid, because she can be a total bitch and she has always wanted Paul.

Not surprised when she asked, "So, you are still around?"

Tamping my temper I turned to her smiling, "Yes, I am."

Eric took my hand in his. With his support I turned to her with a smile.

"So you and Paul aren't together anymore?" Her question came out a little more enthusiastic after Eric took my hand, but I didn't want to let her have any enjoyment on my account.

"No, we are together. This is my friend Eric and his girlfriend Alison. Guys this is Abby, an old friend of Paul's." I can play nice when I need to.

"So this little guy..." She tried to touch Mason. I pulled him away as she finished her sentence, "... is the illegitimate son?"

Yep! A total bitch. It's not like her words affected me like they used to so I can blow her off in a heartbeat. Of course she continued, "I just don't understand why Paul is so dedicated to you when you run off like that. Plus in those clothes you fit the part of welfare house wife."

A hand wrapped around my waist as Paul moved between us kissing me on the forehead before addressing Abby, "I don't know what you are talking about Abby. Jess is absolutely adorable, and this little guy is 100% mine. Can't you tell? He has my brown eyes, the same nose as me. Even his mouth and lips are like mine all the way to his dimples." Paul's eyes scanned my face realizing that Mason looks like his daddy. Shit, this isn't how I wanted to tell him.

Mason had already stretched his arms to Paul, so he took him to his chest where Mason laid his head down. Adoring them together I wrapped my arms around Paul's waist and reached up to whisper to him, "You're not lying."

Everyone around us disappeared when Paul turned to me lifting my chin up so I had to meet his eyes. Hoping this is what he wanted I found tears in his eyes as he stared at me. The only word that he got out of his mouth was, "Finally." Until Abby had to open her mouth again and ruin the moment.

"Jess, you might want to start dressing like a girl if you want to keep Paul here interested in you. You've gone downhill in the last year."

Giving Paul a silent apology. He pulled me close but spoke to Abby, "I think you have more important things to do than insult me and my family. You should leave now."

Paul gave me the best gift I could have ever gotten from him. Abby stormed off, and we moved to sit in the bleachers with Eric and Alison. Alison comforted me, "Ignorant people are very stupid, Jess. Don't let her get to you."

Paul turned me to him and pulled me close, "I like the way you dress, Jess."

That didn't feel like a complement because I did look dumpy. He traced his hands along my face looking into my eyes, "It's like a secret that only I get to share with you."

If my day could get any better than this I wouldn't know how to handle it.

We watched as these little guys rode around the track wild and crazy. I found it fascinating and scary that these little bitty kids could ride like this. Our adventure over for the night we headed back home. The kids road with Alison and me, while Eric road with Paul. There's something that Paul wanted to pick up before heading home and he asked Eric to help him. Probably another lawn mower or something like that.

We got the kids in and we were getting them cleaned up when the guys pulled up. Paul yelled for me desperately so I ran out of the house worried that something happened to Eric. What I found isn't what I expected. They guys were unloading a mini bike. Making my way to them I asked, "What is this?"

"It's for Mason." Grinning from ear to ear; expressing his happiness and pride that he got our son a mini bike.

He can take that right back to where he got it from, "I don't think so."

"You said you thought it was cool that those little boys could ride."

"Paul, no! This is not right."

"Jess, come on. It will be cool."

Glaring at him I scolded, "He is just a baby. My son is not going to ride those dangerous things." I stormed away from him, but not fast enough because he's storming right after me.

"Jess, what! You said it's cool."

I huffed and stormed into the bedroom slamming the door, but he continued to yell at me the whole way, "What are you so mad about?"

Paul:

What's her problem now, "Jess, I didn't mean to make you mad."

Standing at the door contemplating what I'd do next. Deciding if she is going to be mad at me anyway I might as well make her extremely mad. Storming back down the hall, through the living room, and out the door; I grabbed the bags of clothes and headed back in. Steam had to be coming from my ears because now I am mad.

Eric tried to stop me, "Hey, take it easy. You just caught her off guard."

Glaring back at him, "Can you take Mason outside? We're going to get this all out once and for all. If she is leaving then I need to be okay with it. But Mason is also part of me and she will have to share him now."

He backed off, "Paul, it's clear to me that she loves you."

"Yeah, well then everything can be settled today."

Pushing my way passed him I stormed down the hall and shoved my way into the bed room. Throwing the bags on the bed, ready to clear the air once and for all, and ready to voice my opinion. When she turned to me her eyes dripped tears. Not wanting to let her go, but not wanting to worry every day that when I wake up they'll be gone. She never threatened, but she also never gave me a clue when she left last time.

Her eyes glanced over at the bags, "What's all that?"

"CLOTHES!" I didn't mean to yell, but were fighting. Right?

The green in her eyes popped out at me encased by red. What do I do now that this hit her harder than I believed it would? She continued to stare at me and my knees wanted to give out, but I will not cave this time, "Jess, what? What is it? What did I do wrong now, because I don't understand how to make you happy! That is all I've ever wanted, but it seems like I can never do that. What is it that you want for me, because I am tired of walking on egg shells worrying that you are going to up and vanish again?" Pausing for a breath hoping she will at least yell back, but nothing as she stood there staring at me. Fine I'll keep going. "You do understand that I can't take another round of you leaving and I just need to know right now what it is you want! What it is that you are planning on doing? You have got me all tangled up inside saying we'd get married and then brushing me off like it's not what you want."

Still as if I am not even yelling at her. Maybe if she understood what this does to me, so I whispered, "What do you want from me?"

She walked up to me with tears running down her face. I am not going to give into her little crying fits of getting her way. This is it and she has to be up front and honest with me. She wrapped her arms around my waist and put her head to my chest. I am not caving in. She is not going to win this argument. She has to tell me what she wants and right now. If she rips my heart out I must have killed Anne and this is my punishment.

Almost falling to my knees when she whispered, "I'm sorry."

So much for not giving in to her. She is meant to be right here wrapped in my arms where I can hold her tight. How am I supposed to deal with her fighting dirty like this? "What is it that you want from me, Jess?"

She raised her face until her eyes met mine and spoke in a whisper, "You are the daddy and you can buy your son anything you want from now on."

If she keeps staring at me like that I am never going to get my answer. She'll dance around my questions with a touch here, a kiss there. Yep, the kiss under my chin is breaking me. Determined to stay strong I eased her back half a step to see into those eyes.

Then she continued, "But I am the mommy and it's okay for me to be scared that he will get hurt."

I nodded, but what did this have to do with what she wanted?

She took a deep breath, "Paul, I want a partner, someone that will work together with me. Not someone who will give into me every time I want something, or demand to be the boss of everything. That someone will be my equal but will also love me so deeply that life would be miserable to be without. I love you, Paul, but if were together we will be partners."

Taking her face in my hands I pulled her close kissing her deeply. Not having her close enough I pulled her into my arms. She wrapped her arms around my neck and her fingers entangled in my hair pulling me closer to her. Wanting all of her I picked her up holding her tight to me and she surprised me by wrapping her legs around me. This is it. She is giving into loving me with every part of her. Intending on giving her all of me I walked to the bed, knelt on it easing her down as I kissed her. I didn't want to let her go ever. Holding back to clear my head I hovered over her. As I wiped the hair from her face I had to make my point. "Jess, I am completely in love with you, but I need to know if you are staying. It is killing me worrying that you will leave me again. Mason is my son so you need to promise me that we will talk about everything before we make any life changing choice."

She nodded, "You need to promise *me* that if you buy anything big like this for Mason we will talk about it beforehand. That's so I can prepare myself, and Paul, I don't want to leave."

"Then marry me."

"It's not the right time yet."

"When will it be the right time?"

"I'm not sure."

Pressing my lips to hers I pleaded, "Please, Jess, say you will marry me."

"That's what I am saying. We will get married someday, Paul, when it's the right time."

This girl and her off the wall answers still confuse me. She says she will marry me, but she doesn't want to commit to a time.

"Paul, Eric and Alison are still out there."

Scrunching my eyes closed in frustration. All I want is to be alone with her. So tell me again why they are here? The softness of her lips traced mine, "Paul?"

She is right we need to get back out there so I pushed to get up but she grabbed my shirt pulling me closer to her, "Paul, I love you."

Removing my body from her embrace I gave her a quick kiss. As if she could sense my frustration she grasped my hands in hers and stared up at me with eyes that told me she needed me. I shook my head not because I'm telling her no. It's because I can't believe I am walking away from making love to her right now. Thinking of Mason stuck out there with them and how uncomfortable he is helped me control my raging needs to make her mine again. In one quick tug I pulled Jess to her feet and into my embrace. With the brush of a kiss to her forehead I whispered, "We'll be alright Jess. I promise you."

Heading straight to Alison who held a screaming Mason, I held my arms out to take him and make everything better. The only thing that irritated me is the smirk grin on Eric's face telling me I gave into her again. Not letting myself punch him the face I took Mason cradling him against my chest, "There, there, little man. Daddy's got you." The way his body shuttered against mine while catching his breath; and the way he grasped ahold of my shirt begging me to never let him go made up for not making love to Jess today. Yes, I will always want to make love to her, make her mine again, but this came in a very strong second on my feel good scale. Pacing with him back toward the kitchen Jess stood there with the sweet little smile that she always gives me when I am taking care of Mason.

Not wanting to leave Mason again my plan is to have him down before we went out for the night. My mom and dad showed up to take care of Mason and Masey. Eric and Alison were in the kitchen making something for Masey to have for dinner. My dad sat on the couch flipping through the channels, and my Mom had disappeared down the hall where Jess seemed to be taking too long trying on all her new clothes.

Alison asked from the kitchen, "So what is the name of your band?"

"We didn't have a name. Some people called us the unknown."

"You are kidding. I saw your band at the festival like a year ago January."

Eric spoke up, "Yeah, that's when I came up to see you before I left."

"Yeah, didn't you guys get interrupted by something?"

I laughed remembering the night very well, "Yeah. When I saw Jess I quit playing and chased her."

Jess walked out, "What are we talking about?"

Eric explained that they'd both been at that concert when I walked off the stage to chase her.

Alison wrapped up in the kitchen and mad her way to the living room. "You were good."

We weren't all that good. "That song I sang that night is Jess's song that I wrote for her."

Now Jess rolled her eyes while Eric chuckled out, "You do a lot of things for Jess."

Did he mean that I'm pussy whipped?

His tone now sincere, asked, "Why did you quit?"

"Because she was more important than anything that I did at that time. I would give up everything to have her back." That sounded stupid. If Jess loved me, then I shouldn't have had to give up anything.

Jess walked over to me, "I never asked you to give it up. It's the promising to be there and then not showing up, or brushing me off. I have always been yours ever since I can remember."

My mom blurted out, "That is true."

Then of all people my dad spoke, "she followed you around like that dog. We thought for sure she had a crush on you, but you were so broken to even see it."

"I didn't see it that way. Since Theo put me to work she has been my life line."

Both mom and dad nodded, but Jess walked right up to me staring me in the eye. Holding her gaze is harder than everything else right now because she is in a frilly tank top, tight fitting jeans, and a leather half jacket, and staring at me. I think I just twitched in my pants from the excitement she created.

We headed out for the evening. When we got there Matt came over enthusiastic. He talked me into doing one set with them. Not practicing for a long time it didn't seem too hard for me to get back into it. When it came to

Jess's song I kept my eyes on her. I wanted to be with her alone again. That is what makes me happy; just us hanging out playing with Mason and then sneaking a kiss here and there from her. After a couple of songs I gave up singing going to her and dancing. We used to be good at this and I missed it. Holding her close to me even during fast songs because I didn't want anyone else to have a chance to dance with her; she is all mine.

We were home by 12 so my mom and dad could go home. Of course we took Masey with us to our room again. Knowing they were leaving tomorrow it gave Jess more time with her and then I'd have Jess to myself again.

The morning went fine. This time Masey, Mason, and me made French toast. We didn't make as much of a mess with this.

When Jess was saying her good byes to Eric I still wanted to hit him. I didn't like that she would kiss him on the lips and be in love with me.

Shaking his hand we said our good buys, maybe my good riddance. He surprised me with a wink, "Everything is going to be fine after tonight."

I didn't like that they shared some kind of secret. Jess gave that away when her cheeks colored.

18

An eerie quietness fell on us after they left, making it awkward between us again. It's almost like we're afraid to be alone. She got up and started to make dinner about 6 pm. Even though I went to the kitchen to help her I accomplished nothing accept getting in her way. She shooed me back out to play with Mason insisting I spend time with my son. When she left the kitchen my attention followed her down the hall until she went into the bedroom. The uneasiness of being alone again enticed me to get up to follow her down the hall. Not making it all the way to the bedroom before she emerged from the bedroom coming back down the hall towards me. As she passed me she gave me a mischievous grin making her way to the TV. She put in a DVD and waved for me to come over.

When the scratching on the door distracted us we both smiled. Letting Freedom in she mentally told me she needed to warm her bones. She walked in and nuzzled Jess's legs, then laid down in front of the TV. Something is about to happen: it's in the air and I am breathing it all in like it or not. Jess motioned for me to sit down so I grabbed Mason and took a seat wearily. With a comforting smile she explained, "I have something for you to watch. There is only one thing that I need you to promise me…"

How can I promise when I'm sure what I am agreeing to? But this is Jess so…, "Of course, whatever you need."

Already knowing that I would give her almost anything she asked she then finished her statement, "When I shut it off that's it. You will not go any further than that! Okay?"

A mixture of feistiness radiated from her, but the serious side won out until I nodded.

After hitting play she went back to the kitchen. Having conflicting thoughts of keeping my eyes on her or the TV, so I decided I'd glance at her as much as I needed to while the DVD played. It wasn't until the movie started to play that my full attention remained on the TV. Jess laid in a hospital bed her belly bigger than her. It's obvious that she is showing me Mason's delivery. Captivated by what is happening on the screen I moved to my knees placing Mason in Freedom's care. One last glance at Jess for answers told me I'd have to ask later. She carried on with dinner not turning around at all. Now hiding behind the TV so she wouldn't see my reaction, because I have no idea what this is going to do to me. I am already reminded that I missed it, but happy that she is sharing it with me now. Jess had so much pain on her face, her breathing harsh, and the groaning and screaming too much to bear, but I did. Gripping the top of the TV; positioning myself to catch Mason's delivery right from the screen. Tears filled my eyes as she reached for someone pleading, "Get Paul. I need Paul here. He has to be here. I'm sorry I should have..." She screamed in pain again. Peeking over the TV verifying that she stood there perfectly normal, not hurting in any way. That's when my mother's voice came from behind the camera. No, that can't be right. Why would my mother be there and not me? There it is again, that comforting stern voice that said *no* to calling me to the hospital and to Jess. She had asked my mother to be there. My mom knew and yet she didn't tell me. Was this a conspiracy against me? When Jess's voice pleaded once again I wanted to walk to her, pull her in my arms, and take away the pain she suffered. Taking a quick peek at her to assure myself that she isn't in pain now, but then quickly focused back on the scene before me on the TV. My mind filled with questions, but I didn't want to miss any of this. If she turned it off it would be over, and I had to see Mason come into this world. Finding my hand on Mason's real head as it showed up on the screen; where my eyes tried to focus through the tears that now filled them.

My throat swelled to thickness, my chest heaved, and then I held my breath when Jess screamed until Mason's head came completely out. His little face scrunched with dislike, and keeping his eyes pressed tightly shut. He didn't like it as much as Jess didn't. Thinking about his first cries he shed in my care it's the same face he had then. The doctor explained that all it would take is one more good push. Jess shook her head no saying that she can't do it and that it's too hard for her. She needed me there that is more than evident. I would have given her the support she needed instead of our mothers. Being emotional has never been my thing, but as the doctor cradled Mason's head in his hands my chest constricted. Her body took over with a contraction that forced her to push again. This time it took everyone's effort to help her push him out, including the doctor's gentle pull as he exclaimed, "That's it Jessica. He's out."

Her body collapse to the bed, but her arms stretched out for him, "I want to see him. Please let me have him."

Someone had taken him away from the picture as the screen searched the room but Jess's voice screeched out in the background, "Why isn't he crying? They all cry right away, so why isn't he crying?"

The doctor tried to calm her which didn't seem to be possible without Mason making any noise. The camera stayed on Mason as they sucked his nose her pleading becoming hysterical in the back ground, "He's not alive. I killed him going to that god damn place."

She blamed herself for him not being okay and my eyes filled with tears. A whisper escaped my lips, "He's okay Jess. There just cleaning him up." But the Jess on the screen didn't hear me. She would have if I'd been there.

Tears spilled from my eyes when Mason let out a long loud squeal. Picking him back up they brought him to her where they laid him on her chest. She touched every part of my heart as her fingers delicately traced over his face, body, and taking his messy hand in hers bringing it to her mouth. She kissed it with relief.

They laid him against her as she cried. I should have been there. A part of me is angry that she didn't give me that choice. The other part of me is happy that she recorded it so I'd experience my son being born. My eyes stayed focused on the love of my life holding the gift from heaven, that we made together, in her arms. Alarms started to go off in the back ground making me wonder what had happened. When her eyes met the camera they were empty, then she glanced around the room worried before her body went slack. Everything went hectic including the camera that now showed the ground. My mother's voice rang out, "If she doesn't make it, Paul will need to…"

The TV shut off in front of me not showing me what had happened. My eyes snapped up to Jess holding the remote in her hand as she shrugged, "That's it. You can start it over again if you'd like."

Stunned to silence I stared at her until she gave up and went back to the kitchen. Where do I begin, because she died in that video. Glancing down at Freedom we exchanged the same thoughts. If she died, and I lost her forever they would have had to put me in a padded room to keep me alive. If she died how is it that she is here and alive now? When I made the promise I didn't understand how extreme this would be. Reaching for answers I pressed play again, thankfully it started where it had left off. No pictures just the sound of everyone scrambling to help her.

Jess came over again shaking her head, "You promised. That is not for you."

"But you died?"

"No, it's not like that. Plus I don't really remember it so I don't want to see it."

I stood up following her to the kitchen, "You died!"

"No, I still heard everything."

"But you died?"

"No." She was shaking her head. "I heard a voice tell me to come back. That you needed me. The next thing I remember is waking up in the hospital room."

In my head Freedom's voice rang loud and clear, *"You heard me."*

Not wanting to take my eyes off of Jess ever again, but with Freedom's statement we both turned to her. Jess made her way to Freedom with her head tilted and it seemed like she understood her too. In need of understanding myself I followed into the living room.

Freedom continued to explain, *"Jess, my responsibility isn't Paul. It is you I came back to watch over."*

Jess knelt down holding Freedom's face in her hands, "But Paul's the only one that understood you telepathically."

Freedom's words in her brain not only entered my thoughts, but also in Jess's, *"You weren't ready."*

Jess hugged her but the moment interrupted for me as the food on the stove began to boil over. Taking over for Jess I ran to the kitchen pulling the pan from the stove and turned back to their embrace. Annie had been sent back to protect the love of my life. So many things going on in my brain right now I wondered what to ask or of whom. This is too much to handle.

Freedom got up moving towards the door, *"You have the truth now. Everything is settled. Your son is tired and I am warm. You two need to figure things out."*

She got up and walked to the door. Jess walked over and let her out. She glanced at me and went back to finish getting the table set for us to eat like that whole scene didn't happen. Stunned to the core my body and brain didn't want to work at all numb to everything. What am I supposed to do? If she died, I'd lost her forever without knowing she had my child.

Moving through the motions we ate in silence as Jess tried to give Mason a little of the soup she had made. Unanswered questions kept running through my mine one after another, but not really sorting anything out as I finished my dinner. After getting a bottle ready I went over to pick my son up. Needing more time with Mason as if I had missed so much time with him, but the reality is I just missed the biggest day in his life so far and that seemed to hit home a little harder than I thought it would. Not sure why but I asked Jess for permission, "Do you mind if I put him down?"

So many emotions, so many questions, and so much information to process its hard to sort it out and organize it. My heart raced while trying to stay calm for Mason. To put him to sleep I needed to relax. When his heavy eyelids finally remained shut I laid him down in the crib. His little face so perfect, a combination of Jess's and mine. How did I even think that he could be someone else's child, but the pout is totally Jess's face. With that thought I headed back out to join her in the kitchen. This girl could tell me to eat dirt and I would do it to prove my love to her.

Moving in next to her at the sink, trying to pull myself together, and organize the questions in my head before I come off as a roaring fool. Her little body turned to mine where she ran her hand over my bicep, her voice faint, "I'll be right back."

Glancing down at her out of the corner of my eye I wondered if she is going to avoid my questions again. Those green eyes peaked back up at me while her lips press against my shoulder briefly. Deciding that she isn't avoiding me I finished the dishes while she went to the bedroom. When she came back out to the kitchen she shoved me into a chair talking directly at me with determination, "I can't do this anymore."

My throat swelled as my heart fell to my stomach twisting and turning making me want to pass out. Why would she go to all the trouble of showing me Mason's birth if she is going to walk away now? Pacing in front of me back and forth with her finger pressed to her lip pondering what she needed to say to me. I tried to keep my mind on what she's thinking, but that's when I noticed her bare legs. Allowing my eyes to wander over the rest of her I found her wearing a nighty that is as green as her eyes. Every step she took made it flow contouring her thighs, and it fell nicely around her waist. The best part is the way it cut deep in the chest allowing me to think about teasing her nipples, but way different then when I helped her feed Mason. Has she said a word? I hope not because all I can think about right now is running my hands over every inch of her body. Anger or turned on she has me on the edge of my seat.

Finally she walked up to me. Opening my legs for her to move closer to me she stepped in between them. Not able to look in her eyes for fear of not seeing the love I kept my focus on her waist and lightly put my hands to her sides waiting for the punch.

Flinching when she finally found the words she worked so hard to find, "When I talked to Eric about us, he said you may have needs."

Eric the asshole made me shallow in her eyes. Hell no! I am not going to let this happen, and this silky green thing is as soft as I thought it'd be. Skimming my thumbs against it I replied, "Jess, the only thing I *need* is to have you here so I can see you every day of my life."

Her body heaved a deep sigh, and then her fingers came under my chin pulling it up so I would have to gaze into those startling green eyes of hers. If my eyes met hers I am so in trouble, but of course I let her pull my attention all the way up to her eyes. Witnessing the sadness in her eyes I knew she'd be breaking my heart tonight. Why did she have to wear this silky soft thing if she is telling me she is leaving, it's so distracting?

Her whisper came soft, "Paul, I have needs."

That is something I already accepted, "Anything you want or need it's yours, Jess. All you have to do is tell me what you want."

Her eyes turned to a sparkling green, a grin peaked from the corners of her mouth, and then her tongue came out to lick her lips before biting on her bottom one. My heart jumped out of my stomach back to my chest, and something else jumped to attention. If I am reading this wrong it's not a good time for it. Removing my stare from her I closed my eyes leaned forward pressed my lips to her stomach gripping her sides a little more forcefully testing the waters. Her hands cradled my head, her fingers gripping my hair, and the quite moan she made sent the blood in my veins directly to my tool where it forcefully push against its confines. This girl, no woman is going to be the death of me with the back and forth on the emotional scale. Quietly I asked to make sure this is what she wants, "Like this Jess?"

"Yes."

Where do I start, how do I make her feel things she has never felt before, how do I make her completely mine now and forever? Lowering my hands I let the hem of her nighty fall between my thumbs and pointer finger as I traced my fingers up her back side bringing this silk sexy nighty up her body until I could feast on her bear skin. Opening my mouth to devour her stomach she let a squeak out as my hot breath brushed against her belly. Liking her response I licked from her belly button up and then blew my breath against her skin. She shivered from the coolness or maybe from the excitement I am causing her. It really doesn't matter because we are taking everything to the next level and I am going to cherish every little second I can along the way.

Letting the nighty fall I placed my hands at her waist once again enjoying how soft and luxurious this thing she is wearing felt against my grip. I'm not trying to torture her, but I couldn't handle stopping if we let this go any further. Pushing her back a couple of step her breath came out in a huff. Not only do I want to do this I also need to, "Jess. You're sure this is what you want?"

There are so many places on her body that I want to touch not only with my hands, but with my mouth tasting every inch of her. The first and only time we had been together resulting in Mason, it had been so long since we were here in this place together. Taking me off all my thoughts she pulled my shirt from my back causing an interruption of touching her. Her hands cradled my cheeks as she leaned forward pressing her determined lips to mine, as her body moved into my lap straddling me. Her need apparent in her kisses full of need and want. Easing my arm around her waist I pulled her body against mine feeling every bump and curve pressed against my straining body. The heat of her core rubbed against the stiffness of my desire making her moan out, "Oh Paul."

If she's going to make noises and call out my name I am going to burst at the first sensation of warmth and wetness. My pants are about to bust open the zipper now. When her hands skimmed down my back her nails dug in scrapping as they came up it almost ended me. Pleading, "We should move this to the bedroom!" That wasn't a question because I needed full rain of her whole body.

She stepped back as if we'd move to the bed room, but she pressed her hand to my head shoving me back to the chair. When my eyes met hers I knew that she wanted it here in the kitchen on a chair. Who am I to tell her no so I waited for her to come back to me? When her hands slid up under the nighty and slowly came back down her legs laced with her panties on her thumbs I gasped at the sensation that pumped through my veins. Stunned at her forwardness I sat there in awe.

As she stepped forward she straddled my right leg so I gripped her hip there waiting for her next move. When her hand pressed against my bulge my other hand wrapped around her pulling her to me tasting her lips. Moaning my desires into her mouth as I devoured hers lips and tongue just short from biting her hard with need.

My instinct is to make her mine once again, but with that I want to make this even better than the first time we made love. Our needs are getting in the way for the beauty of making love to my Jess, but I want her to have as much pleasure in this as I will. It's not the same for her with the release and I have to give her that! Reaching down to stroke her needy flesh searching for the nub that will build her enjoyment, all while staring into her needy eyes and planting tender little kisses everywhere I could reach. I didn't want her to come like this but she rocked against my hand showing me I had discovered the little nub that will drive her mad.

The strain of confinement released when I felt the tip of her finger play with the opening of my rod swirling it around. Keeping time with her movements I did the same movements to that delicate little nub making her rock into my hand once again. Her fingers wrapped around the stiffness that is her doing as she nibbled on my lip with need. This time I bucked to her stroke and groaned with need. If I don't get her around me soon it will end prematurely.

Growling out, "If you do that much longer baby, you will never get him inside you."

Her smile rose to her eyes as she pulled back from me staring into mine. Everything put on hold, because those eyes stopped time in my world. Need and passion took ahold of both of us. She stepped back, I stood pushing my pants off, sat back down, and reached for her in a matter of seconds. The only difference now is our eyes stayed locked on one another as she stepped over and straddled me. Reaching for her core I ran my fingers against her wet folds until I found the center positioning her above me as I teased her with the tip. She lowered a little tempting me with her warmth. If she's standing over me she wants the control, and I am not one to argue. I would let this woman do anything to me she wanted to as long as she is choosing me to be the one here with her. When she rose away from me I protested with a whimper of need. She moved a little closer lowering again a tad more than last time, again she rose away from me. My hands found her waist gripping tightly waiting for the full consumption. Stepping closer one last time, her hands gripped my shoulders and when she lowered onto me she took me all the way to the tilt.

"Jessica," escaped from my lips without a thought. The sensation a mixture of warmth, wetness, and tightness around me made me shutter at the sensation. All the while her eyes connected to mine saying take me home. Her body's need took over moving to me as I gripped her hips helping her to reach the spot within her walls that would drive her home. Two bodies entwined together moving to our own rhythm. The release so near I held her tight stopping her from moving. She bit her bottom lip before she begged, "Please don't stop."

Shaking my head, I had to let her know one thing, "If we keep going it's going to be over, and that's how we ended up with Mason. If you don't want another one we have to..." As she leaned forward she took my earlobe in her mouth pulling, sucking, and whispered, "I took care of it. All I need now is the pulse of you against this very spot," She shoved herself against me and without argument I pulled her hard to me driving everything to that one spot she showed me until I exploded into her.

She screamed out, "Oh yes!" as she rocked against me a few more times sucking every ounce of fluid from me. Pulling her into my embrace holding her there without letting go; this is where she belongs, in my arms forever.

Her body relaxed into mine, her head on my shoulder. If my legs weren't going numb from sitting in a chair I would have remained here until Mason woke up again. Kissing her cheek, while speaking softly to her, "Should we move this to the bedroom?"

Shaking her head, she replied, "No. I don't want to let you go yet."

Allowing each minute to pass; withstanding only a few minutes I picked her up from her bottom. Trying not to remove myself from her, but with it all spent like that, and her soaking wet it slipped out when I took the first step. She moaned her disapproval, but it wouldn't be long before he rose for another one with her naked body pressed to mine. Having every intention of making it to the guest room I surprised myself with another idea when I passed the bathroom.

Lowering her to her feet slowly letting her body slide away from me I turned the shower on taking the soap in my hand. Not only will this rejuvenate us, it would be fun. I'd get to touch every inch of her without complaint if I used washing up as an excuse. While the soapy caresses felt amazing she still protested when I wanted to wash her core, but through sweet persuasion I got my way. As I knelt before her she gulped and asked, "What are you doing?" The frightened child came out, but this is a grown woman that I want to experience everything with. I lifted her foot to my thigh, took the soap to a lather, and then washed her foot stroking between her toes. The giggle brought laughter to our explorations while I moved to the other one. Rinsing took things to a whole new level of pleasure. Kissing the inside of her knees, up her thighs she relaxed allowing me to try everything with her. Her fingers entangling in my hair kneading her pleasure of each caress I enticed her with. It wasn't until I kissed her core that she protested, "What are you doing?"

Grinning from ear to ear I didn't stop to explain. Taking one long lick until I found her clit where I pressed my lips and sucked her into submission until her knees went week. She moaned through her second climax of the night. Her head fell back as I rose to hold her tight, only her eyes burned with lust, "I want you in me now, Mr."

Who am I to argue the point so I gave her exactly what she asked for, which is only too easy when all her moaning had engorged me again. This time it's not going to be gentle, the pain in my balls needed a release and she begged me for another round. Not as strong as the last time it left me wanting more than the 10 minutes it took. Grabbing the towel I slowly wiped the beads of water from her skin and wrapped a towel around her. Quickly I took care of myself and we headed to the bedroom. She went to our room, while I moved to open the guest room. We both laughed as she came to me, gave me a peck on the lips, and I escorted her into the room. She is in for a full night of touching, playing, and pleasure beyond anything she'd ever want again.

Totally exhausted I held her close to me while her leg trapped over mine, her head on my shoulder, and her hand resting on my chest. Her breathing grew deep and slow acknowledging her sleep. This sensation of being in Heaven here on Earth is new to me. Completely satisfied I dozed a little here and there. It's my fear of waking from this only to find that it had all been a dream kept me from fully submitting to sleep.

When Mason decided to wake up he cooed instead of crying, but Jess didn't move at all. Running my hand up her back to coax her awake she begged for more sleep. That's when I got up and took Mason to the kitchen for some man time with my little guy. Grabbing all the fresh vegetables we have in the fridge setting them on the counter I pulled out the blender next. I messed with blending different mixtures letting him taste things as we mixed. Some of the faces he's making are hilarious. After feeding him sweet potatoes I had to wake Jess; she's missing all of the fun in this. Bringing

Mason with me to the bedroom to help me wake her. As I set him next to her on the bed he leaned over slobbering his mouth against hers. She smiled, and I touched her face, "Jess, you have to come see this little man's face. He likes real food."

She grabbed his face and kissed him but kept her eyes close, "Paul, can you take him out of here? I am not dressed."

Chuckling at her protest, "Jess, he doesn't know the difference. He misses you."

"Paul, need more sleep."

As I took Mason out of the room I glanced back at her. The fact that its caused me to worry about her sleeping this long. Not satisfied I set him in his crib, "Give me just a minute buddy I need to check on your mommy."

In a rush I went back into the other room moving over her, "Jess, hun, are you going to get up?"

She traced her hands up my sides and reached for kissing. Giving her the kiss she wanted didn't last long because she dozed off again so quickly. Overwhelmed with worry torn on staying to coax her awake or tend to Mason. With his reminder yell I went back to him. We headed to the living room, where Freedom's scratching at the door told me I'd have help with Mason. Mason and Freedom found a spot on the floor in front of the TV. My life is getting better and better. My eyes wandered back down the hall, but Freedom assured me, *"She is weak, Paul."*

Bring my attention back to her I wondered how she knew what I'm thinking.

"Don't worry so much. I have always heard your thoughts and you have a lot of guilt built in. You did not cause my death; it was an accident that is all. It wasn't my time, so I got to come back. She's my connection to you. I feel her and she just needs rest, Paul. She is okay."

While Freedom is here to play with Mason I went back to fixing food for him. My whole day consisted of making food and storing the stuff he liked. Letting Jess sleep I only went to check on Jess a few times finding her still asleep. The more she slept the more worried I became. Freedom stayed the day with me to play with Mason only going outside while he took his nap. Trying to preoccupy my time I checked in with the guys and planned on working tomorrow. If Jess didn't come around soon I'd have to call my mom for help.

At the end of Mason's and my day I crawled in bed with Jess not being able to stay away from her. She gave me a kiss but went right back to sleep. Bringing her body next to mine I held her while I tried to sleep myself.

When I woke in the morning Jess had disappeared. My heart raced and panic raged through my veins as I stood up stumbling to get to the door.

Searching the other room I found that all of their stuff remained. Relief washed over me as I took a huge breath calming myself as I heard her giggling in the kitchen and Mason cooed at her. Following the sound of her I made my way to the kitchen. When my eyes finally fell on her I rushed to her squatting in front of her gazing up into her eyes. Reaching to stroke her check with my fingers in awe I asked, "Are you okay?"

She grinned with a confused expression, "Yeah, I am fine. He loves this food. He has been squawking at me for more."

Just then Mason screamed and cooed. We both laughed as she went back to feeding him. I stood up and kissed her forehead, "You slept a whole day. It made me worry."

She glanced up at me, "I think I am weaker than I thought. I was going to call Doc for a checkup."

Very happy that she agreed with me, "When were you thinking?"

"Nap time today. I just was so tired and I didn't have any energy to get up, all I wanted to do is sleep and sleep, and sleep some more."

"I have to work a little this morning but I will be home by eleven. Do you mind if I am here?"

"No, I want you here."

I went to work so worried that she wasn't getting better. Distract with thoughts of Jess not getting better it took me longer at work than I thought it would and I didn't get back till after noon. I pulled up finding her sitting outside on the steps in her underwear and a muscle shirt pulled up. Completely confused with her lack of clothing, I got out of the truck, "Are you okay?"

She smiled at me, "Yes, I am just fine."

"What are you doing?"

"Getting some sun."

"Don't you think you should put a swimsuit on?"

She smiled at me as I walked closer. Pointing her finger at me she turned it curling it for me to come closer. I'd do anything she wanted me to do especially with that grin on her face, and those, eat me alive, eyes.

Moving until I hovered over her, "What did the doctor say?"

"That we should make love as much as possible, because it will help me to build my strength back up."

Was she serious? "He did not tell you that!"

Grinning with mischief she replied, "No, not exactly, but he did say I needed to build my strength up and what better way than to make love to you."

Torn between the thought of this being too much for her and the body splayed out in front of me a smile crept to my face. Scooping her up in my arms before pressing my lips to hers we stumbled into the house. All the while she unbuttoned my pants, pulled the zipper down, and shoved my pants down my legs. We barely got in the house when my pants dropped to the floor. Kicking them to the side I clung to her pulling her against my body. When she put her hands to my chest pushing me away I growled with disappointment. It's a premature reaction, because her next move did me under. Reaching down she slid the little panties she wore down to the ground shoving them to the side. Pinning her backside to the door with my body I reached down to find her so wet that she must have started without me. Hungrily I devoured her lips while pulling her leg around my waist. The day's separation wouldn't keep us apart any longer as I eased into her warmth slowly penetrating each layer of her sweetness. Completely emerged she instinctively wrapped her other leg around me so that the door and my weight held her up. Withdrawing as slowly as I entered I fought the need to grind into her depths with ferocity. Her whimper clued me in on her need of fulfillment. Giving her what she wanted I eased back into her full tilt, but stopped there wondering if this is too much for her, "Jess, you slept a day the last time. Should we be doing this?"

Taking my face in her hands her eyes met mine. The need and desire apparent in the depth of her eyes she pleaded, "Yes, Paul. Yes! Make me scream your name." Keeping my eyes locked on hers I made my way in and out diving deeper, retracting almost completely, and then driving home again until her nails dug into my shoulders. Tears filled her eyes, her gasped heavy now, and the rasp of her voice, "Yes, Paul, oh Yes. Please Paul, YES!" The warmth of someone wrapped around you bringing you to that uncontrollable point of pleasure. Her climax fulfilled I dove deeper, faster, and harder allowing myself to the release I had to have filling her with my seed with three solid thrusts. My body relaxed pressing her against the door completely expelled. That is until she kissed my face everywhere and whispered, "More?"

It's not that I didn't want more. I just didn't want her to sleep another day away, because I wanted to spend as much time with her as I could. If she's sleeping then it's more like I miss her. Shaking my head no, but explained, "I am scared."

"Please?"

"You slept a whole day."

"I am better and I need you."

I pulled her face to gaze into her eyes again. Her needs apparent in the depth of her eyes, and me not being rational enough to refuse her after waiting to be with her, this encounter is inevitable. If this is what she wanted then who am I to tell her no. Caving to her every need I held her firmly to my body heading to the closest most comfortable place to take care of her needs.

In the rush of things before we hadn't even stripped down, so I pulled my shirt over my head while she discarded hers. New blood pumped through my veins seeing her lying before me in all her nakedness. Where do I begin, and where will she end it. Making a playground of her body I kissed, licked, and sucked every part of her body until she screamed out my name once again. The more I turned her on the faster I became ready to fill her. This time I did not torture her with slowness, her body wouldn't allow it meeting me thrust for thrust. This time we moved as one combined unit, not as two bodies, but as one. Where one body ended the other began we climbed to ecstasy together. Not only did she say my name repeatedly I chanted her name over and over confirming she is mine from now through eternity. Collapsing next to her I cradled her body to mine. Apparently she exhausted herself once again, because she dosed off before I pulled out of her. This is supposed to be a guy thing, and here my Jess is the one falling asleep on me rather than me falling to sleep on her. What I wanted is a little different from this because the need for telling Jess that I loved her beyond what words can explain didn't get to happen. Instead I held her, traced her face with my fingers, and watched her sleep peacefully.

If I had to spend another day watching her sleep the day away it would drive me crazy. Not even her eyes twitch when I glide my finger over her lids. This worried me deeply.

Mason's nap time soon ended with a loud screech from the bedroom. She surprised me again when her eyes popped open, "Mason."

I grinned, "You're awake?"

"Yeah, it's just so tiring."

I pulled a blanket down around her and pushed to get up, "I will get him."

If I want to keep making love to my Jess, she is going to need a lot of sleep. It's not like I could turn it off now that she turned on the flood gates of desire in me.

19

If there's one word to explain our relationship it would have to be *Perfect*.

Wednesday I got home by 11:30 am. She met me by the door pulling off my shirt as I came through it and then leading me down the hall. Surprised with her aggression, but not refusing it either. We have a whole year of making up to do and she wants to do it as fast as possible. We spent all three hours playing in bed together. She made my world a better place.

Thursday she surprised me with leading me down to the workout room. Full of mischief, I followed her to the bench. She pushed me down to sit there, while she walked over to the radio and turn it on filling the room with bluegrass. My eyes must have been bugging out when she turned to me slowly walking over to me. She laughed and pulled my shirt up and over my head. Of course I let her, she has been enticing me each and every day, the only thing different is the way we experience each other. She moved over me straddling me tracing her hands across my chest. Not in a hurry I let her explore the way she wanted. Thankfully Mason slept long and hard now. I traced my hands along her thighs, "Jess, what has gotten into you?"

Tilting her head with puzzlement and a touch of hurt sounded in her voice, "You don't like this?"

"Oh, no, it's not that. I am surprised; pleasantly surprised."

She leaned forward kissing my chest as I pulled her shirt from her. Her mouth traced downward to the top of my pants as she moved away from me. A foolish grin spread across my face as she undid them. Helping her I lifted myself as she pulled to remove them. All realization gave me a chuckle knowing that she's always been the girl of my dreams. I couldn't have wished for a better person to love me. The way she traced her hands over every inch of my body showed me how much she truly loved me as a man. Working her way back up my body she kneaded my calves then my thighs. It pumped the blood to all of my extremities, including the erection that grew with each beat of my heart. It's her nose that made first contact as he ran it along the bottom of my shaft causing a shiver to convulse over my body. When the heat of her tongue grazed the tip of me I bucked without consent. Until she put her lips around the tip of me I managed little control but now she pushed me to animal need growling out her name, "Jessica." Using her tongue she swirled it around and around blowing any sense of coherency on my part. When her mouth took me in I crumbled to pieces in her hands. If this girl does not marry me I will hold her captive for the rest of her life. Oh my god what this girl did to me and my heart. When the sensation stopped I opened my eyes reaching for her in need of more. The core of her needs, wet and hot, rubbed against me giving me a hint of what is to come. Sitting up I pulled her closed to me as she eased down over me consuming the very need she created with that wicked mouth of hers. Which I might add has a satisfied smirk, that is until I devoured it rocking into her. My hand pressed to her lower back steading her while I dove deep and then twirled my hips to get arouse from her. Air rushed from her with a gasp. Not knowing where I wanted to put my other hand with so much of her that I want to touch. Surprising myself my hand found her face holding it so I'd get to experience her release from the depths of her eyes.

Her breath came out as a whisper, "Paul?"

That sounded like a question, not a statement. Her eyes turned soft and needy as she repeated with another breath, "Paul?"

"Yes Jess please?"

Tears filled her eyes as we rocked together and once again her breath came out with my name, "Paul?"

If it wasn't the gaze of her eyes it's the breaths with my name on them that undid me. Squirting hot lava into her womb taking down all walls of hurt and pain we had endured over the last year. Her body convulsed against mine. But that wasn't enough because her body craved more. The walls of her heat sucked me in, squeezed it tight milking everything I have to give, until she whimpered with her second release. Wrapping her arms around me her grip grew tighter as if she never wanted to let me go again. I rested my forehead against hers not wanting to break this beautiful connection I finally replied, "It's always been that way for me, Jess." Her body relaxed into mine and I tucked her face into my neck holding on for dear life. If we didn't have Mason I would have stayed here in this position until I could give her another round of deep, meaningful loving.

"Kids, where are you?"

Our eyes met full of surprise and panic as we heard my mom's voice holler out. My mom is here and coming down the stairs. Jess moved from me grabbing our clothes whispering, "Laundry room." I followed and kissed her as the door closed. She laughed all the while we tried to get clothes on, but I couldn't stop myself from kissing her. I could have spent hours making love to her and my mom shows up not only at my house, but moving through it searching for us. We were grabbing clothes from the dryer. She had on my shirt and my boxers as my mom yell out again.

I whispered to Jess, "We have to hurry, or she is going to wake Mason."

Just then we both heard him scream. We started to laugh, and I yelled to my mom, "I am in my office mom, can you get him?"

"Where is Jess?"

"She's here helping me. We'll be right up."

We giggled and kissed more while we stood there trying to calm ourselves down but not working with all the kissing. Taking me to another place she reached up and placed a kiss on my chin, "I love you, Paul."

I hugged her so tight that she squealed. I opened the door for us. My dad happen to be standing there as we fell out of the room entangled in a kiss. He coughed to let us know he's right here. He seemed as embarrassed as much as we were. Jess kissed me quickly and ran for the stairs, "I'll get Mason."

My dad had this look about him that brought fear in me of a scolding.

"So what are you two doing here?"

He laughed, "I could ask the same thing."

I shook my head pulling on a shirt. He shook his head, "Don't you think it's time to ask this girl to marry you?"

I was surprised, "I have."

"So..."

"She needs time. I mean she says someday, but she won't set a date."

"But you're both at it again and now you probably have number two on the way."

"Dad, no. It's not like that."

"Yeah, okay you two always go to the laundry room to get dressed and come out kissing."

Trying to get him off the subject of Jess and me not doing laundry together I said, "If you have any suggestions on how I can get her to give me a date I am all for it? I want her to be my wife. I have wanted that since she was 15 years old."

He glared at me, "Did you give her a ring?"

"Yeah, before she left for South America."

His eyes narrowed, "She still has it?"

I shook my head, "No, but I just asked her Sunday again. She says yes, but she gives me the same *it's not the right time.*"

He furrowed his brows, "You got down on your knee and purposed to her again?"

"No, not like that. Just every time we're cuddling and I'm staring at her I can't help myself and it comes out of my mouth. I want her to marry me." I glanced back at him with wonder, "You knew Mason was my son all along, didn't you?"

He laughed, "Yeah, this little girl loves you so much that she didn't want to trap you with doing the right thing. She brought him here hoping you could accept him, but it's also test for you."

"What kind of test?"

"She wants you to really love her. Not just marry her because of Mason."

"But I do love her. Mason is a bonus."

"I am glad you feel that way but I think you need to make sure she knows."

He put his hand around my shoulder to guide me up the stairs and he whispered to me, "Try the old fashion way. She might like that."

He let go and headed up the stairs. The old way? What was the old way?

My dad gave me an idea and the plan started tonight keeping her up most of the night playing and loving her. With her going into a deep sleep after making love it would give me time to plan out our day. After getting rid of my mom and dad I took advantage of my plan and made love to Jess every chance I had. There isn't a room in this house that shouldn't be christened by our love making.

Mason and I had big plans today. Still worried about Jess I called Katelin to come over and hang out at the house in-case Jess got up before we got back. Matt came with her and they were full of questions but this time I wasn't going to share with anyone except for the one person that can't talk.

We stopped at a store getting tons and tons of candles. Putting a few by his nose made him sneeze if he didn't try to eat them. He had a very cute sneeze. Next we went to the mall in search of a new ring representing a new start to our life together. We went to the jewelry store where Matt's mom, Heather, or Mrs. Cavinaw works. She smiled as I walked in coming around the counter to take Mason from me, "I was wondering when you'd bring this little guy to see me. He is so hansom. How is it going, Paul?"

"I need help. I need an engagement ring, and maybe a wedding ring that goes with it."

"Paul, didn't you already have one for this girl?"

"Where starting over and this might be what I need to get beyond where we are."

She smiled handing Mason back to me. He squealed with glee when she spoke to him, "Your dad's loves your mommy."

Confirming that, "Yes I do and I need something elegant, special, and perfect."

"From what I understand; Jess is a little thin these days?"

I nodded as she traced her hands around the counters searching for something special. She smiled and pulled out a tray. I followed around the counter to where she had stopped, while she put one in a box, "Do you have a price range?"

"No, anything that will make her set a date this time."

She laughed a little as she opened the box and turned it for me examine. I held it up to Mason asking, "What do you think little man?"

He pushed it away. I handed it back to her, "What else?"

Rolling her eyes I could see it irritated her that I let Mason decide. She walked a little further and pulled out another set. She handed it to me and I held it up for him to look at it. He pushed it away so again I handed it back to her. She shook her head, "This one just isn't as fancy but it's got a little better clarity." She handed it to me and in turn I held it up for Mason. He screeched. I grinned, "It will be this one."

"Oh, are you sure dear. This one is a lot more."

"He made his choice, and no one knows his mommy as good as he does."

She nodded and wrapped it up for me. I put it in my inside pocket and we headed toward the exit. Coming to a halt in front of a shop that had a dress in the observation window I imagining Jess in it. At that moment I knew I had to get it for her, and Mason confirmed it clapping his hands on my face making all kinds of noise. Not wasting any time we walked in, spoke to a girl that got Jess's size, rang it up, and we got out of there in no time. The dress will be a perfect complement to my proposal, classy and elegant. What a better way to look when you are proposed to. We headed to the grocery store next with a grand dinner planned I picked up steaks and lobster tails for two. Mason didn't complain once the whole day.

When we got back we found her still sleeping. I called mom and dad asking them to pick Mason up at 5 pm. I told them the plan. They were both very happy for me and were glad to come get Mason for the night. Too excited to get the evening started I headed in to wake her.

Crawling next to her I whispered while tracing my fingers along her face, "Jess, time to get up." Only the smile that appeared so quickly already faded back into sleep mode. Stroking her belly I nibbled her ear, "Come on baby. Time to start the day. We have plans."

Caught off guard by her hand wrapping around me grabbing at my shirt I backed away from her and scolded, "None of that right now. Mason wants to see his mommy."

That bottom lip of hers came out in the way that tears me to pieces just begging me to cave to her desires, but not today. It just isn't going to fit the schedule. I pulled the covers from her as I scooted off the bed. Grasping her ankles I pulled her down the bed to me putting her feet to my chest. In her attempts to play sleeping she didn't protest one bit. I lifted on foot to my mouth kissing it briefly before sliding her underwear over it, then I repeated to get the other foot through the opening. When she realized what I was doing she went limp as a rag doll. I slide her bottoms all the way up, then worked on the T-shirt and then shorts. Not helping with any of it she lye there and let me work twice as hard as this needed to be. She had to get up to spend time with Mason or she wouldn't see him again today. I pulled her to her feet, "You have to get up and see Mason for a while. We have plans for tonight and my mom and dad are going to come get him."

After explaining she got up and motivated right away to go to him but only after wrapping her arms around my neck and kissing me softly. I smiled for her as her finger traced my dimple. I shook my head and turned her to the door, "Your son would love to see you."

"What are we doing?"

"Surprise."

"Do I need to get dressed up or is this a naked affair?"

The smirk on her face told me we'd get naked, but she's in for a romantic evening that we are going to take slowly. "Jess, you need to spend time with Mason and we will do everything else after he leaves."

20

Jess:

Lying here in the tub surrounded by tons of candles made me wonder what Pauls' up to, enjoying this pampering way too much. The bubbles helped to sooth away anything that could be distracting. He told me to take my time, but if I stay here much longer I'dfall asleep. A knock on the door brought me back to reality. The door slowly opened, and I held my hand out for his, "Are you joining me?"

He took my hand and came to sit on the edge of the tub, "Do you understand how tempting that is?" His pause allowed me to entice the thought of swiping away the bubbles. Shaking his head with that adorable grin on his face his hand reached out to glide against my check, "I have something else planned for us this evening. Whenever you're ready just let say the word and we'll go to the next thing on our agenda."

"I could stay here longer if you came in here with me."

He got up from the edge of the tub moving to the sink where he stared at himself a little too long. I could see that his mind was somewhere else.

"Paul, is everything okay?"

Those dimples came through as he glanced at me in the mirror, "We could start now if you want to get out."

Not really sure what his plans were, but I wanted this man deep in me. That need for completion has become what I wanted every moment of every day. I stood up watching for his reaction in the mirror. He closed his eyes with that funny grin on his face, "Jess, please don't tempt me yet. We have all night and when you do that it drives me crazy." He turned wrapping a towel around me.

While he dabbed the towel against my skin I kissed his neck just below his ear then whispered, "So what are we doing tonight?"

He didn't raise his face to me, he was so quiet and almost distant, "There's something for you to wear on the bed. Take your time, pamper yourself, but don't take all night." He kissed my cheek and walked out.

Getting anxious with the way he's acting I wondering what he has planned for us. Was he going to do or say something I didn't want? Determination to make it hard for him to hurt me in any way; I'm going to fix myself up so good that he won't be able to resist me. Though I still looked like a bag of bones with skin on it. I did my hair, my makeup, and slowly moved to the room. I found the other bedroom door closed and found myself sad that he needed to dress in separate rooms. It's almost like he's separating himself from me.

What I didn't expect to find happen to be an off white dress made with satin material. As I let it fall down over my body the silkiness against my skin made my nerve endings come to life imagining each swipe of material is Paul's hands gliding against me. A simple dress, nothing fancy about it, but it allowed me to pull off classy. The top complimented my small boobs giving me cleavage. It fit well down to a drop waist making my waist give shape to my rear. I laughed as I turned in the mirror to notice that I still had curves. Draping against my skin down just below my knee in a simple yet flirty lose way.

If he intended on slowing things down then he bought the wrong dress. It brought me confidence in how I felt about myself, him, and us together for the rest of our lives. Taking once last glance in the mirror and a long deep breath I forced myself out of the room. The other bedroom doors stood open now, so we aren't separated from each other at this moment. Now all I had to do is find him. Slowly I walked down the hall tracing my hands along the wall as the living room came into sight glowing with candle light dancing on the walls. My heart began to race with delight that he's doing something romantic for me. He anticipated my arrival as I peeked around the corner. He stood still when our eyes met and then he stalked towards me determined to consume me. The need mutual after running my eyes over his body finding him in khaki pants, a light blue dress shirt, unbuttoned, and a smile that told me he liked the dress on me. Gasping might be a strong word but the air left my lungs as my eyes lingered on his torso. My nipples may have hardened with just his eyes devouring them.

When he moved close enough he reached out his hand for me to take. I melted into his gaze as my heart beat to escape my chest. I am so in love with this man that he didn't even need to do this, but I found myself pleased that he thought so much of making this night special.

He pulled me forward and took my hand to twirl me in front of him. The dimples came through with his smile as my eyes moved back to meet his.

"You are amazing."

I laughed lightly but stared at him with pleading eyes to explain what he's doing to me.

His grin slight, he pulled me close, and whispered to me, "I made you dinner."

My body trembled with excitement him treating me so precious. I followed him without a word as he pulled the chair out for me to sit.

"I didn't know if you would like lobster, so I made you steak as well."

He moved to the oven pulling out two plates already made up, placing them in the two spots for us. Then he went to the fridge pulling out a bottle of wine. He glanced back at me without letting our eyes meet as he poured two glasses. Holding one out for me when he came back to the table I took it as he said, "Try it. Tell me if you like it."

I only took a sip, and it was delightful. A mixture of sweetness, with a bite of tart rolled over my tongue. Glancing back up at him cautiously, "It's perfect."

He chuckled, "Sparkling Grape juice."

Surprised I asked, "No wine or champagne?"

"Nope, I didn't want to cloud your brain."

This mysterious man sitting next to me brought nervousness. It's the way he would watch as I put a forkful of food into my mouth, the way his eyes glistened when they met mine, and even in the way he played with his food barely making it to his mouth. Wanting to touch his arm and reassure him that he didn't need to do all this because I already loved him so much. Wondering if we were past the point of disbelief that this could be forever, I decided to flirt with him while we ate in quiet. Licking my fingers as I dropped a piece of buttered lobster tail into my mouth, followed by wiping my lips off with a delicious run of my tongue against my lips, as his eyes lingered there. His next bite he took aggressively and hummed out the approval. Playing with the mashed potatoes I flipped my fork over and used my tongue to pull it into my mouth, but as graceful as I am I missed my mouth a little leaving a little in the corner of my mouth. This being the first touch he reached over to me with one finger and scooped it away. Tingles ran up my spine, pin pricks at the back of my neck, and my pelvic clinched when he licked it from his finger. My body burned everywhere with need of his touch. The eating slowed to a pace that neither one of us seemed hungry for food any longer. Reaching out again he ran his fingers along my arm down toward my hand. Wanting him to touch me I turned my hand up to him. His fingers traced and danced along my skin as we both watched, until he stopped with his finger pressing against one finger. He grasped it gently turning my hand back over staring at that one finger. The ring finger that once held the ring he had given me. Pulling it closer to his face he opened his mouth and kissed me there like he's kiss me with a full open mouth kiss. Consumed by the hurt he must be going through I wanted to pull him to me to tell him that everything that we want together will happen someday. Reaching out to him with my other hand I wrapped it around his neck pulling myself closer until his eyes met mine once again. He needed to know that all this special treatment isn't what I needed. I want the everyday, lifetime together kind of love. Not this special occasion kind of love that will fizzle out when we don't make it this special anymore.

"Paul, I thank you for this but you know I love you. Why did you go to all this trouble when you know I don't need it?"

"There is more, but first let me put the stuff away."

He got up and moved around the kitchen putting stuff away. I got up to walk away from the table but surprised by his hand on my arm, "Jessica, we're not done here. Please sit down for a minute."

A lump in my throat grew along with my worry. Why's he going to all this trouble? And is there going to be pain involve? It seemed to me that usually with something so grand there's an apology coming and worry filled my bones. He guided me back to the chair, sat me down, and continued to put things away.

When he finally came back to me he pulled his chair close to mine as he sat a box on the table. My eyes flinched at the sight of this size box then swiftly back to his with a hint of tears filling them.

No... no... no... please don't tell me that we're not going to work out. I LOVE YOU PAUL. Oh shit this wasn't going to be good. He's going to apologies for something he did in the past to me. When he opened the box it wasn't what I thought, to my relief. Taking the ring out, he stared at it in his fingers.

"I tried to think of what I wanted to say to you tonight, but nothing I came up seemed right, to apologize for the things I have done to you before you left. This is the forever ring that I gave to you a long time ago. Intended for someone else but Jessica you have always been my forever and I want you to continue to be my forever." He took my hand as his eyes came back to mine, "Will you wear it?

Cradling his face with my hand I replied, "Yes." Though, I wanted to scream the word YES to loving this man for the rest of my life

He slid it onto my pinky with shaking hands. I leaned to kiss him but he stood up quickly, "No, not yet. I have more to say."

More than promising to be his forever, what else could there be. Taking my hands in his he pulled me to my feet leading me to the fireplace. I didn't understand why he had planned out the evening only to stretch it out so long into the night. That's the most perfect apology that anyone could have given me, so he really didn't have to go any further.

He pulled me to a stop in front of him. He glanced over at the mantel where another box sat. Swearing under my breath at the tears welling in my eyes sure that he intended to make me cry tonight. Glancing at the box myself noticing that it's the same size as the last. Shaking filled my body while asking the silent question in my head. Is he going to purpose now?

Lifting both my hands to his lips to press his lips there as he shook his head no, "Don't worry baby. This is not what you think it is."

Giving me time to settle my heart so it didn't explode. A little disappointed I gained control of my emotions. My attention made its way back up his body to find his eyes warm and caring, his smile sweet and crooked, and his eyes sparkled in the fire's light.

Taking a deep breath he continued, "Again, I tried to think of the perfect thing to explain this box and what it means to me, but I failed again." He opened the box to pull out the engagement ring he had once given me, "This, the ring I gave you so that you would be mine."

Oh shit!

Slowly he examined it along with me held between his fingers. He took another deep breath, "But you cannot have a possession of another being, so when I gave it to you I was wrong in how I thought, but not wrong in how I felt. If you'll wear this ring it will represent all the years that we have loved each other."

Waiting for my approval he stood silently. Vowing to myself to never tell this man *NO* again I nodded to his plea. Not getting the ring on fast enough I fidgeted to get to the good part. If I had the guts to do it now I would drop to my knees and give him the same pleasure he filled me with tonight. He took my right hand in his and slipped it on my ring finger. I didn't fully understand because I didn't get if he was asking me to marry him or not, but I nodded because he was asking me to wear the ring he gave to me. I reached up to kiss him and he shook his head completely smiling, "No, not yet Jess. Just give me a minute."

Wanting to stop my foot in protest like a two year old, but he had planned this out so perfectly I would let him lead me into the night with this schedule. Letting my hands drop he jogged into the kitchen, grabbed a chair, and came back setting it down on the rug in front of the fireplace. He guided me to sit down on the chair.

"Paul, what are you doing?"

"Just a minute. One more and then you can kiss me all you like."

That comment made me worry even more. There's more to his confessions? He knelt down in front of me taking both my hands in his. Whatever he's going to confess, someone else in my absence, hating me for leaving him, having his son without him, or whatever this confession I would forgive him. All that matters is that we are together now, and I wanted it forever. His head bent forward staring at my hands building strength to continue. Wanting to relieve the pressure from him I pulled my hands away from his and lifted his chin so that he'd understand that I will not hold anything against him. Only when I pulled his face up his eyes had leaked tears, causing the same reaction in mine. His pain is not his alone. We were as one unit now and he needed to understand that if he'll have me I am here to stay.

A slight grin came to his face as he reached up to wipe my cheeks, "Jessica, I am completely and utterly in love with you. You have given me every reason to live, love, and be completely happy with my life." He opened anther box to uncover a new delicate perfect little ring of simplicity. I gasped as he moved closer to me, "I know that I have not been a perfect man, and I will not be perfect because we all make mistakes."

He took another big breath as tears traced down my face he continued as he gazed into my eyes, "If you say you will marry me I promise to always be truthful, I promise to always be faithful, and I promise to love and cherish you for the rest of my life. Jessica Jenson, will you please marry me?"

I blubbered with happiness as I nodded and said yes. He took my now convulsing hand pushing the ring onto it. I threw my arms around his neck hugging him so tightly crying into his shoulder. He pushed me away cupping my face in his hands, "Does this mean you will give me a date?"

Nodding profusely I replied, "Tomorrow."

The shock on his face filled me with laughter as he asked, "Tomorrow?"

"Yes, or the next day, or the next. The sooner we do this the sooner we will be a family."

His mouth came to mine hard and passionate as he laid me down on the rug pushing the chair away with his foot. Giggling I kissed every inch of his face. Pulling away he stopped a second staring down at me and asked, "Do you want a big wedding?"

I shook my head, "I only want to be with you. I don't care if it's big or small; whatever you want."

He kissed me luring again, but stopped for more questions, "Who do you want to marry us?"

"Priest, minister, justice of the peace, Paul, I don't care. I love you and whatever you want you can have."

He moved to kiss me again and again. When he stopped this time he glared at me, "Are you playing with me? I mean you really don't care about any of that?"

I shook my head pulling him back to kissing me. He stopped again frustrating me beyond words, "What about a dress?"

I grinned, "This one is perfect for a small wedding on the dock with a few family members around, don't you think?"

His kiss came deep and hard but he stopped again, "If you are going to wear this don't you think we should get it off of you?"

I laughed and nodded as he slowly helped me from the dress but only moved to lay it across the chair that was now laying on its side. He came back to me to love me the way I needed him to completely and solely.

Two months later we found ourselves on the dock with a few friends and family; gathered to watch us finally unite our lives together.

Happy Paul didn't want or need a big wedding. We had done everything wrong in our start but we were going to end it the right way; together for the rest of our lives.

After a few months had gone by I went to Paul asking him for something to do during the day while Mason napped. He offered to make me happy, but I needed something more than being a mom and pleasing my husband. Being supportive he offered going back to school, but we discussed the importance of my needs, which meant I needed a lot of attention from him. If I ran off to school he wouldn't be able to give me the special time I needed with him to feel completely love.

With determination to keep me at home with him and Mason he handed me all the routes and schedules of the guys. He asked me to figure a way to make everything more efficient. When he's gone at work and Mason slept I worked feverishly to come up with ideas. I had finally reworked everything, changing routes, and schedules so that the guys could make more money by staying in one area and not waist time driving around crossing each other's paths.

So excited to show him my idea, I fidgeted all through dinner. Mason, on his feet now, got into everything so Paul made himself busy with putting safety latches on everything. After I got Mason down I pulled Paul into the back room where I had set up a table for my diagrams, posters, routes, and jobs.

I set him down in my chair and went through the whole thing without any interruptions from him. When I finished he just sat there staring at all the information.

Torturing me by not saying a word I found myself anxious to hear what he thought. I finally yelled at him, "Paul!"

He glanced up at me, "You are amazingly perfect. Do you know that?"

Shocked and stunned, but he came at me with the biggest hug and kissed me profusely. I knew I did good when he took me upstairs for the best sex we have had in a while. As we lay there, I realized I'm happy in my life more than I could imagine. He whispered to me, "Jessica Reese, you are now the proud partner of your own business. How does it feel?"

I laughed and pinned him down as I stared into his eyes, "I did good?"

"You have no idea."

21

Things are so good between us and in our lives together that I'm not sure how to tell my dear sweet husband that I did something that we promised to never do. I'm hiding something from him and today I'm going to tell him, but the how is what I am not sure about.

I walked out onto the deck finding him overseeing Mason playing with Freedom and her puppies. Mason is smarter than a whip now. It's a blessing that Paul and I made so much time for him. He's only three but talking in full sentences, recognizes letters, numbers, and some words. He can even read simple books which is almost unheard of, but when you read to your child five times a day and actually get down on the floor to play with them it's bound to be a positive outcome.

The business that we shared is going so well that it's made me comfortable for this, but deep down I still kept a secret from my perfect husband after promising each other we'd never do that.

Mason screamed and came running towards Paul. He got up quickly running to pick him up hugging him trying to calm him, "What happened buddy?"

"He bit me Daddy. You bite him back."

Paul chuckled as did I, but I listened to Paul's reply with satisfaction, "Oh, buddy, he is a baby like you were once and he doesn't know that he hurt you."

Just then there was a yelp. I glanced over where Freedom scolded her pup. The pour thing cowered to his mother after she scolded him with a nip. Paul pointed, "There you go. Freedom scolded him."

Paul set Mason back down letting him run back to Freedom tackling her with a huge hug. He laid on her kissing her. Paul turned to sit again but spotted me observing them. He opted to make his way to me. He came up the steps and wrapped his arms around me so that we'd keep an eye on Mason together.

Taking the deepest breath in preparation, because it's time for my confession, at first I spoke softly to try to keep him calm, "Paul, do you remember when we promised that if we're going to make a big decision that we would discuss it first?"

He turned me to him keeping his arms wrapped around me, "What have you done?" His tone did not scold. Actually he chuckled while asking. This could go in my favor yet.

"I made a mistake, and I made a big decision without you."

His face still held a grin as he asked, "Did you buy new furniture?"

I grinned shaking my head.

"Did you buy a new car Jess, because I think we should go with a minivan?"

I shook my head with regret, "It's a little bigger than that."

Now his face faltered a little, but he didn't lose his cool, "So... what is it?"

I pulled the stick out of my pocket that revealed a plus sign on it handing it to him. He released me taking it from me as he inspected it. He stared at it with wonder. The realization hit him as the grin on his face grew, "Does this mean that we're having a baby?"

His eyes came back to mine, but a tear escaped me when our eyes met. He swept me into his arms kissing me, "You have made me the happiest man on the planet. You can keep these secretes anytime you need to if you are going to make me this happy."

*****

Paul shoed me from the house to put my feet up; the boys were going to make dinner. Mason read the recipe for Lasagna as Paul and Kyle put the layers into the pan. I walked out to the porch grabbing my book to get in a few chapters. We spend so much time raising our boys that I had to give this one special attention while it's still in me so I read out loud. It's so weird to see our sons growing up into little men. Mason is seven now and little Kyle four. The hardest part for me is that we're having another one. Paul was so great with my pregnancy with Kyle, that when he pleaded for another baby I agreed, even though the fear of pain still crosses my mind from time to time. However, delivery went much better with Paul in the room with me, and after I don't even remembering changing a diaper for the first month. I traced my hand slowly over my stomach as this one moved inside me tracing it's little hand or foot against my hand. Paul came out curling up with me on the oversize chair. He traced his hand along my huge belly as he nibbled on my ear, "So, is that it?"

He experienced the movement inside my belly. His expression priceless as I grinned at him, "It feels loved already."

He smiled and kissed my cheek, "I would like a girl this time."

I shrugged, "It doesn't matter what we have, Paul."

"Jess, I want you to have a girl. I need to be a protective daddy. With boys its different."

I shrugged again, "Paul, you will be happy no matter what it is."

He smiled pulling me up with him, "You are right. You are giving me another happiness and I cannot ask for anything more."

I got to my feet, my stomach rolled a little. He eased me into the house, but the way my body is acting I knew that today is the day this one would come into the world. Not able to eat I watched Paul help Kyle with his food, and Mason, what a little man he is now, so much like his father. Paul's glance followed me as I got up holding my stomach, "Jess?"

Smiling sweetly at him hoping he understood without words. When I got to the phone I called his mother, "It's time. Can you come take care of the boys?"

Paul's eyes penetrated me with a mixture of fear and excitement. He hurried to clean up Kyle, but he's still hungry, so Mason took over helping him eat. Paul scrambled to get the bag and helped me walk to the truck. This man of mine so sweet as he traced his hand slowly over my belly talking to the little one inside, "Hold on little one. We need to get to the hospital before you can come out."

His mom and dad pulled up to see Paul help me into the truck. The contractions started a while ago becoming stronger and stronger with each one, "Paul honey, this one is not going to takes it's time. We need to..." The pain engulfed me.

Paul's dad came to kiss my cheek, "You make my son so happy. We love you Jess, and we'll see you in a day or two."

I nodded as I grimaced in pain. Paul grabbed my hand trying to talk to me as the pain increased.

My eyes went wide with the last one. I gripped Paul's hand tightly to get his attention and groaned out, "We have to hurry!"

*****

So glad Paul is taking the boys fishing while Sarah is napping, that way I can get a real nap. Paul rocked her to sleep which allowed me to relax on the porch. This is my favorite place to read, relax, and talk to my new baby that is inside of me.

Noticing Mason as he got the supplies ready to go down to the boat, Kyle followed right behind him carrying more supplies, and little Trevor tried to pull the tackle box behind him when he couldn't carry it any longer. I laughed as I gazed at each one seeing how much each of them a replica of their father. Mason now 13 is starting his last year of middle school in a couple of weeks. Time is going by so quickly that it made me a little sad. Kyle is still growing into his own body at the age of 10. Still awkward but determined to be as good as Mason is. Little Trevor at six is more determined to prove that he is just as strong and smart as the other two. I chuckled as they headed down the yard to the boat, "Hey, life jackets please."

Paul walked out the door, "She is sleeping. Do you need anything before I go?"

Shaking my head as I gazed at him, "No, my sweet, have fun with the boys."

"Promise you baby we'll be back before Sarah gets up."

Reminding him that I am not incapable of taking care of my only daughter, "I am okay to take care of her."

He shook his head crawling over me pulling my shirt up. He traced his hands along each side of my belly and kissing it in the middle. I entangled my fingers in his hair because I loved when he did this. Now with all the kids it's a lot less often that I get the attention I need. He glanced up at me, "How about I drop the kids off later at my mom and dad's so we can have an evening alone?"

Giggling with delight, "Do you remember the last time you did that?"

He smiled and kissed my stomach seductively, "Yes I do. That's how this happen."

Filled with joy I shook my head disapproving. He glanced up at me again as he kissed my stomach more and raised his eyebrows, "But I can't get you pregnant now."

"Dad, do you think this will be the last one? I don't want to go to high school while mom is still having babies."

We both laughed at each other as Paul moved away from me, "Mason, that is enough. It took me a long time to talk her into having more so I would like to thank her for each and every blessing she has giving me. It's up to her when she will be done."

"Fine," Mason walked over to me sitting down pulling my shirt back down, "He just loves when you are helpless, do you know that?"

We all chuckled as I glanced up at Paul. I took Mason's hand in mine, "You are so right and that's how it was when I had you. I was very sick, and he took care of you on his own so let him enjoy this."

He laughed looking back at his dad, "He is kind of wimpy when it comes to you."

I smiled, "I hope so. I plan on keeping him for a long time."

They were off to go on there fishing trip. Paul made sure to only go out far enough that I could still see them on the lake. Me with my separation issues with all of my babies.

After a little while I headed in to relax on the couch; the air off the lake a little chillier than I wanted. As I got in the house pain engulfed the lower part of my stomach making me fall to my knees. The pain unlike anything I've ever felt in the past. It's not a contraction, but the pain stretched over the bottom of my stomach making me cry out. Only five months along the fear made me pull out my phone and call Paul.

He answered, "I know I promised to give you attention but can we stay out just a little longer?"

"Paul?"

"Jess?"

"I need help."

The motor started before I explained anything. Listening to his rapped breath as he made his way to me comforted me enough to stay calm. He came running in the house with Trevor on his back, Kyle at his hand, and Mason running in after him. He let go of the boys as he came to trace my face while I lay there on the floor, "Jess, what's wrong?"

Scared to move at all, because the pain wasn't like anything before, I gave him a pleading look as I quietly whispered, "Pain, afraid." I closed my eyes as he lifted me to him barking orders to the boys. Mason went to get my stuff in a bag. Kyle went to get Paul's keys, and little Trevor brought Paul the phone. He called his mom and dad and they were on the way. Just then Sarah let out a loud cry. Mason went to get her. She's still a baby, and this may scared her. Grabbing Paul's arm I gasped out, "Tell Mason to keep her out. This might scare her."

He yelled for Mason but Kyle told his dad that he would take care of Sarah. He ran back to her bedroom as Trevor sat down in front of me crying. Paul pulled him to his chest, "Buddy, it's okay, but I need your help."

His teary eyes stared up at Paul waiting for his dad to tell him what he needed him to do. Paul gently explained, "I need you to be strong and help Kyle with Sarah until Grandpa and Grandma can get here. Can you do that?"

He nodded as Paul wiped his tears away and kissed him, "Mommy is going to be okay. Can you go help them by getting her bottle?"

He nodded and took off running. I smiled at Paul, "They are all like you."

He smiled back at me pulling me into his arms, "They are all good men because you are a wonderful wife and mother."

After hours at the hospital and a few ultrasounds Doctor Feriday came in smiling, "Well, we need to discuss something that's not all bad."

Paul took my hand moving closer for the bad news. Doc smiled at the both of us and then continued, "You know when I first met you Jessica I never thought your body would adjust to having so many healthy children."

He's telling us that our luck has run out and this one is not going to be healthy? Paul squeezed my hand tightly, "Jess, we will be fine. We can handle anything together."

Doc laughed, "Yeah, well this one is going to be a challenge."

Confused with his laughter we both stared at him, but Paul asked, "Is there something wrong with it?"

Dr. Feriday's grin grew. If this is bad news he has a bad sense of humor. "Well, this one is going to be double trouble."

Paul grinned at me as he glanced back to the Doctor, "We can handle it. Quit beating around the bush."

He laughed out loud at our expense, "Jessica, the pain you are experiencing is stretching. When you grow with having a child your muscles stretch like this."

He put his hands together with his fingers in between each other and then he moved his hands apart a little.

"So this is just stretching. It hurt so bad that I thought I lost this one."

"Well, you are feeling it more this time because there is more than one in there."

Did he just say we're having twins? Paul turned to him, "She is okay?" He nodded.

"There is nothing wrong with the baby?"

Doc corrected him, "No, nothing wrong with the babies."

I started to cry, "That is it Paul. I am not having anymore. You are never going to touch me again!"

He turned to me cupping my face in his hands and he leaned forward to kissing me, "No, no more. I love you Jess." His mouth taunted me, with intention of making me forget that there are two babies in me. Doc move to the door, "I will give you some time, but when you're ready I bet you'd like to see them?"

In Paul's excitement he kissed me hard after replying to Doc, "Yes, please."

We watched as he showed us the ultrasound where they both sat in my belly. Doc turned to Paul, "Things will have to be a little different with this one."

Paul eagerness became irritating, because it isn't his body that had to endure this. Two more? We are going from four to six kids in the next four months.

"Paul, no more lifting anything for Jessica. Jessica, I want you taking it easy. Lounge around and take it easy. Let those boys take care of you and little Sarah. Paul is good at this and you need to let him."

I nodded letting my attention fall to Paul. He's so happy and I'm so miserable.

*****

Mason's graduation day is here and we're heading out the door. Paul had the twins dressed and ready to go. Since they came into this world Paul works more at home than ever in the past. Guilt for making me endure two at one time, and the only C-section I had happened to be with Dylan, the second twin. The one and only man that I've loved made his way back to me, taking me in his arms, and pressing a kiss to my cheek,

"Aren't you glad we had so many. You can let him grow up and still have a house full."

Pride, love, and sadness were having a grudge match in my head. I shook my head, "But they are going to grow up too."

He smiled at me, "Yeah, but by the time Brandon and Dylan are graduating you are going to be so happy to get rid of them that you won't be sad at all.."

I chuckled as he wrapped his arms around me to kiss me gently. He still had my heart in his hands making me weak in the knees.

"You two are horrible. We need to get going or I am going to be late for my own graduation."

Paul turned to Mason, "I only hope you find someone as special as your mother."

"Tracy. I am marring her."

"I don't think so. Not yet, you have college to think about."

"Um, I wanted to talk to you two about that. You two started young and everything worked out so we decided to get married and start having kids right away."

Glancing at Mason, thank god I saw him hiding a grin, because if he wasn't kidding his dad would beat him good.

Paul turned to him, "I talked to you about this."

"Dad you are so gullible. She is not and we are not going to get married for four years. We will both be done with college. By the way dad, you did a better job than you give yourself credit for."

He walked out and Paul put his head to my chest, "I thought I'd kill him."

I pulled Paul's face to mine, "You can't blame him. He has a great dad."

Paul held me in his arms while his hand came to my face with adoration, "You are the most beautiful woman in the world. Thank you for letting me be part of your life."

I kissed his nose, "Thank you for being my life."

We headed out chasing all the kids out the door.

Look for Melissa M Marlow's other works

Forever Yours
Wasting Away FY Book 2
Growing Tears FY Book 3

Push Away

Losing You
It's Not Over